BOLINGBROKE
CHIT

LYNN MESSINA

potatoworks press
greenwich village

THE BOLINGBROKE CHIT

CHAPTER ONE

Earning the nickname Lady Agony was no minor accomplishment. Plenty of girls lacked conversation. Indeed, every season, at least a dozen green misses emerged from the schoolroom unable to speak intelligibly on a variety of subjects or engage in the lighthearted banter that was the lingua franca of the *beau monde*. No, for a simple exchange with a young lady to be deemed "agonizing" by the *ton* required a particular talent. It was not enough merely to be tongue-tied in the presence of an attentive listener; one had to make the attentive listener tongue-tied as well.

Lady Agatha Bolingbroke did this beautifully. With her deprecating manner and her dispiriting mind-set, she was a conversational vortex, a swirling whirlpool of dampening sentiment that drained all lively thought from those around her. Consummate flirts, poised hostesses and men noted for their address all found themselves trailing off as they stared into her severe black eyes. Even Sally Jersey, who famously earned the sobriquet Silence for her tendency to prattle, ceased her endless chatter in the company of Lady Agatha.

As Lord Wittleton had once observed within unintentional earshot of the girl's papa, the Bolingbroke chit was like a wet cloth or blanket draped over a gathering.

1

It was little wonder, then, that the girl's mother all but despaired of marrying her off and engaged in an endless string of ploys in the hope of somehow arranging a suitable match.

Understanding the motives behind her mama's machinations, however, did little to make Lady Agatha amenable to them, and she watched Lady Bolingbroke with a piercing stare as the woman sank into the seat next to her.

"Well, I say, this is remarkably comfortable," Lady Bolingbroke declared as she looked around the well-appointed box, situated to the middle left of Drury Lane Theater. It was an enviable location, for it required only a slight tilt of her head to observe the occupants of the box to her right and no tilt at all for the occupants opposite to observe her. "I am delighted to be here. Are you not, as well, Aggie dear?"

"Yes, of course, Mama," her daughter said with a sharp frown, her fierce eyes focused on the lace trim of her white silk gloves. "Foisting myself upon strangers is among my chief delights. I'm grateful to you for providing me with this opportunity."

"I know you are," replied her parent with undaunted gaiety, "and you must not be. As your mother, it's my duty to provide you with as many opportunities as possible. You should, of course, thank the Duchess of Trent when she arrives with her sister. 'Twas remarkably gracious of her to invite us to attend the theater with her. I say, this is the veriest treat. Now, do be a dear, Aggie, and hand me my opera glasses. Without seeing the shape of the mole on Mr. Carpenter's nose, I can't tell whether it is the heir or his younger brother."

With a sigh, Agatha withdrew the ornate spectacles from her reticule and handed them to her mother. If there was one thing she disliked more than foisting herself on strangers, which her mother required she do with alarming regularity, it was being called Aggie. The absurd appellation bespoke her mother's habit of infantilizing everyone. Agatha's father was Bolly, her maid was Ellie, and her governess had been Stony.

Agatha loathed diminutives.

Lady Agony—now, *that* was a nickname.

She knew, of course, that the term was used by the *ton* to describe the unpleasant experience of trying to converse with her. She understood that its intentions were cruel, but she felt only satisfaction in the fact that *her* intentions were understood. Lady Agatha Bolingbroke neither desired nor sought the good opinion of society and had more important things to do than spend her days thinking up sufficiently engrossing chatter about horseflesh or Lord Byron.

Not that she couldn't rise to the occasion if she chose to exert herself—Lady Agatha knew herself to be a creature of mild intelligence—but she could not envision the circumstance that would inspire her to make the effort. After four seasons, she'd experienced all that the marriage mart had to offer and found it sadly lacking. The good aspects, which were few and far between, could be best enjoyed in silence: plays, operas, museum exhibitions, fireworks displays.

"Providence!" Lady Bolingbroke chirped as she lowered the opera glasses to smile at her daughter. "The mole on the nose is shaped like a leaf, not an apple, which means we are sitting across from the elder sibling. Smooth your hair, dear, and straighten your shoulders so that he may see you at your best. You do recall, do you not, that you danced with him at Almack's your first season? It was a minuet, I believe. You made such a delightful pair with your complementary coloring. At the time, I was not enamored of the match, as his family's seat is quite offputtingly far in the north. But that was some time ago and my definition of *far* has altered slightly."

Agatha was not surprised to hear it, for if Lady Bolingbroke had had any particular qualifications for her daughter's husband when she'd first made her debut, they had long since been abandoned in the name of expediency. After four long, unsuccessful seasons, Agatha knew both her parents would happily accept the proposal of the first gentleman who asked, which was why she worked so diligently to make sure none did.

"I do not know what you mean by complementary

coloring," Agatha said, intentionally rounding her back so her shoulders slumped. She would certainly not improve her posture upon her mother's command. "We both have the same sallow complexion. If anything, we made one another look more sickly."

This deflating statement, which would have caused her father to sputter in annoyance, only made her mother chuckle. "How droll you are, my dear. I've always said your sense of humor is your most attractive trait."

Now Agatha smiled with genuine amusement, for if her sense of humor was really her most attractive trait, then she was truly sunk indeed. Her appearance certainly did not show her to advantage. In addition to stern black eyes, she had coarse dark hair that refused to comply with the elegant hairstyles of the day and narrow lips that seemed permanently pinched with displeasure. To be completely fair, she actually had very fine features—eyes evenly set and well proportioned to her face, a delicate nose that turned slightly upward at the end—but the underlying architecture of her face was so severe as to undercut even these compensations.

As an artist, Agatha appreciated the value of good bone structure, but as a young lady making her come out, she knew her sharp cheekbones and chiseled jawline indicated a strength of character not welcomed in a girl of marriageable age. She understood why this was, of course, for no matchmaking mama wanted a daughter-in-law with a strong will and no gentleman desired a wife of decisive opinions.

To her credit, Lady Bolingbroke had done everything she could to raise a milk-and-water miss of little resolve, and it was her enduring frustration that her daughter could not be taught how to simper or demur or even trill enchantingly. Agatha's laugh in particular had long been a source of disappointment, for the sound always rang with sincere and heartfelt enjoyment. Oh, the number of times her mother had explained that a true lady was never genuinely amused! Rather, her mirth was calibrated to the particular circumstance in a series of complex calculations designed to produce the perfectly regulated response. She knew her daughter was clever, but after years of futile lessons, she had to concede it was the wrong sort of clever. Sure, Aggie could toss off a remark so cutting it eviscerated its listener, but she could never figure out how to imbue a chuckle with the amount of warmth suitable to the situation.

Other mothers would have abandoned the field by now, but Lady Bolingbroke was made of sterner stuff than most and her campaign to rid her daughter of all signs of intelligence continued unabated.

"Mr. Carpenter appears to be sitting next to Sir Winston, who is, I believe, a Whig crony of his," Lady Bolingbroke added. "You might also describe his complexion as sickly, but I suspect that's from an unfortunate overapplication of powder. Do take a look, dear, and offer your opinion."

Although Agatha did not relish a close-up examination of Sir Winston's spot-marked face, it was more appealing than quibbling with her mother about her lack of interest in Sir Winston's spot-marked face and she calmly accepted the opera glasses. As slouching forward actually required more effort than her usual posture, she sat up straight in her chair while she looked across the way. Her gaze landed first on Mr. Carpenter—yes, her mother was right, it was a leaf-shaped mole—then on Sir Winston, who did appear to be sporting an unusually heavy application of white face powder, no doubt in an attempt to cover up the unsightly blemishes on his chin and forehead.

"It appears to be a cosmetic choice, although it is a case of employing a lion to get rid of a dog," Agatha explained as she returned the spectacles to her mother.

"I think he looks very well," Lady Bolingbroke observed.

"A moment ago, you said he was sickly," Agatha felt compelled to point out, even though such bold about-faces were commonplace for her mother, who regularly issued statements that contradicted the ones that immediately came before.

"Sickly becomes him," Lady Bolingbroke explained as she raised the glasses to her eyes. "Perhaps he will start a fashion, and applying face powder will become all the crack. It could be delightful."

"And you can lead the revival of powdered wigs," her daughter suggested. "Several relics of my grandfather's are moldering in the attics."

Lady Bolingbroke dismissed this proposal as manifestly absurd, for she herself was not what one would call an arbiter of style. "But if a true arbiter of style should take up the mantle, I would gladly follow."

Agatha knew this only too well, as her mother gleefully fell in line with all the dictates of fashion, no matter how ridiculous or physically inconvenient. Just that afternoon, she could be seen strolling the lanes of Hyde Park in a bonnet piled so high with silk ribbons, ruched taffeta and ostrich plumes, she could barely hold her head up. Several times, she had to discreetly grip the hat with her left hand to alleviate the pressure on her neck, which felt as if it were bending like an old tree branch. Despite the discomfort, she maintained a spirited conversation with Lady Tilby and refused to admit to any irritation.

Although her mother hid her obstinacy behind an ingratiating smile, she was just as strong-minded as her offspring and would not give up until Agatha was firmly tethered to a gentleman of respectable breeding. Rather than fly up into the boughs, Agatha calmly went where she was bid and dampened the proceedings as best she could. Her hope was that people would stop inviting her places, but so far that desire had proven futile, as evidenced by that evening's invitation to view *The Merchant of Venice* with the Duchess of Trent. She didn't know how Lady Bolingbroke managed to arrange the outing—as far as she knew, neither of her parents counted either the duke or his wife among their intimates—but her mother was very pleased with the coup and could not contain her excitement. Indeed, she had talked of nothing else for a week.

For her part, Agatha had been dreading the excursion, for she considered the new Duchess of Trent to be an entirely insufferable creature. Before marriage elevated her to the realm of respectability, Miss Emma Harlow—or the Harlow Hoyden, as she was more commonly known— indulged in a series of reckless larks that should have by rights ended in her total disgrace at best and her utter ruin at worst. Among her most outlandish exploits was a curricle race from London to Newmarket to break Sir Leopold's long-standing record by more than two minutes.

Although Agatha had never actually met the young lady in question, she knew her to be naïve, arrogant, childish and petulant and believed she rightly deserved whatever comeuppance she got. For years, the Harlow Hoyden had managed to skirt the line of propriety, somehow always ending up on just the right side of the border. Her recent wedding to the very worthy and well-regarded Duke of Trent had secured her place among the *ton* in some quarters—people such as Lady Bolingbroke were happy to forgive a duchess anything— and the marriage struck Agatha as a fitting end for the impertinent miss. The illustrious gentleman was not known for his sense of humor or easygoing manner and was in fact thought to be stiff and toplofty by those who knew him best. Surely, marriage to such an upstanding gentleman would prove stifling and chastening to a woman of high spirits.

When the Harlow Hoyden arrived at her theater box a few minutes later, however, she did not appear to be oppressed by her decorous marriage. If anything, she seemed to glow with good humor, as did her sister, Lavinia Harlow, who, as her twin, shared her sleek blond hair and peaches-and-cream complexion. Agatha, who had never aspired to beauty, only to be left alone to pursue her art, did not resent the women for their lovely appearance. Rather, she resented them for their liveliness and their relentless enthusiasm and the way they seemed to find everything highly amusing. Their unfailing cheerfulness was so overwhelming, Agatha couldn't think of a single deflating thing to say.

And yet *she* was considered the wet blanket!

"*The Merchant of Venice* is one of my favorite plays," the

7

Duchess of Trent announced as she glanced down at the pit, then across it to the boxes opposite, several of which were still filling with arriving theatergoers. The curtain would not rise for another twenty or so minutes. "I'm desolate to have missed Kean's performance as Shylock. By all reports, it was remarkable."

"Undeniably, yes," Lady Bolingbroke rushed to assure her. "I was fortunate enough to have seen his performance and it had a profound influence on me."

Hearing this review, which did not comply with the original one given on the night of the performance—or, rather, in the middle of the performance—Agatha said, "It is true. Mama demanded a pound of flesh from her neighbor, whose infernal cough—I do believe that's how you described it, though perhaps you said *damnable*—made it impossible for her to hear any of Mr. Kean's speeches, which she felt were a trifle overdone in their inflexible malignity, creating such an unpleasant theater-going experience that she swore never to return."

"Yet here we are," her mother said without a trace of embarrassment, "returned to the scene of the crime, as it were. I trust everyone is in fine respiratory health? To be completely honest, I myself felt a dry tickle at the back of my throat around nuncheon today, but I had a cup of tea with honey and it immediately passed."

"Well, that is a relief," her daughter said, "for I would have been wretched if we had to cancel. I've been looking forward to this evening with particular anticipation."

The inflection in her voice left everyone in the box with little doubt as to the true state of her desolation, but no one chose to remark on it. Instead, the duchess inquired about Lord Bolingbroke's health. "I trust he suffered no ill effects from last night's long meeting of the British Horticultural Society. It took quite a while for Vinnie's membership to be approved."

At the mention of her father's beloved organization, in which a group of grown men—no, not just men now, for as the Harlow Hoyden had observed, her sister now ranked among them—met regularly to discuss the trivial matter of gardening, Agatha rolled her eyes. Almost all of her parents' conversation consisted of her father lecturing her mother on how to best cultivate flowers. Although Lady Bolingbroke's interest in horticulture extended only to ensuring that the bouquet in the drawing room did not clash with the drapes, she always listened to these drawn-out speeches as if she found the information to be the most engrossing she had ever encountered. She considered it her duty as a wife to provide her husband with an attentive ear, even if her spouse could not provide her with attention-worthy material.

This slavish devotion to tedious oration was another reason Lady Agatha discouraged suitors.

"He was a little shocked by the result of the vote to admit Miss Harlow, for he did not think her membership application would be approved," Lady Bolingbroke admitted with an apologetic glance at the duchess's sister. "Like most men of his ilk, Lord Bolingbroke does not appreciate the value of change and allowing a woman into the august society is a rather large change. However, now that the watershed event has taken place, he's determined to put a brave face on it and accord Miss Harlow all the respect she deserves as a fellow member of the society."

"How very broad-minded of him," the duchess said with an ironic grin. "I'm sure Vinnie appreciates his forbearance."

Having followed Miss Harlow's candidacy, which had caused quite a stir after a wager was placed in the betting book at Brooks's that she would not succeed in her goal, Agatha knew how ardently the Duchess of Trent supported her sister's cause and wasn't at all surprised by the archness in her tone. That the other Harlow girl needed her twin's ardent support was not in doubt, for the young woman had scandalized the *ton* with her determination to win entrée into the masculine domain. A more modest lady would have immediately declined the invitation, which had clearly been issued as a joke, but Vinnie Harlow used it as an opportunity to achieve her true goal: nabbing a husband. Everyone knew she was dangling after Felix Dryden, Marquess of Huntly, the famous naturalist who had recently returned from a two-year expedition to the South Seas. Her pursuit of such an eligible bachelor—he had wealth, good looks and a quick wit—would be unremarkable save for the fact that she had only just emerged from deep mourning for her fiancé, Sir Waldo Windbourne. The flagrant lack of respect for a man whose life had been tragically cut short offended all proper feeling.

Ordinarily, Agatha's supply of proper feeling ran short, a circumstance her mother frequently deplored as unnatural, but on the matter of Miss Lavinia Harlow and her hoydenish sister, she had a substantial surplus. She couldn't say why exactly the behavior of the two girls affronted her so much, but there was something about them that set her teeth on edge.

To be fair, Agatha had never actually paid much heed to Vinnie, for she had always seemed like the sensible twin, complying with the strictures of society without complaint like any proper young lady. But her zealous resolve to gain membership to the British Horticultural Society proved she was cut from the same cloth as her sister.

"Oh, but I *do* appreciate his forbearance," Miss Harlow insisted now with so much humility Agatha had little recourse but to doubt her sincerity. "I did not expect to gain admittance to such a prestigious organization and fully anticipate there will be a period of adjustment for everyone. I'm grateful for all the support I can get."

Just as Miss Harlow uttered the word *support,* reinforcements arrived in the form of Sir Charles Burton and the Earl of Moray, two members of the horticultural society who appeared to require no period of adjustment in accepting a woman among their ranks. The earl, in particular, seemed delighted with the turn of events and pledged to guide Miss Harlow through her first meeting, which would coincide with an exciting lecture from an American naturalist who would arrive from New York on the morrow.

Sir Charles applauded his friend's generous offer and urged Miss Harlow to accept it. "We in the society take much pride in our protocols, of which we have dozens to provide order and efficiency. I don't doubt a young lady such as yourself might get confused trying to follow all of the rules, and Moray can be relied upon to ably translate complex ideas into simple terms. I will also be on hand to help make your first meeting a pleasant experience."

"I cannot imagine a more gracious offer," Miss Harlow said. "Of course I'm happy to accept. Thank you."

"Naturally, my sister is pleased to return the favor, for she's quite adept at understanding complex ideas, as well. Just this afternoon, in fact, she perfected her invention of the Brill Method Improvised Elasticized Hose," the duchess explained. Then she looked at the two peers with bright blue eyes wide with innocent curiosity. "What devices have you gentlemen recently invented?"

Sir Charles coughed awkwardly while the earl pulled out his fob and pointed to a knot securing the red-and-gold ribbon to his watch. "This bow is of my own creation. I call it the Moray Maneuver. If you like, I shall demonstrate it for you."

The duchess was saved from responding by the arrival of Mr. Edward Abingdon, yet another member of the British Horticultural Society who felt compelled to assure Miss Harlow of her welcome.

Observing the scene, Agatha couldn't decide if she was amused or disgusted. It was embarrassing to witness so many accomplished gentlemen—Mr. Abingdon, for example, was a noted whipster—making a cake of themselves over an assertive female who had elbowed her way into their private club. What flattery! What fawning! What absurd currying of favor!

Truly, she'd never seen anything like it.

At the same time, however, there was something irrefutably hilarious about watching her father's beloved and esteemed institution devolve into a miniature marriage mart for the use and benefit of Miss Lavinia Harlow. The British Horticultural Society was clearly prime husband-hunting ground, and Agatha could not entirely blame Miss Harlow for working so tirelessly to gain entry into it. She was, after all, four-and-twenty years old and had already lost one fiancé to an unfortunate accident—suffocated by his own corset, if the rumors were to be believed. A woman of her advanced years could not have many options left, especially if she had scholarly interests such as inventing things. Yet now, suddenly, her life was rife with possibilities, for if she failed to catch the Marquess of Huntly, the Earl of Moray seemed happy to impale himself on the hook.

If Lady Bolingbroke had realized the society's potential for securing a spouse, she would have petitioned for her daughter's inclusion years ago.

Agatha's gaze sharpened as an image took form in her mind. She pictured the society's stately lecture hall, where the great Sir Joseph Banks himself once gave a presentation on the uses of eucalyptus, redecorated to look like Almack's. Amid the crystal chandeliers, large wall mirrors and orchestra, she envisioned the twenty-six members of the society tripping over each other to sign Miss Harlow's dance card.

She would call the tableau the British Wedding Society.

No, she thought, shaking her head. The cadence wasn't right. The title of the drawing had to sound more like the organization it was ridiculing. Perhaps the British Matrimony Society. It was a vast improvement, no question, but it still fell short of capturing the rhythm. She closed her eyes for a moment, the image so clear in her head she felt as if she could touch it, and saw the perfect name write itself along the bottom of the picture: the British Matrimonial Society.

"You can't do it, my dear."

The male voice, suspiciously close to her right ear, startled Agatha, and her eyes flew open. Standing beside her was a blond gentleman dressed in the first stare of fashion—exquisitely cut coat, elaborately tied cravat, lavishly embroidered waistcoat, pristinely pressed pantaloons without a hint of wrinkle. Every aspect of his appearance, from the slope of his pocket flap to the gleam of his Hessians, spoke of a keen attention to detail and hours spent before a looking glass inspecting the results.

Agatha, who could not imagine taking that much care

with her toilette—or, in fact, any care—looked at him in shock, her heart tripping in fear that he'd discovered her secret.

Impossible, she told herself. This tall stranger with the amused brown eyes could know her secret. Nobody knew it—not her father, not her mother, not even the estimable Mrs. Biddle, who owned the print shop in St. James's Street. Only her lady's maid, Ellen, knew her alter ego was a famous caricaturist, and she certainly had not told this preening dandy.

Assuring herself that she had nothing to fear, however, did little to calm her nerves, and she felt an almost irrepressible impulse to deny his assertion. *Yes, I can do it*, she wanted to shout. But to admit such a thing would be absolute madness, for she didn't know what she was claiming to be able to do. A far better response would be to deny that there was anything to deny: *I didn't say I could do anything.* That was risky, too, though, because denying that there was anything to deny could have the unfortunate effect of implying confirmation—confirmation of what, she didn't know, which was just as bad.

Completely in the dark and unable to think of a reply, Agatha found herself speechless for the first time in her life.

"It's an appallingly dressed crowd, I know," the gentleman said, "but you can't simply close your eyes because it hurts to look at the world. I've tried on repeated occasions—most recently when the Count de Fézensac arrived at Viscount Morton's ball sporting a chartreuse-and-lilac-striped waistcoat with sequined buttons—and I always wind up walking into a drum table. Better to steadfastly face the truth head on: Few of one's acquaintance own any claim to sartorial elegance. That might seem too excruciating a fact to swallow, but I assure you it's less painful than a bruised shin."

As grateful as she was to finally know the topic under discussion—she wasn't accustomed to ignorance and did not relish the sensation—Agatha still had no idea what he was talking about. The gentleman's conversation was too absurd to digest (drum tables? bruised shins?), and she continued to stare at him with her black eyes wide with confusion.

"There are a few bright spots and perhaps it would help if you focused your attention on those," he announced, warming to his theme. "My coat, for example, with its delicate windowpane design. Note how small and uniform the pattern is. It provides a soupçon of ornamentation, just enough to entertain the eye without knocking it over. Needless to say, I would ordinarily feel mortification at offering a compliment to my own person, but the coat and, in fact, my entire ensemble are the work of my tailor, not myself, so the only compliment is to my having the good sense to find the right one."

Agatha knew from experience that the best way to bring an end to an unwelcome exchange was to say something cutting, a skill that came as naturally to her as breathing, but as she looked at the gentleman in his delicately patterned topcoat, she couldn't think of a single set-down. The more he chattered about ridiculously inconsequential things, the slower her mind worked. She did not know to what to attribute the effect, other than being unaccustomed to someone talking so long in her presence. Usually by now the other person had curled under her withering gaze.

Perhaps my gaze isn't withering enough.

With that thought came another, and she said sternly, "You cannot knock over an eye. You can poke it or blind it, but you cannot knock it over as if it were a chair or a small child."

As far as famous Lady Agatha conversation-ending ripostes went, it was hardly up to her usual standards, but it gave the gentleman enough pause to halt his rambling monologue.

He tilted his head to the side, then conceded with a nod. "You are correct," he said. "Of course you are. The number of abuses one can afflict on the eye are limited and do not extend much beyond pokes and blindings. I suppose you can roll an eye, but a roll is not a knock, and regardless, it can be done only by oneself. I beg your pardon for not choosing my words more carefully, but I'm afraid I always get a bit beside myself when discussing topcoat ornamentation. I hope you can forgive the excess."

His expression was entirely sincere—he even managed to draw his eyebrows together in a show of contrition—but Agatha could not suppress the feeling that he was making fun of her. Nobody apologized so effusively for what was merely a turn of speech.

Determined to end the conversation once and for all, she said, "No, I cannot." The brusque refusal of an apology was one of Lady Agony's most reliable tactics: The rudeness was so abrupt and unexpected, the apologist either retreated in stunned silence or stood mutely while Agatha walked away.

Not this gentleman. No, this dandy with the expertly tailored topcoat and the excessively sincere apology simply laughed and said, "Right you are. It was an unforgivable offense."

Now he was mocking her outright!

If there was one thing Lady Agatha Bolingbroke did not know how to be, it was a figure of fun, and she stood there, teetering between anger and embarrassment, unsure which emotion she felt more strongly.

Anger, she thought decisively, as the hot flush of embarrassment washed over her cheeks.

The moment clearly called for a scathing insult, something caustic and biting that would send him scurrying back to his dressing room, where he belonged. But she saw the amusement on his face and realized he didn't have the gravity of mind to take anything seriously, let alone recognize when an insult had been heaped on his head. He was a fop, a frippery fellow with his mind firmly planted in his wardrobe, and nothing she could say would give her the upper hand.

Lady Agatha dearly treasured having the upper hand.

Even if she couldn't put him in his place with an acerbic retort, she could at least make her displeasure known. She was, after all, the daughter of an esteemed peer and the guest of the Duchess of Trent. Surely, she deserved better treatment than to be laughed at by a cavalier coxcomb with more hair than wit.

Protesting, however, would only earn her another overly effusive apology.

Before she could decide on a response, the gentleman took her hand in his own and raised it to his lips for the briefest of kisses. "My dear Lady Agatha," he said gravely, "it has been a pleasure."

Astonished by the blatancy of the lie, for nobody had ever uttered anything remotely similar to her, she exclaimed, "No, it hasn't."

Once again, he laughed, his deep, rich baritone ringing with pure humor, and Agatha found herself oddly struck by the warmth in his bright brown eyes. She ordered herself to turn away but could not.

"You're right," he agreed easily. "It's been dreadfully dull and you should apologize for forcing me to endure such an unpleasant experience."

His playful tone stunned her—nobody teased Lady Agony!—and she stared in silent amazement as he stepped past her to pay his respects to her mother. He inquired after Lady Bolingbroke's health and asked a series of questions about her fondness for Shakespeare, after which he had an equally sensible conversation with Miss Harlow. He responded to her questions with perfectly reasonable answers that made no reference to windowpane patterns or chartreuse waistcoats.

Observing the lively scene—the easy way Miss Harlow and the gentleman conversed with each other—made Agatha feel strangely unsettled, as if something worthwhile was happening and she was deprived of the opportunity to enjoy it. The notion was absurd, of course. The only thing she'd been deprived of that evening was the pleasure of not foisting her presence on complete strangers. It was her mother's fault that she was standing by herself in a crowded theater box with an awkward sense of not belonging.

"We should allow these ladies to get settled before the performance starts," Mr. Abingdon announced to his friend, who was smiling at something Miss Harlow said.

The earl, who had been cut out of his conversation with Miss Harlow, immediately seconded this idea and suggested that Mr. Abingdon and his friend leave at once. Unfortunately,

Sir Charles also agreed that the ladies should be given a few minutes to settle and insisted they make their good-byes.

As soon as the gentlemen left the box, Agatha turned to her mother and asked, "Who was the man who accompanied Mr. Abingdon?"

Although Lady Bolingbroke took great pride in her vast knowledge of the *beau monde,* she was too distracted by the events across the way to recite her usual assortment of facts such as lineage, current address and estate value as well as snippets of gossip she deemed relevant or accurate. Instead, she raised her opera glasses, leaned forward in her seat and supplied her daughter with only a name: Viscount Addleson. Then she said with curious excitement, "Mr. Carpenter has been joined by two ladies. The woman in the blue turban is vaguely familiar and is most probably his aunt Calliope Redburne, whose husband is the ambassador to Russia. But I've never seen the younger one before. Her brown curls are very pretty, and her eyebrows arch charmingly. She must be his cousin."

Agatha didn't give a fig about Mr. Carpenter or his relations, but she knew better than to inquire further about the viscount. Even with her attention drawn elsewhere, Lady Bolingbroke would immediately recognize an indication of interest on her daughter's part and pounce. Viscount Addleson would suddenly find himself invited to tea and rides in Hyde Park and intimate dinners at home with the family. It had happened before with poor Mr. Sutherland, whose only crime had been to have extraordinarily symmetrical features, a fact Agatha had the shortsightedness to observe in the presence of her mother.

Two years had passed since Mr. Sutherland hopped a boat to India to escape her mother's invitations—at least, that was how Agatha thought of his unexpected, seemingly unplanned journey—but recalling the horror still made her shudder.

Having learned from her mistakes, Agatha gaped at Lady Bolingbroke in surprised fascination. "Charmingly arched eyebrow? I must see that. May I?" she asked, holding her hand out for the glasses, which her mother surrendered with great reluctance.

Although Agatha saw nothing remarkable in the arch of the young woman's eyebrows, she devoted several minutes to praising first it, then the curve of her chin. While she spoke, she scanned the theater looking for the viscount, who was seated several rows to Mr. Carpenter's left. The two boxes were close enough in proximity that she could examine Addleson without raising either her mother's or her subject's suspicion.

Now that he wasn't prattling nonsensically about clothes or blatantly mocking her, Agatha could appreciate his aesthetic qualities—the broad swath of his shoulders, the straight line of his nose, the deep rose of his generous lips. He wore his blond hair calculatingly disheveled in a perfect approximation of the windswept style.

He was not handsome—at least, not in the classical way of Mr. Sutherland, whose physical perfection made her want to place him in a variety of tableaux. If the gentleman had been willing and society permissive, she would have leaned him against a fireplace, stood him before a ruin and sat him upon a horse in full regalia.

But the aspects of appearance that fascinated her as an artist did not necessarily interest her as a woman, for as she looked at the viscount now she thought there was something very appealing about his uneven features and open demeanor. She wondered about the attraction as she switched her attention from Miss Redburne's chin to her ears, marveling at how beguilingly jaunty they were.

Lady Bolingbroke's fingers twitched with the nearly overwhelming desire to snatch the glasses from her daughter's hands, but she managed to contain herself and merely begged for an opportunity to admire the beguiling jauntiness herself.

"Yes, of course, Mama," Agatha said agreeably, tightening her grip. She simply was not ready to relinquish her view of Viscount Addleson just yet. She was far too intrigued by the way his eyes crinkled when he laughed.

The Merchant of Venice started a few minutes later, and

unable to justify looking across the way when the action was on the stage, Agatha returned the glasses to her mother. Lady Bolingbroke required no justification for the brazen observation of her fellow theatergoers, and she kept her eyes trained on the boxes opposite for the whole of the performance.

Agatha could not imitate her mother's unabashed curiosity and limited herself to darted glances at Addleson. Despite the activity around him—Mr. Abingdon was deep in conversation with the gentleman to his right, who seemed to be trying to teach himself how to juggle apples—he was engrossed in the play. Agatha wanted to be engrossed in the play, too, and was genuinely annoyed at herself for being unable to concentrate. She resolved to focus on only the stage, which she managed to do, but the effort required was almost as distracting as the viscount and she missed most of the dialogue.

Conceding it was hopeless, Agatha abandoned all attempts to follow *The Merchant of Venice* and decided to think of something else—the British Matrimonial Society. While Shylock raged at the Venetian judicial system, Agatha laid out the scene in her head: Miss Harlow would stand in the middle of the lecture hall's famous rotunda, looking bemused by all the attention, a pretty blush on her cheeks. Her suitors, also known as the esteemed members of the British Horticultural Society, would be gathered around her, their hands held high like schoolboys craving attention. Two or three would be lying on the floor, having tripped over themselves in their rush to court Miss Harlow. A large orchestra would be arrayed along the back wall, opposite the speaker's podium, and next to it would be a table with a bowl of the notoriously weak lemonade served at Almack's.

Yes, she thought with silent satisfaction, that would do very well.

The play ended with a standing ovation, which her mother enthusiastically joined despite not having watched a single moment of the performance, and it was universally agreed that they would not stay for the afterpiece. The duchess cited her own fatigue, but it was her sister who in fact looked exhausted.

"Well, that was a treat," said Lady Bolingbroke as soon as she and Agatha were in their carriage. "I cannot recall the last time I've enjoyed myself so much. The duchess and her sister are charming, and the acting was sublime. I do believe I shed a tear at the end."

Given that *The Merchant of Venice* was a comedy, Agatha could only suppose her mother had cried because she had to leave off watching her neighbors.

Lady Bolingbroke recounted the delights of the evening during the drive home, which was mercifully short. Once inside the Portland Place residence, she requested a light repast to be served in the drawing room, but Agatha excused herself to work on her illustration. She did not say that to her mother, of course, claiming instead to be too tired to eat anything. Her mother would be horrified if she knew the truth and would most likely disown her. She was impatient enough with Agatha's stubborn insistence on painting with oils, rather than making tasteful watercolor daubs like other accomplished young ladies of marriageable age. That her daughter had a genuine talent for painting was a source of embarrassment for her and seemed of a piece with her inability to appropriately calibrate her laughter. Both indicated a deplorable lack of moderation.

Agatha abided by her mother's wishes that she not put her portraits on public display and hung them in the privacy of their own home, mostly in her bedroom, with a few in her father's study. The majority of her work was piled in stacks along the walls of the small downstairs room given over to her studio. She was also under strict orders not to inconvenience the staff in her never-ending hunt for subject matter. She complied with this request as well by seeking out the servants in their natural environment and drawing quick studies that she filled in later at her easel. Only her maid Ellen was able to sit for her and that was because her mother thought it took hours to make Agatha's coarse hair presentable. In truth, it took mere minutes; the rest of the time was given over to posing and painting.

Having made these concessions to her parent, Agatha had to have some outlet for her passion. It wasn't enough to paint in obscurity and display her portraits in secret. She craved—nay, hungered—for her work to be seen and admired and discussed. If drawing caricatures for Mrs. Biddle's shop in St. James's Street was the best she could do, so be it.

Lady Agony had been thwarted enough in her twenty-two years to be grateful for anything she could get.

With this melancholy thought in mind, she donned a smock, lit several candelabras, retrieved a fresh piece of paper and got down to work.

CHAPTER TWO

Although Miss Lavinia Harlow had never before demonstrated a new invention, she felt quite certain that six servants, three family members and one fiancé were a large enough group for a satisfying exhibition. Her sister, Emma, disagreed and insisted Vinnie wait while she gathered an audience more appropriate to the occasion. To that end, the Duchess of Trent was down in the kitchens assuring Mrs. Chater that neither she nor her staff would suffer any ill consequences if the potatoes currently in need of peeling were a little under-cooked at supper.

Emma did not also immediately assure Mrs. Chater and her staff that they would suffer no ill consequences should they decide not to drop everything to admire her sister's handiwork, and it fell to her husband, Alexander Keswick, Duke of Trent, to make that fact clear.

"But it goes without saying," his wife insisted.

"No, it does not," her husband countered.

Twenty minutes later, Emma strode into the conservatory with the entire kitchen staff, Dobbins from the stables and yet another footman in tow, causing her sister to wince.

"There's no need to make a fuss," Vinnie said, disconcerted by all the attention. When she'd entered the

22

room an hour before, she had not intended to make an elaborate presentation. Her plan had been simply to test her watering hose to confirm for her own edification that the device actually worked. Confirmation was necessary because the only successful occurrence had happened the day before amid a profusion of tears and looking back now she couldn't be sure if she or the hose had produced the stream of water.

Ordinarily, Vinnie would not have been working on an important project while sobbing uncontrollably, but her sanity had required she come up with some distraction to keep her mind off her own misery. The previous evening, only minutes before she was to make the speech to the British Horticultural Society that would decide her membership to the organization, she had bared her soul to the Marquess of Huntly, and other than look at her with utter shock, he had not formulated a response. More than a dozen hours later, she had been beside herself with anxiety.

The reason the marquess had not issued a prompt reply—either positive ("I love you, too") or negative ("I appreciate the sentiment, Miss Harlow, but cannot return it, as I'm appalled and disgusted by you")—was he had been racketing around the countryside in search of her father to ask for Miss Harlow's hand in marriage. While he had been seeking the disinterested Mr. Harlow, Vinnie's heart had been slowly crumbling. By the time Huntly returned to London, she had been thoroughly wrung out by the emotional turmoil of the long day, but his declaration of love, ardently stated and ably demonstrated, revived her to such an extent she hadn't minded going to the theater with Lady Bolingbroke and her famously standoffish daughter. Naturally, she'd tried to extricate herself from the engagement, for she had an adored fiancé into whose eyes she wanted to happily gaze, but she submitted graciously to her sister's demands and thoroughly enjoyed the outing. Not even Lady Agony's sour puss could dull her high spirits.

And now, obligation fulfilled and uncertainty behind her, she was eager to test her invention for a second time. If only Emma would let her.

"There's every need to make a fuss," her twin insisted. "The Brill Method Improvised Elasticized Hose is the single most exciting scientific innovation in the history of gardening."

Vinnie smiled faintly at this elaborate and clearly overblown assertion. "You know nothing about the history of gardening."

"A matter that can be easily rectified," Huntly said, his eyes glinting with humor. "Only say the word and Vinnie will provide you with a full accounting of the Archimedes screw pump."

She had done precisely that to him on their first meeting, which occurred in that very room several weeks before. After almost two years at sea, Huntly had entered the conservatory to reacquaint himself with his friend's orchid collection and found his person summarily doused by an exploding hose—one of Vinnie's early prototypes. As surprised as he was by the unexpected soaking, Vinnie stammered a reply so nonsensical, the marquess naturally assumed her attics were to let.

It was a bizarre first meeting, hardly indicative of a great love, and only someone such as Emma, with her perverse notions, would have concluded they were fated to make a match of it.

"It's not accurate to say I know nothing about the history of gardening," Emma said. "I know it's deadly dull and your hose is absolutely thrilling—which is why a large and admiring audience is required."

Vinnie split a quelling look between her betrothed—teasing her about their dreadful first encounter!—and her sister. Then she raised an eyebrow as she surveyed the crowd. "I trust the audience is suitable now?"

Emma wrinkled her forehead as she considered the question, and her husband, anticipating her response, forestalled her with a raised hand. "Don't say it, imp." Then he turned to Vinnie and told her to proceed at her leisure.

Although she hadn't planned on making a speech, Vinnie felt some explanation of what her observers were about to see was necessary, for what they were about to see was something very underwhelming indeed. Only Emma would gather two dozen people to observe a hose expel a stream of water in a calm and steady fashion.

"Thank you for your interest," Vinnie said, with a self-conscious and apologetic smile at Mrs. Chater, who surely had more important things to do than stand around the conservatory watching flowers get wet. Despite potatoes to peel and fish to debone, the cook had an attentive look on her face. Everyone did, even the dowager duchess, an intimidating matron of the *ton* who had sternly disapproved of Vinnie's application to the British Horticultural Society. "As some of you know, especially Tupper, who has had to clean up many of my failed experiments, I've devoted considerable time in the past few months to trying to improve the modern watering hose. The problem with the hose is it's made of leather stitched together. Leather is not a very flexible material, so it tends to burst rather than stretch. My idea was to take the method by which Mr. Samuel Brill, a shoe manufacturer, used India-rubber to increase his shoes' imperviousness to water to improve the elastication of leather. I have succeeded in that aim, as I intend to demonstrate right now."

Her brief explanation done—and Vinnie was very proud of herself for being so concise and not veering off onto a tangent about turpentine—she lifted the hose and tested its suppleness. Satisfied, she reached out her hand to turn the device on, her heartbeat elevated from either excitement or uncertainty or both, and just as her fingers made contact with the pump, the dowager's daughter burst into the room with a wild look on her face.

"There you are, Mama," Louisa said, her tone exasperated and annoyed as she marched over to the dowager, waving a newspaper in her hand. "I have been looking everywhere for you and I assure you it has been an ordeal. The entire house is deserted. I had to open the front door myself. Do you understand the magnitude of the inconvenience of opening a door for oneself? Are we monkeys? Do we live in a zoo? And what if the prince regent had come to call? Would he have been forced to open the door for himself? Imagine the mortification."

The dowager knew her daughter's dramatics too well to dignify this absurdity with a response, but Emma could not resist. "I imagine the prince regent travels with an entourage well schooled in the operation of the door knob."

Louisa turned to her brother's troublesome spouse suddenly, as if surprised to see her. Her attention had been focused so intently on her mother when she'd entered the room that she hadn't noticed anyone else. Now she looked around and saw scullery maids and stable hands in the conservatory. Good lord, was that Mr. Colson, who kept the household accounts?

Although she knew just whom to blame for the unusual gathering, she addressed her next question to her mother, not the hoyden. "What is happening here?"

The dowager smiled. "To be completely honest, I'm not entirely sure, my dear. I believe we are celebrating the engagement of Huntly and Vinnie in the manner in which horticulturally inclined people celebrate engagements." She glanced at her son for confirmation. "Is that not correct?"

Before Trent could answer, Louisa gasped in horror and her face paled. Although she had the same coloring as her younger brother—rich brown hair, deep brown eyes— marriage to an obstinate man and being mother to two irrepressible children had given her a gaunt appearance ill served by the lack of color. "But that's horrible. Tell me it's not true," she implored the marquess.

Vinnie felt her own color drain as the force of Louisa's words hit her. She knew she wasn't the ideal wife for most fashionable gentlemen, as her passion of drainage systems made her worse than a bluestocking—a greenstocking perhaps—but she would defy anyone, Louisa included, to come up with a spouse better suited to Huntly than she.

Even knowing how perfectly matched they were, she felt the sting of Louisa's disapproval. She hadn't expected Trent's sister to delight in the news, but nor had she prepared herself for such fervent objection. Her vehemence was so astonishing, Vinnie could not think of a single thing to say.

Fortunately, she didn't have to, for a forceful chorus rang out in her defense. Emma's outrage, of course, was the loudest, but it was joined by Huntly's anger, the duke's indignation and the dowager's horror at having raised a child with such appalling manners. Even the butler Caruthers voiced his censure with a deeply felt, "I say, ma'am."

Taken aback by the unprovoked attack, Louisa stared at her family as if they were all bedlamites, then whistled sharply to gain their attention. "You misunderstand me. I have no objection to Miss Harlow marrying Huntly. Why in the world would I? I think she's a dear girl, albeit with an eccentric hobby that is quite outside the bounds of what is the standard. Do I think that hobby is so encroaching it may adversely affect the care of her children? Perhaps. But, I assure you, that's no business of mine if she chooses to ignore her family."

While Vinnie tried to decipher the meaning of this bizarre speech, Emma opened her mouth to object to its falsely conciliating tone. "Now, see here, you—"

"No, Emma," the duke said with a firm shake of his head. "Calling my sister names, while no doubt gratifying, will not aid the situation. The same applies to you, Huntly. Now I suggest we all retire to the drawing room and have a sensible conversation." Then he turned to Vinnie and added, "I fear your demonstration will have to be postponed for the moment, but we will reconvene at a later hour. I know we are all eager to see the Brill Method Improvised Elasticized Hose in action."

If Vinnie had found it embarrassing to have such a large crowd assembled on her behalf once, it paled in comparison with her mortification at the thought of it being assembled again. She did not, however, want to appear churlish or ungrateful, so she agreed to this plan and removed to the drawing room in the wake of her sister, whose sotto voce complaints about Louisa were clearly meant to be heard by everyone.

Once they were settled in the drawing room—a formal affair with classic English furniture arrayed in tasteful colors—the dowager invited Louisa to explain herself. "And choose your words carefully, for as you yourself have pointed out, this is not the zoo. Don't rattle the cages."

Louisa sat in a wingback, her shoulders stiff and straight against the chair's maroon leather. "Of course, Mama, I always speak with forethought and circumspection, even if others don't. I could, of course, take offense at how willingly my family chose to believe the worst of me, as I have done nothing to earn such distrust, but I will rise above the insult and explain that my objection is not rooted in Miss Harlow's unsuitability but Mr. Holyroodhouse's offensive drawing."

Huntly laughed as he recalled the lampoon the famous caricaturist had drawn depicting the members of the British Horticultural Society as flowers at the mercy of a grotesque woman who looked vaguely like Vinnie. She was clutching the tulip bearing the Marquess of Huntly's face in her hands over a caption that read "Plucked!"

"I appreciate your concern, Louisa, but I've long accepted my situation and don't cavil. In fact, I enjoy being plucked by Miss Harlow," the marquess announced with a warm look at his fiancée, who promptly turned a shade of red so bright, she would have glowed if someone had extinguished all the candles.

"That is old news. Literally," Louisa announced, with a cluck of her tongue as she laid the paper on the table for everyone to see. It featured a new drawing by the talented Mr. Holyroodhouse, one in which the soaring rotunda of the British Horticultural Society, where just two nights before Vinnie had made the presentation that had earned her acceptance, was transformed into a ballroom. Surrounding Vinnie, who stood in the center, were the twenty-six members of the horticultural society clamoring to sign her dance card. Beneath the picture were the words *The British Matrimonial Society.*

In an instant, the color drained from Vinnie's face and she inhaled sharply as she absorbed the impact of the abuse. Unlike her younger sister, she wasn't accustomed to being the subject of mockery. Before she had decided to pursue membership in the society, the most unconventional thing she had done was plant narcissus next to *Allium cepa*, a daring move that could result in an upset stomach if an untrained eye mistook a daffodil bulb for an onion.

Now she had been held up for public ridicule twice in as many weeks and she realized with sudden clarity that it would never stop. Like a naïve child, she had assumed her notoriety was only a temporary condition, a nine days' wonder swiftly supplanted by the next sensation, but she had failed to account for Mr. Holyroodhouse's bottom line. He was an ink-stained fiend, to be sure, and as long as jeering images of her sold prints, he would continue to produce them.

When the first drawing appeared, she had responded with her usual practicality and attempted to withdraw her candidacy to the society. Without question, she had been mortified to see herself portrayed as a monstrous harridan with jabby elbows, but it was the ruthless treatment of Huntly that proved the decisive stroke. She could not allow him to be the subject of so much derision. Unaware at the time of the depth of her feelings for him, she did not know why the notion so unsettled her, only that it did.

Unimpressed by her grand gesture, Huntly had promptly informed her that she would not be withdrawing. Instead, she would make her presentation to the society one week hence and the matter of her application would be decided by a vote, not by a toad-eating dandiprat with a pen.

Indeed it had been decided, somehow in her favor, and Vinnie, who'd had no real expectation of gaining admittance to the esteemed institution, found that her delight in the accomplishment had lasted—she glanced at the clock over the mantel—precisely twenty-six hours and forty-three minutes.

Such a small window of enjoyment, she thought now, as she contemplated the usefulness of trying to resign. Huntly would not allow it, she knew that. Neither would her sister, who had compiled dossiers on all the society's members in order to give Vinnie a tactical advantage. Trent would oppose it, too, for he had long been her champion and had done everything possible to advance her cause. Even the dowager, who considered membership to the British Horticultural Society to be an absurd affectation for a woman, would disavow any suggestion of quitting. Having achieved her masculine goal, Vinnie should at least have the fortitude to see it through.

They were all looking at her now, waiting for her response, and as much as she wanted to concede the field to the unscrupulous Mr. Holyroodhouse, she resolved to hold her ground. For weeks, she had been trying to convince her intrepid sister that she had the same indomitable spirit, and crumbling at the first available opportunity would hardly demonstrate that point.

Smiling brightly, though she knew the color had yet to return to her cheeks, Vinnie said, "I am happy to see my elbows were given fairer shrift this time. They are not so pointy that I'm at risk of eviscerating passersby on the sidewalk."

"Yes," Emma said with a thoughtful nod, "but the bump on your nose is larger."

Huntly agreed with both assessments and said, "Your lips are thinner."

"And you have a charming hump," Trent added.

His mother scoffed at his absurd observation. "That's not a hump, my dear, it's Huntly's hand. Your confusion is understandable, however, as it looks like a joint of ham."

Trent leaned in closer for a better look. "So it is. Sorry, old man, but your fingers would be vastly improved with a regular regimen of exercise. I could refer you to Gentleman Jackson for a program."

Huntly held up both his hands for the room to examine. "I appreciate your concern, Alex, but as you can see, the joint-of-ham aspect is merely artistic license."

The dowager nodded approvingly. "Now that we've resolved that pressing matter, let's ring for tea. Lavinia, could you please do the honor, as I know your heathen sister will open the door and holler for the servants like a chimney sweep."

As Emma protested this characterization on the grounds that chimney sweeps do not have servants, Louisa emitted a low squeal, as if she were a bagpipe slowly losing all its air. The sound grew louder and louder, increasing in pitch and vigor, until it was an ear-piercing shriek.

Her mother, who was in the middle of chastising Emma on her pedantry, broke off her speech to stare at Louisa in surprise. "I hardly think—"

"No," her daughter said angrily. "*I* hardly think! I came here out of the kindness of my heart because I do not want the people I care about to be the object of censure and ridicule. I have other responsibilities that require my attention, including but not limited to the rearing of two brilliant but strong-minded children, but I put them aside out of concern for my family. And for my efforts, I get talk of ham and climbing boys. You are all mad. Yes, Mama, I said *all*," she added defiantly. "I used to be able to depend on your good sense and reliable disposition, but in recent months, I've noticed a frivolous streak that I find quite discomforting. I am not implying it is my sister-in-law's fault, for I had seen indications of it before her, most particularly when you insisted on training a parrot to sing 'La Marseillaise,' but it has become more marked in the months since Trent's marriage and for that I don't believe she can be held entirely unaccountable."

Although Louisa had expressed this thought in many varied ways during the past seven months, it was the first time she cited the dowager's parrot as evidence of previous frivolity and Emma insisted on knowing the full story: how, what and, for God's sake, why.

"It was for Prinny's birthday," her mother-in-law explained. "Sir Reginald—you know how droll he can be—noted that the French national anthem sounded precisely like the squawk of a parrot, which Prinny found highly amusing, so naturally I was obliged to demonstrate the truth of the observation. I must confess the results were mixed, for the parrot's tone wasn't quite as nasally as—"

The thought went unfinished as Louisa shrieked for a

second time. Her tone was more forceful still and could be categorized as an outright scream.

Once again, she had the full attention of the room, and not wanting to risk losing it to another inconsequential diversion (though the embarrassment she felt over the parrot incident could hardly be described as inconsequential), she said, "Although I am happy for Vinnie and Huntly and offer them my felicitations, you must comprehend why we cannot announce their engagement."

Huntly smiled and assured her that wouldn't be a problem, for they had no intention of announcing their engagement. "We plan to marry by special license as soon as it can be arranged," he said, "and will send notice of the wedding to the papers."

Louisa's sigh of relief was quickly supplanted by a gasp of horror. "Absolutely not! Miss Harlow is just out of black gloves. Her fiancé died only seven months ago. Every sensibility would be offended by such a hasty marriage."

No, Vinnie thought, not *every*, for her sensibilities were quite fine with it. Her late fiancé, Sir Waldo Windbourne, was a villain and a traitor who had sold England's secrets to the highest bidder and maimed her brother, Roger, in a failed murder attempt. The only reason Sir Waldo had courted her in the first place was to gain access to her brother's secret papers, for he knew Roger worked as a spy for the Home Office and hoped to ascertain confidential information.

Emma had taken an immediate dislike of Windbourne. She'd found him pompous and verbose, a combination that led her to call him Sir Windbag, and she'd despised the condescension with which he had treated her twin's skill with plants, as if it were a children's toy to be abandoned at the first opportunity. Her antipathy had been based on nothing save personal preference, though she would argue it was intuition, not opinion, but her instincts proved remarkably accurate. It was she who discovered Windbourne's treachery, and in the most hoydenish act of a very hoydenish career, she'd chased him through the countryside to intercept a message that could have proven fatal to the future of England.

She'd achieved her goal in the end but not before risking her life and ultimately her sister's, and it had been Vinnie, who, mere seconds from being gutted by a fish knife when Windbourne broke into their town house in the middle of the night, shot her fiancé dead with a pistol.

Although she had suffered no physical harm in the confrontation, Vinnie had not emerged from the ordeal entirely unscathed. Her confidence had taken a pummeling as well as any faith in her own judgment. Clearly, she could not be relied upon to recognize a black-hearted villain when he turned up on her doorstep feigning adoration. Adjusting to the fact that she had taken a life also required some effort. She felt no guilt over the deed, for it had been a matter of survival—her own or Windbourne's—but nor could she dismiss it entirely. It was now part of who she was: Miss Lavinia Harlow, murderess.

And not just a murderess—a liar, as well, for she had had to pretend to grieve the death of her fiancé, lest the *ton* discover the horrible truth. For six long months, she had to wear the willow for a man she despised.

The truth had been covered up to protect Vinnie, yes, but it was also a state secret, for none of the actors could be revealed without endangering lives or embarrassing the Crown. The list of people who knew the truth was very short—Vinnie and Emma, their brother and his wife, the duke and his cousin Philip—and had recently expanded to include Huntly. To no one's surprise, the Home Office was determined to keep the group as small as possible.

The need for secrecy created an intolerable situation that was hardly conducive to forming a lasting attachment, and yet somehow in the midst of her fake mourning, she had developed a real tendre for the Marquess of Huntly. She had not expected to. In the wake of her disastrous relationship with Windbourne, she had not believed it even possible. That the marquess returned her regard seemed like nothing less than a miracle, and she would not deny herself one moment of happiness to satisfy an empty social convention.

"I appreciate your concern," Vinnie said calmly, "but we are resolved to go forward with our plan."

Louisa stared at her in shock. "Resolved to go forward with social ostracism? My dear girl, think of what you're saying."

"That's enough, Louisa," her mother said sharply. "You have made your point, and everyone in the room has heard it. Personally, I believe you are overstating the matter slightly, for no one would dare ostracize the Marquess of Huntly's wife. And don't forget who her sister is. To be sure, Emma is a confirmed scapegrace, but she's still the Duchess of Trent and she has acquitted herself reasonably since her marriage. I don't think anyone would dare give Miss Harlow the cut direct, and if they did, they would have to answer to me."

This sentiment, entirely unexpected from a woman who had stridently objected to Vinnie's candidacy to the British Horticultural Society, was as affecting as it was surprising, but before Vinnie could voice her gratitude, the dowager forestalled her with a raised hand.

"No, my dear, don't be flattered or touched," the dowager said, her tone cool. "Your happiness, while not entirely inconsequential to me, is not as important as my consequence. A fine arbiter of taste and fashion I would be if I could not carry off one slightly scandalous marriage." She turned to her daughter as Tupper carried in the tea tray. "You have always been a high-strung child, for which I accept full responsibility. I did not take care to make sure you got enough mutton when you were in leading strings."

Louisa did not know what to make of this charge of meat deficiency, for she did not believe there was a connection between temperament and lamb consumption. Moreover, she did not think her mother believed it either. The woman was simply being frivolous again. For some reason, she found it amusing to support Miss Harlow's wedding and would not listen to a single word against it. The dowager's recalcitrance was another alarming development, and Louisa wondered how to address it without running the risk of having her disposition described as overly sensitive.

Luckily for the dowager, Louisa was denied the opportunity to respond by the arrival of the twins' sister-in-law. Mrs. Sarah Harlow was a tall woman with a slim build and calm brown eyes that sparkled when she was amused. Her posture was excellent, her temper was even, and she had a refined manner befitting the daughter of a viscount. For years, she had been responsible for squiring Emma and Vinnie around town, a duty she had performed with mixed results, as some of the Harlow Hoyden's most outlandish exploits had occurred under her aegis, most notably a neck-or-nothing race from London to Newmarket to break Sir Leopold's three-year-old record. That escapade, which beat the standing time by two minutes and seven seconds, had been carried out with the full blessing of the twins' brother, Roger, but the gossips still laid the sin at Sarah's feet. Men could not be relied upon to act sensibly, especially where curricle races were concerned.

She had fared far better with Vinnie, whose willful streak did not emerge until after she had moved into the Duke of Trent's town house. Although she was genuinely happy for Vinnie that she had achieved her goal of being accepted into the horticultural society, Sarah was at a loss to understand why she would want to.

Looking at her former charges now, comfortably ensconced in the duke's elegant drawing room like a pair of gracious young ladies, she wondered how two such harmless-looking girls could have caused her so much anxiety.

"Good afternoon," Sarah said with an amiable smile. "I got here as fast as I could, but I fear I may be too late."

"I can not confirm or deny that supposition," the duke said, striding over to greet his new guest, "until I know for what you are here."

"The demonstration, of course," she explained.

Vinnie sighed loudly and glanced at her sister with exasperated chagrin. "You invited Sarah?"

"And Roger and Philip and Mr. Berry from the horticultural society," Emma noted calmly. "In order for an audience to be large, it must contain a large number of people. I don't know what happened to Philip, but Mr. Berry sends his regrets and assures you he looks forward to your demonstration at the society."

As Vinnie hadn't originally planned to do one presentation, the news that she would now have to do two was not entirely welcome. It wasn't Sarah's fault, however, that her twin was pathologically supportive, and she quickly assured her sister-in-law that she hadn't missed a thing. "The demonstration will take place shortly. Please have some tea in the meanwhile."

"Yes," Louisa said, the light of triumph in her eyes as she sensed an ally in their midst. Mrs. Harlow was a sensible woman of good breeding. Surely, she would immediately grasp the untenability of a hasty marriage. "Please do join us for tea. We were just discussing Mr. Holyroodhouse's most recent work."

With a moue of disgust, Sarah sat down on the settee and accepted a cup of tea from the dowager. "Has that dreadful man struck again?"

"He has," Louisa said, presenting the offending illustration to Sarah with an eager flourish, and was duly rewarded for her zeal when the other woman cried out, "Oh, no. How wretched!" Then she reached out and grasped Vinnie's hand in a comforting squeeze.

Gratified by the response, Louisa said, "I'm relieved to see that *someone* in this family understands the ramifications of such catastrophic prescience. Please explain to them, Mrs. Harlow, why they can't possibly get married now."

The request was so puzzling to Sarah that her brow immediately furrowed as she looked from Vinnie to Emma to Huntly to Trent, trying to figure out what Louisa meant. She knew of no impending marriage, but when she looked at Vinnie again, she saw the bright eyes and giddy smile and squealed in delight. Then she enveloped her former charge in an enthusiastic hug and congratulated Huntly on his very good sense in selecting Vinnie for his wife.

"You are perfectly suited and I'm sure you will be very

happy together," she said. "I know your brother, Roger, will feel the same way when he hears the news. Oh, this is the best possible development."

For Louisa, Mrs. Harlow's enthusiastic support of the match was the worst possible development, as it proved conclusively that she was the only reasonable person in the room. Everyone else was either mad or a victim of willful ignorance. Even if Vinnie were not just out of black gloves, the cutting insight of Mr. Holyroodhouse served as a sufficient deterrent to matrimony. How could any member of the British Horticultural Society marry the new female member when it had been so recently ridiculed as an annex of the marriage mart? She would have assumed Huntly's pride could not bear the insult.

And yet the future bridegroom seemed not the least bit perturbed by the mockery, and Louisa, conceding defeat, announced her intention to leave. Emma, however, was unwilling to surrender a single member of her large audience and insisted she stay for the demonstration, which was once again delayed as the duchess rounded up a crowd of spectators appropriate to the occasion.

Finally, Vinnie was given the signal to proceed and rather than reprise her speech from earlier, she merely turned on the hose and watched with giddy pride as her device worked exactly as it was supposed to. Cautiously, she increased the water pressure and grinned with delight as the contraption held—no tears, no bursts, no unfortunate soakings of innocent bystanders.

Her audience, perceiving the importance of the moment if not the significance of the accomplishment, clapped enthusiastically, while the Marquess of Huntly took very great advantage of his new position and kissed his fiancée imprudently on the mouth while the entire household staff looked on.

"Now, *that* is what I call a demonstration," Emma said approvingly.

CHAPTER THREE

To say that Jonah Hamilton, Viscount Addleson, was unimpressed by *Agastache rupestris* would be to understate the case significantly. It would be more accurate to declare with unequivocal certainty that he found the flower—commonly known as sunset hyssop—to be the least interesting cultivar he'd ever had the displeasure of examining through a magnifying glass.

"Its ability to withstand high temperatures and arid soil makes it particularly well suited to the desert regions and mountain ranges of the American West," Mr. Caleb Petrie explained as he directed Addleson's attention to the plant's spidery roots and spoke for five minutes on the benefits of a shallow root system for maximizing water absorption.

Previous lecture subjects had included the flower's startlingly vibrant orange petals, reminiscent of a sunset, of course, which was how the plant got its name, and its usefulness in attracting bees.

Why anyone would want to attract a horde of insects that stung its quarry with random ferocity the viscount could not fathom. Nor could he comprehend why anyone would fret about the amount of water a plant absorbed during a three-month period in a climate of moderate dryness.

And yet Mr. Petrie continued to discuss these subjects at length with barely contained enthusiasm, his pale blue eyes glowing with excitement as he focused his magnifying glass on a spindly brown root. He was an unusually tall gentleman with a graying beard, and after fifty-two years of looking down on his fellow enthusiasts, he had started to consider them beneath his notice. This predilection explained why he failed to see the glassy-eyed boredom in his lone audience member's gaze. "You see, it's exactly as I said," he observed eagerly.

Like any titled gentleman of impeccable breeding, the viscount did not mind being bored to flinders. Indeed, he considered it one of his chief obligations as a member of the peerage. Dinner hostesses, business associates, simpering misses, ignorant cawkers, swells of the first stare—they all conspired to keep him in a semipermanent state of ennui. Addleson wasn't an impatient man, merely a quick-thinking one, and few people or things presented sufficient stimulation to maintain his interest. To his late father's irritation, he had the deplorable ability to immediately identify a problem and present a solution, a skill that assured his estates ran with unprecedented efficiency but left him with few challenges. Vingt-un had been a consuming occupation for a while—before he realized he could keep track of all the cards in play and was no longer surprised by the revelation of a hand.

As tolerant as he was of boredom, however, Addleson was willing to shoulder only his fair share of it, and the fact that he was Mr. Petrie's sole victim bothered him hugely. If the lecture had been addressed to the entire room, which was, to be sure, stocked to the ceiling with plant devotees, he would not cavil. But it was directed exclusively at him and there was no good reason why he alone should be singled out for the honor. His interest in flowers extended only to the presenting of them to Incognitas and courtesans and even then he performed such courtesies infrequently. A man of his ilk—cultured and tailored to within an inch of his life—had no business knowing the word *cultivar*, let alone how to use it correctly in a sentence.

Indifferent to the viscount's shame or, perhaps, even oblivious to it, the thoughtless Mr. Petrie had foisted that knowledge on him as he had other information, a development Addleson deeply resented. There were few experiences more unpleasant to an Englishman than to be educated against his will.

Of course, attending the soiree had been a mistake. A gathering to welcome an unknown naturalist from the wilds of North America was hardly Viscount Addleson's natural milieu. A gathering to welcome a well-known one was no more his scene, but that at least carried the cachet of meeting a celebrated figure. In this case, however, he had been unable to resist the enthusiasms of his cousin, who had sworn up and down that the evening would be the most thrilling affair of the season. The viscount, being almost thirty years of age and suspicious of all superlatives, doubted very much that the event would rise to the level of entertainment vehemently professed, but his sense of humor was such that it compelled him to witness firsthand exactly how *un*thrilling it was. For his perversity, he'd earned a private audience with the evening's guest of honor, whose success among other unknown naturalists from the wilds of North America was mentioned several times by the visitor himself.

The viscount found it difficult to believe there were any other American naturalists, let alone additional unknown ones, but he held his tongue and waited out his punishment. He knew it was pointless to try to interrupt a man who traveled with his own magnifying glass. Had Petrie produced a monocle or even a loupe like a jeweler, Addleson would not have hesitated to change the subject, for the reticent nature of those devices implied an openness to new ideas. But Petrie's magnifying glass, with its mother-of-pearl handle that freed its user from all physical constraints, indicated a dominant mind unwilling to be swayed.

"No, no, no," Petrie said suddenly and vigorously, as if confirming the viscount's thoughts, which would have been an impressive feat, for the speaker seemed entirely unaware that his lordship had any. "You must not ask me about the soil quality of the Atlantic coastline, for my assistant, Mr. Clemmons, is not here and he knows all the precise details of my research, which is, as of yet, incomplete. You are right to point out the several articles I've published on *Ammophila breviligulata,* as they caused quite a stir in my home state. I look forward to working further with those subjects when I return to New York. I suppose I could have declined this trip to pursue my study, but an invitation to speak at the British Horticultural Society is too great an honor to turn down. If only my assistant were here. He had been all ready to board the ship with me when he was suddenly and inexplicably overcome by a hideous stomach ailment. But that is neither here nor there, for your interest is only in the suppositions that I hope to confirm as soon as I return to New York, which has several promising islands in the immediate environs of the port. However, since you asked, I will discuss the tolerance of *Ammophila breviligulata* to intense heat, excessive sunlight and drying winds."

The truth was, of course, that Addleson had not asked about the soil quality of the Atlantic coastline, and he strongly doubted the American would have heard the question if he had. Like all bores, he preferred his own thoughts and opinions to the exclusion of others and had changed the subject from *Agastache rupestris* to *Ammophila breviligulata* without any prompting from his victim. Addleson's father had been the same way, pontificating at length on topics of interest to him, but the late viscount had the additional debility of limited intelligence, which made him suspicious of everyone, including his son.

Smothering a sigh, Addleson glanced around the parlor, a comfortable room decorated in quiet shades of blue and gray, and spotted his cousin by the window in deep conversation with the Earl of Moray. Edward wore an expression of amazed wonder as he nodded agreeably to everything Moray said. No doubt they were discussing the vital importance of sun to *Flowericus randomonus.* A few feet to their left was Lord Bolingbroke, a tall, stout gentleman whose imposing stature was undermined by the look of rapt fascination on his face and a coquelicot waistcoat two sizes too small. Examining him, Addleson could not decide which of his host's offenses was greater: his complete indifference to the suffering of one of his guests or his offensively bright, ill-fitting, red waistcoat.

No, thought Addleson with a small shake of his head, it was easily the waistcoat. Obliviousness could always be dismissed as the unanticipated effect of excessive excitement, but there was never an excuse for displaying poor sartorial judgment. If one could not be relied upon to show faultless taste at all times, then one was obligated to hire a valet who would. It was the single most important rule of being a titled gentleman, after cooling down your horses properly following exercise and giving your servants generous Boxing Day presents.

As understanding as Addleson was of his host's distraction, he still could not help being irked by it. Yes, the waistcoat was the graver sin, but its unappealing color did not entirely overshadow Bolingbroke's failure to attend to his duties as host. Even if he did not notice Petrie monopolizing the viscount, surely he should have noticed the *viscount* monopolizing *Petrie*. After all, the man was the guest of honor, the reason the large and elegant crowd had gathered in the blue-gray parlor, and yet nobody had tried to claim his attention for—Addleson looked at his watch—twenty-three minutes. Certainly by now a kindly onlooker or an impatient admirer should have saved the naturalist from the viscount's clutches with a pointed interruption. Addleson was not possessive of his victimhood. He didn't care who was thought to be the sufferer as long as it was acknowledged that *someone* in the conversation was suffering.

"It has not been confirmed yet," Petrie said, continuing his monologue unabated, "for I have not had the chance to complete my research, a development that I attribute to this delightful visit, which I may have mentioned before—please forgive me if I repeat myself. At a certain point, one acquires so much knowledge one cannot keep all the facts and figures straight in one's head without a chart or an assistant, such as the helpful Mr. Clemmons. I do wish he were here so he could give you the particulars you seek. However, as I was saying, it's my belief that *Ammophila breviligulata* is less vigorous in stabilized sand. This theory is based on the curious fact that *Ammophila breviligulata* is harder to find inland than along the coastline. From my astute observation, I can naturally suppose that it thrives under a certain circumstance."

Finding coastal plants no more interesting than root systems, Addleson looked at his watch again. Over the years, he had developed a method for surreptitiously checking the time so as not to give offense, but he did not bother to employ it now, for it was clear to him that Petrie would not notice. Nobody in the room would notice, he thought with a chagrined look at his cousin, who remained in thrall to Moray. Damn Edward! Bolingbroke was no better, nor was Lord Waldegrave, with his ingratiating smile at his host's wife, or Mrs. Clydeon, who was bent over a modest pamphlet with a green cover, or—

Shifting his head, Addleson suddenly found himself the object of Lady Agatha's frank appraisal, her black eyes steady as she watched him. He was startled to discover himself unknowingly observed—had she seen him consult the time? wince at her father's waistcoat?—and assumed his surprise explained the odd little buzzing sound he heard in his head as his gaze locked with hers. It was the strangest thing he'd ever experienced—the way the world seemed to stop and hum as they stared at each other, as if immobilized by a swarm of bees circling above their heads.

Lady Agatha did not look away. She did not flinch or cringe or recoil or jump or show any reaction at all at being caught in so blatant a study of him. She did not pretend to suddenly be fascinated by the seam of her glove or a spot on the floor. She kept her head straight and her eyes fixed and her expression blank.

Addleson remained still, as well, his own gaze as constant

as hers, as the seconds ticked by. He couldn't say what he was doing exactly. Not staring. No, sir, for he would never engage in such deliberately boorish and rude behavior. Observing, perhaps. Lady Agatha, with her severe black eyes, resolute chin and implausibly pert nose, was certainly a curiosity as worthy of close examination as the root of the sunset hyssop. Categorizing the act as mere observation, however, was too feeble and failed to account for the compulsive nature of the moment because, yes, there was something about it that felt a little beyond his control. Maybe it was merely a contest, a battle to see whose will was stronger, and Addleson, a competitive sort, could not bring himself to abandon the field.

The problem with that simple explanation, which the viscount favored because it *was* so straightforward, was it did not account for the buzz that continued to sound in his ears. The hum was an odd development, to be sure, but with his well-established skepticism of superlatives, he doubted that it was truly the strangest thing that had ever happened to him, for how could such a momentous event happen there, in Lord Bolingbroke's tasteful drawing room during his tedious soiree in the middle of a tiresome discussion of beach grass by an international bore?

No, nothing of import had occurred, except, perhaps, the viscount's reluctant acquisition of the word *cultivar,* which he intended to forfeit as soon as he exited the building.

With this concise thought in his head, Addleson decided the bizarre—though, obviously, not *most* bizarre—moment had gone on long enough and resolved to look away. He had better things to do than to stare down an odd female. But before he could bring himself to look away, the appalling girl raised her left eyebrow. The movement was subtle yet calculated, and though she revealed no humor in the curve of her lips or in the depth of her eyes, the viscount could feel her amusement.

If they had indeed been engaged in a contest of stares, then Lord Bolingbroke's daughter had handily prevailed. But just because she had taken the first round did not mean she had won the competition.

Although it felt to Addleson as if several minutes had passed, it had in fact been only a few seconds and Mr. Petrie was still discussing the concentration of *Ammophila breviligulata* along the American coastline.

"What I refer to in my articles as a sand dune, which, if you are not familiar with the term, means—"

Addleson tilted his head to the side. "I apologize for the interruption, Mr. Petrie, but did you just say sand dune?"

The American continued his explanation for another few seconds ("a hill of sand compiled by the…") before he realized the viscount had spoken. "What? Yes. Ah, the sand dune. It's a rather difficult concept to grasp if you've never seen one. You see, it's a hill of sand compiled by the—"

Addleson stopped him with a firmly raised hand. "No need to explain. I know exactly what a sand dune is because just this afternoon Lady Agatha was kind enough to introduce me to them," he explained with a pointed look at the woman in question. "She has a veritable passion for sand dunes, and I couldn't live with myself if I deprived her of the opportunity of discussing them with another devotee."

At once, Mr. Petrie's face lit up and he looked eagerly at his host's daughter, who was, as per her habit, standing by herself at the edge of the room. Her customary pose, which typically included an intimidating frown, had caused the Earl of Halsey to observe that the Bolingbroke chit wasn't so much a wallflower as a wallweed.

Mr. Petrie, either knowing nothing of her reputation or too overcome with enthusiasm to consider it, strode to her side in four quick steps. "What a pleasure to discover an enthusiast," he announced, his smile wide and bright. "You must tell me where you've attained your knowledge. I know it was not from my very insightful article in *Scientifica* because that esteemed journal is not published here, which is part of my purpose in coming to London: I hope to find an English publisher for my collected works. I have several meetings arranged with a variety of respected firms, including Thomas Egerton, whose Military Library series is quite well admired.

I'm sure you await details of my meetings with eagerness, as do all of my admirers, and I promise to report back as soon as I hear good news."

If Lady Agatha was taken aback to hear herself described as an admirer of the obscure American naturalist, she did not reveal it. Her expression, which had darkened immediately upon Mr. Petrie's sudden approach, had remained surly throughout the whole of his speech.

"Sand dunes," Addleson explained, and the black eyes darted to him, displaying none of the steady calm of only a few moments before. "I've informed Mr. Petrie of your love of sand dunes and he rushed over here to share his fondness with you."

This communication did nothing to improve Lady Agatha's temper. If anything, her expression grew stormier as she pulled her eyebrows together, and Addleson, recognizing the expression from their exchange at the theater three days before, knew she was trying to think of something deflating to say. On that occasion, she had failed to issue a cutting reply, a development that had surprised the viscount, who, like many of the *ton,* knew Lady Agony only by reputation.

Addleson had not visited the Duchess of Trent's box with the intention of teasing the notorious misanthrope. He had simply wanted to compliment Miss Harlow on attaining membership to his cousin's gardening club. Although it seemed like a dubious accomplishment to him—wasn't she now *obligated* to attend meetings?—he recognized its significance, for she was the first woman ever to achieve the honor. He'd assumed the call would be brief, but the presence in the box of Moray and Sir Charles ensured that the visit was long and generously sprinkled with facts about drainpipes, as irrigation was, according to his cousin, Miss Harlow's specialty.

Amid the lively chatter of the box—Lady Bolingbroke's liberal use of gardening terms, the duchess's pointed attempts to change the subject, Moray's effusive admiration for Miss Harlow's hose invention—Lady Agatha stood quietly with her eyes unfocused, a look of intense concentration on her face as if solving a great puzzle. Thoughtfulness was not what one expected from the famous Lady Agony, whose features were said to be permanently arranged in a scowl, and his playful sense of humor, always ready to tease at the slightest provocation, could not resist a lighthearted quip. And that was all he had done: made gentle fun of the way she had closed her eyes as if trying to shut out the world, an impulse he understood only too well. In a flash, her eyes had flown open and she had stared at him with a mixture of horror and confusion and, watching, he could almost see the wheels in her head spinning as she tried to figure out who he was and why he was speaking to her. Spurred on by the mischievous imp that incited most of his absurdity, he prattled inconsequentially about his tailor for several minutes and had the pleasure of seeing a series of fascinating expressions cross her face.

No, Lady Agony was not what he had been expecting at all.

Addleson, who found most people to be disappointingly predictable, was pleasantly surprised by the development. His father, a dull-witted gentleman who treated his clever son with suspicion, had been the first disappointment in the viscount's life, consistently responding with anger to anything he didn't understand. When, six years old and eager for his first pony, Addleson had asked his father how high a particular hurdle was in relation to the height of the horse, he had simply been trying to establish a ratio for optimum jumping, not imply his esteemed sire did not know how to take a fence. But his father, vaguely aware of his own intellectual limitations, interpreted every comment by his son, however innocuous, as ridicule—a circumstance the staff couldn't help but note and discuss, thereby exposing the late viscount to the ridicule he had sought to avoid.

To ensure a peaceful existence for himself, Addleson adopted a nonthreatening air of frivolity, and although he was never quite sure his mother understood the extent to which he lowered his intelligence to dodge his father's harsh hand, he knew for certain she never rose to his defense. Her abandonment bothered him more than his father's belligerence, and in the eight years since his death, he had rarely seen her, preferring to spend his time in London or at one of his other estates. The viscountess was welcome to Hamilton Hall.

Whatever personal reasons he had for cultivating a penchant for triviality, Addleson had quickly discovered that the ability to play the fool served him well among the *ton*, for it was always better to be underestimated than overvalued. It was always better to keep people off their balance, never quite sure if your latest idiocy was sincere or irreverent banter. Most people did not know where they stood with the viscount, which suited him perfectly because he always knew where he stood with most people—and that made life dreadfully dull. Spouting inconsequential prattle about clothes or politics kept matters interesting, as evidenced by his conversation with Lady Agatha.

To be sure, his rambling complaint about the unsettling sartorial choices of the *ton* had been absurd, but it was also entirely true. The waistcoat worn by the Count de Fézensac to Lord Morton's ball *had* almost caused him to bump into a table. The color combination appalled his simple but elegant taste, and he couldn't conceive why any right-thinking human being would top the atrocity with sequined buttons. Had nature not been sufficiently offended by the marriage of chartreuse and lilac?

The senseless babble had had the desired effect of disconcerting the renowned curmudgeon, and Addleson had watched in delight as Lady Agatha's countenance underwent a series of changes: annoyed, disgusted, angry and, finally, the deliberate expression she wore now.

One after another, the emotions had flitted across her face, and Addleson, recognizing each as it passed, marveled at the utter transparency of her countenance. No wonder Lady Agony chose to keep her features in a habitual scowl of dislike; anything else would reveal her innermost feelings.

"My lord is mistaken," Lady Agatha said flatly. "I know nothing of sand dunes."

Far from drooping in disappointment, Mr. Petrie's already bright smile grew impossibly brighter. Addleson's own grin widened as he realized the blathering American was too self-important to wonder how the viscount had overestimated Lady Agatha's knowledge of sand dunes so egregiously.

"Ah, an initiate!" Petrie said, relishing the prospect. "It's always a pleasure to meet a newcomer to the subject of sand dunes. To be completely candid, I must own a jealousy of your ignorance, for there is so much wonderful and amazing information you have yet to acquire. You are as a blank slate. It has been many decades since I was a newcomer to anything, and I recall the state fondly. We will start your education at the very beginning, so you don't miss any of the important details—the beginning being, of course, the grain of sand."

"I have no interest in sand dunes," she announced, her shoulders stiff with impatience.

Unperturbed by this additional proof of misleading information, the naturalist merely shook his head sadly. "A common occurrence, in my experience, especially among your compatriots. No doubt you suffered through hours and hours of dreary lectures on geography in the schoolroom, which dampened all interest in the subject, if not the entire process of learning. Few governesses are trained in the finer points of pedagogy, and most are incapable of conveying information in an interesting and useful way. Usually, they are content with the mere recitation of facts, which has the unfortunate, though of course predictable, effect of damaging the student's ability to think. It's much better to engage your pupil in what is called the Socratic method, which employs questions as a didactic device. For this reason, you can be assured that when I teach you about sand dunes, you will have a great deal of interest."

Addleson had to choke back a snort of disbelief when Mr. Petrie announced himself an adherent to the Socratic method, for the man did not listen to questions, let alone ask them, but Lady Agony was not as polite. Her attempts to interrupt him, however, were futile, and she finally settled for speaking over him until he deigned to listen.

"Mr. Petrie, I cannot believe you are familiar with the Socratic method, for your long-winded discourse indicates an inability to hear anyone speak save for yourself, and I can assure you with one hundred percent certainty that the only dreary lecture I've ever had to suffer through in my entire life is this one."

Admittedly, Mr. Petrie had heard only a portion of this unfavorable speech—his own thoughts having concluded about midway through—but the part he did hear was fairly damning. Nevertheless, he took no offense. Rather, he just shook his head with a fond smile and said to Addleson, "Women! Are they not the most darling creatures? So emotional! We try to enlighten them, but they are far too sensitive for the rigors of education. Yet I believe it's our sacred duty to at least try to provide them with some edification, for even a dog can learn how to roll over and sit up." Now he turned to his host's daughter. "Don't you agree, Lady Agatha?"

Her ladyship declined to answer Mr. Petrie's query directly, but the manner in which she abruptly turned her back on him and walked away implied strong disagreement. Addleson did not blame her, for it was never flattering to be compared with a domesticated animal and found wanting.

Mr. Petrie was likewise forgiving of Lady Agatha's behavior and nodded with sympathy. "She is overwrought, the dear girl, which is hardly surprising. My arrival has been a very exciting event for everyone and has caused a minor uproar in the household. Sadly, there was a mix-up with my luggage at the docks, which created all sorts of upheaval, and the first room assigned to me was unsuitable to my needs. I'm sure Lady Agatha understands the need for the temporary disruption, for she is, I think, a credit to Lord Bolingbroke. One hopes for an excess of sensibility in one's daughter. There is nothing more off-putting than a masculine female."

"I don't know," Addleson said consideringly. "I can think of at least one thing."

But the unknown American naturalist was as inured to implication as he was to interruption or insult. "Lord Bolingbroke has been very gracious to me. When I received an invitation to speak at the British Horticultural Society, I had thought—"

Addleson did not care what Mr. Petrie thought. In fact, if he heard one more of his well-considered opinions, he might very well bash the loquacious American over the head with the nearest object, which—he glanced around quickly— seemed to be a rather delicate blue-and-white vase.

For the sake of Lord Bolingbroke's pottery, the viscount hastily made his excuses. "I must check on Lady Agatha. As you have observed, she's overwrought."

"Of course, of course," Mr. Petrie said, immediately perceiving the wisdom of this plan. "Emotionally distraught women are unstable and are likely to do harm to themselves or others. I know this well, for I have an irascible old aunt who can wield a cane with unsettling authority. The secret is to use a gentle and calming voice, as if speaking to a small child. Perhaps I should come with you."

The viscount was tempted—so very, very tempted—to say yes just for the pleasure of watching Lady Agatha break the blue-and-white vase over Mr. Petrie's head, for he could not imagine any other response to his offensively soothing tone. It was rather like a prophesy that fulfilled itself: Treat a grown woman like a child and she will react like a child.

Even Addleson, whose sense of humor was frequently described as perverse, knew better than to subject a lady to that insult, especially in the sanctity of her own home. "No," he said firmly. "I thank you but no."

Mr. Petrie, who was unaccustomed to either being refused or listening to other people, immediately began to plot their strategy, suggesting that he approach Lady Agatha first. "Observe my method and adjust your own accordingly," he said as he followed the viscount across the room.

As amused as he was exasperated by the man's persistence—or was it resilience, a distinctly American trait—Addleson stopped abruptly, glanced around quickly and promptly settled on Mr. Abingdon as his victim. Edward was only a few feet away, well within ear-cocking distance, and that was exactly what the viscount did, tipping his head to the right, as if overhearing an irresistible tidbit. Then he turned to Mr. Petrie and said, "As you appear to have the matter entirely in hand, I shall let you comfort Lady Agatha, whilst I share my knowledge of sunset hyssop with that gentleman over there who just claimed to know nothing of it."

At once, Mr. Petrie was off, darting across the room with his magnifying glass held high like a flag, his eyes aglow with excitement. His impatience was so great, he didn't bother to wait for Addleson to finish his sentence or for him to indicate the interested party. Instead, he waylaid the first person to cross his path and accosted him with facts about *Agastache rupestris.* Waldegrave's confusion was apparent, but the young lord, perceiving himself complimented by the older man's attentions, immediately fell in with the impromptu tutoring session and examined the root system of the flower with an interested smile.

Addleson watched the happy exchange with relief, for he had begun to despair of ever shaking off the cloying American. He imagined himself at home in his bedchamber, Girard laying out his nightclothes with careful consideration as Mr. Petrie, his lecture unceasing, detailed the virtues of North American flowers. Shivering with distaste, Addleson decided it was time to escape rather than risk another incident and immediately sought out his host.

In rapid succession, he thanked Lady Bolingbroke for her gracious hospitality, assured Lord Bolingbroke that he would not attend Mr. Petrie's address at the horticultural society in ten days' time, arranged to meet his cousin at White's later in the evening, complimented the Earl of Moray on the towering achievement that was his cravat and neatly sidestepped Mr. Harrington Corduroy, whose polka-dot waistcoat would have precluded him from conversation with the viscount, even if his meandering discourse had not. Then Addleson exited the parlor though the door to the right.

He sense of accomplishment at having skillfully eluded further conversation was sharply undermined by an unexpected loss of balance. He lurched, then wobbled and teetered, before steadying himself with a firm hand against the wall. Astonished by the awkwardness, for Viscount Addleson never faltered—not literally, not figuratively—he stared blankly at his feet for a moment, his eyes slowly focusing on the rug. He had tripped over a frayed edge, which was, he realized, hardly surprising. It seemed inevitable that a man so passionately devoted to plants would let his house run to seed.

Addleson impatiently straightened his shoulders and lifted his head to find himself once again the object of Lady Agatha Bolingbroke's steady gaze. Naturally, he was disconcerted to realize he was being observed, a development he sought to disguise by striding confidently up to her. He stopped a little closer than was suitable and noted with surprise how firmly she held her ground. Other ladies would have taken a cautionary step back; she inched forward.

"I trust you are recovered from your fall," she said mildly.

Too mildly, Addleson thought, fully aware that her overt consideration was actually covert mockery. He was not, as a rule, a person given to wild surmise, but he couldn't entirely squelch the suspicion that she had deliberately arranged the carpet to bring about his mishap. It was absurd, of course, for it would require divine omniscience to know though which door her intended victim would leave the room.

"I am, yes, fully recovered," he said, resisting the urge to correct her, as his momentary bobble did not quite rise to the level of a fall. "And I trust you've recovered your wit. Mr. Petrie must have addled you a great deal if you were unable to formulate a reply."

Addleson did not have to see the flicker in her eyes to realize how much Lady Agatha despised the suggestion that there was something, anything, she was unable to do. It was immediately apparent in every line of her body—her stiffened shoulders, her raised head, her narrowed gaze.

"On the contrary," she said, her tone as underwhelmingly bland as before, "I found him to be unworthy of the effort. I assure you, I am quite capable of offering a cutting reply when necessary."

Addleson's smile flashed quick and bright. "I am very flattered, then, that you don't find it necessary now. I shall take that as a compliment."

Oh, Lady Agony did not like that—the acceptance of a compliment she had not offered. With deliberate calmness, she looked him in the eye and explained she could not in all good conscience abandon an elder in his time of need. "Decency requires that I remain long enough to establish your welfare. Having ascertained that information, I'm now free to leave. Do be careful on your way out, my lord, as the threshold at the front door is a little steep. Perhaps Gregson can lend you his arm. You must not be too ashamed to ask for help."

With that parting barb, delivered with a glimmer in her eye, Lady Agatha curtsied with all the practiced charm of a girl in her first season and returned to the soiree. When she came to the worn patch of rug he had tripped over, she stepped with exaggerated care and with what Addleson would swear was a grin on her face. He saw it only briefly—just a fleeting glimpse before her expression assumed its customary scowl—but in that moment, Addleson thought she was beautiful. The shine in her eyes complemented the glow in her cheeks, making the sharp lines of her face seem soft and perfect and lovely.

Struck by it, Addleson watched her pass through the crowd, her blue dress darting to the other side of the room, where she stood apart from the assembly like the wallflower she was.

No, the viscount thought, not like she was but like she pretended to be. Lady Agatha Bolingbroke was no shrinking violet, excluded from the assembly on account of crippling timidity. He had never met a less shy young lady, and she certainly did not suffer from awkwardness or discomfiture. If she was separate from the company, it was because she chose to set herself apart.

The question, of course, was why.

As the daughter of a well-to-do peer, she had everything to recommend her: modest fortune, excellent pedigree, circumspect upbringing. Granted, her looks were unconventional, the chiseled features at odds with the ideals of classical beauty, but her appearance wasn't off-putting or displeasing. Indeed, there was something oddly appealing about the unexpected originality of her countenance.

By all measures, Lady Agatha was a prize on the marriage mart, and the fact that she didn't exploit her superior circumstance to attract a husband made her a most curious creature. If anything, she had done the opposite of pressing her advantage, acting with deliberate offense to keep all suitors away. Even fortune hunters seemed sufficiently cowed by her unpleasant disposition to not make the attempt.

Addleson could not imagine what she stood to gain with her unusual behavior, other than a life of loneliness and regret— a strange choice for a woman in the first flush of youth. One dwindled into spinsterhood; one did not vigorously pursue it. Her perverse decision indicated she had an alternative plan for settling her future, one that did not include hearth and home.

It was an outrageous theory, to be sure, but a logical one as well, given the evidence, and Addleson, who rarely showed interest in women toward whom he had no romantical intentions, discovered an odd compulsion to confirm it. Lady Agatha meant nothing to him—his acquaintance with her parents barely extended beyond nodding—yet he suddenly felt a desire to know everything about her.

Naturally, it was the mystery she presented that intrigued him, not the chit herself, and as soon as he unraveled the riddle, he would cease to find her of interest. He knew this because that was the pattern that had repeated endlessly throughout his whole life: Something held his attention only as long as he didn't understand it. Once he figured out the mechanism by which a device or person functioned, how its springs and toothed gears worked together to produce a result, he was no longer interested in its operation. This penchant for boredom was why he had decided to take up his seat in the House of Lords. Even with his high intelligence, the machinations of Parliament, with its backroom deals and political maneuvering, seemed beyond his deciphering. It was, he hoped, too massive a behemoth to grasp in its entirety.

Lady Agatha, alas, wasn't nearly as large. She was, despite her rude glares and steady gaze, a mere slip of a girl, and he didn't doubt he would understand her movements easily enough.

It was, he noted with surprise, an oddly disheartening thought, and incapable of explaining the gloomy feeling that overtook him as he left Lord Bolingbroke's residence, he decided to seek out the simple pleasure of the gaming table, rather than follow his original plan of visiting his latest paramour. Silvie was a riddle he'd deciphered almost upon introduction, and although he found her avarice evenly balanced by her wit, he had begun to tire of her coquetry. A demand for an emerald necklace was a demand for an emerald necklace, regardless of how charmingly the requirement was stated.

Yes, he thought, as he gave his driver the direction of the Elder Davis, it was time to give his mistress her *congé*. He would, of course, comply with her request for an emerald necklace as a parting gift and would even include a matching bracelet and earrings. He would have Stern take care of it first thing in the morning.

Addleson's mouth twisted in a wry smile as he wondered if Silvie should thank Mr. Petrie or curse him, for it was certainly his seemingly endless lecture on sundry North American plants that had made him so decisive. He usually approached the end of an affair with more tact and discretion, gradually severing the connection, but he knew the emerald set would go a long way in soothing ruffled feathers.

With the immediate future neatly settled, the viscount expected his mood to improve, but it did not and he arrived at the gaming hell determined to use his memory skills to beat his fellows at cards. Mr. Petrie had a lot to answer for indeed. The imminent penury of the Elder Davis's patrons was surely all his fault.

CHAPTER FOUR

The problem, Agatha realized, with spending four seasons alienating everyone who tried to establish a connection with you was that when you wanted to find out information about a particular gentleman, you had nobody to ask.

There was always her mother, of course, but such a route necessitated posing the question without appearing interested in the answer, for anything else would enflame the sliver of hope that burned in Lady Bolingbroke's heart despite her daughter's best efforts to extinguish it entirely. Although her mother had been too distracted to properly address her Addleson query at the theater, she would recognize a follow-up for what it was—sustained interest—and most likely send an engagement notice to the *Times*.

Agatha could not run the risk.

Instead, she waited until all the guests from her father's soiree had taken their leave, including Mr. Petrie, who had accepted Lord Waldegrave's invitation to continue their conversation over port at Brooks's, and casually remarked on the success of the evening.

"Such a delightful turnout," she observed as she followed Lord Bolingbroke into his study, where a collation of cold meats had been served at his request. Supper had been provided at the affair, but he had been too busy with his hosting duties to eat properly. Now he was decidedly hungry.

Truman, who had laid the silverware, offered Agatha a plate, but she politely demurred, preferring a cup of tea, which was instantly provided.

"Yes," agreed Bolingbroke. "'Twas a delightful turnout, which was entirely gratifying, as Mr. Petrie is not well known in this country. Gruber"—his lordship's full-time gardener and sometime advisor—"brought him to my attention, for which I'm grateful. The society has never invited an American to speak before, and I'm glad I was able to persuade the membership of Petrie's worthiness. I believe his talk is going to concern sunset hyssop, which is, if my memory serves me correctly, a topic Townshend has written about extensively. I am surprised Townshend did not come tonight, for he knows more about the flora of North America than the entire membership combined."

Before her father could make further comments about society members who had failed to attend, she tried to bring the conversation back to those who had. "Petrie must have some admirers, for even Lord Addleson, who is not known for his fondness of horticultural matters, attended."

Striving for the perfect note of carefully modulated disinterest, Agatha succeeded too well in her aim because her father agreed and quickly changed the subject.

"He came with his cousin Edward Abingdon. They are frequently together," Bolingbroke explained as he broke off a piece of bread. "The truly astonishing guest was Philby Cromer, who is a member of the Society for the Advancement of Horticultural Knowledge, which, as you know, is decidedly misguided in its approach to advancement and science. I would not expect a member of that institution to attend such an event, for its fellows are resolutely unenlightened, embracing their ignorance with both hands."

Lord Bolingbroke continued in the same vein for several minutes more, detailing his disgust with the Society for the Advancement of Horticultural Knowledge and mocking everything about it, from its arbitrary membership rules ("One blackball and a fellow is out—no debate, no appeal!") to its poorly located offices in Cheapside ("As if they are setting up a law practice to prosecute flowers!").

Although the particulars of the tirade were new to Agatha, the outrage was not, for her father frequently disparaged the rival organization. As far as she could tell, the differences between the two groups were so minor as to not exist at all, for were both not devoted to the study and care of plants? But even though the finer points eluded her, she knew better than to dismiss them. Where she saw seventeen different shades of primrose, her father saw yellow.

While waiting for Lord Bolingbroke's ire to run its course, Agatha sipped her tea and called to mind the expression on Addleson's face as he looked down at the frayed carpet—a mix of startled, disgruntled and annoyed. He had worn a glare of such intensity, she had half expected him to demand an apology from the offending scrap of rug.

It was such a small thing to be bothered by, like misaligned buttons on a waistcoat or an untied boot, but the event clearly pricked his vanity, and when he raised his head to discover her gaze upon him, she wasn't at all surprised to see the flustered expression on his face. What she was surprised by was how quickly he recovered his dignity, for nary a second later he was striding toward her with broad, determined steps meant to intimidate her. He stopped mere inches from where she stood, and Agatha was honest enough to admit that he had succeeded. Up close, his scowl firmly in place, his shoulders intimidatingly broad, he was quite daunting, and rather than succumb to the unsettling feeling with a discreet step backward, she embraced it with a bold step forward.

Naturally, she couldn't resist teasing him about his stumble. Without intending to, the viscount had revealed the remarkably trivial matter to be a sore point, and she prided herself on spotting and exploiting sore points. The comment also gave her an opportunity to seize the upper hand, for the advantage had been Addleson's all evening. He had been correct about the encounter with Mr. Petrie: She had been unable to come up with an appropriately cutting reply and walked away in silence as a last resort.

Her inability to think of a more assertive response was all Addleson's fault. Of course she knew how to handle a preening idiot such as Petrie. The man was staying in her house and had been trying to espouse scientific theories in her general direction for three days now. She successfully routed them all, save for a talk on the highly developed root system of the sunset hyssop. She didn't care a fig about the advantages of shallow roots, but the spiny tentacles of the roots themselves, with their intricate, lacelike pattern, appealed to her, and she grabbed the flower without asking permission, promptly disappearing with it into her studio.

No, the reason Agatha couldn't think of a properly dismissive remark to issue to Petrie was the viscount's barely concealed amusement. Delighted by the whole exchange, he stood by gleefully as the naturalist compared her unfavorably to a household pet. He had orchestrated the whole thing, dragging her into the conversation under false pretenses— she, an aficionado of the dune!—in order to humiliate her with Petrie's offensive notions about womanhood.

She had been too furious to think properly, her anger made worse by the fact she was still reeling from the perplexing moment earlier when Addleson's gaze had met hers. What a extraordinarily disconcerting experience that was, to find herself incapable of looking away, to feel as if the room had suddenly fallen silent and everything ceased to move, even the clocks.

The interval ended as abruptly as it began, and Agatha, striving to hide her embarrassment behind a veil of amused indifference, raised one of her eyebrows at Addleson.

Recalling the incident now, she attributed the unsettling moment to the fact that the viscount had caught her staring. Such a thing had never happened to her before, despite the many hours she'd spent examining the *beau monde* with single-minded focus. Her status as Lady Agony—a young lady unwilling to endear herself to others, readily mocked for her lack of social graces—made members of the *ton* oblivious to her attentions. It was as if she were capable of not being seen, a special ability only she had, and she relished the possession of it, for it allowed her the time and the opportunity to get the details right, to fix a scene in her mind so she could re-create it hours later on paper.

But she had not been invisible to Addleson. He had seen her looking at him and returned her stare with equal brazenness.

It was little wonder she could not formulate a sufficient reply to Petrie, with the naturalist comparing her to a dog and the viscount gloating silently and her mind churning with the implications of her sudden visibility. That she could walk away without stumbling herself was accomplishment enough.

Agatha took another sip of her tea, which was cool now, as Lord Bolingbroke congratulated himself on not barring the door to Cromer. "For that is exactly what the Society for the Advancement of Horticultural Knowledge would do to a member of the British Horticultural Society, should one of our numbers so forget himself as to attend a gathering of theirs."

"Of course," she said, nodding enthusiastically at his gracious condescension.

"It goes without saying," he added, "that such an event would never occur, for there is nothing that the absurd travesty of an organization could offer that would interest any members of our illustrious institution. In theory, however, it is easy to predict how they would behave."

Agatha knew her father could predict an endless variety of rude behaviors for the other group and sought to change the subject before he grew too deeply connected to the endeavor.

"Mr. Petrie instructed me on sand dunes," she announced apropos of nothing.

If her father thought the non sequitur was unusual, he made no mention of it as he poured himself another glass of claret. "A subject on which he is an expert. His knowledge is vast and impressive, and you would do well to listen to any topic on which he cared to offer instruction. We are very fortunate to have him as a guest on this, his maiden journey to England."

Knowing very well the state of her fortune, Agatha chose not to dwell on her father's comment and instead observed that Addleson had been the luckiest recipient of their visitor's vast and impressive knowledge.

At the second mention of the viscount in a single conversation, her mother would have had the banns posted and the guest list drawn up. Her father, however, noticed nothing amiss. Unlike his wife, Bolingbroke had more things on his mind than the marital status of his lone progeny. Without question, he was fond of Agatha and hoped to see her comfortably settled with a family of her own, but it made no difference to him if that happy event happened that year or in several years. Sometimes his wife insisted on discussing the matter with him, and ever the thoughtful husband, he always agreed to listen to her concerns, though, to be accurate, he never actually agreed to consider them. Rather, he pondered issues of greater importance, such as which orchid to submit to the horticultural society's annual exhibition, while Lady Bolingbroke chattered away about Agatha's unencouraging prospects.

He treated his daughter with the same benign indifference, appearing interested in her painting while remaining almost entirely ignorant of her passion. When she presented him with a full-size portrait of himself to hang in his study, he could not say which surprised him more: the imperious sneer she had given to his upper lip or the revelation that he had agreed to let her hang the canvas in his study.

Bolingbroke nodded agreeably to her observation. "Yes, yes, Addleson did in fact have the unparalleled pleasure of Petrie's company for an extended time. I almost interrupted once to introduce Petrie to Cromer—a bit of showing off, I will admit!—but I did not have the heart to spoil Addleson's enjoyment."

Agatha smiled at this assertion, for the viscount had looked far from joyful while her eyes had been focused on him. But her father's enthusiasms tended to cloud his perception, altering his reality just slightly.

"I am surprised by Addleson's interest," Agatha said. "He strikes me as the sort of gentleman who's more devoted to being a tulip than raising them."

Her father laughed appreciatively at her witticism, for he himself had recently been represented as a tulip in a drawing by that wicked Mr. Holyroodhouse only a few weeks before. As an obedient daughter, Agatha had felt some qualms about portraying her sire as a flower and appeased her conscience by placing him in the back row, half hidden behind one of Miss Lavinia Harlow's pointy elbows. The alternative—not doing the caricature—had never occurred to her, for she was too much of an artist to forgo the perfect idea out of a vague sense of filial disloyalty. The Marquess of Huntly had indeed been plucked by the Harlow chit and his own arrogance.

In drawing the illustration, she had treated her father no more harshly than she had treated herself, for Lady Agatha Bolingbroke's lack of social graces was far too widely discussed to pass unnoticed by a social commentator of Mr. Holyroodhouse's caliber. Not to lampoon the notorious misanthrope would have raised awkward questions about the cartoonist's identity, so Agatha gamely took aim at herself. Employing the nickname she had heard muttered in her general direction several times, she put it front and center in her first drawing, a depiction of a dark-eyed woman standing alone in the middle of an empty dance floor: "Lady Agony awaits her next victim."

And with that, a reputation had been made.

"Well stated, my dear," Bolingbroke said, "very well stated. Just between us, I will confess that I suspect he's a bit dicked in the nob. He is mostly a reasonable man of passing intelligence, but he's given to long, rambling fits about inconsequential things. He once babbled at me for five minutes on the proper height of a Hessian heel! Without question, I recognized the gravity of appropriate footwear and take great pride in the shine of my shoes—not that I would employ Champagne like Brummel in the pursuit of it, for such a thing strikes me as wasteful—but there is a point at which a preoccupation for fashion passes into madness. I wasn't even wearing Hessians at the time. I was sporting top boots! I fully expected the commissioner of Bedlam to come and carry him off. I think it's above all things absurd for a man with such an uncertain temperament to be allowed to take up his seat in parliament. Obviously, it's his birthright and the Crown cannot administer aptitude tests before allowing the privilege, but surely something should be done to prevent cracked pots from deciding the country's future."

Considering her father's own penchant for passionate discussion of the things that mattered to him, Agatha smiled at his indignation and pictured him trapped in a conversation about boot heels. Despite his claim to care about the luster of his footwear, she knew he thought very little about his appearance. His only concern was that he be presented in the first stare of fashion; the tools required to attain that goal—be it Champagne, claret or gutter water—did not occupy him in the least.

For this reason, she could well imagine his impatient stance as the viscount rambled on: the disgruntled brow, the curled lip, the fingers of his left hand tugging on his watch fob. The scene was so diverting, it took her a moment to properly digest the whole of his statement.

"I'm sorry, Father, but did you say that Lord Addleson intends to take up his seat in the House of Lords?"

Bolingbroke nodded in earnest. "I did, m'dear, yes. Your surprise is understandable, for if anyone seems ill-suited to the rigors of political life, with its three-hour speeches on the leveeing of taxes and its decidedly unaccommodating benches—terrible on the back, I assure you—it is he. But it's not mere rumor. Linlithgow heard it from the gentleman himself. He leans Whigish, you know—Addleson, not Linlithgow."

At once, the idea of Addleson sporting a Whigish wig occurred to Agatha, but the image that accompanied the thought was of the dreary wigs her grandfather and his contemporaries wore. Towering in height and brimming with pomposity, the powdered confections lent themselves easily to satire, as Hogarth's brilliant engraving, "The Five Orders of Periwigs," beautifully demonstrated. There was nothing about the formerly popular adornment, however, that aligned it with the Whig party. Headpieces in general, she realized, were politically neutral in their bearing, unlike, for example, the scarlet ribbons worn by French nobility during the Terror to denounce the voracious use of the guillotine.

Although she could not come up with a type of wig that had an essential Whigishness about it, she remained convinced the idea had merit and wondered if she was being too literal in her thinking. The wig didn't have to be accurate in its history.

Or maybe the problem was that she wasn't being literal enough. Perhaps the dim-witted viscount believed that being a Whig meant wearing a wig.

Oh, yes, she thought as the image started to take form in her mind. She could show Addleson in his dressing room donning a wig and the caption would read: "Lord Addleson becomes a Whig."

No, she thought, excitement coursing through her, Lord Addle*wit* becomes a Whig.

As impatient as she was to get started, Agatha was too well bred to dart out of the room like an eager schoolgirl and instead listened politely as her father speculated about Linlithgow's political affiliation. Although Bolingbroke had known the fellow for more than twenty years, he didn't have a clue as to which direction he leaned, a thought that had only just occurred to him. Listening to him parse his friend's horticultural preferences for deeper meaning ("A penchant for reusing topsoil does not necessarily indicate a Tory frugality"), Agatha thought she might pull her hair out at the roots.

Far better to rudely end a conversation than to go bald.

Surely, her mother would concur. Lady Agony was horrifying enough with a full head of disheveled ringlets.

"I'm sorry, Papa, but I must excuse myself. I have work to do," she explained, jumping to her feet.

It was hard to say which startled his lordship more—her abrupt movement or the concept of work. Despite the imposing image of himself sneering down at him from his own study wall, the brushstroke of which even he had to concede was masterful, he continued to consider her painting as a genteel hobby to be cast aside when she married. All her attempts to explain otherwise had fallen on deaf ears.

"What are you doing closeted in here with me, anyway?" she asked, abruptly changing the subject rather than trying yet again to make him to understand. "You should be at Brooks's savoring your triumph, for your party was a stunning success. Did not a member of the Society for the Advancement of Horticultural Knowledge humble himself so thoroughly as to beg admittance? Surely, someone had laid odds against such a development in the betting books. And we can't let Waldegrave monopolize our guest. He hasn't suffered through—I mean, enjoyed the pleasure of—his care and feeding for three days."

Although Bolingbroke was not a possessive host, he could not deny the truth of his daughter's statement. Mr. Petrie *was* his guest and while it had been a pleasure to feed and house him, the experience wasn't without its challenges. The American was very particular in his requirements, to the consternation of Bolingbroke's staff, and yet chaotic in his habits. A tremendous amount of fuss and confusion had been caused upon his arrival at the docks by the fact that he didn't know what his own trunk looked like, a calamity made worse by the much-regretted absence of Mr. Clemmons, upon whom Petrie clearly relied very heavily.

Bolingbroke took a final sip of brandy and stood up. "You are right, my dear, to remind me of my duties as host. I should not have been so quick to abandon Mr. Petrie to the vagaries of London. I'm sure Waldegrave is taking sufficient care of him, but no doubt he wants to review with me the pleasures of the evening. If nothing else, he must be aware of our rivalry with the Society for the Advancement of Horticultural Knowledge and will want to revel in its ignominy. I shall head to Brooks's immediately. You will forgive me, I hope, for cutting our tête-à-tête short?"

Agatha smothered a smile as she gave her father a second kiss on the cheek, for she was positive he had forgotten the first one. Unlike his wife, Lord Bolingbroke was dismayingly easy to lead astray. "Of course, dear. Don't tease yourself a single moment more."

While her father called for his valet, Agatha swiftly exited the room and ran down the stairs to her studio. In all likelihood, Lady Bolingbroke had retired for the evening, for she had said as much after their guests left, but she had been known to ambush her daughter before and Agatha wasn't taking anything for granted. A conversation with her mother now would be fatal, as that determined woman could not be swayed from her purpose by a simple change in subject. No, she would go on at such length, Agatha would lose all opportunity to draw.

Once safely in her studio, Agatha immediately began to sketch. She started with the central figure, elongating Addleson's chin and increasing the size of his ears. She sought perfection and was frequently ill tempered when a likeness fell short of the original, but she was also accustomed to working quickly. Her opportunities to draw were curtailed by the social calendar and her mother's whim. On more than one occasion, she'd been forced to cease painting midbrushstroke to change for a dinner party.

Was it any wonder, then, that she worked so hard not to be invited to dinner parties?

Tonight, at least, she would not be interrupted, and as the hours passed, she drew dozens of sketches of Addleson, each one with a slight variation from the last. She did not usually spend so much time capturing a single subject, but there was something about the viscount that was proving elusive. First, she thought it was the set of his mouth, slightly amused yet somewhat scornful, but then she realized it was the look in his eyes. There was a deceptive stillness about them that she took for emptiness, but his eyes were not empty. She knew this because every time she drew them with a vacant stare, the image looked wrong. The only time Addleson looked like himself was when she gave his eyes a keen knowingness.

That wasn't right either.

Frustrated, she decided to change her approach altogether and settled on a different idea, one that was much better than the original. Rather than donning a powdered wig in his dressing room, Addleson was lifting a bench in the Lesser Hall at the Palace of Westminster. The caption read: "Viscount Addlewit takes up his seat in the House of Lords."

It was, Agatha decided well after midnight when she was finally satisfied, the ideal solution, for not only was the new idea more clever than the original, but it also took the focus away from his lordship's face.

Pleased, she signed the caricature in Mr. Martin Holyroodhouse's florid hand and wrapped it in sturdy brown paper. The responsibility of delivering the package would fall to her lady's maid, Ellen, whose father worked for a perfumer on Jermyn Street. He, in turn, would slip it discreetly under the back door of Mrs. Biddle's shop in St. James's. If there was a note for Agatha, he would find it hidden under the mat on the back step.

Luckily for Agatha, Mr. Smith was a game fellow who enjoyed a mystery so much, he'd happily agreed to help without asking a single question. If he suspected the whole story, he had never indicated as much to his daughter by word or deed.

The delivery procedure was somewhat Byzantine in its complexity because Agatha needed to ensure her anonymity. If Lady Bolingbroke discovered the truth—that her socially uningratiating daughter regularly mocked and ridiculed the members of their set—she would throw away everything Agatha cared about: her paints, her inks, her canvases, her sketch pads, her pencils. She would summarily discard every single thing that made her daughter's life worth living and then banish her to her room to survive on bread and water for years.

Agatha knew this to be true. Her mother flitted around like a butterfly, darting from one shiny object to another on a wisp of laughter, but she felt things deeply and would not be able to easily dismiss the gross social humiliation of having a caricaturist daughter. As it was, she could barely bear the burden of having an artistic one. To be sure, Lady Bolingbroke never wanted to raise a child with a consuming passion. Like all devoted mothers, she wanted her offspring to be proficient at everything, not to excel at anything.

With a tired sigh, Agatha opened the door to her room and was immediately greeted by Ellen, who was reading in a comfortable armchair near the fire.

"Good evening, miss," she said, raising her blond head in greeting as she marked her page in the book.

Agatha smiled wanly in return and dropped onto the bed, suddenly exhausted. "Thank you for waiting up. I did not intend for it to be such a late night. I fear I lost track of time."

Ellen nodded understandably as she unwrapped the laces on Agatha's shoes. "I appreciate your concern, but I don't mind." She dropped the fawn boots onto the floor while her charge stood up to give her access to the fastenings on the back of her dress. "A note came for you from Mr. Floris," she said, using the name of her father's employer, rather than the woman who owned the print shop. It was another precaution they took to protect Agatha's secret. "It is odd, however, because it doesn't seem to be from"—she paused awkwardly as she wondered how to say it without mentioning a name—"the, ah, Mr. Floris."

As Agatha stepped out of her dress, she glanced at her bedside table and noted that the handwriting on the letter did look different. Perhaps Mrs. Biddle had hired an assistant to attend to her business affairs. The majority of Biddle's communications with Mr. Holyroodhouse were curt missives conveying compensation for services rendered. Every few months or so, the shop owner included a longer message reporting on the success of her prints in order to give her a sense of how the public responded to her work. This was how she knew that caricatures of the Harlow Hoyden and Lady Agony sold particularly well.

Yawning, she reached for the letter, then bent her neck as Ellen draped her nightdress over her head. Agatha knew she was supposed to do something with her hair—brush it a hundred times to make it shine or wrap it around strips of paper to ensure curls—but she was too practical for such vanities. Even on nights when she wasn't exhausted to the bone, she refused to submit to anything other than a sturdy nightcap, an eccentricity that both pleased and dismayed her lady's maid. Ellen delighted in working for such a sensible woman with a sense of purpose but despaired at ever having the opportunity of showing her to her best advantage.

Agatha climbed into bed as she unfolded the note and perused it with sleepy eyes.

Dear Mr. Holyroodhouse,

It is a pleasure to establish contact with you, for I am perhaps your greatest admirer and enjoy with all possible pleasure the drawings you produce. Your recent skewering of Miss Lavinia Harlow was a masterpiece, and you captured the situation with such la élégance that I am in awe of your skill. Your accomplishment was so impressive that I didn't even notice the harshness with which you treated the other members of the horticultural society, who were, by all accounts, mere bystanders to Huntly's folly.

Your drawing, however, did not go far enough, for it showed Miss Harlow to be the harpy she is but not the villain.

No doubt you are startled by my applying the word villain *to such a gently bred young lady. Do not be fooled, Mr. Holyroodhouse, by appearances. As an artist, you must realize that there is much we don't see seething beneath the surface.*

In the case of Vinnie Harlow, this is especially true.

I am in possession of sensitive information that is essential to the work you do. Please know that I don't share it with you lightly but with a heavy heart, for I am but a simple, humble farmer, a good and generous person who treats everyone with the kindness they deserve. I wish that Miss Harlow deserved more kindness, but like all villains she has forfeited that courtesy.

Now to the information: Miss Harlow's fiancé's death was not quite the hapless accident everyone believes it to be. Insider reports indicate that she had a hand in it.

You are shocked! A refined gentleman such as yourself cannot conceive of such treachery, and I understand. However, you must believe me when I tell you my source is unimpeachable. A great injustice has been done to Sir Waldo, and it's up to you to bring it to light. I do not mean for you to lay a charge against the woman but for you to subtly but honestly hint at the truth in one of your clever drawings. If she is innocent, then no harm will befall her. But if she is guilty, as I believe, she will begin to act thus and reveal the truth for everyone to see.

I cannot say more at this time, for to do so would be to endanger us both, but I'm trusting you to do the right thing.

With the greatest of faith,

Anon

Agatha's sleepiness fell away as she read the letter, her surprise only surpassed by her disbelief. Miss Lavinia Harlow a murderess! The idea was preposterous. Without question, she and her sister were intolerable, with their smug condescension and unconventional behavior and their reckless disregard for the good opinion of the *ton*.

She could, she supposed if she stretched her imagination, believe it of Emma, for she was wild, selfish and had seemed many times during her career as if she were careening toward a great disaster. But even then, Agatha could not bring herself to believe it would have been anything other than an accident, one of the many unforeseen outcomes of a rash adventure.

Surely, the letter was a joke.

"Where did you say the note came from?" Agatha asked.

Ellen, who was in the process of hanging up her dress, glanced over and noted the sudden alertness in her mistress's eyes. "Is something wrong, miss?"

Although Agatha did not know the answer to the question, she shook her head. "No, I'm just curious about its origins. Was it delivered in the usual fashion?"

"Under the mat at Mrs. Bi—um, under the usual mat. As you know, my father checks regularly for notes, regardless of whether he delivers a drawing. That missive was waiting for him this morning." She furrowed her brow as she saw the frown on Agatha's face. "Are you sure nothing is amiss?"

Agatha flipped over the sheet of paper thoughtfully and noted that it was much better quality than the sort regularly used by Mrs. Biddle. It was also larger than the narrow strips of paper the shop owner could afford.

Clearly, this letter did not originate with the frugal Mrs. Biddle. Nor, for that matter, did it come from a simple, humble farmer. There was plenty of that ilk on her family's estate in Kent, and none employed the word *unimpeachable*. Indeed, even if they did use it in everyday speech, they wouldn't know how to spell it. Agatha herself would most likely get it wrong.

No, this letter clearly came from a gentleman of some education and wealth. The fact that he left it under the mat at Mrs. Biddle's indicated that he did not know her true identity and had been genuine in his attempt to communicate with Holyroodhouse. But to what end? Was his motive as straightforward as he said? Did he simply want to bring a villain to justice? More to the point: Did he truly believe that someone like her, a mere caricaturist with a perceptive pen, had the ability to bring someone to justice? She certainly did not feel as though she had that power.

Agatha folded the note and laid it under her pillow. "All

is well, Ellen. I'm just fatigued. There is a new drawing for your father to deliver. I've left it on my table in the studio."

"Very good, miss," Ellen said as she smoothed a final wrinkle on the gown and carried it to the dressing room. "Sleep well."

Agatha closed her eyes, but she was too busy trying to decipher the mystery of the anonymous letter to drift softly to sleep. As a general rule, she did not like puzzles because they were just distractions. Her mother frequently tried to whet her interest with teasing hints about upcoming events. But this mystery was irresistible. Obviously, she did not believe the information to be true, but try as she might, she could not bring herself to dismiss it entirely, for what motive could someone have to lay such an evil charge against Miss Harlow. Surely, there must be a sliver of truth somewhere for the suggestion to have emerged at all.

Her thoughts returned to the idea of an accident. Perhaps Miss Harlow did not intend any actual harm but inflicted it by mistake. That seemed much more likely than the premeditation the letter insinuated.

The question then became, what had Miss Harlow done that resulted in death? In what horrifying manner had the man died if not by overtightening the stays in his corset and unintentionally suffocating himself? Surely, the universally accepted explanation of his demise was a clue in itself, for what man died in such a ridiculous manner? How did the writer of the letter discover the truth? Was he a relation of Sir Waldo? A friend? A confidante? Did he have a reason to dislike Miss Harlow? And what about his presenting the information to Mr. Holyroodhouse? Did that act make her source more credible or less? Nobody had ever entrusted such a large responsibility to her before. Did her mysterious correspondent genuinely believe that a caricaturist such as she could bring a villain to justice? Did she believe it?

It was hours before Agatha fell asleep.

CHAPTER FIVE

If there was one thing Agatha had learned from her mother, it was how to impose on the privacy of others. The trick, she had observed from years of unrelieved embarrassment, was to pretend absolute obliviousness to the inconvenience one is inflicting. Lady Bolingbroke achieved this effect beautifully by disguising any moment of awkward self-awareness with overly emphatic compliments such as "How droll!" and "You clever miss!" What toll such assertiveness took on her ladyship, Agatha did not know, for her mother was always cheerful and relentlessly positive in her outlook.

Sitting in the Duchess of Trent's drawing room, however, Agatha felt her soul slowly shriveling as she tried to make small talk for the first time in her life. She clutched the cushion of the settee with tight fingers in order to stop herself from flying out of the house.

"This room is lovely, Miss Harlow," she said to her host, who sat in the armchair adjacent to her, the picture of innocence as she filled Agatha's teacup. Her dress in particular—bright yellow and trimmed with florets—seemed especially unlike a murderess's.

But if you were a heartless killer, would you not do everything within your power to look sweet and innocent?

Aware that she was staring, Agatha added, "I like this settee. It's very"—she ordered herself to quickly think of an adjective that suited a mundane piece of furniture—"cushiony."

"Yes," Miss Harlow said with a bright smile, "it does have a pleasing springiness. I've observed that many times."

Having paid few social calls in her career, Agatha could not tell if this comment was appropriately bland drawing room conversation or mocking banter. Fearing the latter, she felt her cheeks grow warm and with nothing else to say, she cried, "How droll!" Her exclamation had all of her mother's vehemence but none of her exuberance, and Agatha felt her entire body turn red.

If her company noticed anything strange in her behavior, she did not reveal it as she insisted on being called Vinnie. "I'm delighted you decided to call, as we did not have an opportunity to talk at the theater. Did you enjoy the performance?"

By asking the question, Vinnie was throwing her guest a lifeline, and Agatha knew it. She was far too skilled in deliberate rudeness not to notice when someone was being intentionally kind. As she responded honestly to the query, explaining what she did and did not like about the production of *The Merchant of Venice,* she wondered if such a well-bred woman could possibly be responsible for a man's death. She knew better than to equate good etiquette with actual goodness, for she realized many people relied on the social courtesies to hide ill intentions, but she felt there was something meaningful in Vinnie's brand of decorum. It seemed unlikely to her that someone who sought to put a guest at ease would choose to end a life.

If Miss Harlow was somehow responsible for Windbourne's death, then it must have been a tragic accident.

Agatha felt her opinion growing firmer the longer she talked to her investigative subject. Vinnie not only agreed with her points about the production ("The scenery *was* dreary and, yes, a few arches does not a palazzo make") but also contributed several points of her own that Agatha appreciated, a rare circumstance for a girl who seldom engaged in conversation. Even rarer still was the genuine interest she felt in the other woman's thoughts and ideas, especially when the topic turned to the matter of her watering hose invention.

"I'm sorry," Agatha interrupted, "did you say watering hose?"

"For my shame, I did," Vinnie said, "and I had firmly resolved before this interview not to make a single gardening comment, for I imagine you must get much of that at home with your father, who is as enthusiastic a member of the horticultural society as anyone I've ever met."

Agatha laughed and assured Vinnie she could sustain a great deal of gardening talk even as she marveled at the other woman's thoughtfulness. Agatha couldn't recall if she had ever embargoed a topic out of deference to another person. Given her history, it seemed unlikely.

"Yes, my father has a lot of zeal," Agatha said, "but if you are persistent, you may get him to discuss another topic. We are hosting Mr. Petrie at the moment. Have you met Mr. Petrie?" she asked, then waited for her host to shake her head no. "He has a decidedly narrow field of interest, so the conversation has run the gamut from the root system of *Agastache rupestris* to the root system of *Ammophila breviligulata*. Or he will try to remember an important fact and then shake his head regretfully and insist his assistant, Clemmons, would know it if only he were here."

Vinnie smiled. "No wonder you decided to visit us."

The comment was made with innocuous good cheer, but it reminded Agatha of her true purpose—to discover whether the woman next to her was a murderess—and she felt heat suffuse her cheeks again. Awkward and embarrassed and discomforted by the unfamiliar sense of duplicity, she exclaimed, "You clever miss!"

The statement was patently absurd, both in its content and its delivery, but rather than cry foul, Vinnie assured her that her watering hose invention was much more impressive, a fact that was immediately proven with a demonstration. If anyone had told Lady Agony Bolingbroke that she would enjoy watering a row of orchids with the Brill Method Improvised Elasticized Hose, she would have laughed in her face. Yet, as she applied the reassuringly sturdy contraption to *Cypripedium calceolus,* she discovered that the activity was entirely pleasing. There was something childishly fun about playing with someone's new invention, and she giggled as she pictured the expression on her father's face when she spoke with authority on recent innovations in watering hoses.

Agatha was so diverted she didn't realize the conservatory had new occupants and jumped when she heard the unexpected drawl of Lord Addleson. "I really must insist that you stand back, Lady Agatha, for that shade of puce does not do your complexion any favors."

Although Lady Agony prided herself on the issuing of stinging set-downs, although she had made her name by dispensing cutting rejoinders, she once again found herself at a loss. Her first thought—her only thought—was that there was nothing near her that could be called puce. The walls were lilac, the floor tiles were jonquil, the desk to the side was mahogany, the chair next to it a deep royal blue. The flowers themselves were a vibrant mix of hues far too many to catalog, and although the lady's slipper she was watering at that moment could be described as a purplish pink, no one in his right mind would designate the shade as puce.

Then again, Viscount Addlewit could hardly be described as being in his right mind.

Yet she was the one standing there dumbfounded like a nick-ninny.

The situation was intolerable! Oh, it very much was, for he was a nodcock who could not lift his eyes above his own expertly tied cravat. His only talent, aside from picking the perfect pattern to match the tassels on his boots, was catching her unawares. To be sure, it was a very impressive accomplishment because aside from these few brief moments of vulnerability, her guard was always up.

Caught now, with a hose in her hand and a childish

whisper still in her heart, she turned Miss Harlow's invention on Addleson. She sprayed him boldly with the device, moving the stream methodically from the top of his head to the tip of his shoes, making no effort to pretend the soaking maneuver was an ill-judged move on her part. Everyone watching knew it was intentional.

When she was satisfied that her victim had been thoroughly drenched, when even the droplets of water clinging to his blond locks had droplets of water clinging to them, she carefully laid the hose down next to the *Cypripedium calceolus*.

"Don't look now, my lord, but your waterfall does not go with your Waterfall," she said, although in fact she did not know enough about cravats to identify the knot he was wearing as the Waterfall.

Calmly, Agatha turned to her host, as an apology was very much in order. Even she, with her negligible social graces, knew it wasn't the thing to soak one's fellow guest to the bone. In truth, she *was* sorry to have created a scene in the Duke of Trent's conservatory. She did not know what had come over her—except she did know and suspected she would do it again.

Standing on her dignity, for it seemed to her to be the only thing she had left, certainly not the high ground or the upper hand, she stiffened her shoulders and raised her head to meet Miss Harlow's horror head on. But there was no horror, only bubbling mirth, and all at once, like the shot of a pistol, the room echoed with laughter. It reverberated not just with the hilarity of Vinnie or her sister or even the duke, who had always seemed like an imposing figure to Agatha, so high in the instep and formal, but with Addleson's as well. Her victim seemed particularly amused, his hand clutching his side as he gasped out raucous chortles of delight. Perhaps the water had dissolved the last wit he had left.

Determined to quit the company as quickly as possible, Agatha did not wait for her host to settle down but rather offered her apology over the laughter. She did not know if Miss Harlow heard her, for she could barely hear herself over the noise, but she took Vinnie's abrupt nod as acceptance and excused herself from the room.

She had just passed through the front door when she heard Addleson call out, "Wait, Lady Agatha!"

On a sigh, she walked down the steps and stopped. She had known this moment was coming. Despite the seeming amusement, no gentleman, especially not a dandy of the first water like Lord Addlewit, could let such an insult stand without issuing his own stinging set-down. She did not cavil at the treatment, for the pleasure she had felt in soaking him was worth any number of harsh words.

Dutifully following instructions, she waited patiently for him at the bottom of the staircase. When he was near, she took a deep breath and turned to face his ire.

"Miss Harlow tells me you arrived in a hack. Please allow me the pleasure of escorting you home," he said.

If Agatha were to try to capture the absurdity of the scene for display in the front window of Mrs. Biddle's, she would draw her own eyes as wide as saucers and have her jaw scrape the ground. She had never in her entire life been as shocked by anything as the viscount's generous offer. He could not be sincere in his efforts.

No, she realized, he wasn't sincere at all. He merely wanted the time and comfort of the journey home to properly take her to task. She was not such a fool as to fall in line.

"Thank you," she said calmly, "I can find my own conveyance home."

"I do not doubt it," he said, seemingly not bothered by the puddle forming at his feet, "but there is no reason for you to make such an effort when my carriage is out front."

Naturally, she was struck by how reasonable he sounded, as if he had no thought in his head other than her comfort, but she was not fooled by it. "Given that I have just soaked you with a hose, I think avoiding an angry reprimand is a very good reason to make the effort."

Addleson's lips twitched as he affected a look of surprise. "I reprimand you?" he asked, as if the idea were as outlandish as eating pie on the moon. "My dear, you overestimate my fondness for dry clothes."

He had a way about him, Agatha conceded as she looked in his eyes, all but gleaming with amusement. There was something likeable about his absurdity, in the humor he found lurking in every corner of a conversation. But having just wielded the hose, she knew better than to accept his pose. "And you underestimate my intelligence. Good day, sir," she said firmly as she marched down the front walk.

Addleson caught up to her in a few easy strides. "Please, Lady Agatha, please," he said, his tone modified to reflect— or affect—actual concern, with none of its usual mockery. "I promise you I'm not in the least put out by your actions. I'm not entirely sure what I did to warrant such a reprisal, but I don't doubt that I deserved it. I know I can be provoking."

Because his manner was so different, Agatha stopped and considered him thoughtfully. The gentleman standing before her bore little resemblance to the fop she had known previously. Indeed, he seemed like another person entirely. She didn't know how someone could alter himself so completely.

"Truly?" she asked, still suspicious. But what purpose did he have in deceiving her? If he wanted to vent his spleen, he could do so right there on the quiet street. "You are not angry at the damage I have caused to your clothes or your dignity?"

Now his smile was as genuine as his tone. "I have plenty of both and put little stock in either."

Standing there, the sunshine dappling the walkway, Agatha found herself oddly entranced by his good humor and goodwill. His temperament appeared to be exactly as it ought, and his intelligence seemed to shine brightly in his eyes.

Perhaps it was a trick of the light.

"Of course," he added with a hint of the old drawl as he led her to his carriage, "I can't speak for my valet, who cherishes his own dignity, which you have decidedly wounded with your actions. He's also very passionate about tailoring and may try to hold you accountable for what he will see as a deeply personal humiliation. Be warned, he is a terrifying Frenchman with a creative vocabulary. If Boney had him as aide-de-camp, he would have not only prevailed at Waterloo but conquered all of Europe as well. We should be grateful that he chose instead to concern himself with the cut of my jacket."

"I shall consider myself warned," Agatha said, settling comfortably in his well-appointed vehicle.

"The secret to dealing with Girard is to wait until he is almost boiling over with rage and then compliment him on his—and this is the very important part—swallow-tail coat. Again, I can't emphasize enough the importance of singling out the swallow-tail coat. During the five years in which I've made careful study of the phenomenon, I've praised his waistcoat, his trousers, his linen and the style of his hair. I even once observed that the pure soundlessness of his dull leather shoes was divine and it did not mitigate his ire one single bit. The only thing that works is admiration for the swallow-tail coat, which is, I believe, why the Waterloo scheme would have ultimately failed, for Girard would immediately cease commanding the troops to preen. Now, come, let me hear you try it."

Agatha did not respond. Why would she when he was so obviously teasing her? Surely, he didn't genuinely believe she would practice making nonexistent conversation with his valet.

"It's a precautionary measure only, I swear," he added, raising his right hand as if taking an oath. "Needless to say, I won't divulge any details about my soggy state, but servants talk, you know, and they have an uncanny way of finding things out. It's the very devil! Even if Girard does discover your name, I won't reveal your address. But he is a resourceful little man, with the aforementioned battlefield skills, and in the unlikely event that he does manage to track down your whereabouts, I want you to be prepared. So do say it with me, 'Your swallow-tail coat is humbling to behold, Mr. Girard.' Note: That is a general compliment that works well for me, but you should, of course, feel free to tailor it to your preferences. You may be as free and easy as you like. I assure you, there's no wrong way to say it."

As he instructed her on what to say, Agatha could not

help feeling as though he was making a May game of her. He claimed not to put too much stock in his dignity, but would he not feel some of it restored by the loss of hers? It was a reasonable suggestion, and she thought such a devious and frivolous revenge would suit a man like Addlewit.

And yet it was the frivolity of the enterprise that was most appealing, for the viscount seemed so eager, so hopeful she would play along, it felt churlish not to comply.

"Very well," she said, swallowing her alarm. "That is a very nice swallow-tail coat, Mr. Girard."

Immediately, he shook his head, "No, that was the wrong way to say it."

Agatha crossed her arms over her chest and bit back an angry retort. Convinced now she was being mocked, she calmly repeated his words with pointed inflection: "There's no wrong way to say it, eh?"

"Your skepticism is fully justified, but please bear with me as I clarify my terms, for I should have made a distinction between a compliment and effusive praise. The latter is what's called for here. So while your compliment was very elegant and refined and exactly what you want to say to Mr. Brummell should you be seated next to him at a dinner party—and do file it away in the case of that eventuality—it would in no way defuse the situation should an angry Gaul turn up on your doorstep. Let's try one more time, shall we?"

Agatha almost said, "No, *we* will not try one more time," but the absurdity of the situation stopped her, for she was riding in a carriage with a gentleman who was still dripping from the soaking she had given him. Addleson's sogginess wasn't even the truly shocking part . Rather, it was the fact that Lady Agony was conversing in private with a gentleman.

It was an unprecedented development.

"I am in awe of your swallow-tail coat, Mr. Girard," she said sweetly, "for it is the most magnificent example I have ever seen."

Addleson nodded appreciatively. "Now that was perfect. You cadence and formulation were exactly right. In five years of toadying to my valet, I have never done better."

To her surprise, Agatha felt a blush creep up her neck at his approval. "Your point is well made, my lord."

"What point?" he asked, surprised.

"On the usefulness of effusive praise," she explained, feeling more than a little foolish for how effectively it had worked on her. She neither wanted nor sought his good opinion, and the triviality of the subject made it entirely meaningless. And yet she was blushing.

The viscount laughed. "You won't let me get away with anything, will you?"

He posed the question in his familiar teasing drawl, but Agatha said earnestly, "No, I don't let anybody.

She knew at once her answer was too serious for the circumstance, for Addleson's gaze sharpened and he tilted his head to the side.

Uncomfortable with the scrutiny, she said, "I did not expect to see you at the duke's house." Of course she was aware of the incongruity of Lady Agony questioning the sociability of another person, but it was all she could think of.

Rather than archly reply that *he* hadn't expect to see *her,* which, she felt, he would have been entirely within his rights to do, he said, "My cousin suggested I seek out Trent's advice on a political matter, given his breadth of experience.."

"You are taking up your seat in the House of Lords?" she asked because she was engaged in a conversation and it was what any thoughtful human being would naturally say next. But as soon as the words were out of her mouth, she felt another wave of embarrassment wash over her as the image of him literally carrying his seat flashed through her mind.

It was not, she discovered, a comfortable sensation to talk with the object of one's ridicule before the object knew of the ridicule. Prior to this exchange, she had assumed it would be the same as talking to the object *after* he or she knew, as she had that afternoon with Miss Harlow. Yes, she felt a little awkward at being the author of some personal discomfort to the other party, but despite one tiny deception as to the identity of the artist, all the cards were on the table. Nobody had secret information about the future.

Now she did and it made her feel like a sharper.

Fortunately for her, Lord Addlewit did not take anything seriously. "Having achieved my life's goal of sartorial perfection—you will note that even soaking wet, this topcoat holds its shape—I've decided to turn my attention to less pressing matters such as reducing the duty on silk handkerchiefs."

"So having achieved your life's ambition, you will now devote yourself to helping others rise to the same level of excellence," she observed, aping his drawl. "How very public spirited of you."

Addleson's lips twitched. "Surely not the *same*. I am a member of Parliament, Lady Agatha, not a worker of miracles. If I could work wonders, my clothes would be dry by now."

Ah, yes, there it is, thought Agatha, the scold for her ill treatment of him. She had known he could not pass an entire carriage ride without making some effort to elicit guilt. He would be happy, though clearly not surprised, to know his comment had the desired effect, deepening her discomfort. Lady Agatha Bolingbroke was not only a sharper but a cad as well.

How charming.

Unwilling to address his remark, for she could neither defend the attack nor apologize for it, she looked out the window as the familiar landscape of Duchess Street slipped by. She was almost home and would pass the rest of the journey in silence.

The viscount seemed content with her plan, for he made no further comment either, and only claimed her attention when they arrived at her town house.

"Ordinarily, I would insist on escorting you to your door, but in the interest of avoiding awkward questions about my sodden state, I think it's best that we say good-bye here," he explained as the carriage rolled to a stop. "You have been delightful company, Lady Agatha, and I appreciate your condescending to let me convey you home."

As nobody had ever described Lady Agony as delightful,

not even her father, who was genuinely fond of her, she had to assume he was mocking her again. His tone suggested otherwise, for it lacked the sardonic edge that usually infused his words, but his eyes—those baffling, puzzling, confusing eyes that she had found impossible to depict last night—remained amused and detached. For the sake of her art, she stared into his eyes, determined to memorize the expression so she could re-create it on canvas. She didn't often choose random members of the *ton* as subjects for her portraits, but Viscount Addleson's elusive nature offered compelling challenges.

But even as she resolved to render the gentleman in oils, she decided she did not like him. There was nothing novel in this conclusion, as she disliked a great number of individuals, starting with but not limited to pompous American naturalists, but she usually liked people in whose company she had passed a pleasant interval. Addleson, with his instruction on how to word a swallow-tail-coat compliment to his valet, had amused her. More than that, he had cajoled her into frivolity, an accomplishment so rare she valued it a great deal higher than sartorial perfection.

The pleasantness of the interval was undermined, however, by her inability to comprehend his true nature. His character seemed to shift from moment to moment, and while this elusiveness made him an interesting subject, it made him an unappealing companion. It was one thing to laugh at one's French valet, for who had not been amused by the capricious ways of their servants, but it was another thing entirely to laugh at one's peers.

Agatha realized that a charge of hypocrisy could be laid at her feet, for did she not regularly laugh at her peers in Mr. Holyroodhouse's cartoons? But there was a difference, and although she couldn't quite put her finger on the exact nature of the disparity, she knew it had something to do with the detachment of her work. Her drawings were not personal attacks against people; she was merely rendering for general consumption an idea that already existed in society. She did not pluck the Marquess of Huntly with her caricature; he had performed that service himself when he nominated Miss Harlow for admittance to his club.

Everyone must be accountable for his decisions, she thought, as she continued to stare into the viscount's eyes.

And then she realized: She was still staring into the viscount's eyes! Or must the activity, which had gone on for seconds or—*gasp!*—minutes, now be described as *gazing deeply?*

Agatha could not think of anything more horrifying and abruptly looked away to give the door handle her full attention. It was so unlike her to woolgather!

"Thank you, my lord," she said, trying to recall the last thing he had said. Something about appreciating her condescension. Yes, of course. "And I appreciate your discretion in remaining here." Even if he hadn't been sodden, she would have insisted on seeing herself to the door, for anything else would have appeared amiable. "If you will excuse me, I'm sure my mother is wondering where I am. Thank you and good day."

Unable to risk further contact, she kept her eyes trained down but even so, she knew his own eyes were amused. Everything amused him, and as she exited the carriage she reaffirmed her dislike of him. How disagreeable to be around someone who was entertained all the time.

After he helped her down, he tipped his hat and said with misleading solemnity, "Good day to you, Lady Agatha."

Addleson immediately retook his seat in the carriage, but his horses did not pull away, and although she knew herself to be provoked, she did not turn around as she walked to the front door. She was so uninterested in his movements, she didn't even peer through the peephole.

After handing her pelisse to Gregson, she found her mother in the drawing room flipping through a fashion magazine. Lady Bolingbroke looked up with a pleasant smile. "Ah, there you are, Aggie. I do wish you wouldn't spend the entire morning painting in your dreary studio, as social calls are much more conducive to one's health and happiness."

"I was out paying a social call," she said for the simple delight of watching her mother stare at her in amazement.

Given that she usually spent whole days painting in her dreary studio, she wasn't at all taken aback by her mother's reaction. Amused, she sat down on the settee and poured herself a cup of tepid tea. "I visited Miss Harlow."

"You *visited* the duchess?" Lady Bolingbroke asked, agog. "You *went* to her house and *chatted* with her?"

"Well, I chatted with her grace only briefly, but I did have a nice coze with Miss Harlow," she explained, recalling with surprise how much she'd enjoyed her one-on-one with the horticulturalist. In truth, she had expected the experience to be long and tedious, but it had been quite pleasant. Sadly, and perhaps inevitably, the visit had ended on a sour note, what with her dousing the Duke of Trent's guest, and she rather thought Miss Harlow had compounded Agatha's faux pas by laughing uncontrollably. As her hostess, Vinnie should have smoothed over the awkward moment, not exacerbated it.

Recalling the incident again, Agatha felt the insult keenly.

Still trying to understand her daughter's unprecedented sociability, her ladyship smiled hesitantly and dropped the magazine on the cushion next to her. "Did you? Did you *really*?" she asked suspiciously. When Agatha stared blankly at her, she tittered and shook her head. "I am so pleased. To be honest, I had a feeling an unconventional woman like Miss Harlow would have a positive effect on you. I know you think I have little patience or respect for your art, but I do understand how important it is to you. That is why I thought Miss Harlow would be such a good example. She has her inexplicable interest in drainage pipes and yet still enjoys social functions. It is possible to do both, Aggie dear."

"Of course, Mama," she said obligingly, wondering if she had unintentionally opened herself up to an extended lecture.

"She is so successful at striking a balance between her arcane interests and society that she has managed to nab not one fiancé but two," Lady Bolingbroke added, her tone bright with admiration. "You will admit, it's an impressive accomplishment, particularly when one is swathed in the unflattering colors of mourning."

Agatha, whose interest in the conversation had been perfunctory, suddenly sat up in her chair. Her mother's observation had been remarkably accurate: It was unusual for a woman in widow's weeds to attach another suitor, for she was constrained not just by her own grief but also by the ugliness of her garments and the strictures of society. No gentleman wooed a lady in mourning.

If Huntly could not have wooed Miss Harlow while she was in mourning for Sir Waldo, perhaps he had wooed her before she'd entered it. Could she have won over a new parti while still attached to the old? She would certainly not be the first or the last woman to treat a beau so cavalierly. But what cause would she have to kill the poor man? Surely, it was better to be known as a jilt than a murderess.

But Miss Harlow wasn't known as a murderess.

Could her motives be that monstrous? Agatha wondered.

"Huntly is, as you know, an exceptional catch. Her first fiancé, though an agreeable enough fellow, was only a baronet. Huntly is a marquess, which is a vast improvement, if," her mother hastened to add, "one thought of marriage in terms of social advancement. I assure you, I do not. Your father and I are not particular in our requirements for your husband, merely that he be from a family of good standing and have a comfortable income. We do not require a title, though if you feel that is the only way you may be happy, we will support you in every possible way."

Agatha had no doubt of her parents' support. She had been assured of it almost weekly from the moment of her come out. To her mother's credit, that good lady had remained remarkably consistent in her requisites for a son-in-law. Even with her increasing desperation, she had never swayed in her insistence on an established family. Agatha rather thought her mother would be happy with a well-educated fishmonger by now.

"I had not heard of Miss Harlow's engagement," Agatha said, wondering if it could be true. As her mother observed, baronet to marquess was an impressive promotion. Was it impressive enough to kill for?

Despite her attempt to create a complete picture, the pieces of the puzzle simply did not fit, for it was impossible to imagine Lavinia Harlow as a coldhearted killer. She recalled her delight in showing off her improvised device for watering flowers—a hose made of an expandable leather that wouldn't burst under pressure. Agatha could not imagine a more frivolous yet more functional invention.

"Yes, she and Huntly are to be married by special license any day now. Moray mentioned it to me last night. I'm not at all surprised. In truth, I don't think anyone is, for obviously Huntly put her name up for your father's club in an attempt to win her good opinion. An unconventional manner in which to woo a young lady, to be sure, but I would never question the choices of others," she explained with an air of complaisance. "From the very beginning, in fact, I had no issue with her joining the society. Your father was entirely appalled at the notion of a female invading the inner sanctum, but I believed it was a fair trade for the duchess's support. We have one of the oldest names in all of England, but it never hurts to be seen in the company of a duchess."

Although Agatha found herself startled to discover why the hoydenish young duchess had suddenly shown an interest in her, she knew she should not be. She herself had speculated as to by what method her mother had wrangled an invitation to the theater, for she had known the event could not have occurred on its own.

Forewarned, she could hardly pretend to have her feelings hurt now.

"Oh?" Agatha said vaguely, hoping to elicit more information from her mother. It would never do to show too much interest, for Lady Bolingbroke might begin to wonder if she had said something wrong.

"Well, you're an intimate of theirs now, so you know how close the duchess and her sister are. Naturally, the duchess wanted to do whatever she could to help ensure her sister's acceptance, so she offered to lend us her support in exchange for your father's vote. Your father was initially put off by the proposal, for he thought a tit-for-tat arrangement quite vulgar, but I pointed out how we make such exchanges all the time—shillings for candlesticks, for example—and the duchess increased her offer to two social events. Your father felt compelled to agree."

Agatha didn't know which was more appalling: that her mother equated her with candlesticks or that she haggled over her price.

It made no difference to her, of course, why the Harlow sisters had taken her under their wing and she certainly had not expected the arrangement to last. She herself was hardly free of blame, for she had used friendliness as a ruse to gather information. Her visit with Vinnie had been fairly conclusive, but she needed to reevaluate the situation in light of this new evidence. Her deductions were based on the assumption that the Harlow girl was incapable of premeditation. Now that she knew she had ruthlessly traded votes for favors—and that she had raised the ranking of her husband-to-be—she couldn't be as confident.

The only way to know for sure would be to draw a caricature and wait for her reaction. An innocent woman would laugh; a guilty one would blanch.

Agatha knew her thinking could be called simplistic, for society demanded that all its members be able to play a part. But the accusation of murder was so startling, so horrible and shocking, she imagined few women would be able to hide their true response. An experienced society matron would no doubt have the restraint to keep her smile firmly in place but not an unsophisticated young lady such as Miss Harlow.

Eager to begin, Agatha put down her cup of tea and announced she had some work to do. Lady Bolingbroke, cringing as always at the categorization of her daughter's hobby as work, refused to let her daughter leave before lecturing her on the proper method for paying social calls. "You take the carriage, my dear. How you arrive is as important as when you arrive.

And showing up without a lady's maid is course and vulgar. I trust you will comply with these rules in the future."

Given the unlikelihood of future social calls, Agatha easily acquiesced to her mother's requests and left the dear lady to peruse her fashion magazine. In her studio, she sketched a dressing room scene—decorative screen, mirror, table, clothes tossed over the back of a chair—and placed a round figure in the center who more or less met an approximate description of Sir Waldo Windbourne. Positioning him sideways, she dressed him in pantaloons, Hessians and a pristine white linen. She wrapped a whalebone corset over his shirt and inserted a young lady to tighten it. The caption read: "There, that should do it."

As a general idea, she thought it had merit, for the concept worked on two levels. On the face of it, it was merely a funny representation of male vanity. The lady helping him into the corset did not have to be Miss Lavinia Harlow. Yes, she had her smooth blond hair, but Agatha had intentionally kept her outfit plain so the woman could easily be taken for a servant. Only those who had their suspicions—Agatha, her anonymous source and the villainess herself—would notice anything amiss.

Indeed, she had little doubt that the thing most people would notice was the lack of ingenuity on the part of Mr. Holyroodhouse. As a target, Sir Waldo should be well beneath the renowned satirist's notice, for the deceased gentleman had been the easily mocked embodiment of male vanity long before the caricaturist took notice of him. Agatha's depiction added nothing to the conversation.

The drawing needed to be refined. She would heighten the color on Sir Waldo's face, perhaps tint it a bright shade of purple to reflect his struggle for breath, and add a few droplets of sweat to his temples. Miss Harlow's face also required adjusting. She had to sharpen her expression to one of satisfaction. That, too, would work on two levels. To the unaware, her satisfied look could stem from the simple pleasure of having achieved a difficult goal, for what woman did not know the challenge of lacing a corset.

With her concept established, Agatha began to work on

the drawing in earnest, adding color and texture and the tiny details that gave movement to a face. She had to stop a few hours later when her mother sent Ellen to change her for Lady Kennington's rout. As always, she resented the intrusion, but in this instance she admitted it was timely. By all accounts, she was finished with the illustration and was making only minor changes. Something about the image did not sit right to her, for no matter how closely and carefully she examined it, she did not feel the usual fissure of excitement that accompanied the completion of a work.

Something was most definitely off.

"It seems done to me, my lady," Ellen said when her opinion was sought. "I think it's as good as anything you've ever done. And really funny, too. Imagine a man that size trying to squeeze into such a tiny corset! I'm surprised he hasn't suffocated himself."

Her maid's comments should have put Agatha's mind at ease, for she had said exactly what any artist hoped to hear. "But does it look like the lady is trying to suffocate him?"

"Lawks, no, milady!" Ellen said with a surprised lift of her head. "She's just helping him. Putting on corsets is no easy business, I can tell you." Then she colored brightly, tilted her head down to study her finger and said, "Not that I've ever had trouble putting on your corset."

"At ease, my girl!" Agatha said on a trilling laugh. "I assure you, the thought never occurred to me and even if it had, I would not care either way. You are free to grumble about tightening my stays belowstairs to your heart's content."

Her mood much improved, Agatha decided she was being too particular in her taste, which she attributed to tiredness. Between her Addlewit drawing and the mysterious letter, she had gotten very little sleep the night before. Clearly, that was why she wasn't quite satisfied with the drawing. Ellen, who appeared well rested, thought it a harmless representation of vanity and suffering. She should be pleased.

I *am* pleased, she told herself, signing the drawing with a flourish. Then she wrapped it for transport to Mrs. Biddle's shop, left it on the table for Ellen to deliver and followed her maid to her bedchamber to change for Lady Kennington's rout.

CHAPTER SIX

As soon as Viscount Addleson saw the drawing of him carrying his own seat in the House of Lords, he presented himself at 227 St. James's Street and demanded to meet the artist.

Mrs. Biddle had heard many such requests in the six years she had owned her shop, for none of the gentry liked to see themselves represented as fools, deviants or scoundrels and often wanted to enact some sort of revenge on the perpetrator. It made no difference if the subject was male or female, as both sexes had easily punctured vanities. She knew what it was like to find yourself under attack—as the owner of a print shop, she suffered verbal assaults almost daily—but she never took the insults to heart. It genuinely did not bother her if Mr. So-and-So thought she had the face of a cow or if Lady This-and-That questioned the legitimacy of her birth. She had a business to run and no time to nurse wounded egos.

Likewise, she had little patience for the righteous outrage of an angry public and had developed a strategy for handling complaints. When she first opened her shop, she had vigorously refused to provide any information about her associates. That practical approach, however, yielded little success, for the sanctimonious targets of cutting satire could not easily be swayed from their purpose. Undoubtedly, another tactic was in order and Mrs. Biddle (née Miss Biddle) found it in the person of Mr. Biddle, a fictitious husband who could never be located when he was most required. He was a very useful creature, for not only was he intractable and often drunk, but also he allowed Mrs. Biddle to side with her victims. She would happily provide the information if only Mr. Biddle would relent.

Mrs. Biddle employed this ruse now as she beheld the elegant figure of Jonah Hamilton, Viscount Addleson. He was a dandy, she could tell that immediately, for only a dandy tied a cravat so elaborately. Mrs. Biddle had a special contempt for dandies because they were the most entrenched objectors. Placing a high value on perfection, they could not bear to see a version of themselves that was less than ideal.

"Sorry, I am. Really. I would gives you the name if I knew it," Mrs. Biddle said, feigning agitation. "Me 'usband, Mr. Biddle, 'e runs the place. I'm jest 'is servant. I'd find 'im for you, really I would, but I don't knows where 'e is. Prolly drunk in an alley, the no good louse! Rumming it up all the time and leaving me 'ere to deal with the likes of you. I don't knows anything, I tell you! I don't knows anything."

Here Mrs. Biddle scrunched her face up and squeezed out one melancholy tear that slowly glided down her pale cheek. A second and third drop followed in rapid succession until her entire body was wracked with anguished despair.

The tears were, in fact, Mrs. Biddle's pièce de résistance. She used to bring them out only as a last resort, but she had discovered through a process of trial and error that they effectively brought all encounters to an end. No man wanted to assuage a crying female with whom he had no familial or contractual obligation.

"Brava!" Addleson cried out, clapping his hands in enthusiastic appreciation. "Brava!"

Mrs. Biddle contrived a sad little hiccup and raised her head slowly to find the viscount grinning at her broadly from ear to ear.

"A magnificent performance, my dear," he said

approvingly. "Quite one of the most impressive I've ever seen." Addleson bowed. "You have my compliments. Now do be so kind as to give me Mr. Holyroodhouse's direction and I shall get out of your way posthaste."

Addleson watched in amusement as the shopkeeper tried to make sense of his response, which was, without a doubt, a first for her. Clearly, she had expected him to react to her own helplessness with either sympathy or frustration or even pronounced indifference, but he was surely the only gentleman to express admiration for her presentation.

And the admiration was genuine. Rarely had he seen a more affecting or sincere performance. Her tears in particular—the way they started slowly and gradually gathered momentum like a rainstorm—were humbling to behold. If he didn't fear she would bash him over the head with a broom, he would ask her to teach him the trick. As a frequent dissembler himself, he knew being able to cry on command was a worthwhile skill.

Precisely because he was a dissembler, he had easily recognized a like-minded soul. As he had said, her performance was impeccable, but she had done little things that gave her away, such as peeking up at him out of the corner of her eye to see how her tears affected him.

Although his response had put a cork in her wheel, the determined Mrs. Biddle refused to abandon her role. "I don't knows wot you're saying, melord, I don't. Was you banged in the 'ead before coming in?"

The viscount applauded again, then smothered a smile when he saw annoyance flash across her face.

"I appreciate your dedication to your craft, Mrs. Biddle, but it is wasted on me," he explained calmly as he rested an elbow on the counter. "No doubt, many an outraged customer has been turned away by your deft simulation of misery and so they should be, for anyone who is fooled by your performance deserves to depart in ignorance. Now, as I said before, point me in Mr. Holyroodhouse's direction and I will leave you in peace."

Mrs. Biddle examined him silently for a long moment,

then sighed. "I'm sorry, my lord, but I cannot help you. It is my established policy not to give out private information for the men who provide me with illustrations."

Addleson wasn't at all astonished to hear the woman speak in clear, modulated tones. Nor was he surprised to hear her talk of policies. As the owner of a large estate, he knew much about the policies of tradespeople, and the policy they held most dear was that money was dear. He, therefore, offered her a tidy sum in exchange for the address.

"I don't know his address," she said.

Addleson doubled his offer.

She shook her head regretfully. "You are killing me, my lord, because I haven't given an honest answer in half a dozen years. But it's the God's honest truth that I don't know where Mr. Holyroodhouse lives. My contact with him is very limited. I promise, however, to convey your anger and righteous disapproval for his drawing in my next communication."

Now the viscount lifted his eyebrows in surprise. "Disapproval?" he asked, his tone full of wonder. "How can anyone disapprove of such a brilliant depiction? I don't want to take Mr. Holyroodhouse to task. I want to hire him to do a large reproduction of the masterpiece to hang in my study at home."

At the mention of the word *hire,* Mrs. Biddle's whole demeanor changed: Her eyes lit up, her mouth softened, and she leaned forward against the counter. "Hire, you say?" she asked softly.

"Hire," Addleson repeated firmly. "As Mr. Holyroodhouse's representative in all business matters, you would no doubt get a cut of that commission."

"And how large a commission will that be?" she asked.

"Very," he said.

Mrs. Biddle nodded and the viscount could see her doing the arithmetic in her head: price of illustration + finder's fee − artist's compensation = large and well-deserved reward for dealing with the inconveniences of owning a print shop.

In truth, Addleson would be genuinely shocked if Mr. Holyroodhouse earned more than 10 percent of the payment.

Satisfied with her calculations, Mrs. Biddle promised to get in touch with the artist that afternoon. "I said I don't know where he lives and that's the God's honest truth, but we have a system for communication. I expect to hear back from him in a day or two. How may I reach you?"

The viscount placed his calling card on the counter and thanked Mrs. Biddle for her help.

"Any time, my lord," she said earnestly, running her fingers over the engraved words. "Any time at all."

"Good day, then," he said, dipping his head.

"We have several prints left, my lord," she said as he turned to leave. "Since you are so fond of the artwork, perhaps you would like to buy a few copies to give out to your friends."

At this suggestion, which was, he admitted, an entirely reasonable one, he laughed heartily. The unexpected sound, so full of sincere amusement, filled the small shop and caused its practical-minded keeper to gawk. "I like you, Mrs. Biddle, and because I do, a word of advice. Get yourself another wedding ring. The one you are wearing is far too fine for the wastrel you've decided to cast as your husband. It's a small detail," he conceded, as she continued to stare at him in surprise, "but details are what make a character believable."

And with that, he left.

***

Although being portrayed as too addle-witted to sit in the House of Lords did little to prick Viscount Addleson's vanity, having this depiction be the *second*-most-talked-about caricature at Lord Paddleton's ball genuinely annoyed him. After all, it wasn't every day a fellow found himself thoroughly mocked in print—and how clever the mockery had been! Mr. Holyroodhouse had summed up the situation with concision, humor and insolence.

Addleson wasn't surprised by Mr. Holyroodhouse's skill, of course, for he had been an admirer of the artist for years and had long hoped to one day secure his notice. The sense of accomplishment he should have felt at finally attaining a cherished goal, however, was undercut by the appearance of a

97

second victim of Mr. Holyroodhouse's pen. It was hardly fair, as the cartoonist rarely produced two drawings in one fortnight, let alone two in a single day. His contemporaries were far more prolific, which made their attention far less valuable.

To be fair, Addleson's ire did not stem only from the fact that he had to share the ridicule with another subject. It was the quality of the other drawing as well, for it was well beneath Mr. Holyroodhouse's usual standards. It did not skewer a convention or deflate an ego or redefine a situation; it merely accused an innocent young lady of murder.

Like everyone else in the Paddletons' ballroom, the viscount was confused by the charge, which seemed to have materialized out of thin air like a spirit. It wasn't as if the *ton* had been speculating for months about Sir Waldo's death or murmuring quietly about his fiancée's guilt. The unfortunate event had elicited only titters of amusement at his humiliating end and resolutions to avoid a similar fate.

And yet Mr. Holyroodhouse had all but declared Miss Lavinia Harlow a murderess.

It wasn't as simple as all that, of course. The drawing itself could be interpreted in a variety of ways, and the woman tightening the corset to a lethal degree looked like Miss Harlow only very, very slightly. But an entire world was contained in that very, very slightness, as he discovered when he'd arrived an hour before to find it the topic on everyone's lips.

"It's absurd, of course," his cousin Edward said reasonably to a group of gentlemen that included the Earl of Hardwick and Mr. Smythson, "for I have talked to the woman personally and cannot believe that anyone who cares so passionately about the proper drainage of watering systems could be so indifferent to the sanctity of human life. At the same time"—here he lowered his voice as if revealing a dark secret—"I can't bring myself to ignore it entirely, for surely Mr. Holyroodhouse would have no cause for making a baseless accusation."

Naturally, Addleson understood the logic of his cousin's deduction—and why the rest of the *ton* had reached the same conclusion—but he was nevertheless annoyed at the simplistic thinking. Gossip was such a destructive force precisely because nobody could imagine anyone being so immoral as to simply make up a story from whole cloth.

Offended on principle, as well as on behalf of the young lady herself, who would surely never hurt a fly, let alone a fiancé, Addleson interrupted Edward to complain about his inconsideration. "You do realize, I trust, that Mr. Holyroodhouse also caricatured me today?" he asked in his most cynical drawl. "The cruel gentleman showed me carrying a chair in the House of Lords like a veritable idiot. Is that not worthy of endless conjecture? Is Viscount Addleson really that addle-witted? Discuss!"

Neither Hardwick nor Smythson knew how to respond to this bizarre demand, other than to think that the viscount's positing of such an outlandish thesis in fact confirmed it. Edward, however, knew how his cousin's mind worked and recognized his nonsense for the rebuke it was. He duly changed the subject to that weekend's race at Newmarket.

Given the parameters of civility, which he himself felt constrained to observe, the viscount was unable to intrude on every conversation that considered Miss Harlow's guilt, but he made considerable progress and his efforts were aided by the Dowager Duchess of Trent, whose look of stern disapproval was more than enough to silence even the most vigorous wagging tongue.

The only person who wasn't furiously speculating as to the immorality of Miss Lavinia Harlow was Lady Agatha, whose back was pinned to the far wall like a swath of linen to a dress form. Her shoulders stiff and her face pale, she observed the gathering with blank eyes, which was, he realized, an unusual posture for the young misanthrope. She was frequently detached from the company, yes, but tonight she seemed removed.

Having just finished a set with Miss Hedgley, whom he had to chastise twice before she would give his caricature due consideration and even then she pretended not to understand it ("All members of Parliament carry a heavy burden, my lord"), he was eager to talk to someone whose intelligence, if not temperament, he respected.

"Lady Agatha," he said brightly as he joined her along the wall, "we must discuss the drawing."

She jumped. There was no other way to describe how her feet left the ground for a fraction of a second at his announcement. Her face, already ashen, grew another shade paler, and her expression took on a trapped quality.

Taken together, these three qualities indicated fright, but what could the indomitable Lady Agony have to fear in the mention of Mr. Holyroodhouse? Not of being mocked by the great man himself, for she had already had the pleasure on more than one occasion. Perhaps the random attack on someone as modest and unimposing as Lavinia Harlow made her realize they were all vulnerable to the scurrilous pen of a scoundrel.

Seeking to put her at ease, he said gently, "I mean, of course, the representation of me as a parliamentary neophyte who does not know what to do with his seat. I contend, of course, that I in fact do know what to do with my seat and that is to replace it with one that has a cushion. I would also, while I'm making changes to suit my superior taste, replace the tapestries. The depictions of the Spanish Armada are magnificent, of course, but too dreary with the weight of history to aid in the production of new laws. In the interest of efficient governance, I would suggest more elegant adornment."

If anything, this speech increased her discomfort, for her impossibly pale complexion seemed to lose yet another shade. In a moment, she would be as white as his shirt.

Her tone when she spoke, however, gave no indication of her obvious distress. "No doubt a reproduction of Mr. Holyroodhouse's illustration would meet your requirements, made larger, of course, so that your clever ministrations could be admired by your peers."

Addleson did not consider himself easily impressed, but Lady Agatha's articulate attempt at deflating his ego while clearly distracted by her own miseries struck him as a notable achievement. "We are as two peas in a pod," he observed with an eager smile, "for I had the very same thought and just this morning commissioned Mr. Holyroodhouse to produce a larger version for my study. I cannot think of anything more pleasurable than looking up from a tedious document on salt importation taxes and seeing that excellent image staring down at me. But I wonder if hanging it in the Lesser Hall would make me appear overly fond of myself, an impression I am loath to give. I wish to appear only the proper amount of fond of myself. Perhaps you can suggest what that is."

Lady Agatha stared at him silently for a long moment, thoughtful consideration knit in her brows. "You are mocking me," she said.

The viscount, who considered mockery to be his mother tongue, felt the unexpected sting of embarrassment at her charge. The truth was, he hadn't meant to mock her, not entirely, for his original intent had been only to bring color to her pallid face. For some reason, he found her air of absolute wretchedness disagreeable to observe.

"I am not," he said simply, his tone quietly insistent as he looked into her eyes. There was something about her eyes—as dark as a cavern, as deep as a pit—that pulled at him. "I understand why you would think that, for I find many things worthy of jest, but I was not offering ridicule but comfort. You seem troubled by something, and I sought to distract you with chatter. I know I can be a frivolous fellow, but I'm actually quite good in a crisis. If you would but tell me what's distressing you, I am certain I could provide some assistance."

Now her dark solemn gaze clouded with suspicion as she wondered what his game was. How surprised she would be, he thought, if she knew he had no game.

He was surprised himself.

Rather than spill her secrets, she tilted her head and asked, "You really want to hang a large reproduction in your study?"

An earnest query about his redecorating plans was not the reaction Addleson was expecting. He hadn't actually thought the severe Lady Agony would break down in a flood of tears or beg for his help, but a rigid shake of her head coupled with an assurance that nothing was the matter would have been more in keeping with her character.

"Yes," he said, curious as to her interest. Perhaps as a fellow object of Mr. Holyroodhouse's scorn, she could not conceive of looking at one of his illustrations at regular intervals. "I genuinely admire the piece for its concept and execution."

A slight blush stained her pale cheeks, and he wondered if she was embarrassed for him. Far from impressing her with his claim of usefulness, he seemed to have now confirmed her belief in his uselessness, a development that did not amuse him nearly as much as it should have.

Her next statement revealed neither opinion. "That's a very nice compliment. I'm sure Mr. Holyroodhouse isn't so lost to all decency as not to appreciate a very nice compliment such as that."

"But he is lost to some decency to have made this allegation against Miss Harlow?" he asked.

The black orbs of her eyes seemed to blaze as she said, "To have done such a thing, he must be. It's so obvious what he meant for everyone to think. How indecent and cruel."

"It *is* indecent and cruel," he agreed, noting how quickly the color had faded from her face. She was once again wan and pale. "I'm gratified to hear you say it because too many of our acquaintances are pondering its truth. But it's also puzzling, for what purpose could Mr. Holyroodhouse have in making the charge? What does he hope to accomplish? Is it an act of revenge for a perceived insult?"

"An act of revenge?" she echoed softly. "Miss Harlow would have had to have insulted him greatly to warrant such malicious retaliation. Could any insult be that egregious?"

The viscount shook his head. "I don't know. For the answer to that, you will have to ask Mr. Holyroodhouse."

Lady Agatha laughed without amusement at the suggestion of tracking down the elusive artist. Having failed at the task himself only that morning, he understood her cynicism.

"I'm relieved Miss Harlow is not here to suffer the snickers and suspicious looks firsthand," she added after a moment of consideration. "That would be intolerable."

"I am of the same mind," he said. "The Harlow Hoyden could, I believe, stand up to such rank speculation without flinching, but her sister seems to be of a more delicate nature. It's best that only the dowager came to defend her honor, for no one would dare talk back to such an imposing woman."

His point was proven at that very moment, as the imposing woman herself, who was several feet away, raised her voice over the orchestra to demand that Miss Hedgley clarify her statement. "It's my own fault for growing so old, but my ears don't work as well as they used to and I didn't hear the entirety of your statement, my dear. Miss Harlow is *what* kind of conniving hussy?"

Miss Hedgley, a one-time flirt of the Duke of Trent currently enjoying her second season, stared in silent terror at the intimidating matron whom she had once aspired to call her mother-in-law.

"Reviving and unfussy, your grace," the girl's mama said, rushing forward with an awkward chuckle. "My daughter merely observed that Miss Harlow is reviving and unfussy. Naturally, she meant it as a compliment and was only trying to understand why such a lovely girl would be the target of such a vicious attack."

At once, the dowager's face relaxed into a smile. "Yes, of course, that makes so much more sense. I don't know what I was thinking to imagine otherwise. Do accept my apology."

Letting out another uncomfortable giggle, Mrs. Hedgley assured the duchess there was nothing to forgive. Then she quickly ushered her daughter away before the indiscreet young lady could get herself into further trouble. The dowager watched them scamper off with a satisfied smile before looking to her left and asking, "What was that, Mr. Orton?"

Mr. Orton, a middle-aged gentleman with irregular front teeth and a slight lisp, immediately walked in the opposite direction. Undaunted, the dowager followed.

Amused by the display, the viscount turned to Lady Agatha and observed, "Even with his twenty-year advantage, Mr. Orton is rapidly losing ground. I fear his only recourse now is to run, which is, as you know, hardly appropriate behavior for a ballroom. Even so, the floor is far too crowded for him to pick up any speed. Oh, no, wait, he's changed course and is headed for the cardroom." Addleson shook his head and tsked softly. "A tactical error, for now he's trapped in an even more confined space with all those tables and only the one egress."

Despite the hilarity of the situation, Lady Agatha's grim mood continued unabated. The dowager's antics did nothing to lighten it, and she watched the scene silently, her dark eyes heavy with misery. Disturbed by her expression, by the bone-deep sadness of her unhappiness, Addleson longed to ask her again what was troubling her. The exercise was pointless, of course, for there was no reason why she should trust him with her confidences. He was but an annoyance to her, a gadfly who buzzed so stridently around her head that she had showered him with water to cease his chatter. He had never been so surprised nor his topcoat so wet.

But what an event that had been—a thorough dousing at the hands of an unrepentant miss!

The viscount was not one to stand on his dignity, and the thought of making a stinging reply had never crossed his mind. Quite the opposite, in fact, for he genuinely admired her ingenuity, fearlessness and self-possession. How calmly she had stood there in the Duke of Trent's conservatory watering him like a lily in a garden as if it were an everyday occurrence. And then to coolly deliver a clever rejoinder in an exemplary imitation of his own cynical drawl.

All in all, it was the most impressive performance he'd ever seen, made more satisfying by the delighted gleam in the young lady's eyes. One did not expect sparkling wit from the deflating Lady Agony, let alone cheeky humor. His purpose in escorting her home in his carriage had been just as he'd stated: for the pleasure of her company. There was more to her than anyone suspected, and he was determined to learn it all. It wasn't only the mystery she presented, which, he admitted now, was considerably more complicated than he'd originally supposed, but Lady Agatha herself. He wanted to understand the woman, not the riddle.

The realization that his interest in her was personal, not academic, was a surprise, to be sure, but the true revelation was how close he was to pleading with her to tell him what had caused her distress. His need to know was so sharp, he might stoop to begging at any moment, and that would never do. Viscount Addleson might not stand upon his dignity, but he didn't slouch beneath it either.

Taking refuge in the familiar, he said, "Upon my word, the esteemed personage to whom the dowager should really devote her attention is Lord Curtlesby, for he is wearing golden buttons on a yellow waistcoat. Without question, the gold button is a difficult adornment to pull off with elegance and few can manage it with any finesse, but such a combination flies in the face of all that is decent. Appearing before Prinny in his shirtsleeves would be less offensive. Or pairing orange and red," he said. Then he shuddered and announced that he had misspoken. 'Twould be better to present yourself at court without a stitch of clothing than to match orange with red.

He kept his eyes trained on the lively company as he spoke, but sly glances in Lady Agatha's direction revealed an unexpected expression: appreciation. Instead of her usual disgust or disdain or even annoyance, she looked grateful for his chatter. The ferocity of her anxiety did not lessen, but it no longer ruled her thoughts, allowing her to make pertinent observations on a topic for which she had little patience. When he paused in his cataloging of Lord Curtlesby's many sartorial sins, she jumped in with a critique of Lady Haverford's elaborate ostrich-plumed headpiece.

"Somewhere, there is a very chilly ostrich," she said.

Addleson agreed with her assessment and wondered why ostriches didn't form a union to lobby Parliament for better treatment at the hands of society matrons. The turban itself was entirely à la mode and extremely elegant, but he would sooner bite off his tongue than offer a hint of criticism to Agatha. He didn't want to say anything to upset the moment.

When they finished abusing Lady Haverford, for her large emerald-green fan made her dainty hands look distressingly small, the viscount pointed out the droop in Mr. Herring's Oriental, which was the result of not enough starch in the cravat. It was, he explained in resigned tones, a common mistake made by many valets, though not by the faultless Girard.

As if taking his cue, Lady Agatha said, "I am in awe of your Oriental, Mr. Girard, for it is the most finely starched example I have ever seen."

Addleson laughed at this sally but didn't otherwise call attention to it. Instead, he noted that the Earl of Thynn's breeches lagged behind the current style by several years. Silently, however, he thought her remark was sublimity itself, and although the fathomless black eyes did not reveal a hint of sparkle, he thought he detected a lightening of her mood.

Lady Agatha seconded his observation about Thynn's breeches by calling them Jacobean, and Addleson agreed the article of clothing bore a striking resemblance to trunk hose and knee garters. He then commented on the Elizabethan quality of Lady Fellingham's neck ruff, an entirely unfair characterization of the delicate lace that lined her collar. Verisimilitude, though, was not the point of the exchange but rather to make the more outrageous comment. For as long as he could—and sadly, it was only thirty minutes more before Mrs. Mobley claimed him for a quadrille—he stood against the wall swapping absurdities with Lady Agatha.

It was a game, to be sure, but more than that, the viscount thought, it was a conversation.

CHAPTER SEVEN

Although the Harlow Hoyden had been skewered by Mr. Holyroodhouse on no less than seven occasions—the last one showing her waltzing with Trent on the back of her mother-in-law—she had never considered hunting him down and cutting out his heart with a knife until he depicted Vinnie tightening her fiancé's corset to a fatal degree. The usual forbearance one was obliged to show cartoon-drawing villains was not required when they painted one's sister as a murderer.

There was no person less of a murderer in the entire kingdom than Miss Lavinia Harlow. She had shot a man, yes, and took his life, but she had done so only out of defense of herself. What was the more palatable alternative? Let him kill her with a fish knife and her sister, too, and perhaps the entire household because shooting a man point blank was considered ill bred by the *ton*? It was patently absurd to believe anyone would blame Vinnie for her actions.

And yet society was frequently absurd.

Emma knew the truth must remain secret for Vinnie's sake, for her twin already felt herself guilty—wrongly!—of murder. Vinnie understood the necessity of Windbourne's death and did not regret it, but nor would she let Emma cast the event in an entirely heroic light. Having never sent another human being to his grave, the Harlow Hoyden was impatient with what she considered to be her sister's martyrish behavior, and she had been greatly relieved when, instead of extending her suffering, Vinnie had told Huntly the truth and agreed to marry him.

Now, thanks to Mr. Holyroodhouse's efforts, Vinnie had called off the wedding, which was supposed to take place two days hence. Mistaking fear for honor, she refused to expose him to the ridicule and humiliation of having a widely suspected murderess as a wife.

Huntly and Emma had spent hours and hours trying to reason her out of her ridiculous position. Everyone had: Trent, the dowager, their brother Roger, his wife Sarah. Even the duke's sister, Louisa, whose response to any caricature remotely connected with her family was to board up the town house and repair to the country, insisted Vinnie was overreacting. Like the dowager, she had no idea the charge was actually correct and shrugged it off as overreaching nonsense.

"The drawing's mendaciousness is its undoing," she said. "If Holyroodhouse had been so clever as to include one or two elements of fact, I could understand how the representation as a murderess would discomfort you. But this illustration is so unmoored from reality, it is naught but an overdone joke that exceeds its ambitions. If you want the gossip to stop, simply go through with your hastily conceived marriage and the *ton* will rightfully return to being horrified by how quickly you threw off your mourning."

Emma, seconding the argument, found herself in the unusual position of praising her sister-in-law's good sense. What an upside-down world it was when the perpetually hysterical Louisa was held up as a totem of reason.

But Vinnie would not accept reason or logic or even a clearly articulated gut feeling. No, she was far too determined to save Huntly from herself.

It was infuriating, and Emma would be arguing with Vinnie still if Trent had not pulled her out of her sister's bedroom at a little after three in the morning to let the poor girl get some sleep. By the time the duchess had come downstairs at ten to resume her arguing, Vinnie had already left the house.

That was three hours ago and all she had done since then was pace from one end of her study to the other, back and forth like a horse trapped in a corral.

Suddenly, the door flew open and in stomped Philip Keswick, the duke's scapegrace cousin whose bearing was as resolute as his words. "Let's go!"

Emma did not have plans for the afternoon, let alone an engagement with the young cawker, but she immediately spun on her heels and strode toward the door. Yes, they had to go. Pacing accomplished nothing. Indeed, less than nothing, for she would wear a hole in her floor while the wicked Mr. Holyroodhouse remained unmolested.

Not while she still drew breath and had access to a knife.

No, not a knife, for that would be too good for him. The incision would be clean and exact, almost painless in its surgical precision. She needed a tool that would be difficult to maneuver through skin such as a fork or, even better, a spoon. Yes, she would hunt down Mr. Holyroodhouse and spoon out his heart with a soup ladle. Then she would bury his body in a shallow plot and dance on his grave.

In the hallway, Emma turned right as Philip went to the left. "Hey, where are you going?" he asked, trotting to keep up with her.

"To the kitchens," she said briskly, "to get a spoon."

Assuming she would also retrieve food to go with her cutlery, he shook his head in disgust. "We don't have time."

Unaccustomed to heeding the wisdom of Philip, whose ramshackle ways recently led him to knock over a lady with his hobbyhorse in Hyde Park, Emma conceded the truth of his statement and decided she could get the utensil elsewhere. Given the unreliable cleanliness of the establishment she intended to visit, any spoon found there would most likely be filthy, which was even better for gutting alive repellent caricaturists.

Abruptly, Emma spun around and resumed her march to the front door. She nabbed her reticule and pelisse from the newel post where she left them despite her mother-in-law's pleas to show a little decorum—her ways could be ramshackle, too—and strode outside to Philip's curricle.

The young man, who had managed to acquire a little town bronze during his year in the capital, considered himself a tolerable whipster, but he knew better than to try to take the reins in the presence of his cousin's wife. Previously, when they had dashed out of the capital together in pursuit of the treasonous Sir Waldo, she had insisted on holding the ribbons, claiming superior skill. Naturally, he'd found the idea of being driven around the countryside by a woman humiliating, but her boast turned out to be true: Where he showed keen proficiency, she demonstrated expert skill and talent.

As the carriage pulled into the street, Philip announced, "Your assistance was very much missed at the ball last night. The dowager was a regular out-and-outer, inserting herself into a dozen conversations at once and never losing her temper, not even when Miss Phelps-Bute said she had always known there was something dangerous about a woman who knew how to wield a drainpipe."

Emma, whose hoydenish escapades had long kept her on the fringes of polite society, tried to call up the image of Miss Phelps-Bute. Was she the red-haired girl with brown freckles on her nose or the brown-headed girl with red spots on her nose?

It didn't matter. Had Emma been present to hear the slight against her sister, Miss Phelps-Bute's appendage—either freckled or spotty—would have been bloodied. Her pugilistic impulse was precisely why she hadn't attended the affair. Although at first she had resisted Trent's argument on the grounds that she was perfectly capable of controlling her baser instincts, she had ultimately conceded his point: If she had gone, she would have turned the ball into a brawl.

"The dowager said you were not entirely useless either," Emma observed.

A blush crept up his cheeks as he accepted the high praise. "Really? I, uh, rather thought I'd annoyed her when I stomped on Sir Reginald's toe for describing Vinnie's charm as *lethal* or when I spilled a whole glass of ratafia on Lady Douglass's dress for suggesting Huntly needed to hire larger footmen to protect him."

Emma applauded his innovative approach to gossip squashing. "The dowager did not mention any of that, but I'm wildly impressed. I don't think I could have done better myself."

Now the flush deepened and swept to the tips of his ears. "Just did what I could," he mumbled, delighted by the light of admiration he saw in her eye. "It's not right, everyone talking about Vinnie as if she did something wrong. How is the old girl today? Still refusing to marry Huntly?"

Emma slowed the horses as they approached a corner. "I don't know how she is because she snuck out of the town house before I even came down. According to Caruthers, she went to pay a morning call on Lady Agatha Bolingbroke."

Philip would not have been more surprised if Emma said Vinnie had paid a morning call on the prince regent himself. "Lady Agatha? What does Vinnie have to do with that sad sack?"

"You remember our dossiers, of course, and the various agreements we made with members of the horticultural society to ensure their votes?" she asked. "Our agreement with Lord Bolingbroke was that we would try to bring his daughter into fashion."

"But Vinnie abandoned that route in favor of a more honest approach," he said.

The duchess nodded. "She did, but Lady Bolingbroke refused to acknowledge our revised agreement with her husband and insisted we honor our obligation. That is why Lady Agatha and her mother joined us at the theater last week."

"I thought that was queer, your going to the theater with the Bolingbroke chit," Philip said.

"It *was* queer," Emma said. "She made very few comments and spent almost the entire evening glowering at me. I don't think she likes me."

Philip shrugged. "Lady Agatha doesn't like anyone."

"No, and yet she paid us a social call two days ago," she explained, remembering her surprise when she discovered with whom Vinnie was bracketed in the drawing room. "Out of nowhere, she appeared on our doorstep to visit with Vinnie. Is that not strange? And then she ended the visit by turning Vinnie's hose on Lord Addleson and soaking him thoroughly."

His eyes widened with disbelief. "She didn't!"

Emma giggled. "She did. Right there in the conservatory. Naturally we all broke out into peals of laughter, for it was remarkable that Addleson would get the same treatment as Huntly, though, obviously, this time the drenching was intentional and not the result of a malfunctioning prototype. After spraying the viscount, Lady Agatha made a very clever remark about his cravat—I don't recall it exactly but something about the effects of the falling water on his waterfall—and in that moment I found her entirely likeable. But then our laughter made her realize the glaring impropriety of her actions and she immediately left. The whole episode was vastly amusing from beginning to end, and I would have congratulated her on her audacity if she hadn't run off."

"What does the gel have against Addleson?"

"I have no idea. But perhaps Vinnie will find out today. Presumably, she went over there to apologize for our behavior and to avoid further conversation with me or Trent or Huntly. She is determined to martyr herself and won't listen to anyone. If only events had unfolded differently," Emma said, recalling the terrifying moment when she had woken in her bed to find Windbourne's hands around her throat. In the ensuing struggle, she'd managed to grab a heavy candlestick, but before she could disable him with it, he'd pressed a knife, cold and sharp, against her neck. The terror she had felt was as sharp as the knife, but before Windbourne could do her lasting harm, Vinnie was there, a gun at his back. With chilling calmness, she'd ordered him to release her sister, and promptly he'd complied. But it was a trick, for no sooner had he lowered the knife than he spun around, pushing the knife toward Vinnie's stomach, and Vinnie, her blood hot while her head stayed cool, pulled the trigger and the nightmare was over.

But of course it was not over, for Vinnie continued to live in fear of the repercussions of her singular act of heroism, thanks to small-minded little toads such as Mr. Holyroodhouse.

Well aware that the present was ill served by regretting the past, Emma swallowed a sigh and maneuvered the horses around a bend.

As if suddenly alert to his surroundings, Philip looked at the road behind the curricle and then at the stretch in front of it. "I say, where are you going?"

Emma gave him a sideways glance. "Where are *you* going?"

"To Mrs. Biddle's shop," he said, as if stating an obvious fact. "We must demand she halt publication of the offending illustration at once. We must also insist she never run anything like it ever again."

Shifting the ribbons to one hand, Emma laughed and patted her cousin-in-law gently on the head. "I don't care what Trent says, you are adorable."

His face turned pink again, and he slid his head away from her touch. "Puppies are adorable," he said with as much dignity as he could muster. "I am determined. Mrs. Biddle must be stopped."

Emma rolled her eyes at the notion. "That heartless harpy would sooner run naked down St. James's Street than give up a single penny of profit. No, we will not waste our time trying to convince Mrs. Biddle to act honorably. We are going right to the source."

"The source?" he repeated, his eyebrows drawn in confusion. "You mean the artist?"

"Exactly," she said with satisfaction. "But first we must find Mr. Holyroodhouse, so we are heading to the Rusty Plinth."

At once, Philip bolted upright in his seat. "No."

She spared him a glance as she maneuvered around a dip in the road. "Yes," she said with deceptive mildness.

Philip shook his head and said no again. He reiterated it six more times, his resolution growing more firm with each repetition.

Emma smothered a laugh, for she did not want to seem amused by his distress—although she did think it was funny how thoroughly intimidated the young man was by his older cousin. "Yes."

"No. I promised Trent I would never take you to the Rusty Plinth," he explained, a pleading note entering his voice. "It's a matter of honor. A man is only as good as his word. Surely, you understand that."

"But *I* am taking *you*," she pointed out with blithe assurance. "Honor is satisfied."

Although her argument was well reasoned—after all, she did clutch the reins to the curricle in her hands—Philip knew it wouldn't hold water with the duke and could already feel the weight of his cousin's hand on the side of his head. For God's sake, he was twenty, too old to have his ears boxed. "I must insist that you turn this carriage around immediately," he said with what he hoped sounded like stern authority to Emma. His own ears heard a wheedling plea.

To his surprise, she complied, bringing the horses to a complete stop. "You may climb down here," she announced.

Aghast, Philip looked at the shrubbery by the side of the road and then at his cousin-in-law. "What? Here?"

Emma was too impatient with her husband's attempts to restrict her movements to have sympathy with the young man's plight, which, she knew, was awkward. She didn't doubt that he considered his oath to Trent to be a sacred thing. But as she was not consulted on the tendering of the oath, it had no bearing on her behavior.

"Yes, here," she said matter-of-factly. "You have two choices, Mr. Keswick: Either accompany me to the Rusty Plinth, where I will confer with Mr. Squibbs on how to locate Mr. Holyroodhouse, or return to Grosvenor Square on your own. I will leave it to you to decide which option best suits your notion of honor."

The duchess waited silently as he contemplated his situation, her cornflower blue eyes wide with curiosity and expectation. But his situation was such that there was nothing to contemplate. Trent would have his head if he let Emma travel to the docks alone.

"I shall go with you," he announced graciously, as if the idea had been his all along.

"Good," she said, tugging the reins to move the carriage back to the road. "Believe it or not, I'm grateful for your company, however reluctantly it is given. You did me a great service today when you strode into the room and insisted we do something to help Vinnie. Prior to that, I had been fuming uselessly in my study."

"I would appreciate it if you did not describe our outing to the duke in quite those terms."

"Very well," Emma said with a laugh. "But you are being overly cautious. Surely by now Trent knows me well enough to apportion blame properly. If he didn't, I never would have married him."

This fond sentiment, though charmingly expressed, struck Philip as far too optimistic for the situation. The last time Emma visited the Rusty Plinth in the middle of the day, she wound up trailing Windbourne all the way to Dover and almost getting herself killed. Philip, who had the fortune—or misfortune, depending on one's point of view—of catching her on her way out of town, had accompanied Emma on the mad pursuit and had gotten a bullet in the knee for his trouble. Knowing he had helped save England from a French invasion, however, compensated for much of the pain and several months of enforced inactivity.

Letting the matter of Trent's reaction drop, Philip passed the rest of the journey in silence, for he had enough sense to admit Emma's plan was better than his. The capable Mr. Squibbs was sure to locate the infamous cartoonist in a matter of hours. The gentleman was not only the finest lock pick in London, he was the linchpin of a well-honed network of scouts and spies who lurked in every corner of the city.

What he or his associates could not discover in a twenty-four-hour period was not worth knowing.

Emma had first come into contact with Mr. Squibbs while she was investigating Windbourne and had required tutelage on how to open a locked safe. Unable to uncover proof of the baronet's perfidy through conventional means, she'd resolved to break into his apartments, and although the illicit search turned up nothing of use, it had forged an unlikely friendship between the lock pick and the hoyden.

Several months later, when Emma needed help gathering data on the members of the British Horticultural Society to advance her sister's cause, Mr. Squibbs and his team promptly supplied all the information she needed to compile useful dossiers on all twenty-six members, including her husband. It was that kind of ruthless thoroughness, as embarrassing as it had been for Trent to see his mistresses listed in chronological order for his wife's perusal, that was necessary now.

They arrived at the Rusty Plinth a little before two, and although Philip felt an unexpected rumble in his stomach, he knew better than to request a meal at the dockside tavern. The establishment was large but crowded with battle-scarred tables at which its questionable clientele drank tankards of ale and grumbled among themselves. The door that admitted Emma and Philip also let in a large amount of sunlight, and the patrons nearest to the door groaned at the intrusive brightness.

As Emma's gaze swept the room for the familiar figure of Mr. Squibbs, Philip warily eyed four gentlemen whose interest had not returned to their conversation at the shutting of the front door. He recognized the voracious look on their faces as they examined Emma, whose pretty blond curls and neat walking dress could not be a common sight in the rundown tavern.

He leaned over and whispered in Emma's ear. "If Mr. Squibbs is not here, perhaps we should come back later."

She waved off the suggestion with an annoyed shush, and Philip reminded himself that the Duchess of Trent was no helpless victim. He had watched her calmly point a gun at

Windbourne and even shoot when the villain had failed to follow her command.

But that situation was vastly different from this one, for on that occasion Emma had been armed with a gun, and on this one she had no weapon at all, not even a spoon because he had been too impatient to let her visit the kitchens. Additionally, her standoff with Windbourne had been evenly matched, and now they were outnumbered four to two. And not just four to two but four large, brawny ruffians to one lady and one gentleman whose intention to train at Gentleman Jackson's salon had never turned into reality.

One of the ruffians stood up and Philip gulped.

"Yer grace," the man said, smiling to reveal two missing teeth. "We wasn't expecting you today. Does Squibbs know yer about?"

To Philip's horror, Emma not only recognized the gentleman but held her hand out in greeting. He watched as her fingers disappeared into the large man's grasp and somehow reemerged unscathed.

"Mr. Horn," she said warmly, "it's a pleasure to see you again. I trust your mother is well?"

Amazingly, the large man's cheeks turned dusky pink at this consideration. "Yes, yer grace. Very well. She'll be complimented ye asked."

Emma nodded and gestured to Philip. "Mr. Horn, I'm pleased to introduce you to my cousin-in-law Mr. Philip Keswick. Philip, Mr. Horn was one of the gentlemen who assisted Vinnie and me in our horticultural society endeavor. He discovered a particularly useful piece of information on the Earl of Moray."

Mr. Horn shrugged and blushed more deeply. "'Twas nothing."

Although Philip didn't doubt that Emma could spend the rest of the afternoon making polite conversation with all the patrons of the Rusty Plinth, he thought it was better to move the process along. "It is a pleasure to meet you," he said ingratiatingly, for there was no reason to alienate a man whose girth was twice his own. "I wonder if you could help us with Mr. Squibbs. Do you know where we could find him?"

Mr. Horn jerked his head to the left, indicating the back of the tavern. "'E's meeting with an associate right now but should be done soon. Ye can wait 'ere with us."

Philip could not imagine anything more awful than sitting at the dirty table with four roughs, unless it was drinking ale at the dirty table with four roughs. Then suddenly he heard a sound that truly made his blood turn cold.

"Emma!" Trent called from across the room.

The Rusty Plinth fell silent. Every single person in the taproom—patrons, barkeeps, serving wenches—immediately stopped what they were doing to watch the Duchess of Trent greet her husband.

Only Philip turned away.

As if not the least discomforted by the duke's unexpected presence or his angry tone, Emma turned to Mr. Horn and thanked him for his gracious invitation. "If you'll excuse me, I see my husband is here and would like to confer with me on a matter. Perhaps we can have a proper visit when my business with Mr. Squibbs is concluded."

Although Philip held the Harlow Hoyden in the highest esteem and applauded her daring, he thought this statement was a little much, even for her. "Emma," he said warningly.

Emma dismissed his concern as needlessly anxious. Yes, the duke was glowering at them as if he'd caught them in some inappropriate embrace, and, yes, he did seem as though he was about to carry them off like recalcitrant children. But Emma knew she had done nothing wrong. Perhaps Philip had broken his word to Trent, but all she had ever promised was not to come down to the docks again by herself—and she hadn't. Her proof was trembling right by her side.

Calmly, Emma weaved through the tables toward the back of the room, where her husband stood next to the gentleman she had come to see. As always, she greeted Mr. Squibbs warmly and thanked him for being available for an unscheduled meeting. Then, aware that the best way to deflect criticism was to offer one's own, she turned to her husband and said, "Shame on you, Alex. I expected better of you."

The duke's foreboding expression did not lighten. "As *I* expected better of *you*." Then he shifted his gaze to Philip. "And you."

Philip's shoulders drooped at the charge, but Emma lifted her head and said, "Don't try to turn this around, you associate-poaching scrubber. Mr. Squibbs is my most trusted ally, not yours. If you want to have a resourceful lock pick on retainer, then I suggest you start poking around the docks now and leave Mr. Squibbs and me to our business."

Now the duke's lips twitched as he said, "I thought *I* was your most trusted ally, imp."

She scoffed. "You are obviously not trustworthy at all, for you clearly went behind my back to ask Mr. Squibbs to locate Mr. Holyroodhouse. That is the purpose of your mission, is it not?"

Her husband shook his head. "I know what you are doing, Emma, and as much as I admire the strategy and how well you employ it, I will not let you change the subject. You swore to me that you would not come here again."

"Alone," she said with quiet vehemence. "I agreed to your unreasonable demand not to come here *alone*. And I did not. I came with Philip."

"Yes, and what about that?" he asked with an accusatory look at his cousin. "I had your word you would not bring her down here."

Annoyed at the passivity of his comment—as if Emma Harlow let anyone bring her anywhere—she said, "I kidnapped him."

Philip's eyeballs popped out at that outrageous statement, for although he might have been manipulated into the adventure, he had most certainly not been abducted against his will. "Now, see here—"

Trent leaned against the doorjamb and smiled at the ridiculous ploy. "You expect me to believe you carried off a grown man against his will."

Grateful for the doubt, Philip said, "Here's the way—"

Emma did not let him finish. "Snatched the reins from a grown man and it was easy enough. And now *you* are trying to distract *me* from the larger issue, which is your attempt to control me. You can't tell me I can't come down here by myself and then eliminate all my possible escorts. That's not playing fair."

"What's not fair is your charge of unfairness," the duke said. "If you will recall what happened the last time you came down here by yourself and what would have happened had Mr. Squibbs not intervened. A note would have been sufficient to bring him to Grosvenor Square. You did not need to come down here."

"Exactly," Emma said with satisfaction, as if he had just proven her point, her eyes squinting just a little as a shard of light from the open front door reached even that deeply into the building. "A note would have been sufficient for your needs as well but you didn't send one because you were too much in a rush to get help for—"

"Vinnie," Mr. Squibbs said, not bothering to smother a smile as he inserted himself into the marital dispute. Although he had not had the pleasure of witnessing the duke's every attempt to protect his wife from her own reckless nature, he'd observed enough of them to know neither participant would win.

Emma nodded at Squibbs, grateful for the assistance of her trusted associate. "Yes, Vinnie, because we are all too worried about her to—"

"No," Mr. Squibbs said, pointing to the door, where another newcomer now stood. "Miss Lavinia Harlow is here."

Shocked, Emma and the duke turned their heads in unison to see Vinnie standing with her back to the door and an uncertain expression on her face. It was not fear at the rough company but curiosity and then delight as Mr. Horn introduced himself and promptly pointed to where her family stood at the back of the room.

Vinnie nodded with gratitude and quickly made her way through the maze of tables, all eyes following her as the most unusual business meeting the Rusty Plinth had ever hosted grew even more interesting. With a pert step that indicated a heretofore unseen optimism about her situation, Vinnie stopped in front of her sister.

Emma gaped at her in amazement as Trent tried to process the fact that his gentle and kind sister-in-law had blithely stepped into one of the roughest establishments in London.

Equally horrified, they both said, "How dare you come down here alone!" at the exact same time. Then Emma looked at her husband and requested the right to chastise her first, as Vinnie was her twin.

"A valid argument, imp," Trent said. "Have at it."

Vinnie ignored their foolishness and greeted Mr. Squibbs with a polite handshake. Then she looked at the company and added, "Am I right in assuming you have already been given the assignment of identifying and locating Mr. Holyroodhouse?"

But Emma was not to be put off so easily. "Vinnie, do you have any idea how dangerous it was for you to come down here on your own? There are some lovely people here, of course, including Mr. Squibbs and his associates, but the Rusty Plinth is, by and large, a den of iniquity. You could have been killed or worse."

"Your understanding of the situation is heartening, Emma," her husband said, "for you had seemed not to comprehend it at all."

Emma sighed heavily. "But *I* did not come alone."

Unlike her sister, Vinnie was instantly contrite. "You are right to take me to task, Emma, for I did act impulsively. I had not intended to come here, but as I left Lady Agatha's house— and please do not take me to task for making benign morning calls, for I had to do *something* to take my mind off the matter— it suddenly occurred to me that someone doesn't just know the truth about what happened to Sir Waldo, someone knows the *truth*," she explained, her voice lowering to a whisper as she finished the sentence. Mr. Squibbs, the soul of discretion, walked a few paces away to give them their privacy. "Someone knows our secret. Once I realized that, I didn't stop to think but came here as fast as I could to request the resourceful Mr. Squibbs's help. We have to discover that name."

Aware of the elevated level of interest in their business, Mr. Squibbs suggested they continue their conversation in the backroom, where they could finalize the details of his assignment without being overheard or interrupted.

"An excellent idea," Trent agreed, "but we might as well wait."

"Wait?" asked Philip, who still felt aggrieved by Alex's and Emma's treatment and hoped to defend himself better once they were alone. "Wait for what?"

"I'm sure it will be only a minute or two," the duke added.

"*What* will be only a minute or two?" Philip asked.

"Just a little more patience," Trent advised as the front door opened to let in another patron. "And there it is."

Confused and frustrated at his cousin's persistence in not answering his questions, Philip gasped, "What?" just as Emma grasped Trent's meaning. Vinnie, seeing the enlightenment on her sister's face, turned immediately to the door to watch her fiancé navigate the taproom of the Rusty Plinth with cautious experience.

"May we adjourn to the backroom now?" Emma asked, her blue eyes glinting with mischief as she greeted the marquess with a cheerful nod. "Or do you expect the dowager to arrive in a moment, perhaps with Caruthers in tow for protection? Or will she come alone like Vinnie?"

Although still a few feet away, Huntly was close enough to overhear this comment and his face immediately turned ashen. "What?"

Vastly amused, for surely everything was going to be all right now that the capable Mr. Squibbs was on the case, Emma linked arms with Vinnie and led her through the doorway to the backroom, a considerably brighter and cleaner space than the public hall. "On second thought, you are probably better off not acquiring a husband. As soon as they have a ring on your finger, they start making unreasonable demands."

Outraged, Huntly said, "Not coming alone to the most dangerous enterprise in town is *not* an unreasonable demand."

Emma smiled knowingly at her sister as if her point had just been proven.

CHAPTER EIGHT

If attending a ball at which everyone was speculating about a certain young lady's murderous past because of an illustration you drew was painful, then entertaining that same young lady in your own drawing room was pure agony.

As she sat down on the sofa, Agatha could not figure out where to rest her eyes. Looking directly into her guest's smiling visage was most definitely not an option. How Miss Harlow managed to accomplish that—smile when a charge of murder had been leveled against her—was beyond Agatha's comprehension. If the situations were reversed, she would be unable to leave the house without a scowl firmly affixed, let alone pay a social call as if nothing untoward had happened.

Agatha, who could barely stand under the weight of her own guilt, found the other woman's attitude very unsettling. Anger she could understand or despair or even defiance, but this overt cheerfulness was so inexplicable it felt like an elaborate trick to gull her into confessing.

Or perhaps this was merely what true innocence looked like. Miss Harlow's conscience was so clear, she didn't know to be mortified.

Struggling to stem her own mortification, Agatha glanced at the spot on the wall to the left of her guest's shoulder and asked, "Would you like some tea, Miss Harlow?"

"Vinnie, please," she insisted before announcing that a cup of tea would be delightful.

Agatha blanched at the informality—as if they were friends!—and reached for the teapot. Pouring the hot brew gave her something tangible to focus on, and she drew out the process as long as she could, fussing over the simple task with far more care than it deserved. To her utter desolation, however, she could not linger over the distribution of sugar cubes indefinitely, and eventually she had to raise her head to meet the clear blue eyes of Vinnie Harlow.

It required all of Agatha's self-possession not to flinch. Inside, she recoiled as if slapped on the cheek by a hulking brute, but outwardly she remained calm as she tried to think of an innocuous topic. Her ability to make polite conversation, hampered in the best of times by a genuine indifference, was thoroughly incapacitated by a stricken conscience.

Unaware of her host's sudden muteness, Vinnie leaned forward and said, "I must apologize."

The announcement was so bizarre, so unexpected and incongruous, Agatha immediately heard a strange hum in her ears and she wondered if her anxiety had brought on a fit of apoplexy.

No, she thought, giving her head a slight shake to see if she could dislodge the sound. To her dismay, she could not. No, this was part of Miss Harlow's cunning plan to trick a confession out of her. She knew who was responsible for that hideous drawing and rather than confront her directly, she intended to torture her until she revealed every gruesome detail herself.

It would not work, Agatha resolved. No matter what the provocation, she would keep her silence. It was not only that the secret of Mr. Holyroodhouse's identity must remain secure, but also the unbearable fact that she had been a dupe. Someone had wanted to cause Miss Harlow great pain and had used her to accomplish it.

And how readily she had complied!

She should have known something was wrong. Indeed,

she *had* known it, which was why she had relied on Ellen's opinion to calm her misgivings. What an act of madness that was! To expect a lady's maid to see the whole picture—to be able to identify a likeness to Miss Harlow, to know the facts of Sir Waldo's death, to have the worldliness to question the straightforward narrative of the image. The dear girl knew nothing of the ways of the *ton*, neither its players nor its machinations, and would have no cause to wonder at the drawing's hidden message.

Even before Agatha had entered the Paddletons' ballroom, she had realized she'd made a gross miscalculation. Lady Bolingbroke, who had been unable to speak of anything else during the carriage ride, made it clear that none of her friends would be able to speak of anything else either. As soon as her mother said Miss Harlow's name, Agatha had known what was coming. She'd managed to quiet her qualms but not silence them entirely, and there seemed to be a horrible inevitability about the gleeful speculation in which her mother indulged. Agatha's head began to throb and she tried to beg off with the headache, but Lady Bolingbroke, assuming the usual dislike of social outings, dismissed her complaint and insisted she would be fine once she heard the lively trill of the orchestra.

The opening strains of a quadrille did nothing to improve her anxiety, but discovering that Miss Harlow was not present and would not appear calmed her nerves slightly. Feeling as if she had evaded a well-deserved punishment, she planted herself against the wall and determinedly closed her ears to all gossip. It was not difficult, for she was too enmeshed in her own misery to notice anyone else, and Addleson's approach passed unperceived until he was standing directly in front of her.

What fresh torture that had been—to be confronted by yet another victim! Consumed by guilt and despair, she had entirely forgotten about the viscount, and it was only when he insisted that they had to talk about his caricature that she remembered she'd injured two people that day. Her shoulders tensed as she prepared for a lengthy and bloated rant against the awful Mr. Holyroodhouse, which, she assumed, would include some outrage, unfounded, to be sure, about the villain's sartorial inadequacies. Her head still throbbed—oh, how it throbbed—and her entire body ached from the effort of holding itself upright, but she managed to remain on the spot. She stood there, determined to suffer the abuse she knew she had earned.

But no abuse came! Only praise for Mr. Holyroodhouse's cunning and skill.

At first, she'd interpreted his request for a larger drawing, which had arrived that afternoon from Mrs. Biddle in an envelope marked URGENT, as proof of his inanity: Lord Addlewit was too thickheaded to recognize an insult when it was perched atop his shoulders. No doubt he thought the drawing was a tribute to his physical prowess. But when he had stood before her at the ball she had seen the look in his eyes, that bright elusive gleam that she had tried and failed to capture on paper. It was, she had realized with shock, the keen light of understanding.

Viscount Addleson wasn't a joke because he *was* the joke. The dull-witted dandy who couldn't see beyond his shirt points was a fiction, a character invented by him for his own amusement. How dull-witted *he* must find *them,* eagerly accepting his inconsequential prattle as the genuine article.

No wonder her drawing did not bother him: It was a lampoon of a lampoon. With her cunning and skill, all she had captured was a shadow, an image cast upon a wall by a clever puppetmaster.

Without question, Agatha's ego felt the sting. To be revealed as a fool while mocking another for his foolishness was not a pleasant sensation. As a trained observer, she had been schooled in the art of seeing beneath the surface to the underlying structure that gave it shape and she should have realized all was not as it appeared. She had caught a glimmer of the truth while drawing his image but had literally turned it away, settling on a profile because it was easier.

As severe as the blow was to her vanity—and it was particularly disheartening to realize she was obtuse on the day she'd discovered herself to be a dupe—it didn't bother or discomfort her. She was simply too grateful to learn she hadn't caused him pain to worry about her deficiencies. She had done enough damage without adding him to the scrap heap.

Still reeling from the truth about Viscount Addlewit, she was further surprised to hear him dismiss the charge against Miss Harlow. She had known him to be smart, yes, but she had not expected him to be shrewd. Acuity of the mind was a rare thing among the *ton*, who would rather adopt the feelings and opinions of their friends than think for themselves—a fact demonstrated by how quickly the implication of her drawing had been picked up and circulated. Mr. Holyroodhouse had said jump and the members of the *beau monde* obligingly hurled themselves into the air. Only the dowager duchess, whose private suspicion of the worst would not stop her from publicly rejecting it, had mounted a defense of the girl.

For the second time in as many minutes, Agatha felt a deep well of gratitude toward the viscount, and in that moment, she liked him better than any other person she had ever met. She realized it was strange to be so amiably disposed to someone she had so recently scorned, but it didn't feel strange or odd or even the slightest bit peculiar. It felt entirely natural, and when he launched into a ridiculous tirade about the unsuitability of Lord Curtlesby's gilt buttons, she drew her first easy breath of the evening.

It wasn't the ruse itself—inane chatter to alleviate her anxiety—that yielded results but his effort in employing it. She could not fathom his concern for her welfare, for what did it matter to the lofty Viscount Addleson if she was distressed, but she recognized his behavior for the act of kindness it was and could do nothing save respond in kind. She was not as skilled in ridiculous banter as he and felt ridiculous herself when she compared the Earl of Thynn's staid breeches to seventeenth-century garments, a misguided comment that clearly indicated how ill suited she was for the game. Yet Addleson adeptly picked up the ball with all the insouciance of a skilled player and gently lobbed it back to her. The conversation that followed, as silly and as spirited as a children's game of hide-and-seek in the garden, gratified her so much, she was actually disappointed to see it end.

That was certainly a first for Lady Agony.

Thinking about conversations she wanted to see end recalled her to the present, where Miss Lavinia Harlow—Vinnie—sat before her intent on offering an apology. Agatha could not imagine a graver injustice and, smothering a cry of protest, said stiffly, "An apology isn't necessary."

"You are being too kind," Vinnie said, compounding Agatha's misery with the gracious compliment. If only the other girl knew how very *un*kind she had been! "But it's true. As my guest, you deserved to have every courtesy extended to you, and I failed to fulfill that basic social obligation by laughing at your mishap with the hose. I fear you took my…our…laughter as scorn, but I assure you we weren't laughing at you. To prove it, I brought this."

Vinnie produced a white cloth from her reticule and held it proudly aloft as if displaying Princess Caroline's jewels. Her satisfaction with the item hardly seemed appropriate to its presentation, for the cloth was really just a worn bit of fabric streaked with black grime and frayed at the edges, and looking at it Agatha suspected another trick. Miss Harlow could not actually believe the tattered rag was an object worthy of exhibition, let alone admiration. Its condition was so wretched, it seemed unworthy of the Duke of Trent's trash pile. The cloth should be thrown into the murky waters of the Thames at once, if not sooner.

Smothering a fissure of alarm, Agatha said, "It wasn't a mishap."

She'd hoped to disconcert her visitor with the truth, but Vinnie smiled brightly and a dimple peeked out. "I know that. I was just trying to give the incident a little dignity out of respect for you, and I'm delighted to see you don't need it. So now, this blackened rag," she announced with authority, "is the cloth I reached for to dry myself after one of my hose prototypes malfunctioned in the presence of the Marquess of Huntly and exploded water all over his dignified person. This was our introduction and he was so crushingly polite, although he denies it and claims he was merely civil, and I was mortified to the tips of my toes, and seeking a distraction, I took this cloth here—this very same filthy, dirty, shockingly soiled cloth—and dried my face with it. I trust you can imagine what happened next: I wiped black smudges onto my cheeks as I stood before the impeccably courteous marquess whose disdain was palpable despite his excellent manners. Or, rather, because of them. I tell you this to explain why we laughed. The story was known to all of us, and there was something irresistibly funny about seeing it happen again, as if the hose itself has a destiny it must fulfill. And I bring this cloth to show you that it could have been much, much worse."

As Vinnie spoke, Agatha felt something inside her crumble and thought it must be her spine because suddenly it was very difficult to remain upright. Indeed, she felt an overwhelming desire to coil herself into a ball like a small child, and it was only her rigid self-control, honed through years of humiliating episodes with her mother, that kept her shoulders straight.

She'd thought she had known the extent of her wrongdoing prior to this interview, as accusing an innocent young woman of murder was a horrendous offense. But as the duchess's sister explained her behavior, Agatha realized her sins were far worse than she'd believed, for she understood now that her malice had been motivated by spite. Having paid a call on Vinnie with the express purpose of discovering her guilt, she had left the town house convinced only of her rudeness to a guest, and that, it seemed, was enough to expose her to Mr. Holyroodhouse's wrath. Her knowledge of the crime had not improved, nor her opinion of its likeliness altered, but rebuffed by Vinnie's laughter—by everyone's laughter—and mortified by the realization that Vinnie's interest in her had been coerced by Lady Bolingbroke, Agatha had struck back with the only weapon in her possession.

It was a devastating realization for Agatha, who had always prided herself on Mr. Holyroodhouse's detachment. Her paintings were inspired by passion, by an irrepressible need to capture something compelling on canvas, and she threw her heart into every brushstroke. Her drawings for Mrs. Biddle, in contrast, were an exercise in observation, an opportunity to examine the *beau monde* and its foibles with disinterest. Her caricatures, done with a light hand and a raised eyebrow, were never personal. She was merely reproducing the world as it was.

What a foolish conceit—to imagine any representation of the world could be made without prejudice. No human being was wholly impartial, especially she, whose opinions had been formed by years of repression and restriction. All she had wanted to do was paint, and having been denied the pleasure by her parents, she had taken to making snide pictures about their friends and associates. She had mocked the members of her father's beloved institution by turning them into tulips precisely because he held the organization in such high esteem. Then, of course, there was the apparently not very minor fact of Vinnie herself, the sister of the hated Harlow Hoyden, who did what she wanted regardless of society's condemnation. Emma's sister had seemed cut from an entirely different cloth, but by pursuing admission into the all-male society, she had revealed herself to be a hoyden as well.

Agatha's motives, seen through the clear lens of hindsight, were as plain as day.

Crippled by this revelation, she could hardly think and she absolutely could not bear the sight of the filthy rag, which seemed to represent all that was good and honorable in the world. On the morning after being accused of the single most horrendous crime possible, Miss Harlow had presented herself in Portland Place to apologize. Rather than defend her own position, she had sought to put another's mind at ease.

Agatha had long known she was selfish, but she had never grasped the extent until now.

The situation was intolerable. No, it was heartrending

torment, the likes of which she had not suffered before, and as much as Agatha wanted to fall at Vinnie's feet and beg her forgiveness, she stiffened her shoulders and said, "I'm sure the smudges were endearing in a street urchin way."

Vinnie laughed. "Think chimney sweep and you would be closer to the mark. I didn't even realize until later when Emma pointed out the streaks to me. I assure you, as foolish as you felt, I felt ten times more ridiculous. I would have had the revolting cloth destroyed, but I forgot about it until yesterday. I hope you will accept it as a token of my esteem."

Agatha would not have credited Miss Harlow with a mischievous sense of humor, and that she revealed herself to have one now, when it was too late for them to be friends, made her inexplicably sad. The sadness was inexplicable because Lady Agony wasn't on the prowl for friends, and even if she were, she would not rummage through the despised Harlow Hoyden's family tree for candidates.

Exhausted by the sweeping mix of emotions she'd experienced during the short interview, Agatha nevertheless managed a lively reply. "You are far too generous," she said, accepting the filthy rag as if it were in fact a cherished jewel of their princess. "I shall treasure it always."

"I think perhaps it should be displayed in the drawing room," Vinnie said with unexpected earnestness. "All it wants is a proper frame."

Agatha shook her head at the preposterous notion. "Absolutely not. It belongs in my bedchamber, where I can look at it every morning upon rising and think, *As bad as things are, they could always be worse.*"

"A salutary lesson for all of us," Vinnie said with just enough solemnity to remind Agatha of her trespasses.

Appalled by her actions once again, Agatha closed her eyes, as if absorbing a great blow, and when she opened them a moment later, she noted the flush of pink that stained her guest's cheeks. In a horrifying flash, she realized Vinnie was embarrassed to have embarrassed Agatha by alluding to Vinnie's embarrassing situation.

Suddenly, the world was too awful a place to exist—human interaction was too fraught, emotions were too fragile, misunderstandings were too easy—and Agatha wanted to run from the room as if chased by a fire-breathing dragon. The only thing that kept her rooted to the spot was concern for Vinnie's feelings, for she knew the other woman would interpret her abrupt departure as a desire to separate herself from a growing scandal.

No doubt, several members of the *ton* had already done that. Perhaps nobody had given her the cut direct, but surely invitations had stopped arriving.

Determined to put her guest at ease, a novel experience for Lady Agony, Agatha asked about soil density, a concept devised by Miss Harlow to describe the compactness of a soil sample of which she'd heard her father speak admiringly. Agatha was not a devotee of drainage systems—indeed, she could not conceive of anyone feeling passionately about irrigation—but she listened politely as Vinnie explained the importance of accurate measures and even found herself interested in the challenges of attaining the right combination for optimal growth. There was enough in common between the mixing of paints and the mixing of soil for her to respect the process.

With Lord Bolingbroke's interest in gardening, Agatha was adept at holding a thoughtful conversation on cultivation, but she had never exerted herself on anyone else's behalf before. Conversing with Miss Harlow was not as easy as conversing with her father, but nor was it very difficult, and Agatha found with relief that the next half hour did not drag. Before she knew it, her visitor was rising to her feet to take her leave and appeared satisfied with her mission. She said as much on her way to the door, assuring Agatha of how pleased she was that there were no hard feelings between them.

Agatha, keenly aware of the hard feelings that should be between them, said with overbrightness, "There are few fences a filthy rag won't mend."

As soon as Vinnie left, Agatha returned to the drawing

room and threw herself on the divan, thoroughly exhausted by the effort of appearing to be a good person.

She was not a good person. She was a horrible person, and she deserved whatever evil thing happened to her on account of her horribleness. She had scarcely concluded that thought when Gregson announced she had another visitor.

Two visitors in one day was unheard of for Lady Agony, and even Gregson looked confused by the development.

"Who?" she asked, opening one eye. She knew it was undignified to address the butler from a supine position on the cushion, but she wasn't ready to sit up yet. The interview with Miss Harlow had been so emotionally grueling, she doubted she would ever be ready to sit up.

"Mr. Luther Townshend," he said.

"He is an associate of my father's from the horticultural society," she said, relieved to discover she wouldn't have to move just yet. "Please inform Lord Bolingbroke that Mr. Townshend is here to see him."

"I would, my lady, except Mr. Townshend asked for you," Gregson said.

She tilted her head and looked at him askance. "That is odd."

"I agree, which is why I asked Mr. Townshend twice to confirm. He insists that he'd like to speak with you."

Sighing deeply, Agatha reached for the back of the divan and reluctantly pulled herself into sitting position. "All right," she said, unable to imagine what business the gentleman could have with her. Although she had never attended a single meeting of the British Horticultural Society, she knew Townshend's temperament by reputation, for he was, according to her father, a man given equally to bellicosity and conciliation. As the deputy director of Kew Gardens, he was accustomed to issuing orders to dozens of minions and he sometimes forgot that his fellow members were not likewise obliged to comply with his every request, a situation that frequently led to angry outbursts immediately followed by earnest apologies. "Please give me a minute to gather my thoughts before sending him in. And ask Mrs. Brookner to bring a fresh pot of tea."

He nodded his head obligingly, collected the tray of tea and left Agatha to puzzle over Mr. Townshend's unprecedented interest in her as she straightened her disheveled appearance. She was still smoothing the wrinkles from her dress when Gregson showed Mr. Townshend in. For a man reportedly given to fits of anger, he had, she thought, a rather benign grandfatherly look about him: tufts of gray hair, a generous middle, droopy cheeks.

With her reputation as a conversational vortex, Lady Agatha had very few callers and she was at a loss as to how to receive one of her father's associates. She would be respectful, of course, out of deference to Lord Bolingbroke, but she did not relish the idea of having to come up with topics of conversation. She had just spent an hour closeted with Miss Lavinia Harlow. How much small talk was one young lady required to make?

Truly, if this constant stream of visitors was what having a real season was like, she was vastly relieved to have never made the effort.

Plastering a smile on her face, which surely looked as false as it felt, she greeted Mr. Townshend forthrightly. "I am surprised by your intent in asking for me. Are you sure you would not rather see my father?"

Mr. Townshend's eyes glowed with startling fierceness as he looked down at her from his superior height and said, "No, absolutely not. I've got the right person."

Unsettled by the intensity of his gaze, for it seemed to hint at some sort of romantic interest, she told herself not to be absurd and indicated the armchair adjacent to the sofa. "Please sit down. The housekeeper is bringing tea, although please don't feel that you must stay for a cup."

"I appreciate your directness, Lady Agatha, and will be direct in return," he said, as he sat down. "I admire your work as a caricaturist and look forward to continuing our association."

Agatha's heart dropped to her toes. Swiftly, like a rock falling from the roof of a building, it plummeted to the floor with determined velocity. She felt her breath leave her body, as if her chest had been pummeled by a great force. The hum began in her ears again as her left hand started to tremble.

She pressed against the arm of the sofa to still the movement as she mustered a look of feigned amusement. "How very droll you are, Mr. Townshend," she said, her voice as calm as a placid pond. In this moment when it mattered the most, a moment she had been dreading for three years, even as she thought it would never come, she managed to control herself. "Now do please tell me how I can help you. Does it concern my father? I know he can be stubborn on certain matters, but he's never impervious to reason. I'm sure together we can win him over."

"Admirable attempt, my lady," he said warmly, "although not quite the right approach to throw me off the scent. If I were not already certain I had the correct person, your agreeableness would confirm my suspicions. Were you not Mr. Holyroodhouse, you would have said something cutting and had me thrown out. Your reputation as Lady Agony precedes you."

Hearing Mr. Holyroodhouse's name spoken aloud in the refined confines of Lady Bolingbroke's drawing room caused Agatha's arm to quiver again, and she ruthlessly stifled it by pressing more firmly against it. "I am merely extending the courtesy owed to you as a friend of my father's, but if you'd like for me to revert to my usual manners, I'd be more than delighted to toss you out on your ear. Shall I ring the bell now?"

Mr. Townshend laughed. "Yes, yes, deny away. Of course you must. But do be quick about it, as we are wasting valuable time. Here," he said, pulling a folded sheet of paper out of his pocket, "is my idea for our next salvo. I think it's rather clever myself."

Agatha's horror at being unmasked was so profound, she did not pause to wonder at his motives for seeking her out. She thought only of her parents' reactions—her mother's fury, her father's shocked disappointment—and accepted the sheet of paper with pronounced indifference. It was only the expression of unadulterated glee on his face that induced her to actually look down. She noticed immediately that it was a drawing, but it took her a few extra seconds to realize what she was seeing. It was not only Mr. Townshend's limited skill that made comprehension difficult, but also the wild premise of the cartoon, which depicted Miss Lavinia Harlow applying a solution of weed killer to a tulip that looked suspiciously like Sir Waldo Windbourne.

To give herself time to think, she pulled her brows together as if seriously considering the drawing. She tilted her head at what she supposed was a thoughtful angle and said, "Hmmm."

Next to her, Townshend practically purred in delight.

The image explained a lot. Townshend was clearly her mysterious letter writer, and delighted with the results from their first collaboration, he was eager to work on their next. She didn't understand everything, of course, such as why he was set on ruining Vinnie and how he discovered her identity.

Impatient with her silence, he said, "It's brilliant, isn't it? It keeps to a theme while suggesting all is not as it seems."

Agatha stared at him, aghast. Brilliant? He thought this amateurish piece of drivel was brilliant? By what impossibly low standard did he measure brilliance? "It says weed killer," she observed.

"Yes," he agreed cheerfully.

"Right there," she said, pointing to the words written on the spray bottle the poorly drawn Miss Harlow held. "You wrote out *weed killer* in large capital letters."

Unaware of her censure, he said, "Exactly. So there can be no mistake."

She stared at him in disgust, amazed at his obliviousness. He'd somehow managed to figure out her secret identity, something nobody else had accomplished, and yet he was clearly an idiot. "No self-respecting caricaturist spells out the elements of a drawing at all, let alone in large capital letters. It's lazy and sloppy and so unsubtle, you might as well write, 'This is funny' across the bottom. I'm appalled that you think

I would ruin my reputation as a skilled and insightful satirist with such incompetence. It's time for you to leave."

Agatha didn't think it would be that easy to get rid of him, and although she wasn't surprised that he remained firmly seated in the armchair, she was somewhat taken aback when he countered her criticism. "That is your opinion," he said stiffly, "and I respectfully disagree."

She snorted in disgust. Respectfully disagree with her? He was a gardener, an administrator, a glorified secretary with a staff of lackeys too intimidated to question his authority. Well, she wasn't a lackey and she wasn't intimidated.

"You have not earned the privilege of disagreeing with me," she announced firmly, as the outrage poured through her. "You have neither the experience nor the skill to assess the components of successful satire. You are just a doodler who thinks he's clever. Yes, I am Mr. Holyroodhouse, and I don't know why you wasted your time coming here, because I will not do anything you ask. You may leave now before I decide to draw a caricature suggesting you killed Sir Waldo and I will not have to use large capital letters to make my point."

So saying, she marched to the door and held it open.

"Sit down!" Townshend barked, his eyes blazing hotly, for her name calling had turned his enthusiasm into anger. "We *will* work together despite artistic differences because I know who you are and one word from me will destroy your reputation so thoroughly your children's children will have to reside on the northern edge of Yorkshire lest they find themselves run out of London for being descendants of yours. Now let us come to terms and I will remove myself from your charming company."

Townshend did not have to make the threat for Agatha to know what was at stake, and she returned to the sofa without speaking.

Taking a deep breath, the deputy director of Kew said, "I think it's reasonable to conclude that your squeamishness with the assignment affects your view of my drawing. When I began our association, I had no idea Mr. Holyroodhouse was a woman and I would never have established the connection had I known. That said, I cannot alter the fact of your sex and am forced to deal with you as you are. To that end, I hope it will ease your delicate sensibilities when I assure you Miss Harlow is guilty of this heinous act. If you understood how guilty she was, you would have no qualms about writing *weed killer* on the bottle. I believe Shakespeare used a similar device in *Hamlet* and nobody cried amateur when the asp appeared."

Agatha was no simpleton and she readily grasped the seriousness of her situation, but that did not stop her from appreciating its humor as well. Having never regretted her lack of friends, she suddenly felt the absence as she realized she had nobody with whom to share Townshend's outstanding peevishness. She immediately thought of Addleson and knew he would get no small enjoyment out of Townshend's insistence that his blunt hand was as subtle as Shakespeare's.

"There is no need to be squeamish, I assure you," he announced with authority. "I am far too honorable to make any charge, let alone one so severe, against an innocent woman, and we are, I believe, in the closing phase of our campaign. Your first drawing, which was quite good, by the way—not what I had in mind, but certainly effective in its own way—has made inroads into Miss Harlow's spotless reputation. People are starting to look at her as the manipulative beast she is. Our next move is to print a rendition of the drawing I've presented to you, the satire of which, as we discussed, is more sophisticated than your feminine mind can grasp. That cartoon will destroy what is left of Miss Harlow's good name and our association will be at an end."

As he spoke, Agatha decided it was not his continued insistence that his facile drawing was brilliant that convinced her he was disturbed, though that did seem to indicate an unbalanced mind, but his assertion that Miss Lavinia Harlow was a manipulative beast. After her experience with Viscount Addleson, she was willing to admit her ability to see below the surface wasn't as highly developed as she'd supposed, but nor was it entirely nonfunctioning. Vinnie Harlow, with her filthy rag of a gift, was not evil. She may not be altogether good, for nobody was, but she was not the dyed-in-the-wool villain Mr. Townshend believed her to be.

Without question, there was a story to be uncovered, some sequence of events that explained his vehement dislike of the mild-mannered beauty. Considering the tenor of his wrath, she concluded that the matter in question had not been resolved in his favor. His mission was one of revenge, not justice.

If she was going to extricate herself from this scrape, she would first need to gather information about Mr. Townshend, for surely he had some weakness she could exploit. Everyone, no matter how seemingly invulnerable, had a fault that would lead to their downfall. Achilles' was his heel; hers was her painting. She would find Mr. Townshend's. The place to start was his disagreement with Miss Harlow, for discovering the root of his hatred would almost certainly reveal important information.

Before she could begin her investigation, she had to extricate herself from this conversation. "Very well, Mr. Townshend," she said, "I will comply with your request, except that you must give me time to come up with an alternate idea. I would sooner be exposed as the infamous Mr. Holyroodhouse than the author of such an amateurish drawing."

Townshend opened his mouth as if to protest, for how could he let such an insulting characterization of his work stand but then thought better of continuing the argument. His goal was the destruction of Miss Harlow, not establishing aesthetic dominance over Lady Agatha. "Very well, my dear, I agree to your terms. You have three days to come up with an alternate idea. If I don't see publication of the cartoon by Thursday, I will announce your true identity at Lord Kendrick's ball. It is meant to be a festive affair, to celebrate the many years his lordship has been happily married to Lady Kendrick, and no doubt the revelation of your secret identity would add an extra dash of felicity."

Seventy-two hours was a meager allotment for ascertaining every pertinent detail of another person's life, but it was more than enough time for Mr. Holyroodhouse to conceive and execute a drawing. "Let us say four days, for I cannot guarantee the efficiency of Mrs. Biddle's shop. She works with several caricaturists and must answer to their demands as well."

Mr. Townshend wrinkled his forehead, as if suspecting a trick, and Agatha, sensing his reluctance, added, "Mrs. Compton is hosting a musicale on Friday and no doubt the revelation of my secret identity would add more than a dash of felicity to an otherwise tedious affair."

Hearing his own reasoning repeated back to him made its logic irrefutable, and he agreed to her proposal. Satisfied with the interview, he stood up to leave. "I am delighted you have decided to be so reasonable, Lady Agatha," he announced agreeably. "I've always found your father to be a pleasant and congenial man and it's lovely to see those traits in his child. Needless to say, we will keep this matter between ourselves. I'm sure Lord Bolingbroke would be as surprised as I was to learn Mr. Holyroodhouse's true name."

Although she was eager to see him leave, Agatha could not help extending the conversation, for there was one piece of information she had to know. "How *did* you learn my name, Mr. Townshend? I have quite an elaborate system in place to protect it."

"Yes, leaving messages under the doormat was quite clever and my man watched the building for several days before he figured out how you and Mrs. Biddle were communicating. Even then, he found it impossible to figure out who was collecting the letters. Then yesterday, Mrs. Biddle, in what appeared to be indecent haste to deliver a very important message, broke protocol and presented the note directly to Mr. Floris's assistant, Mr. Smith. He in turn delivered it posthaste to his daughter, who works in this house as your lady's maid. I will confess I considered for a moment the possibility of Ellen Smith as Mr. Holyroodhouse but then dismissed it as far too unlikely. Your admission confirmed it, but do not tease yourself that you gave the secret away, for I had only the tiniest speck of doubt."

Agatha smiled, as if unperturbed by this explanation, but silently she fumed over the unlikely sequence of events. If Viscount Addleson had not made his preposterously generous offer for another drawing, Mrs. Biddle would not have been so overcome by avarice as to dash over to Jermyn Street and give away the game. How the shop owner knew of Mr. Floris and his location was another troubling matter. Apparently, her elaborate system was not nearly as intricate as she'd thought.

Deciding no verbal response was necessary, Agatha merely nodded in acknowledgement and escorted Townshend to the door. He paused with his hand on the knob while he examined her thoughtfully.

"I am in earnest, Lady Agatha," he said amiably, as if commenting on the weather rather than reiterating a threat. "I will expose you to society if you don't comply with my request. No doubt you think you are very clever and will find a way to outmaneuver me. The effort is charming but futile, for, I assure you, no woman has ever bested me and no woman ever shall."

The arrogance of the statement begged for a reply, but Agatha knew better than to provoke him and merely nodded again. Townshend, mistaking diplomatic silence for female compliance, preened with satisfaction at her ready acquiescence. "I look forward to our collaboration."

"As do I," she said with just enough sincerity to cause him to smile.

With a tip of his hat, Townshend took his leave, and Agatha carefully studied his departing frame as it left her home. What a repellent human being.

Now that he was gone, the panic she had managed to control during their interview overtook her and her left hand began to tremble in earnest. She had to find a way to get out from under his thumb. She simply *had* to. Otherwise she would be left with a set of impossible choices: ruin her own reputation or ruin the reputation of an innocent woman.

If she had no alternative, if every attempt to defeat Townshend came to naught, she would chose the former. Of course she would, for she would not be able to live with herself if she caused Vinnie further damage. It wasn't a matter of doing what was right; it was a matter of doing what was bearable.

And yet even as she settled on her decision, she felt the insidious worm of cowardice coiling through her soul. Her own ruin would be complete and irrevocable. Once revealed as Mr. Holyroodhouse, she would be beyond redemption, a pariah who had betrayed her own kind. She would not be able to brazen it out or laugh off the episode as a very good lark. She would simply cease to exist in the eyes of the *beau monde*.

The thought, to her surprise, was utterly intolerable. Yes, she loathed the obligations of society and the demands they made on her time, but now, as she stood on the edge of exile—on the edge, it would seem, of getting everything she had ever wanted—she realized she did not want it at all. She did not relish having to interact with other human beings, but the prospect of being cut off from them entirely felt more lonely than she could bear. There was a value, she'd discovered, in being among one's peers.

In comparison to banishment, Vinnie's punishment would be mild, for the accusation would always remain speculative. There was no proving or disproving the charge of murder. The Bow Street Runners were not going to dig up the corpse of Sir Waldo Windbourne and examine it for suspicious marks. Agatha did not know if posthumous study of a body was possible, but even if it was, nobody would order such an extreme undertaking based on a few renderings of an anonymous artist.

Vinnie might be made uncomfortable by the publication of another drawing—a few sticklers might give her the cut direct, some high-minded hostesses might exclude her from their guest lists—but on the whole her life would proceed unchanged. At worst, her fiancé, Huntly, whom Vinnie herself described as impeccably courteous, might decide he could not abide by the gossip and end their arrangement.

Such a consequence would be regrettable, of course, but it did not equal the pain of banishment from polite society. And, truly, was it not better for a lady to discover the paltriness of her true love's regard before she said her vows?

In a few months' time, the chatter would die down and Vinnie's life would return to normal. Agatha's never would.

Disgusted by these thoughts and angry at herself for having them, Agatha struck her fist against the door frame, which had the immediate effect of bruising her knuckles. Excellent, she thought, nursing her right hand. Now she was disgusted, angry and in pain—an ideal combination for lucid thinking.

Don't forget panicked, she reminded herself grimly. One hand hurt; the other hand trembled.

Action was required—immediate, decisive, inexorable action—but nothing could be done until she cleared her head. Fear and repulsion did not oil the tricky machinery of the mind. The only thing that ordered her brain was drawing, so she presented herself to her studio at once and picked up her sketch book. Her fingers ached as she clutched the pen, but rather than ring for Ellen to bring a cold compress, she decided to suffer the discomfort as the well-deserved consequence of foolish behavior. But it was not the blow to the door frame that she condemned but her entire history as Mr. Holyroodhouse. How idiotic it seemed to her now that she'd ever believed she would be able to get away with the ruse indefinitely, and the throbbing in her hand, a minor sting compared with the pain her soul suffered, felt symbolic of the entire calamity. She had caused her own wounds. To her hand and to her soul—she had inflicted the damage. Vinnie had not.

Briefly, Agatha closed her eyes and for a moment she could see the entire scene clearly: Townshend prostrate on the floor, his nose pressed into the tiles of the Duke of Trent's conservatory; Miss Lavinia Harlow sitting on his back, her eyes bright as she flipped through the British Horticultural Society's bylaws; and the caption that took the triumph out of Townshend's infuriating boast: "No woman has ever bested me and no woman ever shall."

As she drew, Agatha's sense of helplessness gave way to feelings of competence and control. Townshend had been bested once, which meant it could be done, and something that could be done once, could be done again. Of that, she was certain. The key was Miss Harlow's entry into the horticultural society, for it was the most logical way for her to have earned the detestable gentleman's enmity. She recalled the deal the Harlow sisters had struck for her father's support—two outings to make Lady Agony fashionable—and wondered if Townshend had likewise been approached. The existence of that known agreement indicated an attempt to influence the opinions of the voting members. Perhaps where a benign exchange could not be made, a different sort of pressure was applied.

It seemed highly unlikely that the affable Miss Harlow had blackmailed the prickly Mr. Townshend, yet Agatha, unable to think of a better explanation, settled on that angle as the best one to investigate. The obvious place to start was at the scene of the crime itself, for the British Horticultural Society kept impeccable records of its proceedings. All she had to do was convince the manager of the society's business affairs to let her take a look at the record of its recent meetings.

Dealing with Mr. Berry would be tricky, for she knew him to be a kind but straitlaced individual who passionately guarded the dignity of the organization that employed him. She could not simply walk through the front door and as the daughter of Lord Bolingbroke request to see the private accounts. Not only would Mr. Berry emphatically deny her request, but he would most likely report her unusual behavior to her father. Needless to say, that occurrence must be avoided at all costs.

The only thing for it was to pay the call dressed as someone else. She could not imagine any lady for whom Mr.

Berry would open the society's books, for he was far too conservative in his judgments to think a female worthy of their study. No, she would have to adopt the identity of a gentleman in order to get the information, but what gentleman could it be? Someone Mr. Berry respected but was not too familiar with to notice the discrepancy in his appearance.

Mr. Petrie, she thought with excitement. He was an honored guest of the horticultural society. Surely, his request to see the minutes would be granted without hesitation.

No sooner had she conceived of the idea than she dismissed it, for not only was the American's physical appearance impossible for her to re-create—he towered over her from an unnatural height—he wasn't even in London at the moment. The day before, he had left for Bath to meet with a publisher and would not return for five more days.

Borrowing Mr. Petrie's identity was not an option, but the visiting naturalist could still be of use, for there was his assistant, Mr. Clemmons, to consider. The gentleman had been too sick to travel on the same ship as his employer, but that didn't mean he could not have recovered in time to board the next steamer to London. Charged with his first duty since arriving, Clemmons could present himself at the offices of the horticultural society and request access to its private documents in a mission to discover information. Mr. Petrie wanted to set up an analogous organization in the colonies and tasked him with discovering as much as possible about the well-run institution. No doubt that commendatory undertaking would gratify Mr. Berry's ego.

Excited by her idea, Agatha began working on the most daunting aspect of the subterfuge: imitating the American accent. As a gently bred young lady and a skilled artist, she had never had cause to adopt a foreign accent and had no knowledge of the basics. It would be highly irregular if she hired an actress to tutor her—time consuming, as well, for how would she find this helpful thespian—so she contented herself with copying Mr. Petrie's peculiar way of pronouncing words. The key, she realized, was to overproduce her Rs and to flatten her vowels.

Methodically, she worked, honing her accent while adding features to Mr. Townshend's surly face. She exaggerated his eyebrows and doubled the weight of his jowls. She did several versions of Vinnie's expression, finally setting her face into a look of complete indifference, as if she were entirely unaware that the comfortable chair upon which she sat was the humiliated figure of Luther Townshend.

She toiled diligently for almost three hours, impatiently shrugging off Ellen when the maid appeared to announce dinner, and when Agatha finished her drawing, she not only had an acerbic lampoon of Mr. Townshend's vanity but a plan to free herself from it as well.

CHAPTER NINE

Although Viscount Addleson did not frequently decide to drop family members, as he had so few of them whom he liked, he realized as Edward Abingdon stopped his curricle in front of the British Horticultural Society that he had no choice but to ruthlessly remove his cousin from his life.

"I have nothing but respect for your passion for horticulture, as I believe it's important for a young gentleman to care strongly for something as a blind against cynicism. Look at me, I have given my life over to the pursuit of the perfect waistcoat and I assure you it has not been in vain, for every day I grow a little bit closer to attaining my goal," Addleson explained reasonably. "But your insistence that I share your passion is intolerable and, since you are not my heir, as that distinction belongs to a dull-witted squire whose interest in waistcoats is nonexistent, I feel no compunction in permanently parting ways."

His cousin laughed as if a cruel threat had not just been issued. "This stop will only take a moment, and then we shall continue to Gentleman Jackson's salon. I assure you, our appointment there is real and not a fiction I created to lure you here. Despite what you fear, I'm not lobbying for your inclusion in the horticultural society. I cannot think of a worse circumstance than to be trapped in a meeting hall with you. Now do let's step inside so that I may complete my business swiftly and we can be on our way."

Addleson continued to stare at Edward with a wary eye. "I cannot imagine what business has to be conducted en route to Gentleman Jackson's. Surely, it can wait until after our session."

"Time is of the essence," Edward explained as he climbed out of the carriage. "Mr. Petrie's secretary—you recall Mr. Petrie from Bolingbroke's soiree?—he has arrived in town and is in possession of some information vital to my well-being. At this very moment, he is visiting with Mr. Berry and I do not want to lose the chance to consult with him. As I said, it will take but a moment."

Remembering the tedium of the evening, Addleson seriously doubted that the secretary of the infamous American bore would be succinct. He expected this brief errand would consume the rest of the day and began to consider dropping his cousin in earnest. Of course he knew Edward wasn't really trying to recruit him for his gardening club, but his genuine lack of respect for the viscount's time was troubling. His valet took up too many of his free hours for him to accept an additional burden now.

On a sigh, Addleson entered the cheerful quarters of the British Horticultural Society, with its airy entranceway and comfortable wingback chairs. Mr. Berry, an animated man of mild affability who neatly handled the organization's business affairs, was quietly sorting through a stack of publications on his desk. He glanced up at his visitors and immediately rose to his feet.

"Mr. Abingdon," he said warmly, "what an unexpected pleasure. Do come in. Please do. And Lord Addleson, it is an honor to welcome you to the heart of our operations."

"I'm not here to trouble you, Mr. Berry," Abingdon announced, as the clerk rushed to assure him he was no trouble at all. "I've just come to see Clemmons. Moray said he spotted him here over an hour ago."

Mr. Berry nodded eagerly. "Yes, yes, he's here. He came at the request of Mr. Petrie, who is so impressed with our organization that he intends to establish one just like it in New York. Naturally, of course, he cannot establish one *just* like it, as our institution is unique, with a long and storied history that cannot be replicated. I suspect Mr. Petrie will find it impossible to re-create the rigorous academic atmosphere we have established here, although I would never do anything to discourage his making the attempt. I know it is futile and you know it's futile, but misplaced optimism is an essential part of the gardening process."

"As it is an essential part of the American character," Addleson added.

The clerk beamed at him. "You are correct, my lord."

"Where is Clemmons now?" Abingdon asked.

"He is in the library reading the minutes of our most recent meetings," Mr. Berry explained. "I realize sharing our private notes is highly irregular and I fully intended to deny the request, even though I respected his endeavor and, frankly, expected nothing less of Mr. Petrie. When Mr. Petrie was here earlier in the week, I noted a particularly avaricious gleam in his eye as he examined our lecture hall and naturally assumed he would want to create a similar temple to learning in New York. Actually, I *had* declined, but the Earl of Moray, who had spent a quiet morning reading the recent issue of *The Journal of the British Horticultural Society*, insisted I was being needlessly frugal with our knowledge and assured Clemmons it would be no problem for him to review our private materials."

Although Addleson thought Mr. Berry was being needlessly generous with his knowledge, for two words—*the library*—would have been a sufficient answer, he followed the clerk into the large, book-lined room without complaining. Sunlight poured through a south-facing window, providing light for the solitary figure who leaned over a large ledger. Clemmons was so engrossed in his reading, he visibly jumped when Mr. Berry announced visitors. Immediately, he stood.

To the viscount's relief, Mr. Berry was relatively concise

in his introductions, rambling only for a minute about the society's illustrious Mr. Abingdon, a description that amused his cousin, who had never known him to "quake with insight," as the enthusiastic clerk put it.

While Mr. Berry spoke, Addleson examined Mr. Adolphus Clemmons, who cut a rather unimpressive figure, with his slight build and an unfortunate black mole that seemed to cling to the edge of his right nostril. His complexion was slightly off, indicating he had yet to recover fully from his grave illness, and his lips seemed like narrow strips against the broad plains of his face. His dark hair, speckled with a surprising amount of gray for one so young, emerged in clumps from his head.

His clothes, though neat and clean, clearly marked him as an American provincial, for his attempt to ape the elegant style of an English gentleman was woefully inadequate. His tailcoat, single-breasted with wide lapels and narrow sleeves that gathered at the shoulder, was an appallingly bright shade of pomona green. The way he was wearing his pantaloons further highlighted his ignorance, for even the most rural of one's rural cousins knew the straps were worn under the shoe during the day; under the foot was only appropriate at night. Ultimately, however, it was the fit of the garments that proclaimed him a yokel, for they were not at all customized to suit his slim frame. Either Clemmons did not grasp the concept of tailoring or he was wearing another man's clothes. The latter seemed more likely to him, and he imagined the secretary stopping at a charity shop on his way into town from the docks for an added dose of gravitas.

"Mr. Clemmons, I cannot tell you how pleased I am that you were able to make the journey," Edward said with such force, the poor provincial looked positively terrified. His dark eyes almost popped out of his head.

He coughed several times before saying, "Really?"

Edward nodded emphatically. "Yes, yes, for you hold a piece of knowledge I simply must have. You see, I had an extensive discussion with Mr. Petrie about *Simmondsia chinensis* and he was unable to recall a detail that is of the utmost importance to me. He stated forthrightly, however, that you would be in possession of the information. So, Mr. Clemmons, do be kind enough to tell me how one improves the viscosity of jojoba oil during refinement."

The question was so trivial, so unworthy of a stop at all, let alone a detour from a vigorous boxing session, that Addleson said, "What?"

Mr. Clemmons was also surprised by the query, for he, too, cried, "What?" at the exact same moment.

As annoyed as he was with his cousin, the viscount couldn't help noticing something very strange about Mr. Clemmons's exclamation. The quality of his voice was different: higher, less baritone, more—dare he say it?—feminine.

At once, his gaze flew to Mr. Clemmons's eyes, simmering pools of black, and he thought how very similar they were to Lady Agatha's.

Instinctively, he dismissed the notion as outrageous. What cause could she have to appear as thus at her father's revered institution? Clearly, the reason he associated poor Mr. Clemmons with Lord Bolingbroke's unusual daughter was she had been frequently on his mind since their last meeting, a rare condition for him that he found as irritating as it was intriguing. It was simply a trick of the brain—and a rather disturbing one at that—to see Lady Agony in the visage of a provincial American.

But once the idea was formed, it took hold and Addleson studied the figure more closely, ignoring the poorly fitting clothes that had distracted him from a proper first perusal. The hair, he noted now, was such a marvelous creation, it could only be a wig, one that was decades out of date, judging by the flecks of powder sprinkled in it, and the nose beneath the appalling mole tilted up with a familiar pertness. Then, of course, there were the eyes, Lady Agatha's piercing, fathoms-deep eyes that looked at him with scorn. He would know them anywhere.

As shocked as he was to find her in such an unlikely

position, a part of him wasn't surprised at all. He didn't understand Lady Agatha and he couldn't pretend to comprehend her motives, and yet he had the confounding sense that he knew her. Watching her strive for a semicoherent response to Edward's ridiculous question, he felt as if he knew her better than he knew anyone in the world.

"Ah, yes, the coveted oil of the *Simmondsia chinensis*. A very interesting topic, viscosity, but a wretched business all the same," Lady Agatha said, clearly struggling to keep her deep baritone consistent. Every fourth or fifth word it shrieked upward and then settled down again in the lower register. Edward, eagerly awaiting a long-sought explanation, did not notice. "Yes, of course. The trick, you see, is litharge. Are you familiar with litharge?"

"I am not," Edward admitted.

"You are not?" Lady Agatha said, seeming to gain confidence at this profession of ignorance. "Well, as I said, the secret is to use litharge, which is a mineral that forms from the oxidation of galena ores. You add litharge to a formulation of piled glass, calcined bones and mineral pigments boiled in linseed oil."

Listening, Addleson smothered a smile as he realized she was explaining the process by which one made paint—but not the dainty watercolors ladies of her ilk routinely employed. Lady Agatha was describing oils, and Edward, who did not know lapis from lead, was fascinated.

"When the viscosity of the mixture meets your approval," she continued, "you add it drop by drop into your extraction, stirring with an even hand, until you are satisfied with its thickness. And that, my dear sir, is how you improve the viscosity of jojoba oil during refinement."

Lady Agatha concluded her talk with such commanding authority, Edward could do nothing but nod in agreement, even though questions remained. His cousin might be clueless about the manufacture of oil paints, but he was not an imbecile. The recipe her ladyship detailed was fraught with inexplicable ingredients such as piled glass, and even the most generous attempt to accept her explanation would be confounded by the inclusion of unspecified pigments.

Well aware of her vulnerability, Lady Agatha took an aggressive stance to end the conversation. "I trust our business is concluded, Mr. Abingdon. I am here to gather useful information at the specific request of Mr. Petrie and I would hate to fall short because I was too busy engaging in conversation. Given that you are familiar with my employer's habits, I'm sure you won't be surprised when I tell you he does not appreciate people who talk."

Edward wrinkled his brow, as if trying to decide if this observation about Mr. Petrie was intended to be a slight, and Addleson jumped into the conversation before his cousin noticed anything amiss about Clemmons's American accent, which was turning more British with every syllable.

"The gentleman is right, Edward," he said forcefully, "you must be on your way, for you are already late for your appointment at the salon. I shall remain here to improve my acquaintance with Mr. Clemmons."

"What?" Edward said, his tone clearly indicating that he wasn't sure he had heard his cousin correctly.

Agatha, who was equally taken aback by the announcement, found the suggestion so horrifying, she actually sputtered. Unable to form the words of her objection, she stammered, "Bu...bu...bu..." a few times before clamping her mouth shut.

Amused by both their reactions, the viscount wrapped his arm around his cousin's shoulder and steered him purposefully toward the door. The trick to making people behave as you wished was not giving them an opportunity to act otherwise. "As Mr. Clemmons has professed his aversion to conversation, I'm sure it will take me a while to overcome his opposition. I simply cannot ask you to wait. Having been detained from my purpose this morning by you, I know exactly how rude that is and would never subject you to the same shabby treatment. Now don't worry about me," he added over Edward's continued attempts to interrupt. "I shall hire a hack to get home or allow your efficient Mr. Berry to arrange transportation. I will be perfectly fine. Do say hello to Gentleman Jackson for me and remember to keep your toe and heel aligned. A boxer's success depends on proper foot placement."

Despite Addleson's guidance, Edward stopped abruptly at the door and said firmly, "Jonah, I really don't think—"

"Right you are, my boy, don't think," Addleson agreed, pushing him gently toward the threshold. "Unless it is about your stance. A boxer's game is built from the ground up. Heel and toe!"

On that last piece of advice, Addleson shut the door in the face of his stunned cousin. Immediately, Lady Agatha called out in her false baritone, "Lord Addleson, sir, this is—"

He raised a finger to his lips to indicate silence and pressed his ear against the door. Hearing nothing, he counted to ten and opened the door a crack. Edward was gone. Relieved that his cousin could be deterred from his purpose so easily, he turned on a sigh of satisfaction and strode across the room.

As he pulled out the chair next to hers, he said, "I apologize for shushing you, but I wanted to make sure he was gone. Now, what were you saying, Lady Agatha?"

Her response was priceless. Oh, was it priceless. Indeed, he would happily suffer through a hundred explanations of how one improved the viscosity of jojoba oil during refinement for the pleasure of seeing it one more time.

"I'm not—" The protest died suddenly when she realized she was using her regular voice. She laughed awkwardly, still in her normal register, and scrunched her face up in an exaggerated look of confusion. "Why would you call me that? I'm not Lady Agatha. Maybe you're Lady Agatha." She paused and shook her head. "I mean, who is Lady Agatha?"

Addleson, watching the performance with delight, found her absolutely adorable, a description, he was sure, Lady Agony would find more repellent than being discovered masquerading as a provincial American secretary in the library of the British Horticultural Society.

He did not know what her game was, but there were

several clues on the table worth examining, including the minutes from the society's recent meetings. He glanced at the page and noted it contained a discussion of Miss Lavinia Harlow's acceptance. Without asking permission, he pulled the book closer to him so he could read it easily.

"Excuse me," Agatha protested tartly, trying to drag the minutes back into her possession. "I was using that."

His hold remained firm as he skimmed the document for the missing puzzle piece he knew it must contain. Lady Agatha's interest in Miss Harlow was not exceptional, for everyone was interested in her now, thanks to Mr. Holyroodhouse's drawing. But what if her interest *was* extraordinary?

He recalled her expression at Lord Paddleton's ball, the look of pure devastation on her face when he suggested they talk about Mr. Holyroodhouse's drawing. He had meant his own, but she had naturally assumed he was referring to Miss Harlow's. Her demeanor during the discussion, the way she had blanched when he agreed that the caricaturist was indecent and cruel, indicated a more personal interest in the accused woman's misery.

Addleson did not think Miss Harlow and Lady Agatha were friends, certainly not intimates who felt the stings and arrows of the other's misfortune as if they were their own. He had discovered her at the duke's house, yes, but that visit hardly seemed to be a routine occurrence. The house call was not Lady Agony's milieu, so why had she paid the visit? What had been her purpose?

"If you don't release your grip on this book, I'm going to have Mr. Berry eject you from the building," Lady Agatha announced, this time in the tones of a proper British gentleman. She had gotten the register right but not the accent. Again, Addleson found her wholly adorable, especially when she wrapped her other hand around the book and tugged with all her might.

Her other hand.

Noting the callus on her right index finger, he seized her hand to examine it more closely.

Horrified, Lady Agatha stiffened at once and twisted her wrist to wrench free. Addleson held fast. "Release me at once, my lord," she demanded.

Rather than comply with her request, he ran his finger over the callus to gauge its firmness. Many ladies had earned calluses in the maintenance of their correspondences, but their marks were dainty compared with the thickening of Agatha's skin. It could have been produced by a number of longstanding activities, such as writing a novel in the style of Miss Austen or keeping a detailed journal of her experiences. Those explanations, however, failed to consider the other evidence: She knew how to mix paints, she had seemed particularly distressed by Miss Harlow's situation, she had anticipated his desire to possess a larger version of the drawing, and, of course, the most fascinating clue of all, she had pretended to be Mr. Petrie's ailing assistant to gain access to the British Horticultural Society's private records.

He wasn't sure what all those factors added up to, but he was comfortable enough to make the most outrageous supposition he had ever made in his life.

"You are Mr. Holyroodhouse," he said.

Lady Agatha turned white. All the color simply disappeared from her face as if it had never been there.

"You are in some sort of trouble," he continued, unsettled by her stricken look but determined to articulate his outlandish theory all at once so that they could dispense with the denials quickly. "The trouble has something to do with Miss Harlow, whose misery you did not intentionally mean to cause with your drawing. You did cause it, however, and now you are trying to discover information about her that would extricate you from your situation. What the exact nature of your situation is, I cannot say, for my ability to deduce fails me there."

As he spoke, Lady Agatha stared at him without blinking, her dark eyes made blacker by fear and the pallor of her complexion. She looked like an urchin in those mismatched clothes, oversize and ill-fitting, that absurd wig—how it must itch!—pressing down on a head that dipped from the burden.

It was, he realized, all a burden, whatever it was that had driven her to this juncture, whatever it was that made her stare at him in terror, and watching her, he discovered he wanted to enfold her in a hug, lay her head upon his shoulder and promise her everything would be all right.

Unsettled by the compulsion, he pressed his arms to his sides.

"Everything is going to be all right," he announced softly, genuinely surprised that he could still his hands but not his tongue. The need to give comfort was not a familiar one to him, and he hadn't realized how easily it could slip its leash.

Lady Agatha's expression did not change.

"I told you once I'm quite good in a crisis and I assure you that wasn't thoughtless braggadocio. I have a well-ordered mind and can fit the pieces of a puzzle together quickly, which I believe I've demonstrated," he said, providing a list of his good qualities. "I relish a challenge, am completely trustworthy and have nothing but respect for Mr. Holyroodhouse's talent. I want only to assist you and to stand as your friend if you would but let me."

On a heavy sigh, Lady Agatha closed her eyes and remained motionless for a full minute. The tension in her shoulders did not ease, the color in her face did not return, and Addleson, observing the stillness with which she held herself, feared she was beyond his grasp. Nothing he could say would convince her accept his assistance. Lady Agony did not have friends.

When she finally opened her eyes, Addleson prepared for a polite refusal and wondered how difficult it would be to solve the mystery without her help. It would be challenging but not impossible, for he was already in possession of a fair amount of information and had excellent observational skills. All that was left was to pry into the private business of others, a task that the majority of the *ton* indulged in regularly with no ill effects. It would be as easy as it was unpleasant.

The matter of why he insisted on lending his support after it had been rejected was also easy and unpleasant: He liked

Agatha. She bore little resemblance to the sort of female who usually held his attention, as she had no style, no flash, no flirtatious conversation, no calculated charm. Oh, but the traits she did have—rude, clever, prickly, sly, brave, contrary—tugged at him in ways he neither expected nor understood.

As a man of reason, Addleson was not altogether pleased with the development, for he sensed in his inexplicable admiration for the complicated misanthrope a lack of control on his part. He had never made the conscious decision to like her; he simply discovered one day that he did.

"Mr. Luther Townshend is blackmailing me into publishing further cartoons accusing Miss Harlow of murder," Lady Agatha stated calmly.

"This Luther Townshend?" he asked, pointing to the name in the horticultural society minutes as another puzzle piece fell into place. "So you are here to discover information that you could use against him."

It wasn't a question, but she nodded anyway. "Yes, I thought if I could identify the source of his enmity toward Miss Harlow, it might help me find something to use against him. I think his hatred of her is key, for he loathes her with a passion that is out of proportion to her character or the situation."

Addleson pulled his chair closer to hers and placed the book between them on the table. "And what have you discovered?"

"Mr. Townshend was vehemently opposed to Miss Harlow's admittance. The voting protocols of the organization seem quite byzantine and complicated, but from what I've been able to deduce, the members voted fourteen times and Townshend was among the five who held out. Several other members voted against Vinnie and then voted in favor of her and then voted against her again, but Townshend voted no every single time," she explained.

A quick perusal of the pages confirmed her conclusions, for the vote counts were clearly marked. The viscount leaned over to read a scribbled note between tallies. "What's this?"

Agatha tilted forward, brushing her shoulder against his,

and although the contact was brief and slight, Addleson felt a shudder of awareness rush through him. The room was unpleasantly warm as he examined her for an indication that she had experienced the same flutter.

Her voice betrayed no sudden discomfort or awkwardness as she explained, "I assume the letters stand for Brill Method Improvised Elasticized Hose, which is the hose Miss Harlow invented. It improves upon the standard watering hose with its flexibility and can channel a steady stream of water without bursting."

The viscount smiled. "I am intimately acquainted with the steady stream of water the improved watering hose can provide."

Next to him, Agatha gasped, then flushed brightly as the scene played in her mind as it played in his. She stared at him silently for a moment before quietly saying, "You must know how very sor—"

"No," he said, shaking his head firmly, "don't ruin it now by apologizing. I admire nothing more than a brash deed and a clever riposte, and you delivered both beautifully. Perverse as I am, I found the whole interlude to be genuinely entertaining. I know you didn't believe me. You suspected a trap when I insisted on escorting you home, but I was sincere. I take pleasure in your company, Agatha."

The words were out of Addleson's mouth before they had even passed through his brain. He still wasn't sure how it had happened. One moment he was dispassionately focusing on the problem at hand and the next he was speaking with passionate honesty.

His purpose had been so clear: to discuss the matter of Lady Agatha's blackmail—blackmail!—with the same measured detachment with which she'd discussed it. In truth, he did not feel measured or detached. He felt ferociously angry on her behalf and had Mr. Luther Townshend had the misfortune to wander into the British Horticultural Society's library anytime in the past fifteen minutes, he would have happily wrung his neck.

But he knew his anger did not serve a purpose. It would not help extricate Lady Agatha from her untenable position and it would not keep the discussion on an even keel. The evenness of the keel was of the utmost importance to him because he was keenly aware of the impropriety of the situation: closeted together in a quiet room, the midday sun filtering through the window and bathing her in its warm light. He knew how unseemly their situation was, but he didn't want Agatha to be struck by its inappropriateness. Their business was too important to be hobbled by convention and missishness.

As it was, he was feeling missish enough for the both of them. How else to describe the self-consciousness he felt in her presence, his sense of awareness of her body next to his, so close all he had to do was lean forward to feel her shoulder against his again.

Her shoulder against his! What a chaste touch to crave, he thought in silent mockery of himself. Never in his life had he sought such innocent contact. His encounters ran toward experienced women of the demimonde whose expectations were as limited as his own, and having yet to resolve to marry, he had never sought the affections of a suitable young lady. He had always assumed respectable courtship would be a dreary and dull undertaking, like fishing in a placid lake, but he was prepared—eventually—to submit to his duty, for what he said about his heir was true: The gentleman was a country squire with no style or sense.

But that fissure of awareness he'd experienced at the mere touch of their shoulders was far from dreary and the almost exquisite pleasure he felt at the thought of it happening again was the opposite of dull.

Then again, Addleson reminded himself with humor, what they had here was hardly respectable. The deserted library, the dastardly villain, the injured innocent, the wretched wig—it was a farce, not a courtship.

As amusing as he found the situation, the viscount knew his desire for Lady Agatha Bolingbroke was anything but funny—inconvenient, improper and poorly timed, yes, but definitely not funny. It was, he thought wryly, proof of his perversity, for how else was it that *this* Lady Agatha Bolingbroke, dressed like an American yokel in some gentleman's garish coat, could arouse him to an outrageous degree, while the other Lady Agatha Bolingbroke, elegantly attired in the height of fashion, had provoked only his interest. If he had thought about her frequently in the two days since the Paddleton affair, it was because he found her impossible to understand. Everything about her hinted at hidden depths, and he had discovered within himself a need to plumb them.

And now, suddenly, he knew it all. With a minimum of fuss and a surprising amount of grace, Agatha had revealed her secret torment and accepted his offer of help. Although he had actively sought her trust, he hadn't actually expected to receive it, for he knew what she thought of him: Viscount Addlewit takes up his seat in the House of Lords.

He was humbled by her faith.

Determined to prove himself worthy of it, he had settled on a tone of measured detachment and even-keeledness. What she needed from him was a cool head and clear thinking so that he could objectively examine the facts in order to arrive at the best solution to her problem. Railing against the treachery of Townshend or commiserating over the misery of Miss Harlow would just cloud the discussion with emotion. Feelings would not further their investigation; only facts would.

It was a simple enough rule and yet he, unthinking fool that he was—takes up his seat indeed!—had been unable to abide it. *I take pleasure in your company, Agatha.* What a patently stupid thing to say. Now he was unnerved and she was embarrassed and Townshend's chances for succeeding in his evil endeavor increased tenfold.

Damn his unruly tongue!

Addleson knew it fell to him to restore their footing, and all he had to do was come up with something clever to say. In fact, it didn't have to be clever, merely different from an announcement that he took pleasure in her company. Returning the conversation to the general matter of Townshend's villainy would suffice. Such a comment should not be difficult, especially for someone with as agile a brain as his.

"Coercion," Lady Agatha announced loudly, the unexpected sound echoing throughout the silent room.

The viscount, who was ready to concede to an overestimation of his brain's agility, drew his brows in confusion.

"Coercion," she said again in a quieter voice. The pink on her cheeks suggested her discomfort with his statement, but when she looked him in the eyes, she seemed perfectly composed. "I believe Miss Harlow engaged in coercive tactics in order to convince members of the society to vote for her. For example, she traded two social events with her sister the duchess for my father's support. Her illustrious company was supposed to make me fashionable."

Having resolved to keep the conversation focused on the facts—and only the facts—Addleson found himself breaking his own rule yet again. This time, however, he knew exactly what he was doing, for he could not let such a disagreeable sentiment, though indifferently stated, stand. "But you do not want to be fashionable. You want to be left alone to draw and paint."

He had surprised her. Truly, he had, for the look on her face was of awe, as if he had just made the table levitate.

"How do you know that?" she asked.

Addleson shrugged as if this accomplishment were not at all impressive, but he relished the light of admiration that gleamed in her eyes and wanted to see it again. "You should be prime goods on the marriage mart, for you are pleasing to look at, come from an excellent family and are possessed of a generous dowry, and yet you haven't gotten a single offer in four seasons, not even from a fortune hunter. That, my dear, is no little achievement. Clearly, you've worked very hard to discourage all comers. Figuring out that part of the equation was easy enough. What puzzled me was *why* you would wish to remain unmarried. But now that I've discovered your talent for drawing, it makes sense. You would rather devote time to your art than to a husband."

Agatha stared at him long after he had completed his explanation, her eyes blazing with astonishment at how simply and adroitly he had summed up her London career.

"You don't need to look so surprised by my ability to reason," he said good-naturedly. "Despite your opinion of me as Lord Addlewit, I'm really quite clever, as I keep telling you."

As before, this playful reminder of sins she had committed against him caused her cheeks to turn pink and she rushed to offer an apology. Once again, he would not let her finish.

"I assure you, Lady Agatha, my ego is not so frail that it cannot handle a little gentle ribbing, especially when it is so skillfully delivered," he said, his eyes focused on hers because it was important to him that she believe him, for eternal apologist was not a pose that suited her. "What I do take offense at, however, is your continued belief that my ego is indeed that frail. As I said at the time—to you, in fact, though I did not know then that I addressed the artist—I admired the cartoon, for it concisely sums up the general view of my tenure in the House of Lords. So as not to disappoint, I shall make my first order of business the introduction of an act that outlaws the wearing of gold buttons with yellow waistcoats."

"No, you will not," she said, shaking her head decisively. "Rather, you will oppose the Corn Laws and propose measures to improve the working conditions of climbing boys. You may utter all the inanities you'd like, my lord, but I'm alive to your game now. I don't know why you choose to play it, but I am hardly the appropriate person to question another's social conduct."

Although the question was not asked, he chose to answer it anyway. "Utter boredom, my dear. I find a little nonsense enlivens even the most tedious occasion."

For the first time that afternoon, she smiled. "Like a tête-à-tête with Mr. Petrie? You were the perfect audience for him, quiet and attentive. I kept expecting you to interrupt with some nonsense about the root system of the sunset hyssop resembling the pattern on your favorite waistcoat. In fact, I was hoping you would, for the gentleman is incapable of comprehending any form of rebuke, which I know from extensive personal research."

Addleson laughed, recalling his unnatural forbearance of the unknown American naturalist. At the time, the encounter had been mildly torturous, but he was grateful for it now, for it had led to this conversation. "We must come up with a signal, you and I, so you may alert me when nonsensical blather is called for and I will immediately strike the blow. May I suggest an abrupt ear tug like this?" He quickly demonstrated, tilting his head to the side and pulling his left lobe with his right hand.

Agatha laughed at the display, just as he intended, and shook her head. "No, no, that will never do. You look like you are trying to clear it of water."

"I would suggest rubbing your nose, but a lady does not admit to having a nose in public," he said.

"For that matter, I'm pretty sure she does not have ears, either."

"What if you waved your dance card?" he asked.

Now Agatha giggled. "Can you imagine the picture that would present? It would appear to all as if I were begging gentlemen to sign it." She raised the small notebook she had brought with her and waved it aloft. "Here it is, beaus. Right here! Now who hasn't requested a dance with me yet? You, Mr. Pearson? I'm sure that's an oversight. You can add your name right here next to Lord Peters'." She giggled again, an infectious sound that rang gaily through the empty room. "My mother would have paroxysms, although I'm not sure out of despair at how poorly her daughter is behaving or delight at how her daughter is finally desirous of dance partners. I suspect she wouldn't know either. On that point, it is probably best that we can't come up with a signal, for my mother would interpret your attentions as the interest of a suitor and that would be disastrous."

Knowing her as he did—and that was, Addleson realized, fairly well by now—he understood that she thought it would be as much of a disaster for him as it was for her. No bachelor wanted an overly optimistic matchmaking mama nipping at his heels, and yet he did not find the idea as repellent as he ought. He was not a suitor and did not want to be treated as such, but there was still the matter of his outrageous attraction. Somehow, Lady Agatha, her head topped with an elderly gentleman's castaway wig, was the most desirable woman he had ever beheld.

It made no sense, and yet there it was. He would not try to reason it away, for even though he might delight in being a nonsensical blatherer he took no joy in being a fool.

He did, however, see the immediate value in changing the subject and observed, "Your mood seems improved."

As if surprised by the notion, she paused for a moment to consider it. "It *is* improved. My panic has subsided, and I feel hopeful that we will figure out a solution that will extricate both myself and Miss Harlow. I am very grateful for your help, my lord," she said, impulsively taking his hand and squeezing it. He felt the heat rush up his arm at her innocent touch, felt it sweep through his body, but he kept his expression unchanged. Agatha was not as skilled at hiding her feelings and he saw the exact moment when the impropriety of the act occurred to her. She abruptly dropped his hand and looked down at the table, as if utterly fascinated by its teak finish. "The, um, only other person I could turn to for help is my maid Ellen. She, ah, knows my identity, for she is the one who conveys my drawings to Mrs. Biddle, and she is, um, far too kind to come up with a truly diabolical scheme."

Addleson found her reaction charming. "I am deeply gratified that you find me debased enough to be of use."

Amusement tinged his voice, but Agatha, still embarrassed by her recent indiscretion, heard only the words. "I didn't mean to imply—"

"Before you annoy me with yet another attempt at an apology, let us return to Townshend," he said, adopting the businesslike tone of earlier as a matter of necessity. If he didn't get himself under control, he would spend the entire day laughing with her and they would be no closer to saving her reputation. "What you said about coercion is likely, for I recall now my cousin mentioning a cheating scandal at Oxford, which Miss Harlow threatened to disclose to my uncle. Edward was all out of sorts about the ultimatum, dithering about what he should do, which I found truly entertaining. He is twenty-seven years old and should not worry quite so much what his father thinks."

Agatha checked the minutes for an indication of how Mr. Edward Abingdon voted, and noting he had supported Miss Harlow from the very first tally, decided paternal approval had prevailed over personal aversion.

"Perhaps Miss Harlow did not discover information about Townshend, for his voting record indicates no fear of reprisal," she said, her voice dipping into discouragement as she reviewed the ballots. "In practical terms, it would be impossible for one woman—two, if her sister helped her—to uncover useful information about the entire membership of the horticultural society. Not counting Trent and Huntly, whose support was assured, that is twenty-four men. It would require an entire team of Bow Street Runners."

Privately, Addleson agreed with her assessment, but he had heard the disappointment in her tone and did not want to exacerbate it. "Perhaps, but his animus, as you pointed out, is personal, which implies Miss Harlow did something to spur it. Unless he is unbalanced, and I don't think he is, he would not seek such malicious revenge if she had merely gained entry to the club over his objection. There is something there and we must keep looking for it. Have you read the minutes preceding the vote? There might have been previous debate on the matter."

The viscount reached for the record and flipped through its pages until he came across an earlier date. To improve his vantage, he shifted his body forward and found himself once again in alarming proximity to Lady Agatha. Their shoulders were not touching, nor any portion of their arms or legs, but he was so close he could feel her breath on his cheek and, startled, he looked up to see her face mere inches from his.

Her lips were so near he barely had to move his head to touch them.

Oh, what a terrible idea that was. What an awful, horrible, atrociously terrible idea it was. But her lips—those lovely, temptingly sweet lips, red like berries—were parted invitingly and her dark, mysterious eyes stared into his with an innocent need he would defy any man to resist.

It wouldn't be a real kiss, not truly, for it would not be that frenzied feasting that sent waves of inexorable heat coursing through one's body. No, not at all. Rather, it would be a tepid brush of the lips, a mere taste to satisfy a curiosity, a bagatelle that would be over almost before it began.

Really, there was no reason to scruple. All he had to do was tip his head forward and—

"Pardon the interruption," Mr. Berry announced as he entered the room.

10 CHAPTER NAME

Agatha never imagined she would feel grateful for an itchy wig and a poorly constructed tailcoat that had torn the moment she had stretched it across her flattened chest. What a humiliating turn that had been—causing a tear in the tailcoat of one's footman. The poor fellow didn't even know he had lent her his clothes, as Ellen had snuck into Williams's quarters to remove the items without permission. Agatha knew it was underhanded and inconsiderate to steal from the servants, but she couldn't very well walk up to the Bolingbrokes' third footman and request the loan of his pantaloons and waistcoat.

If only Lord Bolingbroke weren't so tall and stout! Then she could have just taken the clothes from his wardrobe, which would have felt considerably less felonious. But her father had been unable to contribute anything to her disguise, not even one beleaguered old wig. For that, she had had to root around the attics in a trunk of her late grandfather's clothes. The wretched thing had not seen the light of day since the introduction of the powder tax and had required a significant grooming to make it less of a relic. Regardless, no amount of trimming and styling could make its fiber any less itchy.

Gathering the clothes, however, had been only half of the struggle, for putting them on proved to be almost as difficult. Her maid had tried to help, smoothing out the wrinkles, finessing the fit and sewing the tear, but Ellen's familiarity with men's clothing was as limited as her mistress's and she was unable to perform miracles. Agatha, her buttons in awkward places and her pantaloons in danger of sliding off, feared she looked like an actor in a theater company with a limited supply of costumes.

Fully dressed, she had turned her attention to her face, using her artist's eye to subtly adjust the shape of her features with her mother's face paints. She thinned her lips, widened her jawline and added an unappealing beauty mark to the tip of her nose to draw attention away from her eyes. She realized the result wasn't entirely convincing, but she also knew from her experience as Lady Agony that people see what they expect to see. Mr. Berry would not be looking for Agatha Bolingbroke under the coarse, speckled wig of Mr. Clemmons.

To ensure a swift exit and minimal parental interference, she had slipped through the window in her studio, a subterfuge she had never practiced before but had thought about with alarming frequency since her come out. How easy to just disappear through a hole and be free.

Now, however, as the clerk of the British Horticultural Society strode into the room, she gave thanks for every itchy fiber of her horrendously uncomfortable disguise, for the efficient clerk noticed nothing untoward in her proximity to Addleson. Thinking her to be a man, he had no cause to suspect inappropriate behavior and naturally concluded their nearness was merely a matter of efficacy. How else were two people to read the same book?

And it *was* merely a matter of efficacy, Agatha told herself, even though for a moment there, for the most fleeting second between breaths, she had believed it was something else. Her heart had raced in unbearable expectation as she waited for Lord Addleson to kiss her.

Even as her blood pounded, she had known her anticipation was misguided. The urbane viscount with the razor-sharp wit did not have romantical feelings toward her.

Yes, he had admitted with startling candor that he took pleasure in her company, but how quickly he had regretted those words! A mix of horror and panic swept across his handsome features so swiftly, even a besotted schoolgirl would have known the truth, and she could almost see his brain scrambling to figure out the best way to explain he'd meant as a king would enjoy a jester's company.

It was actually very funny because in her wig and face paints and Williams's finery she was practically *dressed* as a court jester. Even without the costume, she was like a character in an allegory: Lady Agony, who illustrates how a young lady ought not to behave. She did not doubt that many matchmaking mamas used her as a cautionary tale to keep their daughters in line.

Agatha did not care about that. Truly she didn't, for she had plans that did not include endearing herself to society. But as she'd sat in the quiet library of the horticultural society anxiously awaiting the viscount's kiss, she'd found herself wishing for the ability to endear herself to at least one man.

"It is a very good thing you are still here, Mr. Clemmons," the clerk said as he walked across the room, "for Lord Waldegrave has arrived to see you."

Agatha rose to her feet and smiled tightly. Her new visitor seemed pleasant enough, with light brown hair and gray eyes, but she tensed her shoulders at the prospect of another impossible question. First the Earl of Moray had asked her about the absorbency rate of bloodroot, which Mr. Petrie had sworn his assistant would know, and then Mr. Abingdon had intruded with his query about jojoba. As the daughter of a longtime member of the British Horticultural Society, she knew enough to bluster her way past Mr. Berry—flattery, flattery, flattery—and to make plantish-sounding answers to questions about plants, but there was only so much nonsense she could spout before eyebrows were raised. She had barely squeaked by with a garbled explanation of how a concoction of lead and linseed oil increased the viscosity of *Simmondsia chinensis.*

While conversing with Mr. Petrie, she had noted that the

American naturalist often referenced his secretary when confronted with a fact he did not know. It had never occurred to her, however, that Petrie had done the same with everyone to whom he spoke. If it had, she would have taken the time to come up with another ruse.

This realization highlighted the single biggest fault of her plan: its failure to consider the possibility of pressing horticultural questions. The oversight was understandable, for how could she have accounted for such a thing? They were *horticultural* questions. The fate of the world did not depend on the absorbency rate of bloodroot.

Six, for the record, was her answer: The absorbency rate of bloodroot was six. Moray, who was famous for his conciliatory nature, did not bat an eyelash and graciously agreed her number sounded right. In fact, he had seemed so satisfied, she had felt compelled to babble for a few extraneous minutes about root diameters and rhizome density.

"It is a pleasure to meet you," Waldegrave said now, extending his hand.

Agatha had also not factored a manly grip into her decision to impersonate a gentleman, and as she stiffened her hand yet again in greeting, she hoped she pulled off a reasonable facsimile.

Waldegrave seemed content with her effort. "The pleasure is all mine, as Mr. Petrie's conversation made it quite clear that you are a hugely busy man. I'm grateful you have the time to talk to me. Congratulations on your recovery. Mr. Petrie thought you would be confined to the bed for at least a month."

Knowing how many responsibilities were heaped onto Mr. Clemmons's shoulders and how endlessly Mr. Petrie could prattle on, Agatha was unable to decide whether the secretary's sudden sickness was caused by exhaustion or a desire to spare himself an ocean journey in his employer's company. She refused to believe he had simply eaten a rotten joint of mutton or digested a spoiled beef pasty.

"Leeches," she said. "My illness 'twas nothing that a few judiciously placed leeches could not cure."

"Which is fortunate for us, for the British Horticultural Society is delighted to export its high ideals to the New World and I'm happy to do whatever I can to help you in the establishment of a sister organization," Mr. Berry said cheerfully, as he explained to Waldegrave her purpose in being there. He was at a loss to explain the viscount's. "We are flattered by your attentions, as well, Lord Addleson, but I wonder at your interest in the institution's private matters. The minutes to our meetings are not for the edification of the general populace. They are only for our members"—he darted an apologetic look at Waldegrave—"to peruse."

"That is my fault, I'm afraid," Agatha said quickly in her American baritone, which was getting easier to maintain the more she employed it. "I appealed to him for help, for I could not understand how a large and complex organization could be run with such outstanding, genial efficiency."

Agatha saw Addleson suppress a grin before concurring enthusiastically with her comment. "Being unaccustomed to the ways of the English gentleman, Mr. Clemmons wondered if valuable information had been elided from the record, such as disagreements or disputes. I assured him we have too much respect for one another to get into minor spats over inconsequential things. I have to admit, however, that even for a British institution, your society seems unusually well run and convivial. You make it seem so effortless, I'm encouraged to start my own organization for the examination and cultivation of plants," he said, as if seriously considering the idea. "I would first need to establish a color scheme for the uniforms, for I could not bear to have an ill-matching membership. I don't know how you do it, Mr. Berry, letting everyone assemble in clothes they selected individually with no thought to the whole." The viscount shuddered as if truly horrified by the disharmonious result. "Then I would need to design an insignia—perhaps a heraldic shield with a fleur-de-lis on it, or is that too obvious? Should I dig deeper to find a more obscure floral reference? Now that I consider the details, it actually seems like a tremendous amount of effort. I do not know how you do it, Mr. Berry, and I don't just mean with your apparent color-blindness."

Uncertain how to interpret Addleson's comments, the clerk paused for a moment before deciding that the balance of his observations was positive and thanked him for his praise. If Mr. Berry had further concerns about the viscount's perusal of the society's documents, he did not voice them. Rather, he excused himself from the company, for the coordination of such a large effort did not happen on its own.

"Our Mr. Berry can be loquacious," Waldegrave said as soon as the clerk had left. "He is very proud of the organization and tends to let his enthusiasm run way with him. With that in mind, I shall be brief. Mr. Petrie informed me of a remarkable species of orchidaceae that does not practice photosynthetic nutrition. He assured me you were well familiar with it. I am what my father describes as an orchid fiend and absolutely must know more."

Agatha tried not to wince at the words *photosynthetic nutrition,* but it was difficult to contain her anxiety at the mention of a scientific concept of which she was unacquainted. She could try to decipher what the term meant—*photo* derived from the Greek word for "light"; nutrition had to do with making sure one received proper nourishment—but it was much easier to focus on the part of the question she knew something about: orchids. Like Waldegrave and many of the members of the society, her father was also an orchid fiend, and if there was one thing she had learned about orchids, it was that they were bizarre. Other flowers were fairly predictable, but the orchid came in every shape, size and color, taking on strange, inexplicable forms. Sketch a teacup with an overlarge handle and it could be an orchid. Throw the laces of your shoes on the floor and their haphazard arrangement could be an orchid. Eat half your supper and what remained on the plate could be an orchid. There were simply no rules governing the appearance and behavior of orchidaceae.

"Yes, yes, of course, the non-photosynthetic-nutrition orchid, a fascinating subject, so surprising and unexpected," she said thoughtfully, stalling for time as she tried to come up with realistic-sounding characteristics. If it did not use light to make food, then perhaps it lived somewhere very dark. Where was such a place? "Underground! The orchid spends its entire life several feet below the surface in"—she thought of a place very far away—"Java. Because it doesn't get sunlight, it's a very pale color, almost white, and has no leaves. It is only a stem and it feeds off the roots of other plants nearby." Now all she needed was a name. She recalled her Latin lessons. "It is called *Orchidaceae opscurum*."

"*Orchidaceae opscurum*," Waldegrave said, as if committing the name to memory. "*Orchidaceae opscurum*."

"*Orchidaceae opscurum*," she repeated firmly, more than slightly unsettled by the spark of excitement glowing in his eyes. He had warned her he was a fiend, and she had just given him a new object on which to focus his frenzy. She wouldn't be surprised if he went straight to the docks to charter a ship for Java. At the very least, he would spend the rest of his life muttering *Orchidaceae opscurum* in his sleep.

When pressed for more details, Agatha made up additional traits, each one more outlandish than the last, until finally Waldegrave was satisfied he had exhausted Mr. Clemmons's knowledge. Then he thanked the ersatz American profusely and left.

Addleson barely had time to compliment Agatha on her creation ("Inspired choice making it white, so it will coordinate nicely with all the other *opscurum* flowers buried beneath the earth") before Mr. Berry returned in the company of a ginger-haired gentleman with overly groomed eyebrows and a tentative smile: Mr. Irby, who had been referred to Clemmons by Mr. Petrie and had a question about sand dunes.

Sand dunes!

It took all of Agatha's self-control not to cry out in despair.

As mentally fatiguing as it was to have to bluff her way through another conversation ("Surprisingly, sand dunes are only 78 percent sand"), part of her was grateful for Irby's company. The problem was not that she didn't want to be alone with Addleson but, rather, how very much she did. Desiring a gentleman's company was an unprecedented experience for Agatha and she worried about what it might mean. Clearly, she had feelings for him, otherwise she would not have anticipated his kiss with such eagerness.

His kiss, which her decidedly irrational brain had invented from whole cloth.

It had been a revelation to Lady Agatha Bolingbroke to discover she had a talent for fiction. Perhaps she could write stories to go with her illustrations.

The misunderstanding, she knew, sprang from her genuine admiration for the viscount, for he was unlike any other gentleman she had ever met. Even after he had listed the facts that led to his conclusion, she still could not grasp how he had deciphered the truth about Mr. Holyroodhouse. To anyone else, a callused finger and a knowledge of pigments would indicate a proclivity for painting, not a secret identity as a famous London caricaturist. The accusation had been so breathtaking, she made no attempt to refute it. Denial would not have served her purpose anyway, for he had easily seen through her feeble disguise as Mr. Clemmons. She did not know when exactly he had figured out the truth, but it was not long after he had entered the room.

What a horrifying moment *that* had been—watching him stroll into the library and having to greet him as Mr. Clemmons. Her heart had actually leaped into her throat as she swallowed a strangled cry. For God's sake, what was he doing there?

It was his damned cousin Edward's fault, with his idiotic question about *Simmondsia chinensis*. What matter was it to him how thick the oil was? Did he intend to create a magical elixir out of jojoba? Would he set up shop in Oxford Street and sell it to the ladies?

Mr. Abingdon could have no pressing reason to follow up with Mr. Clemmons except a desire to make an annoyance of himself, a task at which he had succeeded beautifully.

His cousin knew it, for he had thought the question as

trivial as she did. His annoyance, however, quickly gave way to amusement as she struggled not to sound like a complete nodcock. She had seen the twinkle in his eye. The blasted man always had a twinkle in his eye, for the world was endlessly amusing to him.

As she was endlessly amusing. He took pleasure in her company indeed!

Agatha knew he would unmask her in a flutter of high theatrical drama and waited anxiously for the moment. When it came—after his cousin had departed—she had to acknowledge his innate decency. The frivolity with which he treated the world was not just an affectation, for his enjoyment of the trivial was sincere, but neither was it the whole story. Addleson was also capable of great kindness, as demonstrated by the care he took to alleviate her distress at Lord Paddleton's ball.

It was this treatment of her that she had thought of as she tried to resist his offer to help. It had been elegantly posed and sincerely made, but the thought of admitting to a personal weakness was unbearable, for it wasn't merely personal weakness she would be admitting to but an engulfing helplessness. Her ingenious plan had failed. Nothing in Townshend's voting record indicated coercion, and the minutes leading up to the ballot described only sundry business matters and procedural motions.

She had no evidence. Without evidence, she had no direction. With no direction, she had no chance of overcoming Townshend's threats.

All had seemed hopeless.

Then suddenly Addleson was there—Addleson, who appeared to divine the truth out of thin air, who looked at the same square everyone else did and saw a cube, whose perpetual amusement somehow offered comfort.

The viscount had made his plea to help and she'd accepted, for he was everything one sought in a co-conspirator: kind, honorable and astute. If her feelings for him were a little too warm—if, for example, they created nonexistent kisses out of whole cloth—then she would simply deal with the moments as they occurred and put them behind her. One way or another, her problem would be resolved soon enough, and then she would be free of Addleson's company.

For now, however, she longed for it and dreaded it in equal measure.

As Agatha explained how species colonized sand dunes—a description based entirely on her understanding of how the upstairs maid organized the linen closet—she darted a look at Addleson, expecting to see that familiar twinkle. Instead, her eyes met the top of his head, for his nose was buried deep in the minutes.

She felt a stab of disappointment that he wasn't appreciating her clever dodge, which was immediately followed by a burst of disgust, for she was not a jester performing for the king and had to stop acting like one.

"In the end, it all comes down to organization," Agatha said, "for no matter how large and boundless an area is, you never seem to have enough space."

"Yes, of course, that's it!" Mr. Irby said enthusiastically, as if something very difficult and complex had finally been explained in simple enough terms for him to understand. Agatha rather thought it was the opposite. "You are a pleasure to talk to, Mr. Clemmons, and I'm very grateful for your imparted wisdom. Do say you will dine at my town house before you leave."

Agatha, who could imagine nothing more horrible than trying to maintain her disguise through an entire meal, nodded agreeably. "I shall consult with Mr. Petrie about my schedule and send a note."

Irby beamed. "Very good, very good. I understand from Mr. Berry that you are reading our minutes to discover the secrets to our successful society and that the viscount is here to provide you with guidance. As a member, I am a treasure trove of knowledge, so please do not hesitate to contact me if you need further information. Perhaps I should stay to provide firsthand experience."

"Another generous offer. I thank you again," Agatha said, wondering if she could slip her arm around the loiterer to direct him to the door. As a woman, such a gesture would be forbidden, but it seemed appropriate among the casual fraternity of men. Had not Addleson treated his cousin thus when coercing Abingdon to depart quickly? "But I cannot agree. I'm sure you have more important matters to attend to and I could not live with myself if I kept you from them for my own selfish reasons. Now toddle off before I am entirely debilitated by a guilty conscience."

Unable to resist such a pointed plea, Irby thanked Clemmons again for his masterful discussion of a difficult topic, promised to look out for the missive about dinner and conceded that, yes, he did have an important business matter concerning a recent investment in a gold mine to which to attend.

When the door finally closed behind him, Agatha sighed deeply, threw herself in a chair and laid her head on the table. At Addleson's chuckle, which was immediate in coming, she opened one eye, and meeting his gaze, saw the delighted twinkle.

Her heart hitched.

You are not his jester, she reminded herself forcefully.

She would never submit to such humiliating work, but she could understand the appeal of the job.

"I must salute you, Lady Agatha," Addleson announced, "on another concise and brilliant explanation of a natural phenomenon. I don't know how you arrived at your exact composition of the sand dune, but your calculation of two percent bird dung seems entirely accurate to me."

Agatha lifted her head and opened her other eye. "I worry about the existence of Mr. Irby's gold mine if he did not realize my answer was 100 percent bird dung."

Addleson chuckled appreciatively again, then said in a more businesslike tone, "Before your father comes strolling in here to ask about the average temperature of native grasses in Abyssinia, let's discuss our situation, for even if he does not recognize his daughter, he is sure to recognize his wig."

Now Agatha laughed. "Actually, the wig belonged to my grandfather, so it's unlikely he would recognize it. Your point, however, is well taken. My plan to impersonate Mr. Petrie's absent assistant was hastily conceived, but even if I had had a month to think about it, I would never have imagined word of my presence spreading so quickly. No doubt the news has already reached Mr. Petrie in Bath."

"All plans have unforeseeable complications," the viscount said with a shrug of his pair of very fine shoulders. "Now, while you were trying to distract me with your implausible explanation of how pioneer species colonize, I reviewed all the minutes from the last year."

Aware they had no time to waste, Agatha did not bother to deny the allegation that she had been trying to distract him. Instead, she chastised herself for noticing the quality of his shoulders and asked if he had learned anything useful.

"I'm not really sure," he said, sliding the book toward her and flipping to the middle. "On the face of it, no, for there isn't any specific information we can use against Townshend. As you know, the minutes are mostly devoted to procedural matters. It tells us what issues were voted on and how each member voted, who attended each meeting, who added agenda items for each meeting. Go back twelve months and you will see that many of the agenda items were added by Mr. Berry. There are exceptions, of course, such as when your father proposed inviting Mr. Petrie to speak or Sir Charles suggested an increase in dues. Six months ago, Townshend added an agenda item, which he had not done once in the six months preceding. Then, over the next two months, he added four more items and each time it concerned Mr. Petrie's visit."

Startled, Agatha looked down at the entry to which Addleson was pointing and leaned in closer to get a better look. It was there in black-and-white—agenda item number five: Mr. Petrie's Invitation to Speak.

Addleson turned to the minutes for the next meeting and she saw it again: Mr. Petrie's Invitation to Speak. He flipped ahead two weeks and pointed to the third item on the agenda: Mr. Petrie's Invitation to Speak. He thumbed through a half dozen pages and waited for her to find it: Mr. Petrie's Invitation to Speak.

Agatha could not imagine what it meant. She herself had noted Townshend's interest in Mr. Petrie's visit, but it had not struck her as peculiar. She merely assumed the deputy director of Kew was eager to meet a fellow naturalist from another part of the world. Having not gone as far back as Addleson, she failed to see the three other agenda items or to place them in a larger context.

But now that the viscount had identified a pattern, she realized there was something unusual about his interest and felt a tinge of excitement. Unusual was evidence. With evidence, she had a direction. With a direction, she had a chance of overcoming Townshend's threats.

Her heart racing, Agatha looked at Addleson. Far from twinkling, his eyes were deadly serious.

Before either one of them could say a word, the object of their speculation marched into the room and strolled forcefully across the floor. A smiling Mr. Berry trotted behind him, trying to catch up.

"You will never believe it, Mr. Clemmons," the clerk announced, slightly out of breath as he covered the last few steps to the table, "but yet another one of our members has paid you a call. At the risk of sounding hyperbolic, I must say you are the single most popular visitor we have ever had here—excluding lecturers, of course. I don't mean to imply that you are more popular than the many accomplished men who have spoken here."

While Mr. Berry clarified his statement, Agatha stared at him aghast, dumbfounded by the situation and clueless as to what to do next. Should she look at Townshend? He was there to see her. It would be strange, would it not, if she refused to look at the person expressly there to visit her? But how could she look at him? He might recognize her, even dressed in her footman's clothes and her grandfather's wig.

The wig!

That confounded contrivance itched so much she felt like a flea-ridden mouse on the back of a flea-ridden dog, and it felt as if it would slide off at any moment.

Was it crooked? Had it shifted? Was it about to tumble to the floor?

She was afraid to move her head and knew she must not raise a hand to touch it because that would look bizarre. Gentlemen did not straighten their hair.

Addleson, whose mind was not overwhelmed by doubt and fear, greeted the newcomer with an easy smile and an extended hand. "I don't believe we've met. I am Jonah Hamilton, Viscount Addleson."

Mr. Berry, who considered all greetings and salutations to be within his purview, immediately jumped in to complete the introductions.

"Townshend," the viscount said curiously, "of the Beaminster Townshends?"

"No, my lord," Townshend said firmly.

"Of the Snodland Townshends, then?"

He shook his head. "I'm afraid not."

"Ah, so it must be the Glossop Townshends. Lovely people. I once borrowed a sheep from them that I failed to return. They have never brought it up once. You will convey my apologies, I trust?"

By the scowl on his face, it was clear that Mr. Luther Townshend was not of the Glossop clan either, but rather than extend the conversation, he agreed to comply with the viscount's request with all possible haste.

"I would expect nothing less from a Glossop Town-shend," Addleson replied approvingly. "As I said, lovely people."

Agatha listened to the exchange, fully aware the viscount was giving her an opportunity to collect herself. His ruse had worked, and by the time Mr. Berry introduced Clemmons, she was able to calmly meet Townshend's gaze.

People only see what they expect to see, she reminded herself.

Thankfully, the deputy director of Kew saw very little of interest in her, as his glance met her own only briefly before turning to Addleson to inquire as to his interest in the society's private matters. Mr. Berry reddened at the question, for the disapproval was clear, but the viscount answered the query in exhaustive detail, outlining his short-lived intention to start his own flower club and earning Townshend's scorn when he explained that designing a uniform *and* an insignia was simply more effort than he could expend on a single project.

Mr. Berry, who still did not know what to make of the odd viscount, laughed and said, "I'm sure Lord Addleson is joking."

"I'm sure he's not," Townshend said pleasantly.

Agatha took another deep breath and felt her heart rate slowly returning to normal. She was comforted by the exchange, for the gentleman from Kew had bought the Lord Addlewit act without any hesitation. Having dismissed the viscount as a fool, he had looked no further nor suspected a gambit. That incurious nature would work to her benefit because it meant he would not wonder at Mr. Adolphus Clemmons's ill-fitting tailcoat or look askance at his hair.

"Since we've established that the founding of a noble institution is not suited to your talents," Townshend said, "perhaps you should excuse yourself to find something that is. Your presence in this library is highly irregular, and I question Mr. Berry's judgment in allowing it."

Within seconds, the clerk's face had turned crimson and when he opened his mouth to speak, only a smothered gurgling sound emerged. He bowed his head in shame. "You are entirely right to question my judgment. I apologize, Mr. Townshend, for violating the society's privacy, which is sacrosanct." He turned to the viscount and begged his forgiveness as well. "As the caretaker of this organization, I should know better than to let my enthusiasm get the better of me. Now, if you will follow me, my lord, I will escort you to the door."

"No need to apologize, Mr. Berry, I entirely understand, for my enthusiasms often run away with me," Addleson said graciously. "How very lucky we are to have someone like Mr. Townshend to keep us in check."

"I do what I can, my lord," Townshend said modestly.

"I'm sure you do," the viscount murmured before turning to Agatha, who dreaded the moment he would exit the room and leave her alone with Townshend. Secure in her disguise, she was not worried—or, rather, not altogether worried—that he would discover the truth, but her last interview with the villain had convinced her that no exchange with him could be pleasant. Even this simple question-and-answer session would be repellent.

God only knew what knowledge Mr. Petrie claimed she was in possession of this time.

"I cannot thank you enough, Mr. Clemmons, for indulging me in my folly," Addleson said, looking Agatha squarely in the eyes and sliding in a sly wink. "I look forward to concluding our business some other time."

"As do I, my lord," Agatha said, then watched helplessly as Addleson turned on his heels and walked to the door in the company of Mr. Berry, whose heightened color had yet to subside.

Taking a deep breath, Agatha ordered herself to remain calm—panicking now would be fatal. Deliberately, she called to mind Mr. Townshend's drawing of Miss Harlow with the words *weed killer* written in large capital letters along the bottom of the spray can.

He's a fool, she reminded herself. All I have to do is get through one brief conversation with a fool. I can do that.

Amused, she affirmed silently that it was always useful to feel superior to one's oppressor and turned to face Townshend.

He took three abrupt steps toward her, stopped an inch from her nose and flew his hand across her cheek.

"How dare you!" he snarled.

Agatha was stunned speechless. Absolutely speechless. She didn't cry out or call out or protest or complain. She didn't raise a hand to nurse her stinging cheek. She simply stood there astonished.

"How dare you show up here!" Townshend roared, his eyes burning with fury. "I paid you one hundred pounds to ensure Petrie would not get on that ship—*one hundred pounds*—and yet here he is making the rounds in London. You fool! I gave you the *exact* amount of arsenic to put in his coffee to guarantee his incapacitation. All *you* had to do was dispense it properly. Just a few grains of arsenic in the coffee on the morning you were meant to depart! It was a simple plan, you idiot! How did you run afoul of such a simple plan? And then you have the temerity to show your face here! How dare you!" He lifted his hand again as if to administer another slap, but it hung in the air for a moment before grasping Agatha by the neck cloth. His eyes were so close to hers, she could see the black lines that rimmed his irises. "Do you think I will give you another one hundred pounds to try again? You imbecile! I will not listen to your excuses!"

Agatha had offered none. Even if words had occurred to her, she would not have spoken them aloud, for she knew silence was her ally. In truth, however, she had no words. She barely had any thoughts. All she had was shock—shock at the slap, shock at the attack, shock at the truth.

She couldn't make sense of it yet.

"I do not know what purpose you have in coming here, but you will not attain it, you scoundrel," he sneered with disgust as his grip on her cravat tightened. His breath smelled of stale tobacco and kippers, and she had to turn her head to the side to avoid the stench. He laughed cruelly, seized her chin and forced her to look him in the eye. His fingers dug into her skin, but she refused to flinch. "You *will* not attain it."

Slowly, Agatha's mind started to process the information: Townshend and Clemmons had a compact to keep Petrie out of the country; Clemmons betrayed the compact either by intention or mistake; Townshend wanted to keep Petrie out of the country.

The elements of a nefarious scheme were present, but she could not figure out what, why or how. Townshend's anger seemed like madness to her.

"Perhaps you think to extort more money from me. How many pounds will your silence cost me? One hundred? Two hundred? A thousand? You are not as clever as you think, Mr. Clemmons, nor am I such a fool. I've kept all your letters. That surprises you, doesn't it?" he asked derisively, his hold on her neck cloth loosening as he contemplated his advantage. His shoulders also slackened and he tipped his head back, giving her access to fresher air. "You assumed I destroyed our correspondence as you had requested, but I have every single letter you've sent me during our four-year association, including the very first one, in which you introduce yourself to me as Mr. Petrie's secretary and offer to provide with me copies of his articles in exchange for a fee."

Townshend was much calmer now, and he smiled thinly as he released his grip on Agatha. Then he meticulously straightened the folds of her cravat. It required all of Agatha's self-control not to shove his hands away.

"Yes, I have every single letter you've sent me," he repeated, taking a step backward to examine his handiwork, "and I will not hesitate to use them against you. Mr. Petrie would be quite shocked to discover you've been feeding me his articles for years, and won't he be surprised to learn of your plot to poison him. In this country, it's illegal to try to kill a man. You may think you can escape the noose by pointing your finger at me, but you forget: This is my country—*mine*—and you are the stranger here, a stranger who has admitted in writing that he intended to poison his employer. I think you'll find English justice is swift and sure."

Agatha nodded, for she agreed with his statement and believed that Mr. Clemmons would be immediately presented to the gallows should the evidence come to light just as Townshend had described. An immoral foreigner would not be able to make a case against an upstanding Englishman with influential friends and a respectable position as a director of an esteemed institution.

But what about Lady Agatha Bolingbroke? She was the respectable daughter of an established peer with many more influential friends than Mr. Luther Townshend. Would her testimony stand against his? Could she use the threat of the truth as a bargaining chip to preserve her secret and Vinnie's reputation?

Even as she considered the maneuver, she knew it was too risky to try. Mr. Townshend could not be relied upon to react in a reasonable manner, for his temper, as he had already demonstrated, was vile, and she could easily imagine his wrath veering out of control if he discovered he had been duped. He'd also proven himself to have a devious mind and would most likely be suspicious of any deal that was not weighted in his favor, as this deal would not. Attempted murder was a far more serious crime than rendering as ridiculous one's fellow members of the *ton*, which was not an actual crime at all but rather a grave social faux pas.

No, the best thing Agatha could do now was to remain silent and still and get through the interview without giving herself away.

Townshend examined her mute form with satisfaction. "Your timidity pleases me, Mr. Clemmons."

Good, Lady Agony thought.

"It's not what I had expected from your letters," he added. "I thought you would be more a brute, but you are actually quite slight. I suppose that makes sense, as a more substantial man would make his way honestly in the world, not scheme behind the back of his generous employer. Your greed and incompetence disgust me."

The irony of his contempt did not strike him: a dishonest man chastising another dishonest man for his dishonesty. Perhaps, she thought, the secret to being a villain was believing yourself to be a victim.

"This is what is going to happen now," Townshend announced in a firm voice that led Agatha to hope the end of the ordeal was in sight. "You will remove yourself from my presence and this island immediately. I do not care where you go as long as you go silently. You are free to die in a gutter as long as it is not an English gutter. Do you understand?"

Agatha started to nod, for there was nothing she wanted more than to remove herself from his presence, but she could not bring herself to abandon Mr. Petrie—poor, long-winded, small-minded, generally-offensive-to-all-women, oblivious Mr. Petrie, who had no idea his articles and theses had been published in another country under someone else's name. She could not simply leave him to his fate, for she did not know what Townshend had in store for him. It could be another dose of arsenic in his coffee or something far more wicked.

Gathering her courage, she coughed roughly and sputtered in as guttural a voice as she was capable, "What about Petrie?"

Townshend sneered at her concern, interpreting it— thank goodness—as another attempt to extort money. "You sniveling cur! I would not let you in on my plan even if you volunteered to pay *me* for the privilege. I will take care of the matter myself, and I assure you I will not dose my own coffee by mistake. Now go!"

Agatha did not need to be told twice. Although she had brought a little book for the recording of notes, she did not bother to collect it from the table, for she didn't want to spend the few extra seconds in Townshend's company. It made no difference, as the notebook was empty anyway.

As she breezed past Mr. Berry's office en route to the front door, the clerk requested a word, but she did not pause to give it. She merely waved her right hand in acknowledgement, which he may or may not have seen from his vantage. That, too, made no difference to her.

Then, finally, she was outside the British Horticultural Society and she walked to the corner and around the block and down the street until she was a good enough distance away to safely allow the terror she hadn't let herself feel wash over her. Her hand trembled, her heart throbbed, and her blood pounded as she imagined the scene with Townshend ending in an altogether different way. She knew it was sheer melodrama to think it, and yet she couldn't help but feel she was lucky to be alive. As easily as he had slapped her cheek, Townshend could have snapped her neck.

"You are utterly ridiculous," she muttered, as she took several deep breaths, savoring the freshness of the air. How stagnant and stale the library had become.

Annoyed by the panic and angered by the helpless feeling it engendered, Agatha flagged down a hack and ordered it to take her to Mrs. Biddle's shop in St. James's Street. She was a human being, a woman with a sound mind and a strong resolve, not a leaf to be buffeted by every strong wind. She would not sit back and wait for fate to deal her another blow. No, she would take matters into her own hands by officially retiring Mr. Holyroodhouse. There was no reason she could not do it in person, for her grandfather's wig and Williams's Sunday best offered her all the protection she needed.

Agatha felt so bold and capable striding into Mrs. Biddle's establishment in broad daylight, she was almost disappointed to find it empty save for the proprietress and a lone customer in a mustard yellow waistcoat browsing one of the shelves. It was Mr. Holyroodhouse's curtain call, and she would not have minded a slightly larger audience. Nevertheless, it was sufficient.

"Good day, madam," she said, using her deepest baritone and standing a few feet from the counter. "Although we have never met, we are longtime associates and I am here to end that association. My name is Holyroodhouse, Mr. Martin Holyroodhouse, and you have published my caricatures for several years. I appreciate your support and cooperation, but our arrangement is officially at an end. Please do not attempt to contact me." Agatha bowed abruptly and noted that the tall man by the shelf hadn't looked up once during her speech. As absurd as it was, she felt somehow slighted by his lack of interest in what was Mr. Holyroodhouse's first and last public statement.

So be it, she thought, before bidding Mrs. Biddle an abrupt good day.

The shopkeeper, whose stunned expression had changed little during Agatha's announcement, suddenly turned panicked as Mr. Holyroodhouse walked to the door. "But what about the Addleson commission? Our arrangement ends after you fulfill the Addleson commission, am I right, sir? All that lovely money on offer. You would not abandon—"

Agatha slammed the door on Mrs. Biddle's desperate pleas and hailed a hack to take her home. It felt like days had passed since she had first donned her disguise as Mr. Clemmons, and as the prickly fibers of her grandfather's wig itched her scalp, she surmised that time must move extra slowly when one was wearing a tormenting hairpiece from another century.

Directing the driver to a street adjacent to hers, she climbed down from the carriage, snuck around the house and smuggled herself into her studio through the same window from which she had escaped earlier. Ellen was just where she'd left her, tending the fire and reading a book, and she looked on in amazement as her mistress grabbed the wig from her head, threw it violently onto the floor and stomped on it a few dozen times before throwing the offending article into the fire.

CHAPTER ELEVEN

Although no eligible bachelor had ever paid a call—social or otherwise—on Lady Agatha Bolingbroke, her mother kept the staff prepared for such an occurrence with monthly practice sessions, which she called drills. It was not, as she assured Gregson at regular intervals, that she doubted his skill and expertise, for he was by far the most capable butler they had ever had at 31 Portland Place. It was merely that she knew how discomposing surprise could be on one's ability to think clearly and she wanted to inoculate the staff against its effects. It was almost impossible to treat a gentleman caller with dignified propriety when one's jaw was skimming the floor.

It was thanks to this preparedness training that Gregson did not bat an eyelash when Lord Addleson appeared on the doorstep requesting an interview with Lady Agatha. His manner perfectly composed, he showed the gentleman into the drawing room and suggested a pot of tea while he waited.

The tea was one of Lady Bolingbroke's contrivances and she had been particularly emphatic about its offering, for she felt it would make the gentleman less inclined to run out of the house when he realized he had called upon the wrong Lady Agatha. The likelihood of such an event happening was considerably less now than in previous seasons, as only two other girls named Agatha remained on the marriage mart and neither had a title, but her ladyship insisted the butler present a pot of tea just the same.

Impatient to hear about Lady Agatha's interview with

Townshend, the viscount was in no mood for tea or for waiting calmly in the drawing room. He accepted the offer, however, with an appreciative nod and sat down on the settee.

He immediately stood up again.

It had pained him greatly to abandon Agatha to the clutches of the ruthless blackmailer. Oh, how it had pained him! He had wanted to stay and considered the value of arguing for his continued presence, but Townshend seemed determined for the society's inner sanctum to remain inviolate and he saw no benefit in riling the gentleman up.

Instead, he'd had thought to linger by the door and listen to the conversation, a plan that would have yielded excellent results were it not for Mr. Berry's determination to move him along. Newly awakened to his duty, the clerk had refused to leave the viscount alone for a single moment, affixing himself like glue to Addleson's side. He had even resisted efforts to linger in the office, where his lordship had been inclined to admire as many of the society's publications as necessary to give Agatha time to emerge.

Mr. Berry had gathered an armful of the society's journals and pressed them on him. "Please read at your leisure," the clerk had said, ignoring the two that dropped to the floor. "There are many wonderful articles that should not be rushed through."

"And what is this beautiful item?" the viscount had then asked, spying a rather drab clay flowerpot next to the windowsill. "The artistry is magnificent."

"Mrs. Berry bought it in a shop in Lambeth," the clerk had replied before observing, with a glance at the window, that a hack had conveniently paused in front of the building. Although firmly assured by the viscount that many other conveyances would pause with equal convenience, Mr. Berry had insisted on Addleson's taking *this* conveyance and would not rest until he had successfully installed his lordship in the carriage. The clerk then stood on the sidewalk, watching and waiting, until the hack had pulled away.

Recalling Mr. Berry's determination brought a slight smile

to Addleson's lips, for the dedicated clerk was surely not accustomed to acting with such forcefulness. Addleson was most certainly not accustomed to being routed so thoroughly.

Once in the carriage, the viscount had decided his concern for Lady Agatha's welfare was perhaps out of proportion to the situation. Without question, Townshend was a blackguard and a schemer, but he was hardly of the criminal class. 'Twas not as if he would secret her away to a foreign location and toss her off a cliff like a villain in a novel by Mrs. Radcliffe. As his earlier behavior demonstrated, Luther Townshend was a civilized gentleman who respected order and believed in following rules. His insistence that Addleson had no place in the library was petty, yes, but also accurate. In asking him to leave, he was not intentionally interrupting a meeting between allies.

Likewise, Townshend's interest in Clemmons was impersonal. He had not tracked Mr. Holyroodhouse to ground in the library of the British Horticultural Society after an exhaustive search, but rather sought out Mr. Petrie's secretary to satisfy a curiosity as half the society had already done that day.

Surely, the deputy director of Kew Gardens had many interests outside the persecution of one gently bred lady with a talent for satire.

These sanguine thoughts had accompanied the viscount on his ride home and had seen him comfortably through a meeting with his steward. It was only several hours later, after he had partaken of a light collation in his study but before dressing for the evening, that his calm deserted him. His positive outlook had been based on the assumption that Lady Agatha would do nothing to give herself away. She was a clever chit who was quite capable of carrying out the disguise she had adopted.

But what a complicated disguise it was—American gentleman. He had borne witness to her pulling it off with aplomb three times in succession, and yet he could not help recalling how easily he had seen through the ruse. What if the register of her voice traveled perilously high in the presence of Townshend as it had in his? Edward hadn't noticed, but how could he assume the deputy director of Kew was as oblivious as his cousin?

He would not take it well. No, Mr. Townshend would not consider it a great lark to discover the object of his blackmail scheme was pretending to be an American visitor to poke around in the society's private records.

Whether he divined her true purpose or not, he would react badly. Would his reaction be equal to a villain's in a gothic novel? Most likely not. The very nature of Townshend's plan—attacking Miss Harlow through the work of an artist—indicated an unwillingness to directly involve himself in the ugliness he contrived. At best, he might scare Agatha with further threats of ruination and perhaps move up her deadline by a day.

These thoughts, as reasonable as they were, could not quell the apprehension that grew within him, and with images of Agatha constrained and gagged in a coach bound for the wilds of Devonshire, he presented himself at 31 Portland Place. The butler's cool reception did little to calm him, for it appeared to him to be almost too cool, as if the entire household were conspiring to hide a great tragedy.

Lady Bolingbroke's smile when she entered the room further discomforted him, as it seemed to him designed to lull a dangerous animal back into its cage.

I am losing my senses, Addleson thought as he greeted her with a bow, and he took some comfort in knowing he had enough sense to realize it.

"This is highly unusual," he announced without engaging in any prior social niceties. He did not care about her or her husband's health.

Her ladyship smiled again with calculated serenity and sat on the settee. "Not at all," she said softly, reaching for the teapot. "Lady Agatha receives visitors all the time. She is very popular."

The extravagance of the lie almost unnerved him entirely, for what cause other then deep subterfuge could

Lady Bolingbroke have to make such a blatantly untrue statement? And where was her daughter that she had yet to appear in the drawing room? Was the house so cavernously large that it would take half an hour to travel from one end to the other?

"I meant the lateness of the hour," Addleson explained, smothering his anxiety. "It is past the time for social calls."

Lady Bolingbroke conceded this with a gracious nod and held out a cup of tea. The viscount, feeling he had no recourse, accepted the beverage and sat next to her on the seat. When he was settled, she added, "But suitors are unpredictable creatures and we have much experience in their erratic ways. After all, my daughter is a sought-after young lady."

The claim that Lady Agony was sought after was so patently absurd, Addleson became convinced a great conspiracy to hide Agatha's disappearance was afoot. While Lady Bolingbroke had been dispatched to the drawing room in an outward display of normalcy, her husband and eight of his most trusted men were on the northern road hunting for Agatha's captors.

Addleson placed his teacup on the table with a loud clatter and opened his mouth to demand the truth just as Agatha stepped into the room.

"Lord Addleson, this is unexpected," she said pleasantly.

Surprised to see her thus—not merely safe in her own home but perfectly composed and lovely, with her black eyes glowing against her porcelain skin—he rose to his feet and stepped forward. "I'm pleased to see you looking so well."

Lady Bolingbroke beamed. "She does look well, doesn't she? The social whirl becomes her."

"My mother likes to believe I am a simpering miss having her first season," Agatha explained amiably as she sat down in the armchair. "To be fair, this is a conscious choice she makes every day and not a delusion. My father assures me it is an entirely natural reaction to having an impossible daughter such as myself. Now she will tell you she doesn't mind my teasing at all."

To her credit, Lady Bolingbroke did not appear the least

bit discomfited by her daughter's honesty. "I truly don't mind," she insisted. "I believe there is value in having an optimistic view of the world and think that the best way to make one's wishes come true is to act as if they already have." She lifted the teapot and looked in the viscount's direction. "More?"

Addleson's desire at the moment was for a private word with Agatha, but he could not imagine how that would happen. "No, thank you. I am fine."

"My mother also believes you are here to court me," Agatha said frankly. "He is not a suitor, Mama."

Lady Bolingbroke smiled serenely. "Not yet."

Agatha sought out the viscount's gaze and rolled her eyes. Then she addressed her mother. "I have something of import I would like to discuss with Lord Addleson, a private matter that concerns another person, a third party with whom you are not familiar. Given that Ellen is here to ensure propriety, I trust you can have no objection," she said, indicating her maid, who had taken a seat in the far corner of the room by the rarely used escritoire.

"Actually, I have several objections, but I'm going to suppress them because I still have to get ready for Lady Fellingham's fête, and I know few suitors feel comfortable under the watchful eye of a devoted mother," she said cheerfully as she stood. "It has been a pleasure, Lord Addleson, and I look forward to seeing you soon." She reminded her daughter to offer the viscount more tea and walked toward the doorway, where she paused on the threshold. "We are leaving this open, of course."

"Of course," Agatha said.

Addleson watched the exchange, a little in awe of how easily and straightforwardly the pair dealt with each other. From the few things Agatha had let drop, he naturally concluded she had a contentious relationship with her mother.

"I like her," he said, as he sat down again.

Agatha nodded. "I do, too, a good deal of the time, but, I assure you, she frequently makes it difficult. In keeping with her philosophy, she calls me Aggie in hopes that one day I will be an Aggie," she said. "But that is neither here nor there. We must talk about Townshend. I have remarkable news."

Addleson nodded firmly. "Yes, we must talk about Townshend. I'm not ashamed to tell you I let my imagination run away with me and imagined dire consequences to my leaving you alone with him," he explained with a hint of amusement. Now that the danger had passed—the nonexistent danger, he reminded himself—he could find humor in his reaction. His response had been highly unusual for him, for he was not the sort to leap to the worst possible outcome. Indeed, he prided himself on doing the opposite and typically withheld judgment until he knew all the facts of a situation.

That Lady Agatha was at the root of his strange behavior he did not doubt. Having induced her to trust him with her problem, he felt a driving need to solve it. The task itself did not daunt him, for he had always relished a challenge, but the assumption of responsibility for another human being did give him pause. For years he had thought of only his own pleasure, and aside from removing his cousin Edward from the faro table when he was too deep in his cups for play, he had not inconvenienced himself for anybody.

Now he was committed to thwarting a blackmailer before he could utterly destroy an innocent young woman. He understood the requirements of honor well enough to know the obligation was there regardless of whether it was sought. Only a cad would abandon a lady to her fate once he'd learned of it.

But this detached evaluation of the situation, neatly arrived at in his agile brain, did not sit right with Addleson. He was not helping an indeterminate young lady in an unpleasant predicament. He was helping Agatha—remarkable, surprising, funny, clever, stubborn, reckless, brave, talented, beautiful, desirable Agatha.

He did not feel these things because he was a gentleman saving a lady. He felt them because he was a man saving a woman.

Although the viscount was not one to shrink from

complicated concepts, he was not as familiar with complicated emotions and decided it would be best for the success of their alliance if he dismissed these thoughts from his head.

"I am agog to hear what you imagined," Agatha said, leaning forward in her chair, "for I love a good adventure story, especially when I am the heroine, but it will have to wait until after I've said my piece. I promise you, my story is far more unbelievable."

Addleson leaned forward, too, and noted with regret how far she was from him still. The Bolingbroke drawing room, for all its cheerful comfort, had none of the cherished intimacy of the British Horticultural Society's library.

"Before I begin," she added, "you must swear to me that you will react calmly. It does our cause no good if you storm out in a temper or, worse, wave your fist in the air while pledging vengeance."

As if by design, her statement made him doubly impatient to hear the details of her exchange with Townshend, but he could not help pausing over her priorities. "By what measure is my waving a fist in vengeance worse than storming out?"

"I would have to sit through it," she explained, "and I cannot imagine anything more tedious."

"Truly?" he asked in a delighted tone. "After an afternoon of explaining scientific concepts you had no knowledge of, *that* would be the most tedious thing you can imagine? I fear you have the advantage over me."

Agatha laughed. "You cannot hoodwink me, Lord Addleson. You thoroughly enjoyed listening to my preposterous explanations. The look in your eye was one perpetual twinkle."

"Jonah," he said suddenly.

She drew her brows in confusion. "Excuse me?"

No, he thought, *excuse me for bringing my complicated emotions into this conversation despite my resolution not to.*

But there was no way around it: He detested hearing the cool formality in her tone, as if they had not been a hair's breadth from a searing kiss just hours before. If only Waldegrave —damn his imprudence!—had not arrived.

"Jonah," he said again, his voice husky now with expectation. He was no schoolboy and knew well the excesses of passion, and yet this chaste longing to hear his name on her lips brought him almost unbearable pleasure. "If we are to be conspirators, you should at least call me by my name."

Although she seemed disconcerted by his explanation, she agreed. "Very well, Jonah. Do I have your agreement to remain calm?"

Distracted by his own perversity, it took him a moment to recall the topic. "Yes, you do, Agatha."

If it caused her any pleasure to hear her name from his lips, she did not indicate it by look or deed. "Good, then we can proceed. As soon as you left the room, Townshend stomped over to me and—please note: This is the part where you are going to have to exert your self-control—slapped me across the cheek."

Addleson heard the words and he saw the action play out in his head and still he said with quiet menace, "He what?"

"Slapped me across the cheek," she repeated matter-of-factly. "It was this cheek here, and you can see there is no mark. The important thing is he did not intend to sl—"

She broke off when his hand made contact with her cheek. He did not blame her, for the feel of her warm cheek against his cool hand surprised him, too. He had not meant to touch her. He'd thought only of examining her face a little more closely to confirm no lasting damage had been done. But then, as if by their own volition, his fingers brushed tenderly against the silky skin Townshend had dared to molest.

"You are wrong," he said softly. "There is a mark."

She shook her head gently. "It is only a small one."

"Yes," he said, wondering how she would react if he kissed the mark, so very small though it was. Something about the way she was staring at him, hesitant yet hungry, made him think she would be receptive. Very, very receptive.

It would be an act of madness, of course, for it would not stop at the one kiss and the door to the drawing room was wide open. Plus, the maid—ah, yes, Ellen—was somewhere close by and was no doubt on the verge of coughing with delicate pointedness to remind him of her presence.

Sighing deeply, he leaned back in the settee and contented himself with swearing silent vengeance against the deputy director of Kew. As his fist was not in the air at the time, he satisfied himself that his word had been kept.

Agatha also leaned back, as if seeking shelter or protection in the depths of the oversize armchair. "As I was about to explain, 'twas not I, Lady Agatha, who was the target of Townshend's wrath. He was furious with Mr. Clemmons. Apparently, the two of them have had a longstanding agreement, which he felt Townshend had betrayed."

As Agatha relayed the story, Addleson found his anger replaced first by surprise, then by cynical amusement. What originally seemed like an unlikely contrivance—an esteemed member of an elite gardening society and a director of the most respected garden in the kingdom cribbing notes from an unknown American enthusiast—struck him in the end as the inevitable course taken by a corrupt gentleman who did not relish hard work. Townshend's actions against Agatha and Miss Harlow spoke already of a weaselly nature, and his penchant for ruffled sleeves, a fashion embellishment as outdated as Lord Bolingbroke's father's wig, indicated a fondness for oppressive regimes. Agatha would dismiss his opinion as frivolous and trivial, but, in all sincerity, he would expect any sort of wickedness from a man whose commitment to repressive eighteenth-century ideals was unwavering.

"This has been going on for years?" he asked.

She bobbed her head sharply. "Four, to be precise. I do not know the actual number of articles that have been plagiarized, but it seemed like a significant number. Townshend knew the truth would likely be discovered once Petrie arrived in London, so he arranged for Clemmons to incapacitate him. He was supposed to put a dose of arsenic in his coffee so Petrie would be too sick to travel but somehow managed to dose his own cup instead. That is why he stayed behind and Petrie traveled alone."

"Fascinating," Addleson murmured as he tried to imagine the scene at the docks the morning of departure—the moment when the beleaguered and not very bright secretary realized he had not only failed to poison Petrie but had also succeeded in incapacitating himself. Oh, the futile rage at his encompassing ineptitude. Oh, the helplessness as that first wave of intestinal distress gurgled through his system. Did he even understand at first what was happening? Had he perhaps assumed it was a plate of ill-prepared eggs that caused his stomach complaint?

The viscount was far too well bred to laugh at the physical suffering of another, but he allowed himself a small smile. Sometimes, justice was self-administered.

Agatha did not view the events in the same analytical light, for she forcefully corrected his description. "It's horrifying."

"Let's agree to compromise: horrifying *and* fascinating," he offered diplomatically. "You say there are letters attesting to this history?"

"Townshend claims to have saved every letter Clemmons has sent him, starting with the missive introducing himself and suggesting the plan. He believes there's enough detail in the recent one to have Clemmons sent immediately to the gallows," she said. "I am not guilty of any crime, nor am I a foreigner to these shores, but Townshend's argument for swift justice based on the evidence at hand was chilling. I think his assessment of the situation is accurate—*if* I were indeed Clemmons."

With very little effort, Addleson called to mind the scene in the library and pictured Townshend towering over a tremulous Agatha, his eyes blazing with fury. Her description of the events, cool and matter-of-fact, painted a very different image and as much as he wanted to believe her account, he knew the whole experience must have been chilling.

For that alone—the sense of fear and helplessness she must have felt—he would seek revenge.

"But you are not Clemmons," he reminded her.

"I am not Clemmons, so I have no cause to fear the letters," she said. "We must find them."

Addleson nodded, for, yes, they did need to locate those letters. Having evidence against Townshend would cancel out the evidence he had against Agatha. But would that eliminate the threat or simply delay it? Given Townshend's record of infamy, the viscount rather thought it was the latter. In order to remove the threat entirely, they would have to come up with a more elaborate scheme than simply stealing the correspondence.

"He provided no details as to the probable location of the letters, but the obvious place to start the search is his residence," she continued. "Other than slipping through the window of my studio—and I've only done that for the first time today—I have no experience secretly entering and exiting secured homes. I am, however, a quick learner and feel certain I can acquire the skill as I am practicing it. Shall we schedule the break-in for tomorrow night? We shall have to come up with a ruse to ensure Townshend is away from his home. Perhaps my father can unknowingly help us with that."

The viscount smiled. How could he not when confronted with such undiluted confidence? "I don't doubt for a moment you could become a champion thief overnight, but you should not invest in the tools for your new trade just yet. Your plan fails to take into account our more immediate problem."

Agatha furrowed her brow, as if suspecting a trick. "The more immediate problem of distracting me with some other issue so you can break into Townshend's house on your own?"

"I'm not that devious," Addleson assured her, while privately wondering to what lengths he would go to keep her safe. Lying about a little housebreaking seemed like a minor offense to ensure her well-being. "I refer, of course, to Petrie's presentation at the horticultural society six nights hence. Townshend can't let him take the podium, for as soon as his friends and associates in the society hear the lecture, they will realize something is amiss. No, he must dispense with Petrie before then. You said Petrie is returning on Friday, correct? That gives Townshend only forty-eight hours to make his move."

Agatha bolted upright in her chair. "Yes, of course. I tried to elicit from Townshend precisely what his plan was, but he thought I—that is, Clemmons—was trying to wrangle more money from him and refused to answer. Certainly he will do something to incapacitate Petrie before the lecture. The question is, will he use arsenic again or something more deadly?"

"Regardless, we cannot take the risk," he said.

Slowly, she shook her head. "No, we cannot. We must gather our evidence immediately."

"We must?" Addleson asked, thinking that they would not have to gather anything. If they played the scene correctly, Townshend would bring the evidence to them and do so obligingly in front of a team of Runners.

"Yes, then we can use the letters as leverage to make Townshend abandon his plan to hurt Petrie and stop his persecution of Miss Harlow and leave off harassing Mr. Holyroodhouse," she said excitedly, before pausing and tilting her head thoughtfully. "My, that is quite an extensive list of sins for one packet of letters to ensure against."

"I agree," Addleson said. "In order for us to permanently neutralize the threat Townshend poses, we will need more ammunition. I have a plan that I think will work, but it requires you to dress as Mr. Clemmons again. How do you feel about that?"

She sighed dramatically. "The wig is a problem."

He recalled the monstrosity she wore on her head and smiled. "Yes, it certainly is."

"I shall have to search the attics for another," she explained, "for the one I wore today is cinders in my fireplace grate."

"I'm impressed with your fortitude. I would have tossed it out the window long before I returned home," he said.

"Then you would have looked very funny climbing out of the hack with your long hair in pins," she said, grinning. "But to the matter at hand: Other than the inconvenience of the wig—and I mean the inconvenience of wearing it, not acquiring it, for the hairpiece was remarkable for its discomfort—I have no objection to once again adopting the identity of Mr. Clemmons. I assume Townshend and I will have another standoff. To what purpose?"

"As you said, Townshend's threat against Clemmons, though chilling to hear, has no bearing on you because you are neither a criminal nor a foreigner. The real target of his threat is thousands of miles away in New York, which he does not know," he said and watched with delight as the light of understanding dawned in her eyes. "So we will send a missive from Clemmons suggesting an exchange of evidence: his packet of letters for your packet of letters."

Excited now by the scheme, Agatha jumped to her feet and started pacing the room. "Because I am a villain, too, and, as a villain, I am far too cynical to come to the home country of my co-conspirator without protection."

"Exactly," he said, rising to his feet as well.

"And, naturally," she continued, clearly enjoying the game, "I'm far too hardened by my life of crime to simply hand over anything. No, first I must insist that we have a little chat about who did what and when and then press for details about how he plans to dispose of Petrie. While this is going on, we will...what?" She looked at Addleson thoughtfully as she ran through ideas. "Have someone on hand who can act in an official capacity. Who will it be? A magistrate? A Bow Street Runner?"

"A team of Bow Street Runners."

With an appreciative nod, she stopped her pacing near the front window and smiled with approval. "That's good. That's really quite good. Newgate prison is a much better negotiating tool than the letters. I'm very impressed, Jonah."

At the compliment, Addleson felt a flush of pleasure that was entirely out of proportion to the praise itself. Its cause was simple. In truth, it was far too simple for him to accept, for all it had taken was the sound of his name on her lips and the light of respect in her eyes. Just those two meager things and he had slipped from admiration to infatuation.

Having never made the journey before, he was an

uncertain traveler and could not understand the odd frantic pressure in his chest. Was it panic? Could it be panic? Was it fear? Was it terror? Was it dread? Should he suddenly remember another engagement and come back in the morning when he had himself better under control?

The idea of leaving made sense, of giving himself time to figure out what he was feeling, and yet he remained rooted to the spot, for how could he leave her now, when he'd just discovered this remarkable feeling, this exultation, this irresistible desire to bask in her presence.

He was not going anywhere.

And yet it was unbearable to stay.

To hide the emotion, which was too intense for the drawing room, particularly one with an open door and a lady's maid, he bowed politely and said thank you.

His voice sounded strange to him, as if there were a difference in vocal timbre between infatuated Addleson and noninfatuated Addleson.

Lord Addlewit indeed, he thought in amusement and felt his heart start to steady. The respite was sweet but painfully short, for in five quick strides she was at his side and somehow taking his hands into her own.

"No," she said, squeezing his fingers with sincere affection and gratitude, "thank *you*. You have been a true friend to me today, and I don't know what I would have done without a friend."

The viscount looked into her eyes, those fathomless black pools that somehow saw everything, and resolved never to look away even as he did just that. Gently, he extricated his hands from hers, for he had no other choice. Either he pulled himself away from her or pulled her toward him.

Using the vacuous tone that had earned him Mr. Holyroodhouse's scorn, he said, "I know. You would have broken into Townshend's apartment without delay, and given the limitations of Mr. Clemmons's tailor, I can easily imagine the sartorial ignominy with which you would have committed the crime." He affected a shudder. "Truly, I can't decide which offense is worse."

Agatha laughed, as he had intended, and took a step back. "You're right about my actions, for I would have done something that impulsive. I take issue, however, with your other charge, for Lady Bolingbroke has a wonderfully austere black gown she wore when her mother died. Add a simple pearl necklace and I would have made an impeccably turned out housebreaker. Regardless, I owe you a debt of gratitude and I'm eager to settle up. How may I repay you?"

The correct response was on the tip of his tongue, but he could not bring himself to utter the suitably benign reply that courtesy required. No repayment *was* necessary, and yet there was so much he wanted from her—knowledge most of all, for she was like a dimly lit room and he longed to take a candle to every dark corner.

"Show me your studio," he said.

Her eyes widened—with surprise, yes, for he could not imagine anyone had ever made the request before, but with trepidation as well. Her studio was not merely the private place where she worked, although she did toil there for hours in happy seclusion; it was also the secret heart of her.

Agatha was too clever not to know it.

"My studio?" she asked.

"Your studio," he said, feeling an unexpected mix of surprise and trepidation himself. He had made the suggestion with his usual flippancy, and it was only now, when she seemed on the verge of refusing, that he realized how desperately he wanted her to agree. His need, he discovered with alarm, was twofold, for he didn't just want to see her private place where she was most herself, he wanted her to trust him enough to let him see the private place where she was most herself. "Please show me your studio."

She shook her head and, flustered, tried to answer. "Why would you... I really don't think... I can't just—" She broke off and looked him in the eyes, seemingly at a loss. "My mother would never approve."

It did not take much imagination to conceive the horror with which Lady Bolingbroke would meet such a suggestion, and to some extent, he himself shared it. Nevertheless, he did something he had never before done in the whole of his twenty-nine-plus years: entreated a lady to behave indecorously. "You mentioned a window suitable for climbing through."

Now she was shocked. His desire to see her studio was baffling but not entirely inexplicable. But this—desiring to see it so much he would climb through a window like a thief— was beyond anything fathomable.

For several seconds, Agatha stared at him aghast, then turned to her maid as if seeking assistance. Finding none, for Ellen was deeply engrossed in the stitching on the arm of her chair, she turned back to the viscount and examined him carefully for another few seconds before deciding to concede. "Very right," she said with remarkable calm, "but you must not expect anything very grand. Despite my pleas for a light-filled atelier at the top of the house, my mother has consigned me to a gloomy closet near the kitchens. As you may guess, it's a continual bone of contention between us. She contends too much sunlight will ruin my milky-white complexion, but in truth she hopes to discourage my painting."

"I admire Lady Bolingbroke's optimistic approach to achieving her goals, but that particular wish seems especially unlikely to come to pass," he observed, wondering how she could speak of her mother's trespasses with so little resentment. His own mother had done far less to thwart his happiness, and he resented her so much, he had barely seen her in the eight years since his father had died of consumption.

As fascinated as he was curious, Addleson put the question to her.

Agatha raised her left eyebrow and examined him with an air of amused cynicism. "*Little* resentment?" she asked mildly. "How would you describe Mr. Holyroodhouse, sir, if not as a seething heap of bitter indignation? I resent my mother so little I might irrevocably destroy her reputation as well as mine."

Addleson conceded the point with a nod, for reckless

behavior often accompanied indignant displeasure. "I stand corrected. You have taken resentment to an entirely new level."

"Indeed, I have made a caricature of the emotion itself," she said somewhat contemptuously. "What seems like calculation now, however, was unintentional then. In the beginning, I truly did not understand my motives in creating Mr. Holyroodhouse. I was several months into the ruse, and by the time I'd realized the truth, it was far too satisfying to desist. Three years later, I have no excuse. And what about you, Jonah?"

The viscount, who, though gratified to hear his name trip easily from her lips, knew he was not so facile as to let such a thing befuddle him. If he did not understand her question, it was because her question did not make sense. "You'll have to elaborate, I'm afraid. What about me what, Agatha?"

"Your creation, Lord Addlewit," she said simply.

"I rather thought Lord Addlewit was *your* creation," he said with a teasing lilt to his voice. Despite his playful tone, her face remained serious, for she was too clever not to recognize the sally for the evasion it was. With a thoughtful frown, she silently watched him and waited for some version, any version, of the truth.

She would have to wait a very long time, Addleson thought, for he was not prepared to lay bare his soul. It was one thing for him to look at her secret heart and another thing entirely for her to look at his.

Having no cavalier reply and determined not to give a sincere one, he changed the subject and suggested a tavern called the Rusty Plinth for their assignation with Townshend.

"Clemmons would be new to London and would not have time to acquaint himself with its more respectable establishments. The Plinth is near the docks, so it's likely he would have seen it when he first arrived, and it's appropriately seedy. In addition, it's large enough to house an entire regiment of Runners without feeling crowded and has a backroom for private dealings," he explained, well aware that dodging the question was a craven response and perhaps the first act of cowardice he had ever indulged. "Townshend is unlikely to be familiar with it, which is another advantage."

If she recognized the tactic for what it was, Agatha did not draw attention to it. Rather, she asked him what time he would advise for their meeting and deferred to his superior knowledge of depravity when he suggested two in the afternoon as ideal. He also proposed writing the letter from Mr. Clemmons, as he knew the exact words to provoke his attendance. Immediately, she expressed concern that Townshend would recognize the hand as unfamiliar, and before he could suggest a solution, insisted she could easily pilfer a sample from Petrie's rooms, which were vacant during his absence.

"A man so reliant on his assistant's services would not travel without at least one note or reminder from the fellow," she observed thoughtfully.

One by one, they worked through the particulars of Mr. Luther Townshend's downfall, with the viscount assuming responsibility for much, if not all, that had to be done: He would write the letter; he would talk to the magistrate; he would arrange for the Runners; he would coordinate with the Rusty Plinth; he would provide a carriage to convey her to the meeting; he would even secure a new wig for her disguise.

"I cannot speak to its comfort," he said cautiously, "for it is a wig, and they are known to be itchy regardless of quality, but I can promise it will fit properly and not be speckled with ancient white powder."

"An improvement, to be sure. Thank you, my lord," she said stiffly, then rose to her feet and walked to the door. She was showing him out. "I trust we have covered every detail for tomorrow. I will, of course, have the note with Clemmons's handwriting delivered to your residence as soon as I lay hands on it. Now, you still have much to do, so I will let you get on with it. I am, as always, grateful for your help."

Her tone was cool—cool and polite and detached as if she were discussing the price of silk with the milliner. He understood her aloofness was a reaction to his earlier rebuff.

He knew she had only adopted the same businesslike manner he himself had assumed when her question rattled him, yet he still resented her attempt to put distance between them. Just because he did not want to share the deeply personal truths of his own life did not mean he didn't want to know every deeply personal truth of hers.

She had agreed to let him see her studio, and damn it, he wasn't leaving until he did.

"The south window?" he asked, striding over to the doorway.

"The south window?"

"The window that is suited for climbing through," he explained, amused by how confused she was. It seemed like an obvious question to him. "It is on the south side of the building? I assume so, as the access is better than the north side."

The impulse was there to equivocate—he could see it in her eyes—but rather than try to put him off, she conceded with a detailed explanation of how to find the correct window and instructions for avoiding Mrs. Brookner's sharp eye. "I'm not saying you must crawl, per se, but a low creep under the window sash would not be inappropriate. I will meet you there in fifteen minutes, which will leave me plenty of time to get the writing sample." Then she called for Gregson and instructed him to show the viscount out.

Although his absence would be temporary, Addleson made a proper good-bye and even kissed Agatha on the hand in front of the butler, an obvious misstep made glaring by the horrified look the lady gave him. Smothering a smile, he sauntered down the front path, climbed onto his curricle and drove to the end of the block. Then he pulled his the carriage to the curb, climbed down again and asked his tiger to exercise the horses. Muttering about cracked nobs, Henry jumped down from his seat and took the reins.

Accustomed to muttered insults from his tiger, Addleson did not feel the least bit put out by the abuse and suspected, as he crouched in the grass under Mrs. Brookner's window, that there was in fact something a little cracked about his nob. Agatha's unrestrained laughter as he pulled himself through the window confirmed it.

"Welcome, my lord," she said, closing the casement behind him. "I would offer you a cup of tea, but I'm sure we do not have time to drink it. At this very moment, the tale of the kiss you bestowed on my hand is spreading through this house like fire through tinder and in a few minutes the story will reach my mother's ears. When it does, she will send down a footman to request my presence and I will be subjected to a full interrogation. If I have not made myself clear, the kiss was an ill-conceived idea and a very poor way to repay me for a kindness."

Although she spoke sternly, a glimmer of amusement lit her dark eyes and Addleson sensed an excitement about her, as if she were pleased to have him there. He also thought he detected an unfamiliar bloom to her cheeks but conceded that might have been the lighting in the room, which was as dark as she'd warned.

Indeed, her caution was well served, for the room was every bit as dreary as she'd said. The space was small, the walls were sooty, the floor was smudged with paint and dirt, and the natural light provided by the window in the daytime would be negligible.

He was amazed her studio space was merely a bone of contention between her and her mother. He rather thought it should be the site of a long-fought war.

The room was chilly despite the fire crackling in the hearth, and he noticed the maid Ellen wore a dun-colored wool shawl that had seen better days. Seemingly unaffected by the cold, Agatha stood by the window and watched him with the unwavering gaze of a cat. He did not blame her for the silent scrutiny, for he was the interloper in her midst, one who had inexplicably demanded entry. The onus was on him to make observations.

But he did not want to make observations. Like her, all he wanted to do was look and observe, and breathe and marvel. There was so much to see, for canvases were piled everywhere, one next to the other against the walls and the sideboard and the armchair by the fire. A lot of them were studies—the same arrangement of fruit painted over and over again from different angles using different methods. One focused on the way the light from a candle fell on the bright red skin of an apple. Another captured the shadows in the hollow between grapes.

Many of them were portraits of the staff engaged in sundry duties such as sewing a sock or mixing a broth. There were a dozen canvases of her maid, each one showing her as she was in the moment: an ordinary servant girl posing for her mistress.

All of Agatha's paintings represented the truth. None of them embodied the scope of history or epitomized the great themes of the day. They were not depictions of famous scenes from the classics or the Bible, nor were they glorifications of regular men. Her studies of Lord Bolingbroke were stunning for their honesty, with the perfect touch of impatience and resignation.

On a table, he discovered stacks of sketches by Mr. Holyroodhouse, some barely outlines, some almost finished and others scribbled over. Among the pile, he found several early drafts of Lord Addlewit, his eyes confronting curious onlookers head on. Something about his expression was off—something that she simply couldn't get right—for the drawings were almost identical except for a minor change here or there: the line of his jaw, the angle of his nose, the light in his eyes. Recalling the final, with its profile view of him, he knew she never got it right.

As he looked and observed, it was easy to marvel, for so much of her work was marvelous, but breathing—well, breathing was harder, for she quite literally took his breath away.

Then he flipped through the canvases in the far corner by the fireplace and suddenly there was she: Agatha in a series of self-portraits, each one less flattering than the last until the full-blown scowl of Lady Agony glowered back at him.

Everything stopped.

For one endless moment, nothing in the world moved. His heart stopped beating, his blood stopped flowing, his lungs stopped expanding.

It was there, all there, in that image of Agatha. Everything he saw when he looked at her: the impishness, the anger, the impatience, the delight, the forbearance, the talent. It was all contained in that single image, and as the world suddenly started up again, as the blood began to pound through his veins, as his heart tripped over itself as if trying to win a race, he realized how foolish he had been to think he could be infatuated with Agatha and not immediately tumble into love.

Addleson was staggered and yet not staggered, for he had known from the beginning there was something about her. He had simply thought that something was the mystery she presented, but there he was, standing with all the puzzle pieces in the palm of his hand, and he was still fascinated.

He would always be fascinated.

Awake to the truth, he felt a schoolboy's impatience to declare his feelings and wondered if he could really do it there, in her humble studio with her maid wrapped in the ugliest woolen shawl he'd ever seen. He smiled and laughed at himself as the answer flitted freely through his mind: yes, he could absolutely do it. He did not care if he made a fool of himself. Indeed, he was eager to do so, for he knew Agatha would appreciate the absurdity.

But the matter wasn't that simple. No matter of the heart ever was.

As a man of honor, he could not propose to a woman whose indebtedness was ongoing. He had inserted himself into her troubles—and thank God he had, for the thought of her resolving the complication presented by Clemmons on her own terrified him, especially when he imagined her breaking into Townshend's apartments to look for letters that could be hidden anywhere. The point, however, was that he had promised his help and that help could not now come with conditions. Agatha must be free and unencumbered by obligation when he spoke. Her love, if she loved, must not be clouded by gratitude.

It was only a day, a mere sixteen hours if one were to quibble.

And, oh, yes, he must quibble, for he was a man in love for the first time in his life confined in a small room with the woman he longed to touch more than he wanted his next breath.

As the viscount struggled to get the heady mix of emotions under control, the object of his desire watched him with the steady patience of a saint. No, he thought with a shake of his head, looking at her now and seeing the riddle he would never solve. She was more sphinx than saint, encased in inscrutability and swathed in serenity. How jittery he would be if their situations were reversed, if she were pawing through his life's work—taking study, making judgments, assessing skill.

Only an hour before, Agatha had asked one probing question and he had immediately retreated into formality.

He did not have her bravery.

Carefully, he leaned the wonderful self-portraits against the wall by the fireplace and walked over to where she stood near the window. Only a few inches away, he rested his back against the table, braced his hands along the edge and crossed one foot over the other. He said softly and calmly, "If Mr. Holyroodhouse is a caricature, then Lord Addlewit is a deflection."

The single biggest confession of his life and it yielded no gasp of surprise. Agatha simply nodded.

"My father was a brutish man with little care for intellectual pursuits and he took my cleverness as a personal affront. He assumed anyone who was smarter than he must be silently mocking him for his inadequacies, so I learned at a very early age it was safer and wiser to make only trivial remarks. Anything else would provoke him," he explained, amazed at how easy it was to just say the deeply personal truths of his own life. He'd always assumed the words would choke him. "Inevitably, of course, my father's fear became a self-fulfilling prophesy, for the more I understood his fear of being ridiculed, the more I ridiculed him. He was never quite clever enough to know for sure if I was mocking him, which just made him dislike me more. The relationship was fraught, to say the least, and I was relieved when he died, for it meant I was released from the obligation of trying to love him."

Agatha's sphinxlike face remained unreadable. "You were not relieved."

He smiled wryly. "No. But I *was* released, and although there was no need for me to take refuge in nonsensical blather any longer, I found it both useful and entertaining to be mistaken for a fool. The expression on your face at the theater on the night we met was without price. You were confused and appalled and disgusted and horrified and annoyed, and I remembered thinking that if I had a face that revealed my expressions so plainly, I, too, would keep my features trained in an impatient scowl."

He expected her to scowl, even hoped for it so that he could know what she was thinking, but her expression did not change. "At that moment, I was working out the details of one of Mr. Holyroodhouse's cartoons and for one terrifying instant I thought you'd figured out the truth."

"I did figure out the truth," he reminded her smugly.

Now she smiled, her fathomless black eyes sparkling with humor, and he felt desire pulse through him, desire so sharp it seemed like an actual knife had pierced his gut. How very close she was and how very far away.

Suddenly, there was a knock on the door and although Agatha jumped at the unexpected sound, she also managed a rueful smile. "There it is—the summons from my mother. Ellen," she said, looking at her maid, "will you please tell Lady Bolingbroke that I will be up as soon as I finish rinsing my brushes?"

Ellen complied at once, rising swiftly from her chair to make her ladyship's excuses, but as she slipped through the door, she cast an uncertain glance back at them. Addleson, who readily understood the look, was amused by the maid's concern, for Agatha's ramshackle studio bore little resemblance to a love nest.

But then he looked at Agatha and saw her eyes glittering with humor—no, not humor, unmitigated glee—as she refined the story she would tell her mother about the kiss ("There was a fly on my hand and while I was swatting it away, my hand bumped your lips") and discovered the setting did not matter at all, for in four brisk paces he was by her side and pulling her into his arms. He heard her gasp of surprise as his lips touched hers and he felt her entire body tense as he pressed his hands to her back, but her mouth moved beneath his, soft and sure. The kiss was sweet and almost chaste in its innocence, for he neither increased the pressure nor teased her tongue, but the fire it sparked was as swift as it was fierce and threatened to engulf everything in its path.

As he drew her body closer to his, honor—that damn self-righteous prig!—reared its ugly head and ordered him to take several steps back. For all of her worldliness and cynicism, Agatha was an inexperienced young lady who deserved his respect and reverence, not his voracious hunger.

Disgusted with himself, Addleson turned cold and forbidding, his features hardening into a glower as he forced himself to meet her confused gaze. With shoulders as taut as his tone, he said, "I must apologize, Lady Agatha, for my inappropriate, inexcusable and disgraceful behavior. I do not know what came over me, and I promise it will never happen again."

He hurt her. It was all there on her face—pain, embarrassment, confusion, sadness. He didn't know which had done the most harm: the kiss or the apology for the kiss or the icy voice with which he issued the apology for the kiss. He knew his agile brain would be able figure it out if he just took a moment to clear his head.

But as long as he remained in Agatha's studio, as long as he stared into her beautiful face and her sad eyes, a clear head was impossible. It was not only that his own emotions were too muddled to understand, though that contributed greatly to his bewilderment, but that her body, so pliant in his arms, undermined his good sense. Alone with her for only a few seconds and the code of honor by which he had lived his whole life had deserted him.

Determined to preserve what was left of his self-respect, Addleson bowed stiffly, thanked Agatha for sharing her studio and bid her good night. Then he silently slipped through the window.

Outside, Addleson took a deep, steadying breath and rested his shoulders against the wall of the building. He didn't bother to call himself a fool, for his actions exceeded even the limitations of that appellation, and he didn't seriously consider returning to Agatha's studio to apologize more kindly. He did unseriously consider it for a few moments because he was foolish and in love, but he knew that would only make the situation worse.

Tomorrow would be different. Tomorrow, when the matter of Townshend was settled and Agatha was free of obligation and he had fulfilled his service, he would present himself at the front door like a decent suitor, declare his feelings and beg for her hand. Tomorrow, he would do everything right.

He just had to get through the day first.

CHAPTER TWELVE

Lady Agatha Bolingbroke had never felt so much like a naïve young schoolgirl as when she was waiting for Addleson's carriage to take her to the Rusty Plinth. That morning, consumed by thoughts of the kiss—oh, that kiss, that kiss, soft and sweet, melting her bones, filling her with light, heating her blood—she had opened her eyes at the first hint of light and found going back to sleep impossible. She had tried. With a determination she usually reserved for thwarting her mother, she had closed her eyes and ordered herself to think sleepy thoughts. But instead of dogs lazing before a crackling fire, she saw Addleson's face in the moment before his pressed his lips against hers, his eyes so serious and intent, and she felt the luxurious play of his mouth against her own. Oh, did she feel it, almost as if he were still in the room with her.

To cure herself of her lovesick swooning, Agatha called to mind the look of unrestrained horror that had swept across the viscount's face the moment he'd raised his head. As hurt as she was by his reaction, as disconcerted as she was to feel the sting of coldness while her body was still steeped in heat, she wasn't entirely surprised, for her mother had warned her repeatedly of the irrepressibility of male lasciviousness. All men, Lady Bolingbroke had explained, even the best of them, succumbed at times to their base desires, giving in to a primitive impulse they could not deny and instantly regretted. Naturally, Agatha had treated this grave pronouncement with suspicion, assuming her mother had exaggerated the extent of the problem to underscore her point, but now that she had experienced the mercuriality firsthand, she believed it. The outrageous lengths to which society went to ensure a young lady was never alone with an unmarried man suddenly made sense.

With this discouraging truth in mind, Agatha conceded the futility of trying to sleep and presented herself for breakfast before Mrs. Brookner had finished toasting the rolls. While she waited, she poured a cup of tea and flipped through the early edition of the newspaper. She tried to read an article about an act regulating the practices of apothecaries, but she could not keep her mind on the story and read the same sentence three times before giving up. Next, she sought out a more frivolous item, and although she succeeded very well with an article about fashionable colors for ostrich-plumed hats, it, too, failed to draw her attention away from Addleson.

Sitting still was excruciating, so as soon as she finished her plate of eggs, she excused herself from the table to the surprise of her mother, who had only that moment settled in for a nice long coze about Lord Addleson. Her attempt to have a tête-à-tête with her daughter the night before had been frustrated by a canister of crimson paint, which had spilled so thoroughly that Agatha spent the rest of the evening scrubbing her skin.

Or, at least, that was what Lady Bolingbroke had been told. She had suspected the canister of crimson paint was a diversionary tactic but had been unwilling to risk her pristine silk dress to prove it.

But it was morning now and her ladyship wore a well-loved morning gown and her daughter's skin was without marks, red or otherwise, which made her doubt the story even more. Lady Bolingbroke did not know which development she was more eager to discuss—the length of Addleson's visit (63 minutes!) or his departing gesture (a kiss on Aggie's hand!). She only knew she was determined to discuss them both in minute detail over breakfast, and she would have, if Agatha had not run off as soon as she had sat down.

While her mother drew her brows in frustration, Agatha

sought refuge in her studio, but the quiet room, which had always been a source of comfort, felt diminished in the wake of Addleson's visit.

How dare he do this to her—invade her space, undermine her confidence, cut up her peace, destroy her focus!

Agatha had never been so surprised in the whole of her life as when Addleson asked to see her studio. Surely, he knew her offer to repay him, as sincerely as it was posed, was merely compliance with polite convention. She didn't actually mean to compensate him for his efforts, for what could she possibly have that he would want? Her shock had been so deeply felt, she didn't have a clue as to how to respond. At a loss, she had sputtered—actually sputtered like a dollydrip who had lost the thread of conversation. And then, worse yet, she had used her mother as an excuse. Her mother! Not since she was a girl in leading strings had she invoked her mother's name to extricate herself from a situation.

She knew better, of course, than to imbue the extraordinary request with more meaning than it contained. Addleson's admiration for Mr. Holyroodhouse's skill had been expressed before he knew the artist's true identity, and his desire to see her workspace likely extended from that respect. His interest was in the functional details of her craft, the mechanics of creating a piece of art, like examining the springs and gears of a clock to understand what made it tick.

But even as Agatha assured herself of the impersonality of his appeal, she could not convince herself that a man of his remarkable perception didn't understand the exact nature of his request. He knew what he was asking—to see her very soul—and because nobody had ever shown interest in that meager apparatus before, she'd found the entreaty impossible to resist. For years, the two people who loved her most in the world had treated her studio like an inconvenience to be suffered, her mother despairing of the paint-splattered surfaces and her father decrying the wasted storage space. Neither had ever cared enough to look.

And now finally someone had.

It had been unnerving, yes, to stand quietly by while Addleson thoughtfully examined her paintings, moving canvases around to scrutinize each work, but what a pleasure it had been, too. Unused to the attention, she had relished the novelty and hoped he saw what she saw when she looked at her work: unlimited potential. She wasn't as adept with a paintbrush as she could be, not yet, but with enough time and training, she would be as good as the best Dutch master.

Addleson must have recognized something, for a change had come over him as he studied the paintings in the corner and all at once he had seemed different. The light in his eyes—that bright, knowing gleam—was suddenly a burning flame, and she had been at a loss to explain it, as the paintings were merely a series of unfortunate self-portraits, each one more dreadful than the last. She had tried so hard to make herself beautiful but could not when the moment came to add a flattering luster to her true image.

Perhaps it was the simple honesty of those paintings, the straightforward truth about herself that she hadn't tried to gloss over, that moved him to speak honestly about himself. She did not know why she had asked the question about Lord Addlewit, other than his easygoing manner made her feel overly familiar, and although she wasn't at all surprised by his rebuff, his sincere and candid reply astonished her. She had known instinctively that she was the recipient of a very great gift and resolved not to spoil it by calling attention to herself. She spoke only when she could not stop herself, and she kept her tone measured and calm.

Listening to his quiet explanation, she had felt the same connection she had felt in the library, and when his lips met hers in a soul-tripping kiss, she thought for sure he felt it too. What a glorious kiss—soft, sweet, gentle, reverent. It had been everything a naïve young schoolgirl dreamed of in a first kiss, and in that moment when his lips touched hers, in that flash of heat and awe, she could see it all: the large attic studio swimming in sunlight and Addleson in the corner reading while she painted, the companionable silence, the mutual respect, the delight in each other's company, even the passion that would flare up when her work was done.

Naïve young schoolgirl indeed!

Had anyone ever built such a towering castle in the air?

The castle came crashing down quickly enough as Addleson announced in that cold, indifferent tone that he must apologize for his inappropriate, inexcusable and disgraceful behavior.

What an exhaustive list of adjectives to heap onto one small act. Had he left any disheartening words out? Could he not have squeezed *horrible* and *repulsive* in there too?

He had cut her to the quick, standing there in her studio, in her sacred space she had never shared with anyone before, rejecting everything she was. For years, she had longed for someone to care enough to try to piece together a full picture from the scattered images in the small, dark room. He had. He had seen the whole and turned away in disgust.

Distraught, she had watched him climb over the window, his fine tailcoat hitching on a nail, his cravat unraveling, and the amused look in his eyes, which reveled in the absurdity of the moment—a privileged nobleman tugging his body over a grimy windowsill—deftly exposed her beloved studio as the paint-splattered storage room it had always been.

No, she thought angrily, pounding a fist on the table, she would not let Addleson diminish her, and she would not let him take the one thing that mattered.

With single-minded determination, she grabbed paper and ink and began to sketch. She had nothing in mind to begin, so she drew what was in front of her: the table, the chair, the window behind them. With each stroke of her pen, she felt less and less like a lovelorn schoolgirl. Slowly, her thoughts cleared, her anxiety eased, and she found the humiliation of yesterday start to subside. Ideas took form as she thought about the plan to outwit Townshend, and before she knew it she had a picture in her head of Townshend in a Newgate prison cell, his complacent grin replaced by a look of utter desolation. She imagined the filth and despair that filled the tiny room, the darkness and anguish that seeped into every corner of your being until you were nothing but a hollow man staring blankly at the destruction of your soul.

With nimble fingers, she quickly drew a long, narrow prison cell with chains on one wall and a tangle of stringy hay for a bed. On the far side, she added a small window, with its black bars and stingy ray of light. She placed Townshend, thin and gaunt with a long gray beard with a family of small mice nesting in its hairs, in the center of the room, the sharp angle of his knee protruding like a bone. Then, in large capital letters, she wrote *filth* on the wall, *despair* on the hay bed and *darkness* on the shaft of sunshine pouring through the window. Next to his figure, she wrote *anguish* and added an arrow so that it pointed clearly to the abject misery on his face.

Satisfied, she signed the drawing with a lavish script, employing her given name for the first time ever. Then she removed the sheet and began another picture of Townshend in Newgate, this time sparing him the wretchedness of the prison cell and advancing him straight to the gallows. She stood his pitiful figure on the scaffold and hung the noose a mere inch in front his head. Above the crowd of spectators she wrote *merciless,* near the rope she wrote *cruel* and into the gallows itself she engraved the word *hopelessness.* Her next drawing depicted Townshend in the prison yard surrounded by cold-blooded murderers and thieves, the high brick walls of the imposing building obstructing the sun so thoroughly no plants could grow. Again, she added identifying tags: *futile* for the dead flowers, *bleak* for the high walls, *pitiless* for the roughs in the yard.

She was in the middle of a fourth drawing—Townshend eating a gray slimy substance (*ruthless*) from a cracked bowl (*desperate*)—when Ellen entered the room.

"This came for you, miss," she said, depositing a black oval tin box on the table next to where her mistress was working. She placed a white envelope on top of it. "There's a note too."

Thoroughly immersed in her work, Agatha looked up from her drawing and stared at the box with confusion for a moment. She hadn't ordered any new art supplies recently, had she? Then she remembered Addleson's promise to provide her with a wig and glanced at the time. Twelve o'clock already?

At once, Agatha jumped out of her chair and reached for the letter, which she hastily tore open. She nodded as she scanned the contents—plan proceeding nicely, Townshend agreed, Rusty Plinth at two, expect carriage at twelve-thirty—and asked Ellen to help her change. While her maid unfastened the buttons on the back of her dress, she removed the wig from the box and examined it closely. It was certainly more modern than the one she had unearthed in the attic, its color a rich brown and its style simple with a queue tied with a leather band. It was also lighter than its predecessor, which she hoped augured well for a decreased level of itchiness.

The rush to transform into Mr. Clemmons—pin up hair, flatten chest, widen jawline—kept her mind so fully occupied that she didn't think of Addleson until forty-five minutes later, when she was climbing through the window of her studio, the same window through which the viscount had climbed hours before. She looked back at Ellen, thanked her for all her help and reminded her to invent a large, messy mishap if Lady Bolingbroke should request her presence.

"I don't expect to be gone very long," Agatha assured her.

"Very good, my lady," Ellen said. "Do be careful."

Following her request, Addleson had instructed the driver to wait for her several doors down from her own, so Agatha climbed into the carriage in front of 45 Portland Place. Although the ride to the docks was uneventful, she felt increasingly agitated with each mile covered and, needing to keep her fingers busy, she compulsively tied and untied the purple ribbon that encased her drawings of Townshend, which she planned to present in place of his letters.

Take that, you sniveling coward, she thought as she imagined calmly handing the packet to Townshend as the fact of his defeat slowly occurred to him.

She smiled in anticipation.

Then the carriage stopped in front of a brick building on

a narrow street, and her heart plummeted to the floor of her stomach as the carriage door swung open to reveal Addleson. Unaffected by the events of yesterday, he wore a delighted grin and sketched a fleeting bow.

"Mr. Clemmons," he said, "how very good to see you again."

For a moment—for just the shortest, briefest span of time—Agatha gave the naïve young schoolgirl free rein and allowed herself to feel pleasure in his company. At the sight of his bright, handsome face, those skilled red lips, the tight knot in her stomach simply unraveled, as if it had been a loosely tied silk bow all along, and she indulged the bittersweet joy of a hopeless passion.

The cherished attic studio, with its bright sunlight and doting viscount, would never be, but for that one brief moment she let herself have the dream. She let herself luxuriate in the fantasy, then, appalled by her own missishness, she slammed the door on the lovely scene and faced reality.

With hard-won calm, she addressed Addleson. "It is very good to see you, as well. I trust everything is in order?"

The viscount glanced at his watch. "Our quarry is due to arrive in a half hour. Come, let's go inside and familiarize you with the setting for our scene."

Agatha nodded and followed the viscount into the taproom, which was dark and grimy and malodorous and every bit as unsavory as Addleson had implied. Rough-hewn men with blackened fingernails laughed and drank and glared at one another at wooden tables.

As the site of Townshend's downfall, the Rusty Plinth was ideal.

"There's a private room in the back," Addleson said close to her ear.

Fascinated by the company, Agatha nodded absently and wondered if she could re-create their worn faces and scarred hands and their threadbare clothes.

"Through here," Addleson added, applying very slight pressure to her back as he directed her into the second room, which was livelier and brighter than the main hall, with emerald curtains and a yellow settee. The smell was vastly improved, as well, for although the stench of tobacco, sour ale and sweat still hung in the air, it was fainter and less sinister.

Agatha took her first easy breath since entering the establishment.

Standing in the middle of the room was a trio of gentlemen whom Addleson promptly introduced as Bow Street Runners. The men had been informed of the plan and were prepared to arrest Townshend should he not agree to their terms.

The sight of the Runners, so imposing and official in their black topcoats, unnerved Agatha, and the silk ribbon in her stomach ably tied itself into another knot. Nevertheless, she managed to greet them calmly as she looked around the room for a nook or cranny commodious enough to conceal four large gentlemen. There seemed to be none, unless all of them could somehow squeeze themselves behind the love seat.

As if sensing her concern, the viscount said, "While you are meeting with Townshend, we shall be hiding behind the curtains. I know what you're thinking, of course."

"Really?" she asked, surprised, for in truth she did not know the answer to that herself. The agitation of the moment had made her mind curiously blank.

"You can't conceive of how a man of fashion such as myself would consent to hide behind a curtain of such an unflattering shade of green. Your concern is warranted, for this garish emerald not only clashes with my olive tailcoat but also gives my complexion an unhealthy yellow tinge," he drawled. "Naturally, I entertained the idea of hiring a seamstress to replace the drapes with a set in a more temperate color such as dark blue, which goes with everything, but our plan required prompt action and left no time for redecoration. You must not despair, my dear, that I'm renouncing a lifelong pledge never to align myself with emerald green, for no sacrifice is too great to ensure your freedom."

His nonsensical chatter, so familiar and dear, at once

broke her heart and calmed her nerves. "Your forbearance is impressive, my lord, for even from this great distance, the emerald drapes are spoiling your complexion to an alarming degree. It is unpleasant to look upon, but I shall demonstrate the same forbearance by not flinching at the sight of your alarming yellowness."

"Your heroism is humbling," Addleson said admiringly.

Because she knew he was joking, despite the sincerity in his voice, she shrugged nonchalantly, as if she were offered effusive compliments every day of the week. Then she changed the subject, for his praise made the silk knots in her stomach flutter uncomfortably. "Is it not time for everyone to take their places?" she asked. "Townshend will be here at any moment."

"You are right," he said as the Runners disappeared behind the voluminous folds of the drapes. "He will arrive in a minute or two and when he does, I want you to remember I am nearby. If he does anything to frighten you, if he looks at you oddly or says something you dislike, all you have to do is call out and I will be at your side."

He spoke forcefully, as if determined to imprint his words onto her brain, and she nodded. "Yes, of course."

Addleson examined her closely for another moment more, perhaps, she thought, trying to find a hint of fear in her eyes, then raised a hand as if to caress her. Agatha froze, anticipating the exquisite torture of his touch, but his arm fell so quickly to his side, she wondered if her besotted mind had imagined the movement.

"Good," he said with one final nod. Then he, too, disappeared behind an emerald green curtain, and suddenly Agatha was alone. She knew she was not really by herself, but as she stood there in the middle of the room waiting for a villain to appear, she felt abandoned by life and circumstance. It was absurd to regret the decisions she had made and in truth she was satisfied with her existence, for it was better to have herself than a husband who would dictate her choices, and yet she felt unbearably sad at the thought of this escapade ending. Plotting with the viscount in the library had given her the same ineffable contentment as painting, and she knew she would never forget the closeness she had felt or that irrepressible yearning to be closer still.

For all her giddy swooning, Lady Agatha Bolingbroke knew she was not a naïve young schoolgirl, as that intemperate creature would be on to the next infatuation by the end of the week.

Lucky her.

These melancholy thoughts were interrupted by the arrival of Townshend, who marched into the room with great thundering strides and slammed the door shut behind him with an unsettling crack. "You are either foolish or stupid, Clemmons, to challenge me like this," he announced, removing his riding gloves. "Quite possibly both. Now hand over those letters immediately and I will ensure that an English noose will not meet your neck through my contrivance."

Agatha knew she should not have been surprised by Townshend's aggressive stance, but she had assumed his attitude would be a little more conciliatory in light of the threat Clemmons posed. She had expected a show of civility, if not a sincere display.

Speaking slowly and calmly to ensure her accent stayed consistently American and the pitch of her voice remained unswervingly male, she said, "I proposed a trade. My letters for yours."

"A trade!" Townshend scoffed. "I would be a fool to think I could trust a scoundrel like you."

"Not at all, for I am prepared to trust a scoundrel like you," she said.

Townshend did not like that. Oh, he did not like that at all, being compared to a corrupt American lackey who had sold out his master. His eyes turned flinty, and he took one threatening step toward her. Agatha decided to use his anger against him, for if they were not going to have a polite conversation about past misdeeds and current crimes, then they might as well have a churlish standoff.

"We both know the greater risk is mine, for you are

more of a scoundrel than I could ever be," she said with an insufferable air of moral superiority. "'Twas you who came up with the plan to poison Petrie and 'twas you who sent me the arsenic to do it. You know it and I know it and in case you forget it, I have the letters to prove it."

Townshend growled and took another step closer. "My plan was foolproof: just a few grains of arsenic in Petrie's coffee and he would have been out of commission for weeks. But you...*you*"—how scathingly he said it—"are a villain and a cheat, taking my money for a service not rendered and then coming all the way to London to extort more gold from me. *Hand me my letters.*"

His eyes were bulging now and the tip of his nose was bright red, and although Agatha thought he looked like a demon out of child's fairy story, she took a step closer to him.

"I will own my deadly sin, sir," she said tauntingly. "I am a greedy man and don't deny that I've enjoyed spending your money in London while laughing at you behind your back. But I am not a murderer. I would never harm another human being for personal gain, and we both know that's not true of you. What will you do to Petrie this time? More arsenic? Perhaps hemlock? Maybe he will fall in front of a carriage with a little help from you?"

Townshend laughed scornfully. "You conniving hypocrite. How dare you! Your failure to poison Petrie wasn't an act of conscience but of incompetence. You have no more scruples than I when it comes to dropping poison into an associate's cup. You were merely incapable of accomplishing the deed without tainting your own drink by mistake. I assure you, when I poison Petrie myself, I won't demonstrate such ineptness. Now, for the last time, hand me my letters."

Agatha listened with relief to his confession. He had announced in front of Addleson and her and three Bow Street Runners that he intended to harm the visiting American. There was no way he could take it back. Now all she had to do was get Clemmons's letters and she would be free from his manipulations.

"I proposed a trade," she said again, "my letters for yours."

"No, I do not like that proposal," Townshend said, his tone surprisingly calm after the recent wave of anger. Then he reached into his coat, extracted a pistol and aimed it with cool steadiness at the figure he thought was Mr. Clemmons. "Nope, I don't like that at all. What I like is for you to hand me my letters and for you to scurry all the way back to New York like the filthy piece of vermin you are."

Agatha noticed the design first—the deep rich wood that might have been walnut, the silver fittings, the intricate inlay of silver wire—and felt the bite of fear in her throat second. She had focused on the aesthetics because the act itself had been too improbable for her mind to comprehend at once: the deputy director of Kew Gardens pulling a gun in the backroom of a seedy tavern. It was like a caricature of a caricature of a villain.

Panicking was bad, she told herself as her heart beat wildly out of control and her left hand began to tremble. Panic would cloud her thinking and she needed to keep a clear head, as the situation was not what either she or Townshend had been counting on. He had come to the tavern to extract, at gunpoint if necessary, a packet of letters from a foreign nonentity with no friends and a record of past criminal deeds. He had not come to point a pistol at Lord Bolingbroke's daughter.

What would Townshend do when he discovered the truth?

Realizing how easily the situation could spiral out of control, she took a deep breath and clenched her fist. The last thing she wanted was for Addleson to dive heroically into the fray, for in attempting to save her life, he could very likely lose his own. The thought of the viscount's death, of his dying tragically and valiantly and stupidly in the backroom of the seedy little tavern on the outskirts of the wharf, caused her heart to beat so violently, she could barely breathe.

A faint now would be fatal, she thought, as she willed herself to calm down. She had to get a grip on her fear before it undid her entirely.

You need to think clearly.

Yes, clearly. First, she needed a plan.

"Let's not be hasty," she said as much to herself as to Townshend. Then she remembered that Addleson and the Runners could hear her as well. "Let's all take a moment and think about our options before someone acts foolishly. Pointing a gun at me is not necessary. I'm sure we can come to an agreement."

Although she spoke with confidence, Agatha wasn't so sure they could arrive at an agreement, for as soon as she gave Townshend the packet, he would know he had been a dupe—then he would be an angry dupe with a gun. Before that moment, before the truth clicked in his brain, she and Addleson needed to act.

"The time for agreements is passed," Townshend said with a firm shake of his head. Then he took one step and another step toward her until the firearm was mere inches from her head. One sudden movement and a bullet would be lodged in her brain. "If you do not give me the letters, I will be forced to settle on another course. Your choice of meeting places was particularly unwise, for we are near the Thames and there are a dozen men in the room next to ours who would happily toss your corpse into it for a few guineas."

Sweat slid down Agatha's back as she stared at the barrel of the gun, so close to her eyes she could almost not see it. Its proximity to her head unnerved her so much, her left arm began to shake again. She clenched her fingers as tightly as she could, driving her nails into her palm, and still her fist quivered. Slowly, she raised her other hand and narrated her actions with soothing calmness, for she did not want to startle him with unexpected movements. "I find your argument very persuasive. I will hand you the letters and you will remove that gun from where it is aimed between my eyes. First, I will withdraw the letters from where they are on my person, then I will tell you when it is safe for you to take them."

Was that clear? Did Addleson understand what she was trying to tell him?

Her tone still calm, her voice somehow still sounding like a proper American male, she said, "I am lifting my coat and raising my arm to pull the letters out from my pocket. Now I am pulling them from my pocket." Her fingers clenched around the packet as she took a deep breath. This was it. The maneuver would come down to a mere fraction of a second. Hand the letters, yell, "Now!" at the top of her lungs; drop to the floor; and hope for the best. It was a risky plan but the only one she had.

Before she could implement it, before she could even formulate the next syllable, Townshend grabbed the neat stack from her hand and grinned evilly at her, his gun trained on her forehead with such steadfastness, she feared he meant to kill her anyway. Then, as fast as it had formed, the smile turned to confusion as the image of his own thin, emaciated face stared back at him.

Now, her mind screamed. Now.

But she didn't move quickly enough, for it was already there in his face, the flash of understanding, the bolt of enlightenment, and she saw the moment his confusion solidified into hatred and the moment he decided he didn't care that she was Lord Bolingbroke's daughter or that pulling the trigger meant the fulfillment of the horrifying future he was staring at and she saw the moment his finger twitched on the trigger.

And then the door was opening and Vinnie Harlow was striding into the room and she was marching toward Agatha and she was slapping her in the face and she was saying, "You are vile, Mr. Holyroodhouse." And then into the confusion and chaos—Townshend's understanding no more keen than Agatha's—Addleson flew from behind the curtain, his body soaring through the air as he unleashed an inhuman growl, and landed on Townshend with a raised fist.

The gun discharged.

Agatha's eyes searched frantically for the spreading splotch of blood, for the telltale red that would reveal who had been hit. But she saw none, certainly not on Addleson, who was vigorously pounding his fist into Townshend's face, and certainly not on herself, for she didn't feel any pain. She looked at Vinnie, whose face was ashen, saw Emma behind her and suddenly felt the hard floor of the backroom as the Duchess of Trent shoved her to the side just a second before a chandelier crashed a few inches from her head.

Uncomprehending, Agatha stared up at the Harlow Hoyden, who, as calm and composed as ever, explained that the bullet had frayed the rope that suspended the candles.

It made perfect sense, but Agatha was still unable to understand it. She stayed where she was, lying on the hard floor of the tavern, watching as the Duke of Trent removed Addleson from Townshend's chest and the Marquess of Huntly wrapped his arms about Vinnie and the Runners dragged Townshend to his feet and Emma called for the barkeep to clean up the broken glass.

Then suddenly Addleson was at her side, helping her sit up with excessive tenderness and examining every inch of her for evidence of injury. Finding none, he gathered her roughly into his arms and hugged her with such crushing force he risked causing the injury he had been unable to locate. He sighed deeply, as if expelling all the air in his lungs, slowly loosened his hold and pulled back until he was staring into her eyes. Agatha stared back, marveling at how his eyes could look so wild when his touch was so gentle, and her head, as if by its own volition, leaned toward his and her eyes fluttered closed as she anticipated the feel of his lips....

"My chandelier!" screeched a shrill voice, calling Agatha to her senses. She jerked away from Addleson and leaped to her feet as a short man with an apron kneeled beside the shattered fixture.

"Who broke it?" he asked accusingly, not at all concerned by other recent events, including the cause of the gunshot that led to the destruction of the lighting fixture. "One of yez broke it. Who did it?"

Addleson stepped forward and announced he would assume responsibility for all damages as well as compensate for any inconvenience endured. The tavern owner's tragic demeanor was immediately supplanted by a look of calculation.

"Me mum picked out that chandelier, milord," he said. "She loved it. She's gone now, me mum, died last spring. That chandelier was all I 'ad to remember 'er."

"No doubt your suffering is great," Emma said with a cynical smile, leading the little man to the door, "but I'm confident you and the viscount will arrive at a sum sufficient to make the pain bearable. Now do excuse us, my good man, for we have a lot of business to settle first."

After she pushed the tavern owner gently out of the room and shut the door firmly in his face, Emma said, "Well, this is quite a morass. Now where should we start sorting it out? Truthfully, I cannot decide between Townshend and Lady Agatha." She looked at her sister, whose color had started to return. "Vinnie, what do you suggest?"

Agatha startled at the mention of her name, for she had thought herself still adequately disguised, and realized now that her wig had come off in the struggle, exposing her secret to the person from whom she most wanted to keep it hidden.

Vinnie turned seething eyes from Townsend to Agatha, then back to Townshend, who was struggling to free himself from the Runner's grasp, and dipped her head. "I defer to you, Emma."

Townshend, however, did not appreciate any deference that was not directly aimed at him and immediately protested that he had been tricked by a well-organized conspiracy determined to ruin him and that everyone in the room would suffer for the injustice inflicted on him. With his customary elegance, Addleson withdrew a handkerchief from his pocket, crumpled it into a ball and stuffed it into Townshend's mouth to cut the clamor off at the source. Then he drew the villain to the love seat, bound his hands and feet with what remained of the chandelier cord and asked the Runners to wait in the taproom.

"I will call you when we are ready for further action," he explained as he shut the door firmly. Then he turned and addressed the occupants of the room. "If no one else is prepared to offer a preference, I'm most curious about the source of Mr. Townshend's great hatred of Miss Harlow. He has been set on her destruction with an obsessive devotion that Lady Agatha and I have found puzzling. He contacted Agatha, vis-à-vis Mr. Holyroodhouse, with the accusation against Miss Harlow, and Agatha, not truly understanding how eloquent an artist she is or how enthusiastically the *ton* laps up any hint of iniquity, drew the caricature with which we are all familiar."

Listening to Addleson make excuses for her, Agatha felt the last remnants of shock, fear and confusion fall away. All those years of mercilessly mocking the *beau monde* for its foibles were finally coming home to roost, and she would not dodge the consequences. She had thought herself motivated by resentment of her parents alone, had believed her crusade to be wholly personal, but now she understood—finally—that her impulse to ridicule the *ton* was actually a desire to punish it for denying her the freedom to be herself.

"When Townshend approached Agatha about a follow-up drawing," Addleson continued, "she resolutely turned him down and—"

Agatha could not listen to a single word more. She stiffened her shoulders, walked over to Emma and looked her squarely in the face. "I have wronged you," she said, her hand trembling with greater vigor now than when Townshend had held a gun to her head. "I have wronged you because you possess the strength I lack to flaunt society's expectations. I have punished you for having the bravery to be exactly who you are. You are foolish and wrongheaded and reckless to the point of stupidity, but you fearlessly live your life, accepting the consequences, and rather than respect that, I resented it because I could not act with the same courage. Unable to bring myself to reject society entirely, I have worked tirelessly to make society reject me."

Next she turned to Vinnie. "When you decided to seek membership in the British Horticultural Society, I tarred you with the same brush because with that single act of boldness you became another hoyden and yet another rebuke of my cowardice. And then," she continued, ruthlessly swallowing the knot that rose in her throat, for she would not let herself unravel until she had said it all. "And then, when I allowed myself to behave impetuously for the first and only time in my life, when I gave myself the freedom to act without caring what society thought, you laughed at me. All of you laughed at me, and I took the shame of that ridicule and put it into the drawing. What Addleson said is correct. I did not realize how clearly the illustration leveled the accusation. I honestly thought it was a code to be deciphered by its subject alone. I was horrified when I discovered the truth. But that is neither here nor there, for it does nothing to exonerate my guilt and I seek no exoneration. Here is what matters: This afternoon, Lord Addleson and I have gathered enough evidence against Mr. Townshend to ensure his silence forever. He will never bother you again." Now she looked away from Vinnie, for she had only so much nerve. "I hope this can be some compensation for the pain I have caused you."

"It is little compensation," Emma announced in a hard voice that did not at all surprise Agatha. The woman whom she had described as foolish and wrongheaded and reckless would not forgive easily. "Because we already had Mr. Townshend dead to rights on charges of treason for threatening to reveal secret government information. On one word from me, the home secretary would toss him into Newgate and throw away the key."

The warmth rose so swiftly in Agatha's face, she thought she might faint from the heat. The one mitigating factor she had to offer and it had no value at all. She had not been seeking exoneration, no, but an offer of penance would not have been inappropriate.

"I see," she said softly, her eyes focused on a candle that had snapped in two during the fall. "Of course."

"Or, rather, that's what I wanted Mr. Townshend to believe," Emma said with a brief glance at the offender, whose face was red with his struggles to free himself, "but clearly he was not the least bit intimidated by my threats, for almost immediately after I issued them he recruited you in his plan for petty revenge. This time, the noose is securely in place and for that I am genuinely grateful."

Agatha's eyes flew to meet hers.

"I would not forgive you," Emma added, "for it seems to me the scale still tips out of your favor, but Vinnie will. In fact, she already has because she is too practical to nurse a grudge, and being too practical to nurse a grudge, she will nag me about the impracticality of my nursing a grudge. As I wish to avoid many unpleasant years of determined nagging, I am prepared to forgive you now. But you must comprehend that I do it only out of concern for myself, not for you."

Agatha had not expected kindness from the Harlow Hoyden, only lifelong animosity, and being forgiven so quickly and so graciously made her dizzy with relief. She had to close her eyes to regain her balance, and when she opened them a moment later, she felt herself smiling. "Thank you. After all the harm I've done Miss Harlow, I would hate to have added the burden of years of nagging."

Vinnie, who did not seem immune to the significance of the moment, for she had given her sister a very fond look, spoke with the same nonchalance. "Years is rather overstating the case. With my skill, it would have taken only months. I appreciate, however, being spared the obligation of having to make the effort."

Huntly nodded with approval, for he, too, was prepared to forgive her. "Although I question your methods, I'm grateful to you for revealing our weak spot where Townshend is concerned. As Emma said, we had thought him well routed."

Agatha looked at Huntly—indeed, she looked at all of them: Huntly, Emma, Vinnie, the duke—and wondered how they could all be so kind in the face of her abuse. She had portrayed Huntly as a helpless hothouse flower in the hands of a conniving, monstrous female.

"You mustn't be grateful," she said with an emphatic shake of her head. "I am glad my actions have been of some use to you, but you mustn't credit me with pure intentions. My goal, first and foremost, was to extricate myself from Townshend's control. Having discovered the truth of my identity, he threatened to reveal it to the *ton* if I did not publish a second or third drawing and that I could not bear. Naturally, I had hoped to discover information that would help Miss Harlow as well, but that was not my primary concern. It is I who must be grateful, for your timely arrival surely saved my life."

At the mention of their timely arrival, Addleson leaned against the door and considered the group of unexpected visitors thoughtfully. "I, too, am grateful for your well-timed entrance, but I'm also curious to know by what devising it was contrived. How did you discover Mr. Holyroodhouse's true identity and how did you know he would be here this afternoon?"

Emma laughed with genuine amusement, for his question made the four of them seem preternaturally prescient. "Rest assured, we had no idea Mr. Holyroodhouse was Lady Agatha until Townshend called her that in their struggle, and I, for one, was entirely shocked. It was very clever of you," she said with an admiring glance at the artist, "to publish caricatures of Lady Agony. Such pointed mistreatment would throw anyone off the scent."

Townshend snarled as best he could from behind the handkerchief as Agatha shrugged in modesty.

"We thought Mr. Holyroodhouse was a footman in her father's house called Joseph Williams," the duke explained. "Our investigator, a remarkably capable man named Mr. Squibbs, had been surveilling Mrs. Biddle's shop to gather information and while he was there, he witnessed an exchange between Mr. Holyroodhouse and Mrs. Biddle in which the former announced the end of their association. He followed Mr. Holyroodhouse back to Lord Bolingbroke's town house and saw him disappear into a window in the servants' quarters. Further inquiries confirmed that the description of the gentleman matched that of Joseph Williams. One of Squibbs's associates had been watching the residence for further movements of Williams and when the man presumed to be Williams left the house through the same window this afternoon, he followed him here. Squibbs alerted us immediately and we rushed to the Rusty Plinth to confront him."

Agatha recalled the scene in Mrs. Biddle's shop, her anxious determination to bring the whole episode to a close immediately and in person, and remembered the patron who appeared too engrossed in a series of drawings to pay any attention to her at all. It had not struck her as strange at the time.

"A tall man in a mustard yellow waistcoat?" Agatha asked.

"Yes, that is Mr. Squibbs. For such an distinctive figure, he's amazingly skilled at making himself seem unremarkable," Emma observed. "Now you know how we came to arrive here in the nick of time. Please tell us your version of events. If you are looking for a place to start, you can explain why you have borrowed your footman's clothes."

"Mainly because my father's were too large for me," Agatha said with a wry glance at her ensemble before launching into a narrative of her recent exploits. Having already apologized for her own egregious deeds, she kept to the facts and offered no opinions, preferring, despite Emma's request, to start at the actual beginning, with the anonymous letter she had received. She outlined her scheme to impersonate the absent Mr. Clemmons to gain entry into the British Horticultural Society, whose minutes were orderly but not teeming with useful information, and detailed her horror when Townshend arrived to castigate the real Clemmons for failing to properly poison Petrie.

When she explained why the deputy director had tried to indefinitely preempt the American's visit, Vinnie exclaimed with disgust, "You appalling man! Have you never written a single word that was not pilfered from someone else?" She shook her head and said to Agatha, "*That* is the source of our enmity. I discovered Townshend had plagiarized much of the text for his book, *Botanicus,* from a dear friend of mine and threatened to release that information if he did not support me in my membership endeavor. He responded by threatening to publish damaging information about me in return—information he could have gotten only from an informant high in the home secretary's office—which led to Emma's threat of treason."

Although Agatha genuinely had no interest in the *ton*'s full-time sport of rampant speculation, she thought a person would have to be inhuman or dead not to wonder about the connection between Miss Lavinia Harlow, the home secretary and Sir Waldo's death. If she were prone to making wild guesses, Agatha would think that Townshend's charge against Vinnie was actually true. For some unknown reason, the very sensible Miss Lavinia Harlow had killed her fiancé, and if the home secretary's office knew about it and if Townshend had opened himself up to allegations of treason, then her actions somehow had to be in service of their country.

Was Sir Waldo Windbourne a spy?

Was Vinnie?

As outrageous as both possibilities were, one had to be true, for the pieces of the puzzle would not fit together any other way.

Vinnie, of course, did not seem to be a spy, but appearing non-spy-like was no doubt the number one requirement of the job. The fact, however, that her family had contrived to save her from Townshend's vitriol, not the forces of the British government, argued for her status as a civilian. Windbourne, then, had to be the one digging for secret information, and the circumstances of his mysterious death and Vinnie's freedom implied he had conspired against the interests of England.

Had he been working for Boney or another foreign regime that sought to conquer their little isle?

Astounded by these thoughts, Agatha struggled to return her mind to the topic at hand. What had they been discussing? The source of Townshend's enmity—Vinnie's attempt to garner his support through blackmail.

"Given your arrangement with my father—that is," she explained, "your compact to make me popular in exchange for his vote—I had assumed you had used similar or a more forceful form of persuasion with the other members. But I was confused because Townshend's voting record indicated no influence at all."

Vinnie, who would have been mortified if she had

known the direction Agatha's thoughts had taken, turned a light shade of pink at the mention of persuasive tactics. "I did propose to several members, if not, perhaps, all of them, certain arrangements in exchange for their support, but in the end I decided to eschew underhanded methods and to gain— or not gain—admittance on my own merits."

Agatha's eyebrow's lifted in surprise. "But if that's true, why did my mother and I accompany you to *The Merchant of Venice*?"

She did not need to hear the answer, for the look the sisters darted at each other said it all.

"My mother would not release you from your agreement, would she?" Agatha said with a laugh that was only a little bit forced. There was nothing else to do when humiliated by one's parent yet again than decide to be amused. "Hoisted by your own petard as they say. That could not have been very pleasant for you." Then, because she feared further comment would reveal an unintended bitterness, she changed the subject. "After I relayed the episode with Townshend to Addleson, he suggested that I, as Clemmons, propose an exchange of incriminating letters to Townshend, which I did. Then he arranged for the Runners to be close by to overhear any profession of guilt, which Townshend helpfully supplied."

At the implication that he had a hand in his own undoing, Townshend intensified his protests, and Huntly, unwilling to listen to the unpleasant screech, inserted a second handkerchief into the prisoner's already stuffed mouth.

Trent's lips twitched as he watched Townshend's eyes bulge from the exertion of expressing his displeasure. "An improvement," he said, "but I suppose the fellow does have a point. We can't keep him restrained in the backroom of the Rusty Plinth indefinitely. We must settle on an arrangement for his long-term care."

"Townshend obligingly pointed out that our proximity to the Thames is rather convenient for the disposal of troublemaking individuals," Addleson observed mildly. "I believe he estimated the cost of having a pair of gentlemen from the other room handle it to be only a few guineas. I am happy to shoulder the entire expense if that means a speedy resolution to our problem."

Although Townshend's high-pitched squeak made his objection to a watery grave known, nobody else in the room gave the suggestion genuine consideration.

"Nonsense," Emma said. "You have gone through the trouble of arranging Runners and we should allow them the courtesy of doing their job. Townshend's crimes are plentiful and undeniable, as half a dozen unimpeachable witnesses will testify to seeing him hold a gun to Lady Agatha's head."

Vinnie nodded. "I agree. Mr. Townshend has shown himself to be far too dangerous to remain at large. For all we know, this Clemmons fellow might have expired from his illness. We have only Townshend's word that the dosage he provided was just enough to make Petrie too sick to travel."

"An excellent point," her twin said admiringly.

But Huntly was shaking his head. "No. The scandal would be too great. We would bring Townshend to justice but at a high cost to you and Lady Agatha, for the truth would inevitably emerge. We must come up with an alternative plan that will not engage the interest of the *ton*."

"Exile," Trent said.

"Yes," Addleson said. "My thought exactly, which is why there is a ship bound for New South Wales with Townshend's name already on its manifest. All we have to do is deliver him to the wharf before the next tide."

Huntly smiled ruefully. "Is there not a ship that leaves soon for the Arabian desert or some other territory with a more arid landscape? New Holland is home to many exotic flowers, such as *Telopea speciosissima*, a rare species with a stunning red bloom, and I can't help but feel that with access to such unusual and interesting flora, Townshend might yet make something of himself."

Vinnie scoffed at the possibility. "Unless New South Wales is home to a budding community of gifted horticulturalists from whom he can steal original ideas, I think it's very unlikely Townshend shall produce anything of note. Exile to a distant corner of the empire is a fitting end for a man whose contribution to civilization has been negligible at best."

"Excellent, then it is decided," Emma said, walking over to Townshend to address him directly. She waited until he raised his eyes to meet hers before speaking. "I have no doubt this treatment at our hands will further nourish your hatred of me and my sister. I understand the impulse and would feel the same. I trust, however, that you will think very carefully before trying to strike back again, for none of our encounters has ended in your favor and none of them ever will."

Townshend had much to say about the resolution of their encounters, but his plaintive grunts quickly faded as the Runners, at a gesture from the viscount, dragged him from the room. They heard a sharp, muffled cry as the former deputy of Kew, struggling to free himself, knocked his knee against the side of a table.

Addleson watched them disappear through the front door, then said, "I will accompany them to the ship and make sure Townshend gets off without incident."

"Very good," Trent said. "Will you be kind enough to send me a note when the deed is done?"

"Of course," he said. "And will you be kind enough to see Lady Agatha home?"

"Oh, but I—" Agatha began, but her protest was summarily cut off by the duke, who assured Addleson that he would insist on nothing less.

Having her immediate future settled without her input disappointed Agatha, but it was nothing compared to the sadness she felt at realizing the adventure was over. With the happy conclusion of the affair, she no longer had cause to conspire with Addleson, a thought that made her very unhappy. A lump rose in her throat, making it impossible to speak, and although she feared the tears it might bring, she was grateful for the enforced silence. Without it, she might plead with Addleson to let her ride in the carriage just so they may be allies in a scheme for a few minutes more.

Her risk of humiliation was further reduced by a gasp of surprise from Vinnie. "These are remarkable," she said, picking up the Newgate drawings and gently brushing off the broken glass.

Struggling to hold on to her control, Agatha managed a polite thank you.

Vinnie interpreted her cursory reply as disbelief in her sincerity and shook her head as she examined the illustration of Townshend on the gallows. "No, truly, Agatha, these are amazing. Your skill is prodigious, and seeing it like this, so visceral and passionate, I wonder at how little damage you have done. If I had been endowed with this much talent, I would have inflicted considerably more harm than Mr. Holyroodhouse in my need to express it."

Emma studied the drawing over her sister's shoulder. "As much as it pains me to offer you compliments, I must agree with Vinnie's assessment. You are very gifted."

"Very gifted," Vinnie echoed. "If you are taking on commissions, I hope you will consider doing a portrait of my brother's children. They are such dear little darlings and we have no painting of them in London."

Stunned by the earnestness of their compliments and still saddened by the end of her alliance with Addleson, Agatha could only stare at the Harlow twins. She could think of nothing to say, not even a simple yes or no in response to Vinnie's request, and merely complied silently when Emma slid her elbow through hers and said, "Come. It has been an eventful afternoon and I'm sure you're in need of rest. We will discuss the commission tomorrow during our ride in Hyde Park."

Agatha did indeed need rest, for she had no idea what was happening. It appeared as if the Harlow hoydens wished to commission a work of art from her, which was, in a day of extraordinary developments, the most extraordinary one of all. Flustered, she opened her mouth to thank them for their unexpected kindness when the rest of Emma's words struck her.

"Our ride?" she asked, puzzled.

Emma nodded as she guided Agatha to the door. "Per our arrangement with your mother, we are obligated to accompany you to the theater *and* ride with you in Hyde Park. We Harlows take our responsibilities very seriously, so don't think you can weasel out of it now."

At a loss, Agatha looked helplessly at Addleson as Emma led her across the room. Amused by her predicament—abducted by the Duchess of Trent!—he offered no support save an encouraging smile. *Don't fight the inevitable,* his look seemed to say.

As a general rule, Agatha did not believe in the inevitable, for it implied an inexcusable abdication of responsibility. Yet as Emma tugged her inexorably toward the threshold, she conceded the advantage in recognizing the things beyond her control: She could not stop her mother trying to turn her into a conventional young lady, she could not deter the Harlow sisters from befriending her, and she could not make Viscount Addleson love her.

Disheartened, she stepped out of the Rusty Plinth and squinted her eyes against the bright afternoon light. Obviously, she had not been so foolish as to expect a lasting union to come of their brief alliance. She had known from the beginning that his offer to help had been motivated by an innate desire to rescue a damsel in distress—any damsel. It had not been inspired by a specific desire to rescue her, Lady Agatha Bolingbroke.

Just like the kiss, she realized: rooted in circumstance, reinforced by nature, detached from emotion.

Inhaling deeply, she climbed into the duke's carriage with his assistance and assured herself she was ready to return to her quiet existence. No, she thought, *return* wasn't the right word, for she would not resume her life as it had been. No longer would she make the social rounds to appease her mother and wedge painting into the remaining hours. This time, she would pursue her painting in earnest, improving her skill and refining her technique, and she would not hide her vocation. She would discuss it openly and submit canvases to be displayed publicly at the Royal Academy of Arts' summer exhibition.

Then, as Vinnie took the seat across from her, Agatha wondered why she must settle for only exhibiting at the academy. Why could not she have the pleasure of attending as a student?

Agatha had no illusions—she knew it was an entirely impossible proposition that would never come to pass. Despite the fact that two women were among the founders, the institution was resolutely male. That said, she *was* sitting in a carriage with the first female member of the British Horticultural Society and the notoriously hardheaded Harlow Hoyden. If anyone had an affinity for impossible propositions, it was these two women. Surely, if they were determined to be her friends, they would rally to her cause.

All those years, she thought with a shake of her head, vilifying the Harlow Hoyden when she should have been allying herself.

The carriage lurched into motion, and Agatha stared out the window as the Rusty Plinth receded from view. To her heart, both melancholy and mawkish, it felt as if the viscount himself were disappearing, and she thought she was a fool to believe she could accomplish anything with this desperate sadness pressing on her chest.

Oh, but no. She was the incomparable Lady Agony, a conversational vortex, a swirling whirlpool of dampening sentiment that drained all thought from those around her. All she had to do to free herself from heartbreak was apply the power to herself and empty her mind of the viscount.

It would be easy.

Although Agatha recognized this misguided optimism for the lie it was, she also knew it was for the best. What was a lasting union but a marriage, and marriage was the death knell for female ambition. One could not become a successful lady painter or a successful lady anything with a husband nearby to demand attention, respect and conformity. Even if Addleson did not require compliance to certain conventions, even if he never insisted that she halt her work to get ready for a dinner party with Mr. Annoying or Lady Inconvenient, she would feel the obligation on his behalf. It was one thing to pursue your passion at any cost and quite another to make someone else pay the bill.

The scene of companionable bliss that her naïve schoolgirl brain had concocted was fantasy in more ways than one, for partners with different pursuits frequently went their separate ways. Her mother knew this, which is why she had adopted her husband's hobby as her own, as she had explained to Agatha on multiple occasions. The interests she'd had before marriage—and Agatha refused to believe they were as inconsequential as her mother insisted—had long been sacrificed on the altar of marital accord. Now, despite caring little for orchids, she could list the growth rates of two dozen species.

Whatever choices she made, Agatha knew in the end her marriage to Addleson would be little more than a mound of resentments heaped on top of one another—she resenting him for sacrifices she had made out of love for him and he resenting her for resenting him for sacrifices she had made for which he had never asked and she resenting him for resenting her for resenting him for sacrifices for which he never asked but had silently hoped for and expected.

In truth, she was fortunate their association was at an end, for marriage to the man she loved would be a misery for both of them.

Knowing herself to be lucky, however, did little to ease her broken heart, and as the carriage turned off the street with the Rusty Plinth, she felt a misery so intense, she could barely breathe. To her horror, she felt tears form in the back of her throat and just when she feared she would weep uncontrollably in front of the Harlow Hoyden and her sister and the toplofty Duke of Trent, Vinnie suddenly leaned forward and held out her elbow for inspection by the entire company.

"Now, I will readily concede that my elbow might be a bit pointy," she said, displaying the joint in various poses and angles, "but I must protest Mr. Holyroodhouse's unfair presentation of it as a spike that could impale a small child. Do say you were exaggerating, Agatha, or Emma and I will be forced to wear padded sleeves as a public safety precaution."

Inexplicably, unaccountably, Agatha laughed.

CHAPTER THIRTEEN

Addleson expected the delivery of Mr. Luther Townshend to the *Sea Emerald* to be quick, efficient and unemotional. Armed with the name of the chief officer, he fully intended to present Mr. Topher with his new cargo and stroll down the gangway of the ship without a backward glance. The problem, as he told Huntly, who had accompanied him to the dock, was he had not anticipated an intense desire to ram his fist into Townshend's jaw again. Having already dealt the villain several punishing blows at the Rusty Plinth, he had assumed the savage need to strike his smug face had been appeased.

Apparently not, for, as he looked at the former deputy director of Kew now, he realized the need to thrash him would never entirely go away. How could it, when the vile excuse for a human being had held a gun to Agatha's head?

The image was so clear to him, Addleson might as well have been standing once again in the middle of the room at the Rusty Plinth.

Only he had not been in the middle of the room. No, he had been trapped behind a drape—a heavy velvet green swath that obscured his view of events and nearly smothered him to death as he waited for the moment to strike. He knew it had been no more than a minute between the moment Agatha had uttered the word *gun* and Vinnie had charged into the room. In practical terms, only the tiniest fraction of time had passed while he frantically ran through his options, which were alarmingly few, but it had felt like an entire lifetime. In that infinitesimal speck, it felt to him as if he and Agatha could have married, raised children and retired together to a blessed plot of earth.

Oh, how he wanted that blessed plot of earth!

Imprisoned behind the curtain, he could do nothing to get it. Indeed, he could do worse than nothing, for moving the slightest in any direction risked revealing his position and surrendering the element of surprise. All he could do was wait for the signal from Agatha—clever, coolheaded Agatha, issuing orders like a fearless general on a battlefield—and worry that Townshend would discover the truth or act impulsively or panic when he realized the depravity of his actions. A man who would threaten a life at gunpoint was a man who was already feeling cornered, and such a man could not be relied upon to behave sensibly. He would shoot first and consider the wisdom of it later.

And still Addleson had to wait, his entire body tense and ready as Agatha narrated her movements, slowly building to the moment when she would give the order for the attack. *I am lifting my coat and raising my arm to pull the letters out from my pocket. Now I am pulling them from my pocket.*

But the order never came, just a moment of silence, pregnant with terror, and then suddenly, inexplicably, the sound of Miss Harlow storming into the room. Her entrance could not have been more perfectly timed—Addleson would give thanks for it for the rest of his life—but the serendipity of her arrival made him lightheaded. Relying on a random young lady to unintentionally interrupt an armed standoff was not an acceptable rescue plan. Addleson considered himself to be clever, but nowhere in his calculations for the meeting did he factor in a pistol. It simply never occurred to him that Townshend's response to a fair and even exchange of evidence would be to demand the return of his own at gunpoint.

That failure had almost cost Agatha her life.

He could not bear to think about it and yet he could not stop himself from thinking about it and imagining worse— her lifeless body on the tavern floor—and as he stared into Townshend's face, already bruised from the earlier beating, he thought the only thing that would drive the image from his mind was another trouncing.

"I understand the impulse," Huntly said, laying a hand on Addleson's arm, "because my own fingers are twitching to form a fist, but we must restrain ourselves. It is unsporting to kick a man when he is down, however deserving of the treatment he is. But do not worry that he is getting off easily. I know for a fact our friend is prone to prodigious seasickness, and the voyage to New South Wales is unlikely to be smooth. He will suffer terribly," he added with a cheerful smile.

"You are right, of course," Addleson said, conceding the point. But as he would not be there to witness the months of queasiness and heaving, he found the prospect extremely unsatisfying and promptly pounded his fist into the bound man's nose. Immediately, Townshend cried out in pain and blood poured from his swelling appendage, which may or may not have been broken.

Feeling much better, Addleson sighed deeply and flexed his fingers to confirm he had suffered no damage from the incident. "It's entirely unsporting," he agreed laconically, "and I resolve from this moment to make a concerted effort to reform my character."

Huntly laughed as the viscount thanked Mr. Topher for his help in removing Townshend from the isle of England. Then he wished the chief officer safe passage and departed the ship. He had planned to return immediately to his carriage, but as he stood at its threshold, he could not bring himself to climb in. Rather, he stared thoughtfully at the *Sea Emerald.*

Huntly, noting the direction of his gaze, strongly advised against getting a tankard at the King's Head, a rundown establishment along the dock. "I assure you, it is so derelict and disreputable as to make the Rusty Plinth look like Claridge's. I would call it ramshackle but that would be an insult to ramshackle buildings everywhere."

"I appreciate the advice, but I was thinking I should like to remain here until the ship sails. I'm reasonably confident that Townshend is in no shape to escape and I don't think

Mr. Topher or the captain, who have been well compensated, would allow him to, but I would still feel better keeping an eye on the situation. You, of course, should feel free to leave. I know I'm being overly cautious."

If the marquess privately agreed with this assessment, his answer gave no indication, for he wrapped his arm around Addleson's shoulder and directed him to the King's Head, which offered an unimpeded view of the *Sea Emerald*. "Let's get a tankard while we wait."

Addleson smiled faintly. "What about all that dereliction and disrepute?"

Huntly shrugged. "As a seasoned explorer, I have held my own in establishments many times worse and having seen how well you applied your fists this afternoon, I'm confident you can, too. I'm sure we'll be fine as long as we stick to the beer. The Blue Ruin will likely dissolve our teeth."

They drew attention immediately upon entering the tavern, for they bore no resemblance to the King's Head's usual patron, and several regulars glared at them suspiciously. One stood up and took a threatening step in their direction, but the barkeep, a giant of a man with a neck as thick as a pillar, leaned forward and said, "Ye will 'ave no trouble 'ere."

Huntly nodded appreciatively and gestured to a table by the window, which, as promised, provided a clear view of the ship. They ordered Truman porter and settled in to wait for high tide. The interval itself was not unpleasant, as the marquess made for excellent company, telling tales of his own vast travels with deprecating good humor. The stories were entertaining, but even they could not make the dockside vigil feel any less interminable. All Addleson wanted to do was see Agatha. He didn't know what he was going to do or say—he imagined supine begging for forgiveness for underestimating Townshend would not be entirely out of order—but he wanted to be near her and next to her and as close as possible without scandalizing her sensibilities.

No, that wasn't true. He positively ached to scandalize her sensibilities.

His impatience must have been palpable, for at one point, Huntly interrupted his own narrative about discovering a new species of auk to suggest he keep lookout alone. "I am more than capable of making sure one conniving gardener does not escape in the unlikely event he jumps overboard. I'm pretty sure the fellow cannot swim."

With wry amusement, for he had thought he was a cooler customer than that, the viscount thanked Huntly for his generous offer and assured him he was more than happy to stay. Then he ordered a second round of beer.

It was dark by the time the *Sea Emerald* set sail, and although Huntly insisted he could hire a hack for travel, Addleson refused to entertain the notion and delivered Huntly to the Duke of Trent's residence.

"I won't invite you in," the marquess said with a knowing grin as he climbed out of the carriage. "Do give my regards to Lady Agatha."

Arriving at the Bolingbroke town house a short while later, Addleson knew he was supposed to present himself at the front door like a proper suitor, but his good sense, most likely corrupted by impatience and most definitely by three tankards of Truman, led him to the window outside Agatha's studio. The hour was late and any other young lady would be dressing for the evening's social event—ball, rout, theater, musicale, Almack's—but not Agatha. His Agatha was exactly where she was supposed to be, standing before a canvas with an intense and absorbed look on her face.

At once, his heartbeat seemed to slow down and speed up, and the pervasive sense that all was right with the world existed side-by-side with an irrepressible compulsion to put the world to right.

If he had doubted his feelings, if the terror he had felt upon hearing Townshend hold a gun to her head had not convinced him he loved her wildly, the baffling incompatibility of these emotions would have persuaded him. Only love could create the impossible mystery of peace and chaos in a single heart.

For a moment, he simply stared through the window,

allowing himself the pleasure of the sight of her. She had changed out of her footman's clothes into a plain walking dress. The fabric was an appalling color, something in the yellow family that undermined her complexion, and splattered with paint. Her hair was pulled back in a loose coil at the nape of her neck, the random tendrils that had escaped ruthlessly held down by pins. He had never seen a more unruly hairstyle and if called upon to give it a name would have to settle for the Muddle.

And yet she was the most beautiful woman he had ever seen.

The viscount was so enthralled by the sight of her, it took him a full minute to realize the subject of the painting was he.

He was the subject of the painting.

It was still early in the evolution of the work. It was only a jumble of brushstrokes, a series of rough ideas that implied a well-thought-out concept, but it was impossible not to see his face in the high brow and broad cheekbones. If nothing else, he recognized the look in his eyes, that faintly amused way he examined the world.

Addleson wasn't a vain man and he certainly wasn't given to self-delusion. He had seen the images Agatha had drawn of Townshend in Newgate—terrifying, haunting, precise—and knew her depictions were not love letters to her subjects. But he couldn't look at the face she had painted, with its jawbone far more chiseled than anything nature had given him, and not feel it was influenced by sentiment. It was impossible for him to look at it and not think she loved him.

His heart beating wildly, he tapped on the pane and saw the surprise, delight and confusion that swept over her face as she crossed the small space to the window.

"My lord," she said, drawing the window up, "I was awaiting a note informing me that all had gone well, not a personal delivery of the information." She stepped back to let him climb over the sash. "All did go well, did it not? You're not here to tell me Townshend evaded exile and is meeting with Mrs. Biddle right now to publish a drawing exposing me as the author of so many caricatures?"

Up close, Addleson could see the paint splatters were not limited to her dress, for she had a brown streak across her cheek and a hint of red along her forehead. Without thinking, without answering, he leaned forward—he was already so close—and pressed his lips against the brown smudge because he could not resist. He had never seen anything more charming than Lady Agatha Bolingbroke with paint on her face and the light of curiosity in her eyes. He had only meant to kiss her lightly, a mere brush before drawing back and declaring himself, but once he felt the warmth of her skin, drawing back became impossible. The tug of desire was inexorable, and as he moved his lips to the red smear above her brow, he placed his hands on her shoulders and pulled her gently toward him. Delighting in the feel of her body against his, he moved his lips down to capture her own.

The kiss was a gentle thing, dewy and sweet, and he felt her body tense briefly with surprise before softening against his. At first, she was uncertain. Her lips were timid and cautious but after a moment, after he moved his hands from her shoulders to her back, after his arms tightened around her, the hesitance gave way to boldness and she pressed herself firmly against him, her own arms sliding up his chest. He heard her sigh, then moan, as he increased the pressure and, feeling her yield, he explored the heat of her mouth with his tongue, reveling in her daring as she responded in kind.

His need rose to an unbearable degree but despite the three tankards of Truman, he held himself in check, luxuriating in the kiss but taking it no further. The feel of her mouth, her lips, her passion was dizzying and somehow enough, and he thought he might stay exactly where he was forever, not moving, not pulling away, even when her maid came to announce bedtime.

Then he felt the stroke of her hand against his skin, her fingers making insistent patterns under his shirt, and all sense of control fled so swiftly, so completely, so irrevocably, it might never have existed at all. His lips followed her lead, tracing a path of searing kisses along her jaw and her neck and her collarbone until they reached the barrier of her dress, which he removed by gently pushing it aside. Her breasts— oh, her milky white breasts—were lush and full and pert and perfect and he stared at her reverentially for a moment before taking the rosy bud of her nipple into his mouth. The hitch of her breath, the dig of her nails into his back, the tilt of her head backward further fed his frenzy and he slid his hand downward, eager to discover more and confident of what he would find.

It was only when he skimmed his fingers over the mound of her womanhood, when he felt her tremble, when he imagined her lying entirely naked on the table with her sketchbooks and pencils, that reason returned. It was a mere sliver, just the thinnest shard of good sense, but it was enough for him to breathe the words *marry me*.

When she didn't respond, when she dragged his head up for another urgent kiss, he said it again, "Marry me."

On a whisper of air, more breath than word, she said, "No."

As if doused with cold water, Addleson released her and stepped back. He wasn't a vain man, no, but neither was he unaware of his appeal and he had too much experience not to have understood her passion correctly. "No?" he asked, his tone more confused than offended.

"No," she repeated firmly, the haze of passion slowly replaced by a burst of mortification. Her face lost all color as she tugged at her dress, pulling it up until it covered not only her breasts but half of her neck as well. Then she took another step back. "Though I do perceive the compliment you've paid me and am grateful for the offer."

With his ability to think degraded by desire and drink, it took Addleson a moment to realize he had completely bungled the proposal. Curse it! It wasn't supposed to be like this—a frenzied offer in a shabby basement room. He had planned the scene for the Bolingbrokes' drawing room:

heartfelt declaration, respectable proposal, restrained passion. Given how poorly he had handled the matter yesterday, kissing her sweetly, then bidding her good-bye coldly, he could easily imagine the confusion and suspicion his savagely ardent behavior had created. He could not blame her for distrusting his motives or his sincerity.

"I love you," he said simply. "I love you wholly and completely and with a ferocity I had not thought possible. I loved you yesterday when I kissed you in this room, perhaps in this very spot, but it seemed wrong to declare myself while the situation with Townshend remained unresolved. But it is resolved now and I love you still. Indeed, I love you more. Please marry me."

Agatha's expression did not change, although she grasped her hands together so tightly her knuckles turned as white as her cheeks. "I cannot."

If she had given any other discouraging answer, if she had just said no or apologized for not returning his regard, he might have taken a pet, bowed stiffly and clambered over the windowsill, all wounded ego and hurt pride. But she hadn't. She had said *I cannot*, as if the matter were somehow beyond her control.

"You cannot?" he asked quietly.

She tightened the grip on her fingers. "Must not."

Addleson found this abrupt response even more baffling than the one it sought to clarify. "I know you are very proud of your reputation as Lady Agony and under any other circumstance I would respect a woman's desire to remain quiet, but I must insist you offer a more thorough explanation of why you *must not* marry a man who loves you quite dreadfully. Does something compel you to refuse?"

Standing before him silently, her face bereft of all color, she seemed almost to be a ghost, and he stared into her dark, fathomless eyes, fearful she might disappear before giving him an answer.

"My conscience compels me," she said, her voice as stiff as her shoulders. "Recent events, including those of this afternoon, have convinced me to pursue my painting in earnest. I will no longer hide my skill or proclivity or try to pretend either is of questionable value to me. To that end, I have decided to apply to the Royal Academy of Arts, which, as I'm sure you know, doesn't accept women as students. I shall make a great cake of myself, and I don't care. But I will not make a cake of you by association. I know what it is like to be perpetually embarrassed by one's family and it has a wearying effect on the soul. As the former Mr. Holyroodhouse, I also know how easy it is to ridicule anything that is different or unusual, how to turn someone's strength against them. I will not expose you to that, and I will not give up my commitment to my art. Therefore, we must not marry. I'm sorry for hurting you, but I'm sure, given your temperament, you will be able to recover from this disappointment quickly."

Addleson decided not to be insulted. It required some effort, for it hurt to hear with what little constancy the woman to whom he had just declared everlasting devotion credited him. She was the human being with whom he wanted to spend the rest of his life, not a waistcoat with an stubborn claret stain. Rather than take offense, he strove to understand her reasoning and to respect her choice to behave honorably. Her reservations, he knew, sprung from a lifelong struggle to get her parents to accept her for who she was, and having undergone a similar battle in his youth, he could not blame her for fearing a husband would do the same.

Addressing her concern with the seriousness with which it had been expressed, he said, "Your honesty means a great deal to me, and I give you honesty in return when I tell you I would be honored to assist you in your endeavor to attend the Royal Academy of Arts. I would suffer no embarrassment."

"You believe that now, but your opinion will change once the novelty wears off," she said with conviction. "Then you will grow to resent it."

The idea that he would grow to resent her or her art or anything she chose to do was so preposterous, Addleson had to stop himself from smiling. He did not want her to think he was treating her deeply rooted fears with triviality. "I wouldn't, no, not even if I lived to be one hundred and twenty years old. I am in awe of your talent and would do nothing to squander it. You must trust me on this, my dear, for I love you far too much to make you unhappy," he explained, noting that the rigidity of her body gave her beauty an unexpected fragility, as if she were a porcelain vase that would crack under the slightest pressure.

"Then I would do it to myself out of concern for you," she said, her tone curiously calm despite the agitation of her hands, which she clenched with frightening vigor. "I would sacrifice myself to spare your dignity and would end up resenting you."

How coolly she made it, Addleson thought, her declaration of love that didn't use the word but embodied the act. The fear that his cause was futile melted like snow in the warm sun. "Do you love me?"

Her eyes, obsidian orbs seething against the pale skin of her face, seared into him and he thought her hard-won control would snap. But she held fast, answering his question with the same calm reserve with which she had conducted the entire conversation. "I do love you, yes, an extraordinary amount, but that is not the point."

Addleson felt the chaos in his heart finally settle into peace. "You have the right to your own opinion, but I most respectfully and most fervently disagree," he said before striding to the door and opening it. He stuck his head into the hallway and called to a footman who had just exited the scullery. The servant was so shocked to see a man in Lady Agatha's studio, he stared in confusion, then looked behind him to make sure the viscount was not addressing someone else. "Yes, you, my dear fellow. Please be so good as to inform Lord Bolingbroke his presence is required in Lady Agatha's studio. Thank you."

He closed the door and turned to confront Agatha's horrified gaze.

"What have you done?" she shrieked, clearly agitated by the prospect of discovery. A clever woman—although even the dullest schoolgirl would immediately grasp the implications—she knew exactly what it would mean for both of them, and she frantically tried to push, then drag, him to the window to remove the evidence before it was too late.

Amused by her energetic and ultimately ineffective attempts to eject him from her studio, he sat down at her table, found a fresh sheet of paper and picked up a quill. "I am a perverse creature and want my humiliation ensured in writing," he explained as he started to prepare a binding contract for the two of them to sign.

Agatha grabbed the sheet from the table, causing him to make a large black mark down its center, and tore it into a dozen pieces, despite the fact that it had only two words written on it. "Are you insane?"

Calmly, he pulled another white sheet from her sketch pad and began the document again. "At the risk of giving offense, I think I am the only sane person in the room."

Growling with frustration, she tried to seize the fresh piece of paper, but Addleson was prepared for a renewed attack and held on with both hands. They were still wrangling over it a few minutes later when the door opened and her father walked in.

"Beddows must have gotten into the cooking sherry again because he said there's a strange man in your—" Lord Bolingbroke broke off abruptly when he spotted the viscount in a tussle with his daughter. For a moment, he was so confused by the sight of their struggle, he didn't say anything at all. Then the intimacy of the scene struck him, for surely he couldn't help noticing Addleson's untucked shirt and Agatha's general disarray, and he yelled, "What in thunder is going on?"

The flush Agatha had gained from recent exertions immediately left her face, and she released her hold on the paper as she stared at her father. "You don't understand. It's not what you think," she said, talking fast and thinking faster. "Lord Addleson and I were having a disagreement about the necessity of quality paper in maintaining one's correspondence. I think good-quality stock is indicative of one's regard, while the viscount believes it's the sentiment expressed on the paper that matters more." Her eyes darting around the room, for she seemed distinctly uninclined to look her father in the face, she walked over to him with a forced smile. "It's a good thing you're here to provide a decisive opinion."

If Addleson had not already been top over tails in love with Lady Agatha, her desperate and yet oddly coherent performance would have won him over entirely. "We are drawing up a marriage contract and will need you to stand as witness to the document," he explained.

Dumbstruck, Bolingbroke looked from Addleson to his daughter and then back again, as if unsure which one to believe. Both stories were equally implausible.

While his lordship bobbed his head back and forth in confusion, Agatha stared at the viscount in stunned silence, her expressive face half hidden by the shadow of the dimly lit room. It disconcerted him not to know exactly what she was thinking, but a man proposing marriage was supposed to be unsure.

Accepting the uncertainty, he picked up the pen and began to write. "Lady Agatha is afraid her love for me will undermine her commitment to developing her skill as a painter. Therefore, I am putting into the contract that she must pursue her art with as much dedication and single-mindedness as she would if she were not saddled with a husband."

Although Bolingbroke's bewildered look indicated he still didn't comprehend what was happening, his understanding extended to grasping certain basic facts. "Naturally, as a wife and mother, she would put aside her hobby."

Addleson shook his head with pronounced disappointment as he looked at Agatha, who had yet to step out of the shadow. "I see now where your reluctance comes from." Then, to her father, he said, "I must remind you, Bolingbroke, that you are here as an official witness to the document. Your input is not being sought. Now, what else do we need to address? Ah, yes, your concern that I might feel embarrassed by your ardent pursuit of painting. Let's add a paragraph stating that under no circumstance shall I feel a single, solitary moment of mortification at my wife's chosen vocation. I will go one step further and mandate the particular amount of satisfaction and pleasure I must feel at her remarkable accomplishments. For good measure, I will insert here an addendum limiting the number of minutes in total I'm allowed to boast about her at a given social event, lest I become insufferable in my pride."

The viscount wrote furiously as he spoke, ignoring Bolingbroke's sputtered offense and looking at Agatha intermittently to observe her response. Her posture had not changed. Indeed, she was as unmoving as a statue in a garden.

Determined to provoke a reaction, for it was unbearable not to know what she was thinking, he added what he considered to be his masterstroke. "Furthermore, I am introducing a clause that specifies the size and location of your studio, which will go on the top floor of my town house on the south side of the building to ensure maximum exposure to the sun. And now I'm including a passage that stipulates the installation of a studio in every one of my homes, including the hunting box in Devonshire, which I've visited on fewer than a dozen occasions. Lastly, I'm adding a section requiring the inclusion of a comfortable chair for my personal usage should you deign to let me keep you—"

But he got no further, for suddenly she was there, near him, next to him, dropping to her knees and taking his face into her hands. She peered deeply into his eyes, her own velvety black ones shining with unexpected force and she smiled sweetly. Then she laid one gentle, precious kiss on his lips and said with ardent tenderness, "I deign."

Deeply touched, Addleson pulled her into his arms for another kiss, this one considerably less gentle than the first. Although he knew it was not at all the thing to ravish a girl with her papa a mere two feet away, he could not stop himself from exulting in the feel of her lips and the press of her body and the joy that had pervaded every inch of his own.

Agatha seemed insensible of the faux pas as well, for her ardor was as ferocious as his own, and she pulled back only when she heard the triumphant tones of her mother cooing, "Now that that's all settled, my loves, let's talk about the wedding."

While Agatha blushed and Addleson, unwilling to break all contact, sought his fiancé's hand, Bolingbroke huffed and grumbled, "I have yet to hear anyone ask my permission."

His wife smiled at him with female condescension, "Of course you did, my dear Bolly, you just weren't listening. Now, I suggest we adjourn to the drawing room to have a proper discussion about your marriage. This paint-splattered closet is not at all suitable."

"That's what I've been saying for years," Agatha muttered to Addleson's delight.

"Don't be absurd," her mother scoffed. "No gentleman wants to climb up a tree and risk disaster to court the woman he loves. Trust me, there is nothing less romantic than a broken leg. Your father had a sprained ankle on our honeymoon, and it was very unpleasant."

"I say, Judith, it was a stubbed toe," Bolingbroke objected, "and a very minor inconvenience at that."

Addleson laughed. "I appreciate your consideration, Lady Bolingbroke, although I am confident I could have managed several stories without incident."

Deeply suspicious, Agatha looked at her mother through narrowed eyes. "You cannot expect me to believe that you meant for a gentleman to sneak into my studio through the window."

Her ladyship dismissed this outlandish notion with a wave of her hand. "I'm a mother, darling, not a soothsayer. I simply saw no reason out to rule the possibility. Now, given your status as a newly engaged couple, I will permit you five minutes alone to cement the arrangement. Gregson will be positioned at the door with a watch and will knock at the five-minute mark and then open the door thirty seconds later. Is that clear?" she asked.

Agatha blushed again and assured her mother it was crystal clear. Having witnessed the earlier display of newly engaged behavior, Bolingbroke was less eager to leave his daughter alone with the viscount, and it required cajoling and then outright bullying from her ladyship to get him through the door. Even then, he insisted that it not be closed, and Addleson watched in amusement while Bolingbroke and his wife negotiated the precise number of inches the door was to remain open. The figure that satisfied both parties, though Lady Bolingbroke more so than her husband, was six.

As soon as they were gone, Addleson turned to Agatha intending to make a comment about Lord and Lady Bolingbroke's antics, but as soon as he saw the glow in her black eyes, he realized their time was too fleeting to waste in discussion of her parents. He took her hands in his and tugged her toward him. "You won't regret it," he said seriously, brushing a tendril that had fallen on her forehead.

"No, I don't think I will," she said with equal gravity. "I want your body far too much, my lord."

Surprised by the bluntness—very surprised, yes, that the Bolingbroke chit would announce her desire so plainly—he straightened his shoulders and raised his head.

Agatha laughed giddily at his reaction. "I have been hampered by convention and denied access to the actual male form. Every attempt I've made to study it has been thwarted. One of the stable hands kindly agreed to pose for me and, I assure you, Pryor has a very fine form, even if he is on the short side, but Gregson decided it would be beneath his dignity—Gregson's, mind you, not Pryor's. Pryor is something of a peacock and was looking forward to exhibiting his plumage."

Although Addleson felt he should take at least some umbrage at his bride-to-be's explicit discussion of another male's very fine form, he was too charmed to make the effort. She was wholly outrageous and utterly inappropriate and entirely his. He was not worried about footmen, peacocking ones or otherwise. Nevertheless, he asked, "Will access to my body whenever you desire it stop you from observing the form of the servants?"

Her grin—wide and playful and unrepentant—made his heart stop. "No, but I promise to limit observations to three times a week. Shall we put that in the document as well?" she asked, her beautiful eyes full of mischief as she reached for the pen.

Although Addleson thought a few additional ground rules would not go amiss, lest his clever wife take shameless advantage of him, now was not the time to add them and he pulled her into his arms for another kiss. Knowing himself to be on the verge of more inappropriate behavior, he walked to the door and smoothly erased the painstakingly negotiated six inches. Then he took her hands in his own and kissed her palms. "Given the extent of your sacrifice, we must make sure you are fully satisfied with what you are getting," he murmured softly before slipping her hands under his untucked shirt and pressing them against his hot flesh. "I do not want you to feel that you are making a poor bargain."

Now it was she who was startled by the boldness, and her eyes flew to his. But even as she looked at him in slight bemusement, her fingers knew what to do, for they began caressing his chest with such slow, measured strokes, he found it difficult to breathe and impossible not to moan. Coherent thought was becoming a challenge.

"We have only four minutes left and there's a lot of territory to cover," she said, her voice husky in his ear as she leisurely glided her hands over the corded muscles of his stomach. "I'm not sure we have enough time for full satisfaction, my lord."

As his fingers danced over—and then under—the edge of her dress, he assured her she had no cause to worry about the brevity of their allotted interval. He felt her heart leap when he brushed her nipples with his hands and then his tongue. "You are skilled in your chosen art, and I am skilled in mine," he explained huskily before capturing her lips in a kiss full of sweetness and desire and joy. He had not expected such unfettered sensuality, such unselfconscious pleasure, from Lady Agony, and although he was surprised by its existence, he was certainly not disconcerted by its fervor. As he had boasted only moments before, he was a master of this particular art, and by the time Gregson swung open the door a few minutes later, they were both well satisfied with their bargain.

EPILOGUE

Given her pivotal role in the creation of the great Adolphus Clemmons mystery, Lady Agatha felt obligated to listen yet again as Mr. Petrie struggled to comprehend what had transpired in his absence. In the twenty-seven hours since he had returned from Bath, he had raised the topic with her six times, which, she calculated out of boredom, averaged one conversation every four and a half hours.

"It's simply inexplicable to me, for how could Clemmons change his appearance so radically as to alter the color of his eyes and where did he get a complete top row of teeth? More important, why would he make these changes? He has a perfectly presentable visage—a little rough, you understand, from all that boxing he did in his youth. The missing teeth, as I said, and the scar above his right eye and the misshapen ear that looks disconcertingly like a head of cauliflower. Certainly, sometimes he scares little children, but his able hand as a note taker and his excellent memory more than compensate for a few unexpected shrieks when you are walking home from a lecture late at night." The American naturalist sighed and wrinkled his forehead. "And you are sure he did not come here looking for me? I am positive he had the address, as he made all the arrangements himself. The first thing he would do upon arriving to London would be to pay a call on the establishment at which I am staying. This is all so baffling."

"He did not call here, I'm sure of it," she said firmly, as she had a few dozen times before.

"It's very confusing indeed. To alter his appearance and then appear at the horticultural society claiming to be under orders from me. I never instructed him to become familiar with the workings of the British Horticultural Society. Why would I? For years, various organizations have courted my membership and I have steadfastly denied them the pleasure because I believe organized horticulture ultimately stifles originality. Clemmons knows my opinion, so why would he make such an implausible claim? And then to simply disappear into thin air? What purpose can that serve? Perhaps he went to Bath to try to find me."

At the mention of Bath, Agatha felt her sense of obligation weaken, for she knew what would come next: a protracted digression into Petrie's disappointing exchange with Mr. Trundle. He had been so optimistic about the meeting, so confident that Worthy & Wormley Press was ideally suited to publish his collective works, that he couldn't comprehend how he had been rejected—and on the grounds that his writing was familiar and derivative. Familiar and derivative!

This development presented Petrie with a second great mystery, for by what measure could his informative and inventive essays about the flora of North America be considered unoriginal? Who among the population of England had ever beheld *Ammophila breviligulata* in its natural habitat? Who among the inhabitants of this tiny island had the knowledge and experience to describe it as well as he?

The answer was nobody.

Agatha knew Petrie deserved an explanation. For all his boorish self-aggrandizing, he was still the innocent victim of a crime. Someone—and Agatha was not convinced it should be she—needed to sit down with him and give a detailed account of his assistant's perfidy. The ideal person for the job, she rather thought, was Lord Bolingbroke, for it was he who had invited the American naturalist to their shores and exposed him to Townshend's machinations. The only problem with her father telling Petrie the truth was he did not know the truth either. Sadly, the responsibility of enlightening that gentleman fell squarely on her shoulders, and she was happy to shirk it as long as possible.

As expected, Petrie launched into a narrative of his meeting with Mr. Trundle and rather than sit through another fifteen minutes of indignant consternation, which, to be fair, she knew the gentleman was wholly entitled to, Agatha sought out Addleson's gaze, raised her right hand and tugged her left ear.

Immediately, Addleson, who was sitting tamely on the settee next to her mother, broke out into peals of laughter just as Petrie said, "The flies in this house are relentless, are they not? I've been meaning to raise the issue with Lord Bolingbroke, for I fear his inadequate storage of fertilizer is to blame."

Before Agatha could rise to the defense of her father's compost heap, Gregson announced the arrival of the Harlow Hoyden and her sister. At once, her ladyship leaped to her feet, forgetting all about the viscount's inappropriate outburst—imagine laughing at Sir Irving's gout!—to welcome the Duchess of Trent.

"What a delightful surprise," Lady Bolingbroke said with a sideways glance at her daughter, whose engagement to a viscount had done little to improve her disposition. She still insisted on spending all her time in her ramshackle studio and she still refused to confide in her mother about the events in her life. Her courtship of Viscount Addleson, for example, remained a complete mystery to her.

With a hasty apology to Mr. Petrie for the interruption, Agatha greeted her guests, and although Lady Bolingbroke entreated the duchess and her sister to enjoy a cup of tea, Agatha insisted they did not have time.

"Do not have time?" her mother wondered aloud.

"Do not have time," Agatha repeated firmly. "They are here for a planning session, Mama, not a social call. We have work to do."

Lady Bolingbroke could not conceive what her daughter meant by a planning session. She was a gently bred young lady, not the keeper of Prinny's daily calendar. "I'm sure that whatever your intentions are you will concede the duchess and Miss Harlow would appreciate a cup of tea."

Agatha was not prepared to concede anything of the sort, for how could they come up with a plan for infiltrating the Royal Academy of Art if they were stuck in the drawing room making polite fiddle-faddle all day long? Addleson, however, was more amenable to her mother's point and suggested she and her visitors could spare a few minutes.

"Oh, very well," she said, sighing heavily as she sat down in an armchair that was several feet away from Petrie. Then she turned her piercing gaze on her fiancé. "You do realize, I hope, that you are now in direct violation of paragraph three, subsection five, of our contract, which clearly states that you are never to impose a social obligation at the expense of a professional goal."

Although this transgression sounded quite severe to everyone else in the room—except the girl's mother, to whom it sounded absurd—the viscount did not appear at all concerned. Indeed, the very idea of it seemed to please him immensely and he promised, in a tone far too warm and familiar for the drawing room, to accept his punishment later.

Naturally, Agatha blushed to the roots of her hair, but it wasn't his words that caused her embarrassment but the look in his eyes. It was the same look he'd worn while drawing up the contract in the first place: smug, confident, devilish. He had known as he'd made his increasingly ridiculous list that he would overcome her objections, and it was this confidence, this unchecked self-assurance, that had ultimately swayed her, for he was clearly a man who knew exactly what he was getting into. He was no naïve schoolboy befuddled by the first rush of passion.

But, oh, what a rush it had been. She had never felt anything like Addleson's lips on her breasts, the way she could have simply dissolved into a puddle of pleasure on the floor. It had been at once debilitating and empowering, for although it seemed as if her bones had turned to jelly, she felt as if she could accomplish any feat of great physical strength.

If anything, she had been the befuddled one, afraid that the intensity of her desire would corrupt her judgment, for how could something so powerful *not* undermine her commitment to art?And then Addleson was sitting at her table, quill in hand, adding items to the most outrageous contract ever written. She'd felt herself weakening even before he'd added a paragraph about the studio, but his inclusion of a light-filled atelier obliterated all her fears, for how could she resist a man who understood her so thoroughly—even down to the chair.

Years later, when she told the story to their children, she will say she married their father because of the forest-green leather armchair in her studio.

Now, however, neither Agatha nor Addleson volunteered further information about the contract, despite calls for elaboration, and her mother, appalled by the idea of having produced a daughter who would negotiate her own marriage settlement, quickly changed the subject to Miss Harlow's forthcoming nuptials.

Agatha, of course, was very happy for her new friend, as it seemed she and her bridegroom were particularly well suited to each other, but listening to Vinnie give gracious answers to pointless questions regarding the time of the wedding (2 P.M.) and the color of her dress (silver) was excruciating. It was all so trivial. Who cared where the wedding took place? In Hanover Square or the Duke's conservatory—it was still the tedious recitation of some boring vows before a doddering old clergyman. The event, though meaningful and felicitous to all those involved, did not warrant such intense scrutiny, especially when there were more important matters to discuss: campaign strategies, dossiers, Royal Academicians.

Perfectly aware of her impatience, Addleson watched her with an amused glimmer in his eyes, and just when it seemed as if Agatha would jump out of her seat with impatience ("And what about your bridal trousseau?"), he tugged his own ear. Immediately, Petrie, whose disinterest in wedding matters exceeded even Agatha's own, flailed his arms in front of him as if trying to dispel an insidious cloud of smoke.

"Flies," he said snappishly. "I am bedeviled by flies. They are everywhere."

Swallowing a ferocious urge to giggle, for the gentleman looked as mad as a hatter swatting the empty air, Agatha nodded with sympathy and stood up. "Yes, they are indeed everywhere. Here, let me help you," she said, picking up the *Morning Herald* from the side table, rolling it up and thwacking the flailing naturalist on the head. Then she peered closely at the gray tufts of hair on the top of his head and announced her mission a success.

It was impossible to say who was more shocked—her mother or the American—and before either one could gather their wits, Agatha shepherded her visitors to the door and explained her intention to remove them to a safer location. What location in particular, she did not say. "Given the fly infestation in the drawing room, it's my duty as hostess to save my guests from suffering a vicious attack similar to the one poor Mr. Petrie has just endured. I trust, Mama, that you can handle the matter in here in my absence" she said, carelessly tossing the useful broadsheet onto the settee, where it slowly unfurled to reveal a new illustration by Mr. Holyroodhouse. Despite his very sincere and very public resignation, the famous caricaturist felt compelled to do one final drawing. In it, Lady Agatha Bolingbroke, her eyes shaped like hearts, her lips curved in a smile so wide it bordered on grotesque, stared devotedly at Viscount Addleson with such worshipful adoration, anyone looking at her could not help but be appalled. Underneath the drawing in big block letters it said: Lady Agony indeed!

ABOUT THE AUTHOR

Lynn Messina is the author of more than a dozen novels, including the best-selling *Fashionistas,* which has been translated into 16 languages. Her essays have appeared in *Self, American Baby* and the Modern Love column in the *New York Times,* and she's a regular contributor to the *Times* Motherlode blog. She lives in New York City with her husband and sons.

What good is a *libertine*
if he won't *seduce* your sister?

Book One in the
Love Takes Root series
Available now!

**Twenty-four years of *faultless* propriety
are about to go down the *drain*.**

Book Two in the
Love Takes Root series
Available now!

**Is she a *simpering* miss?
or a tongue-tied *beauty***

THE FELLINGHAM
MINX

a regency novella

Lynn
Messina

Book Three in the
Love Takes Root series
Free novella available now!

Would she be the *dupe*
of a *handsome* lord?

Available now!

CPSIA information can be obtained at www.ICGtesting.com
Printed in the USA
LVOW10s2158040815

448886LV00003B/140/P